ACCLAIM FOR LAURA MCNEILL

"Laura McNeill has a gift for writing taut prose while delving deep into characters. A harrowing tale that explores love and trust and the lengths one will go to save the things that are most important. Highly recommended!"

—ANITA HUGHES, AUTHOR OF *FRENCH COAST* ON *SISTER DEAR*

"McNeill's debut is a heartstopping, nail-biting suspense novel that held me captive until I read the last page. Evocative writing and a compelling voice add to the mesmerizing effect of this excellent debut. I'll be looking for her next book!"

—COLLEEN COBLE, *USA TODAY* BESTSELLING AUTHOR OF *THE INN AT OCEAN'S EDGE* AND THE HOPE BEACH NOVELS ON *CENTER OF GRAVITY*

"A breathless, gut-wrenching, satisfying page-turner about the real superheroes of the world who stand up to evil and won't back down."

—ERIN HEALY, AUTHOR OF *MOTHERLESS* AND *THE BAKER'S WIFE* ON *CENTER OF GRAVITY*

"A bold and poignant look into an imploding marriage, told in a chorus of assured voices. I found myself so invested in Ava, a woman finally ready to examine the dysfunctional family dynamics that have shaped her and rise to courage. The story took me by the hand, bold and tender, and didn't let me go until its extremely satisfying conclusion. *Center of Gravity* is a compelling, fierce, and ultimately hopeful tale, and McNeill is a writer to watch."

—JOSHILYN JACKSON, *NEW YORK TIMES* BESTSELLING AUTHOR OF *SOMEONE ELSE'S LOVE STORY*

"This powerful debut by a former television anchor is a suspenseful and haunting tale of a marriage spiraling wildly out of control. The story line is particularly unsettling as it mirrors the headlines found in newspapers and court cases everywhere. This title will resonate with readers of contemporary women's fiction and fans of Gina Holmes."

—*LIBRARY JOURNAL* STARRED REVIEW OF *CENTER OF GRAVITY*

"This incredibly fast-paced tale is difficult to put down, mostly because the reader gets invested in the characters and won't want to stop until it all plays out."

—*ROMANTIC TIMES*, 4 1/2 STAR REVIEW OF *CENTER OF GRAVITY*

"Readers will find this tale of domestic suspense deeply compelling as a once-happy family unit disintegrates and a woman summons her heretofore hidden strength. Told from multiple perspectives, McNeill's gripping tale explores family, trust, and how lives are rebuilt."

—*BOOKLIST* REVIEW OF *CENTER OF GRAVITY*

"There's plenty of chills in this thriller about twisted family secrets that will keep pulses pounding."

—*PARKERSBURG NEWS & SENTINEL* REVIEW OF *CENTER OF GRAVITY*

SISTER
DEAR

SISTER DEAR

LAURA MCNEILL

THOMAS NELSON
Since 1798

Published in Nashville, Tennessee, by Thomas Nelson. Thomas Nelson is a registered trademark of HarperCollins Christian Publishing, Inc.

Thomas Nelson titles may be purchased in bulk for educational, business, fund-raising, or sales promotional use. For information, please e-mail SpecialMarkets@ThomasNelson.com.

Publisher's Note: This novel is a work of fiction. Names, characters, places, and incidents are either products of the author's imagination or used fictitiously. All characters are fictional, and any similarity to people living or dead is purely coincidental.

Library of Congress Cataloging-in-Publication Data

Names: McNeill, Laura, author.
Title: Sister dear / Laura McNeill.
Description: Nashville: Thomas Nelson, [2016]
Identifiers: LCCN 2015041860 | ISBN 9780718030926 (softcover)
Subjects: LCSH: Domestic fiction. | GSAFD: Mystery fiction. | Mystery fiction. | Christian fiction.
Classification: LCC PS3613.C58623 S56 2016 | DDC 813/.6—dc23 LC record available at http://lccn.loc.gov/2015041860

Printed in the United States of America

16 17 18 19 20 21 RRD 6 5 4 3 2 1

For Joshua

ONE

ALLIE

2016

In her final minutes as an inmate at Arrendale State Prison, Allie Marshall's body pulsed with tension. Eyes averted, managing any movements with robotic precision, she remained on guard.

Only moments to go.

A sliver of time. Not even a quarter hour. An unremarkable measurement, when held up against the billion other moments in any person's natural life. But after a decade inside, those last twelve minutes seemed the longest span in all of eternity.

To her right, rows of monitors blinked and recorded everything across the sprawling campus in Habersham County. Though the angles differed, the subject never changed: women in identical tan-collared shirts and shapeless pants. Inmates on work detail, in the cafeteria, in dormitories.

A corrections officer sat nearby, her pale blue eyes scanning the screens. To this worker, to all of them, Allie was GDC ID, followed by ten numbers. Nothing more. Inside the thick metal bars, Allie's life was suspended, a delicate fossil in amber.

Until now. Ten more minutes.

Her reflection stared back, unblinking, in the shatterproof glass window near the door. Green eyes flecked with gold, dark-blonde hair tucked in a loose ponytail, barely visible brackets at the corners of her lips.

Maybe, Allie thought, she'd forgotten how to smile and laugh. Happiness seemed unreachable, as if the feeling itself existed on the summit of an ice-tipped mountain shrouded by storm clouds. Indeed, the rush of pure, unadulterated joy belonged only to those with freedom. Allie's memories of it—her daughter's birth, Caroline's first smile, first steps—were fleeting and distant.

Instead, the perpetual motion of prison, the waking, sleeping, and sameness, all blended together, like a silent black-and-white movie on a continuous loop.

Until the news of her parole.

At first, the concept of liberty seemed impossible—a hand trying to catch and hold vapor. The judge had sentenced Allie to sixteen years, and she fully anticipated serving each and every one of them. She didn't believe she'd be granted an early release—she couldn't—until she stepped beyond the walls and barbed wire and chain-link fence, barriers that kept her from everyone and everything she'd ever loved.

Allie focused on breathing, stretching her lungs, exhaling to slow her pulse. Her own belongings, a decade old, lay nearby. Keys that wouldn't open doors. A watch with a dead battery. A light khaki jacket with a photo of then five-year-old Caroline tucked in the pocket, one pair of broken-in Levis, and a white cotton shirt. Gingerly, with her fingertips, she reached for the clothing, then gripped the bundle tight to her chest.

A second guard motioned for Allie to change quickly in a holding room. With the door shut, she pulled the shapeless prison garb over her head and picked up the shirt. The material, cool and light, brushed against her skin like gauze. Allie shivered.

For ten years, all she'd known was the rasp of her standard-issue navy jacket, the scrape of her worn white tennis shoes along the sidewalk.

Back in Brunswick, Allie had filled her closet with easy summer shifts and crisp linen pants. Now her body was different too—the soft curves had dissolved, leaving lean muscle behind. The jeans hung loosely around her waist and hips. The top billowed out in waves from her shoulders.

Nothing would fit, she reminded herself. Not much in her past life would.

And that was all right.

When she walked out of Lee Arrendale State Prison, home to thousands of female inmates, Allie didn't want reminders. No indigo tattoo inked down her back or neck. No numbers or symbols etched into her arms or fingers. The only external validation of time served was a faint scar that traced her eyebrow.

The real proof of her internment lay underneath it all. Below the seashell white of Allie's skin, hidden in blood, tendons, and muscle, the experience indelibly marked on her soul. An imprint made by incident, mistake, and tragedy.

Evidence, and lack of it.

"I'm innocent," she'd insisted to everyone who would listen. Her lawyers fought hard, rallied a few times, but in the end, the jury convicted her. Voluntary manslaughter.

A year later, Allie's appeal failed. Then money ran out. Her father turned his attention back to his veterinary practice after his cardiologist warned the stress of another trial might kill him. Her mother did her best to minimize worry while Emma, her tempestuous and fun-loving sister, assumed the role of doting aunt and guardian to Caroline.

And there was Ben. Sweet, thoughtful Ben. The man who'd

wanted to marry her, who said he would love her always. Even after her arrest, he'd promised to wait for her if the worst happened. Allie couldn't live with herself if he'd sacrificed everything—his rising political career, his reputation, and his life for a decade or more. She'd broken it off, knowing it would wound him terribly. When he'd finally left, when she saw him for the last time, it was as if the very core of her being had been torn away, leaving a vast, gaping emptiness she couldn't fill, despite how hard she tried. Allie closed her eyes. She'd convinced herself it was the logical thing, what made sense. She had done her best to forget him. It hadn't worked in the least.

The days and months blurred. Entire seasons dissolved, shapeless and gray, like the ink of fine calligraphy smeared by the rain.

The squawk of the prison intercom barely registered in Allie's brain. Sharp insults and threats were routine, eruptions of violence expected. Even along the brown scrub grass and wooden benches of the prison yard, there was no escape. Allie always tried to disappear—pressing her body close to the concrete walls, becoming a chameleon against the barren landscape.

The women in Arrendale weren't afraid of punishment; most had nothing left. Some bonded with other inmates for favors; others paid for protection with cigarettes, food, and stamps. For those prisoners who had lost everything, inmates with little hope of parole, life was almost unthinkable.

Clutching her hands in her lap to keep from shaking, Allie watched as a woman collapsed in the cafeteria, stabbed in the jugular with a plastic fork. The next week, a fellow inmate in her dormitory was choked to death, purple fingerprints visible on the woman's throat when the guards discovered her body. Allie was haunted with grief for weeks after a young girl, only four years older than Caroline, tried to hang herself with a scrap of fabric.

Despite it all, despite the desperation that seemed to permeate the very air she breathed, Allie had survived.

In another few minutes, her younger sister, Emma, would arrive, as bus service didn't run from Alto to Brunswick. Tomorrow she'd meet her parole officer at noon. And like every parolee, she would receive a check, courtesy of the Georgia Department of Corrections, enough to buy shampoo, a bar of soap, and a comb for her hair.

Allie blinked up at the clock, almost afraid the time might start going backward. She forced her eyes away, squeezed them shut. If she tried hard enough, her mind formed a picture of her grown daughter's face. In her daydreams, she'd imagined their reunion a million times, rehearsed every possible scenario. She worried about the right words to say, how to act, and whether it was all right to cry. The enormity of it was impossible to contain, like holding back the ocean with a single fingertip.

All that mattered now was seeing Caroline.

The buzzer sounded long and loud; its vibration shook the floor. The burly guard sighed and lumbered to her boot-clad feet. She stood inches from Allie's shoulder, her breath hot and rank from a half-eaten roast beef sandwich.

Locks clicked and keys rattled. The barrier, with its heavy bars, groaned under its own weight. An inch at a time, the metal gate heaved open. Soon, there would be nothing but empty space standing between Allie and the rest of the world.

She felt a nudge.

In that moment, Allie heard four words, precious and sweet.

"You're free to go."

TWO

ALLIE

2016

As the gate closed behind her, Allie blinked, her eyes adjusting to the bright blue midday sky. Heat rose in waves off the blacktop. Sunlight reflected from windows along the campus.

Standing outside the gates of Lee Arrendale was surreal. Allie thought about running, maybe all of the way to Brunswick. She would sprint until her lungs burst and her heart exploded, feeling the rush of wind on her cheeks, putting miles between her and the prison.

Of course, she didn't have to run. Her sister stood there, waiting. Lithe and slender, dark hair catching in the breeze, wrapped in a white dress that hugged her curves, Emma stood out against Arrendale's red clay and gravel.

"Finally!" Her sister opened her arms to offer an awkward embrace. As Emma pulled her closer, Allie caught a whiff of coconut, of the ocean and sun. She smelled like home. "Let's get out of here," Emma said, pulling back with a lopsided smile. "This place gives me the creeps."

Allie sucked in a breath of air. After ten years of following orders, standing at attention, and being counted, the pure silence of the

6

open road sounded like a chorus of angels from heaven. There were no overhead announcements, no inmate complaints, and no scrape of shoes along cement. Just the late model BMW's wheels on asphalt, the steady whoosh of air from bumper to taillight, and the heat through the window warming her arm and hand.

Allie glanced over at her sister. Emma had been the constant in the last decade, her only regular visitor. Morgan Hicks, her best friend, had vanished along with everyone else the moment the police announced the arrest.

Her prison sentence changed everyone. Even living outside the imposing walls and curling barbed wire, Emma morphed into someone else. Someone reliable. Responsible. Allie's rock.

Gone was the boy-crazy teenager who'd sneak out on school nights and drink Boone's Farm on the beach. The girl who took double dares and learned to surf at fourteen. The girl who hadn't ever hesitated to flirt with men twice her age.

Allie had been the safe one, the rule-follower; her sister, the rogue. But every month since her incarceration, Emma drove from Brunswick on Highway 95 to Savannah, then made the remaining trek to Alto. No matter how stilted or strange the visit, Allie was grateful that Emma made the effort. The twelve-hour round-trip took planning, not to mention the cost of an overnight stay.

At first, Allie's parents, Lily and Paul, came on holidays and brought Caroline, who seemed to sprout an inch every few months. The visits, short and uncomfortable, became intolerable for her parents when her daughter developed an uncontrollable phobia to prisons and chain-link fencing. Caroline broke out in hives, the skin on her neck and face getting blotchy and red. According to her mother, she would complain of stomach pain—piercing, stabbing agony—in the hours before a scheduled drive.

It had hurt, but Caroline's aversion didn't surprise anyone. The prison, even on visitation days, was a loud and frightening place. The population, restless and violent, often swelled to collective anger, especially in the summer's heat. Lockdowns were frequent. Shouts reverberated through the walls. Days were filled with the clank of metal on metal, locks clicking into place, the grind of mechanized gates.

When they drove by the turnoff to Commerce, Allie shuddered and turned, tucking her meager belongings behind the seat. The wheels hit a bump in the road and rumbled over deep ruts. The plastic crinkled, then settled into place.

Allie glanced down at her sister's purse, wedged between them. The designer leather satchel, packed full, held Emma's cell phone, an embossed address book, and lipstick. An empty Starbucks mug sat in the cup holder next to an extra pair of Wayfarers.

A long time ago, Allie enjoyed the same indulgences. But for a decade, she had existed without any of it. Maybe, in some ways, she was better off, with all the time in the world to think. She laid her head back and let her gaze drift, absorbing the passing fields, rolling green-and-gold hills, and towering pines.

It was thirty-two miles outside the barbed-wire gates of Arrendale State Prison, in Jackson County, when Allie finally wanted to speak. She wanted to ask about Caroline. She was desperate to know everything, hear every detail. But she swallowed the million questions for just a few moments more, letting the silence envelop the space. *Breathe*, Allie told herself.

"Like the car?" Emma asked finally, glancing in the rearview mirror. "It's a few years old—snapped it up after one of my friends told me it was sitting on the lot outside town." She winked. "A bit of a step up, don't you think?"

Allie swallowed back the sand-dry roughness in her throat. "Definitely." She tried to smile. "Where's the Chevelle?" Allie asked, thinking back to her sister's first car, a sleek throwback to the seventies. She ran a hand along the seat, supple and firm, thinking back to the shiny vinyl interior of the old vehicle. "I miss it."

"Junkyard." Emma laughed at the comment, pursing her glossed lips into a wry bow.

"Too bad." Allie fiddled with the edge of her shirt. Her own daughter was old enough for a learner's permit. She'd be driving soon, if she wasn't already.

"How is Caroline?" Allie asked, the question bursting from her mouth before she could stop it.

Emma's grip tightened on the wheel. Her sister turned her head slightly, flashing a too-bright smile. "She's doing fine," she said, her voice strained but even. "Everything's really good." But then Emma trained her eyes straight forward, as if she could only see the lines on the empty road ahead. She swallowed, licked her lips, and lifted her chin. "I think Mom and Dad are going to try to bring her by."

Try. It wasn't what Allie wanted to hear, but she had learned to be patient. After ten years inside Arrendale, anticipation, which used to be excruciating, was now a dull ache. She could wait a little longer for Caroline.

After a few minutes, Emma changed the subject, offering details about Caroline's school, a guy named Jake she'd had a crush on this year, the clubs she'd joined. Emma kept talking, filling the space above, in, around, and below, the invisible question hovering in the car between the two of them.

How was Caroline? Really?

Was she okay? Was she safe?

But Allie let her sister talk. She'd waited forever already. They'd be home soon and she would find out for herself.

As with all family matters, Allie knew the truth was complicated—more intricate than a spider's web and just as sticky.

THREE

CAROLINE

2016

Caroline believed there was safety in numbers. A circle of friends, like a pride of lions, offered protection and relief from the torture that was high school. The tiled walls, the endless eyes, the scanning and scrutinizing.

Caroline held her breath to slow her racing heartbeat. In her head, she counted back from ten. She began to perspire and wiped a hand across her damp forehead. She wrinkled her nose. Classroom doors yawned open into the hallway, sending out air scented with dry-erase markers and pencil shavings.

The catcalls and gossip floated in streams above her head. Words bounced off lockers, twisting in midair. And words, Caroline knew, could hurt. Words could kill. Not in a take-your-life kind of way, Caroline thought. More like a reputation-bombing, forever-outcast sort of way.

One shot. Aimed right.

Bang. You were dead.

Caroline swallowed back a quiver of worry. She'd seen it happen. When Mansfield Academy's elite zoned in on a particular target, it was all-out war. The victims were random. A nerd with braces. A girl with thick charcoal eyeliner whose clothes always faintly smelled of curry. An awkward freshman unlucky enough to trip over his own Chuck Taylors.

Worst of all, there was no warning. No flashing lights. No danger sign in the road. By a small miracle, Caroline had been saved. In the seventh grade, Madeline Anderson had plucked her from obscurity and drew her into Mansfield Academy's inner circle. Selected Caroline from hundreds of other girls who drove Range Rovers, had trust funds, and spent spring break in the Caribbean. For Maddie, the girl who lived to shock her mother and her Stepford-wife friends, Caroline's family scandal worked perfectly.

Caroline wasn't sure who wanted the relationship more. Being friends with the most popular group of girls at her school was a rush unlike any other. When Maddie flicked her long golden hair off one shoulder, heads turned. When Maddie linked arms and drew her close to whisper, Caroline felt the heat of envious stares. When Maddie laughed, her ocean-blue eyes sparkled, right at Caroline.

They were like sisters. Or at least the sister Caroline never had.

If she could become Maddie's twin—her clone—she would have done it. Instead, she did the next best thing. Caroline memorized everything about Maddie. Her walk, talk, and personality. She even wore Maddie's signature outfit—two-hundred-dollar jeans, slouchy designer tops, and strappy sandals.

Every day she channeled her inner Maddie.

It was so much easier than being herself.

She was, after all, the daughter of a convict. She didn't have a dad, which sucked too. Her aunt Emma had raised her. Loved her so much—a little too much sometimes. It could be stifling, but there was no way Caroline would ever hurt Emma's feelings. Emma had given up everything to raise her and make sure she didn't want for anything.

Emma tried, anyway. No one tried harder.

Her grandparents treated her like fine china. Conversations were always awkward and punctuated with "wonderful" and "great." They never knew what to say to her or how to relate. It wasn't their fault, really. No one knew.

And no one would ever mistake Caroline and her best friend for sisters, no matter how hard she wished. Where Maddie was blonde and tiny, Caroline was statuesque and dark. Over the summer, Caroline had grown another three inches. Her straight frame softened. She'd developed cheekbones and hips. A chest. Her hair grew lush, black, and long.

The changes were so dramatic—and almost overnight—that her aunt threatened to start using time-lapse photography. "I'm going to wake up one morning and not recognize you," Emma teased.

Good, Caroline thought. She didn't want anyone to.

Under her shiny exterior, the big smile, the laughter with Maddie and their group of friends, Caroline spent every day waiting. Wondering when it would all collapse.

"Earth to Caro?"

Maddie's poke in the ribs launched her back to the present.

Caroline's body jolted. "Ow! What'd I miss?" She wrinkled her nose.

"Absolutely nothing, other than I was telling you about *Will*." Maddie shot Caroline a fake reproachful look and then broke out into a wide grin. Will was the latest in Maddie's merry-go-round of never-ending boyfriends. She traded them in faster than Caroline could keep track.

"What did he say?" Caroline mouthed.

Maddie sighed and waved a hand in Caroline's face, causing

her sweet perfume to billow from her wrists. "I swear, you're in another universe today." She rolled her eyes and snapped her mint gum. "It's the dream guy, isn't it?"

Caroline hesitated, glad Maddie couldn't see through to her brain, where all of her real thoughts swirled like debris in a tornado.

"I don't know." She tried to grin.

"Liar," Maddie teased under her breath.

Caroline flushed pink. A few months ago, she'd caught the attention of one of Mansfield Academy's star football players. Tall and muscled, Jake Robinson made her head swim. The way his dark hair fell over one green eye, the way he slung his arm around her and held her close, and especially the way his lips felt on hers.

He'd noticed Caroline when Maddie had practically shoved the two of them together at a party on East Beach. There'd been a bonfire, and Caroline had downed one too many beers. By the end of the evening, she was sitting in his lap. They'd been the high school's "it" couple ever since.

Though Jake made her heart do backflips, she maintained a smooth, sweet demeanor. Calm. In control. Inside, Caroline quaked with anxiety. She felt tall and gangly. An alien, beamed down from Mars, wearing strawberry-scented lip gloss.

"I'm a little jealous," Maddie continued. "You live with your aunt, which is cool enough. Then your grandparents buy you whatever you want. Like, you'll probably get a BMW for your next birthday."

"Yeah, right." Caroline made herself giggle and tugged a lock of hair, wrapping it tight around her finger until it throbbed. She released the strands and made a face at Maddie. It was easier that way, to pretend it was all good.

Caroline *was* lucky. She had no strict curfews, no list of chores, no little brother or baby sister to watch after school. Her days were filled, the calendar jammed with circled dates and Sharpie-marker hearts. Her grandmother spoiled her. Emma ferried her everywhere—the mall, football games, lunches—and never, ever complained.

Though Caroline had been told more than a few times by her grandparents that she was book-smart and a diligent student like her mother, physically, she and Emma looked much more alike. Outside Brunswick, people always confused them as mother and daughter. Same last name, same deep brown eyes and long, wavy dark hair, same lithe build.

After a while, her aunt didn't even bother to correct the confusion. And it never bothered Caroline; she actually liked to hear people call Emma her mother.

Now, though, it was all ruined.

The clock was ticking, the wick burning down. The bomb she was about to drop on Maddie would surely blow her world apart. She tried to form the words. *Hey. My mom's getting out of prison.*

It was one thing to have a mother in jail, locked up and far away. To her friends, the idea was surreal, scary, but fascinating, like watching an anaconda slink behind thick glass. Distance and protection made everything okay.

Her mother, living right here in Brunswick? That was another thing altogether.

Her aunt and grandparents broke the news during a regular Sunday dinner. Over the rising steam from shrimp and grits. "Pass the yeast rolls, please? Oh, and by the way, your mother's getting paroled from Arrendale. Emma's going to pick her up on Tuesday." Caroline's fork had fallen from her hand, clattering to the hardwood floor. Incredulous, she had blinked at Emma.

"How long have you known?" Caroline had asked, her voice cracking.

They'd known for months. *Months.* Grandma Lily had wanted to say something sooner, but Emma insisted they wait. And then the justification started.

"You have school. Your grades," Grandpa Paul interjected.

"We didn't want to upset you for no reason," her grandmother added.

Emma reached over to squeeze her hand. "We were just looking out for you."

Her lips parted to respond, but Caroline couldn't think of a single thing to say. She loved her aunt and her grandparents, but they were so overprotective, treating her as if she were a hand-blown glass figurine instead of a living, breathing teenager.

Maddie nudged her out of her daze. "So, this weekend?"

Caroline jumped.

"Somebody's on edge." Maddie gave her a sideways look and bent closer to the mirror.

Unable to make her mouth work, Caroline watched as Maddie freshened her lip gloss. She'd been talking right along, and Caroline hadn't heard a word.

The confession about her mother was caught—in a tangle of words—just over her heart. Not explaining was worse. Letting Maddie find out from someone else? She'd freak. Besides, everyone would know soon. The whole school, the neighbors. Everyone in the entire state of Georgia.

The bell sounded, long and loud. The ringing penetrated Caroline's brain with snare drum precision. Chatter erupted all around her, and everyone jostled for the door. Maddie was still talking. Her mouth was moving, but Caroline couldn't hear her.

With a wave, Maddie disappeared, melting into the rush of students. She had math. Or Spanish. Something. Caroline had missed her chance.

Throat dry, Caroline edged into the crush of students and shuffled to the next classroom, in a building across campus. Outside, the sun beamed overhead, and a warm, salty wind blew off the Atlantic. Squinting against the bright light, Caroline hurried, clutching her books to her chest like a shield.

She ducked into her seat in the biology classroom. Head down, chin close to her chest, Caroline stuck a hand in her backpack. She found her notebook and flipped open the pages, scanning the words.

They'd been talking about PTSD, post-traumatic stress disorder. Some of the kids' parents were soldiers. A few, just back from Afghanistan, were seriously messed up. Didn't know their own families, couldn't remember names or birthdays. It was like their minds had been scrubbed clean with Drano.

And all entirely normal, according to her biology teacher. The human brain knew what to remember and what to forget. Caroline looked at her notes.

After humans suffer trauma, the body reacts. Amnesia, selective or not, is the body's way of protecting the brain from suffering.

So, Caroline supposed, the key takeaway was this: if life was bad enough, if things really sucked, a person's mind ran its own witness protection program.

Simple.

Easy.

Except . . . Caroline's eyes filled with tears.

She could never forget.

FOUR

SHERIFF GAINES

2016

Sheriff Lee Gaines hit his stride halfway through his five-mile run. It was a perfect day, with wisps of white clouds dotting the azure sky. Had it been a Saturday, he would have driven a few miles across the Torras Causeway, passed the welcome sign to St. Simons Island, and taken Kings Way to the Lighthouse Museum. From there, he'd begin his run, enjoying a spectacular view of the rocky coastline and silver-blue waves under a canopy of leaves and Spanish moss. He loved smelling the sea air as he wound through Beachview Drive and Oglethorpe Avenue.

But it was a weekday, and with Chief, his German shepherd, close to his side, Gaines followed his routine through downtown, near the hospital, with a final loop around the College of Coastal Georgia.

Like an NFL kicker who touched his right temple before a punt or a baseball player who needed a certain brand of gum for good luck, Gaines had his rituals. But unlike pro athletes, these routines weren't for winning or getting a twenty-million-dollar salary.

His life was about discipline.

Sweating in the humid morning air, breathing in the scent of newly paved asphalt, he pushed himself the last hundred yards, sprinting to his front steps.

Last week he'd finally moved into his new home. It was only a few blocks away from the one he'd shared with June, but this one was smaller, with a more manageable yard and a big fence. It was what he needed now.

As he rounded the corner to enter through the back door, he caught sight of the For Sale sign he'd been meaning to dispose of. He hesitated, then opened the back of his patrol car and lifted the sign, sliding it inside. Now at least he wouldn't have to see it— this reminder of loss and change—every time he pulled into the driveway.

Not all reminders were bad ones, though. He twisted the bulky high school ring on his right hand. In his prime, he'd led the Mansfield Wolverines to victory. He'd been quarterback and went on to play second string at Georgia State until a shoulder injury ended his college football career. He'd buried the disappointment, studied criminal justice, and entered the Glynn County Sheriff's Department immediately after graduation. Now, after nearly thirty-five years on the force, he ran the department with the precision of a marine battalion, spent time with his wife, and served as a Mansfield Academy booster and unofficial advisor to the school's athletic department.

At eight thirty, uniform on, boots laced tight, Gaines straightened his tie in the full-length mirror and scowled at the gray creeping into his hairline. After refilling a bowl of water for Chief, Gaines paused at the bedroom door. Something nudged at the back of his mind.

His calendar sat on the corner of his dresser. He strode toward it, flipped it open with one hand, ran a thick finger across the page. This particular week had a line through it, under which he'd scribbled his secretary's name and *vacation* in capital letters.

Shoot. Of course he'd forgotten it was *this* week. His secretary hadn't taken time off in four years or more. She was overdue. And worse than that, she had to be gone. Saturday was her daughter's wedding.

Gaines frowned and rubbed his neck. He'd muddle through, but it didn't bode well for a smooth day. He lifted his gun belt and strapped it on tight. The weapon wasn't optional. It was worn on duty, off duty, to the grocery store, and out to grab a bite to eat.

Overkill, maybe. But folks felt safe, it provided comfort, and it was a constant reminder about who was in charge. Who ran things in Brunswick.

In reality, Gaines didn't need macho accoutrements. He wasn't a Rambo-like fanatic who went around seeking trouble. The weapon was his shield; it provided distance between him and the world, protection from anyone getting too close.

And he had Chief. There was no other partner Gaines preferred.

He'd started the department's K-9 program with one dog a decade earlier. Beau, his first trainee, had served his time well. Since then, there'd been several more, but none as fine an animal as Chief. They understood each other.

If only it could be that way with June.

Thirty minutes later, after fighting the usual rush of morning tourist traffic heading to the nearby barrier islands, Gaines pulled into the nursing home parking lot. Though the outside boasted a manicured lawn and palm trees, he despised every inch of it, from the concrete driveway to the florescent lights inside. He resented the air freshener that didn't quite mask the smell of cleaning solution. His wife didn't belong here, this place where people came to die.

June—brain damaged and wheelchair bound—had been a

vibrant, caring obstetrician who'd helped birth nearly every baby in lower Coastal Georgia.

Now most days she didn't remember where she'd grown up, whether she'd gone to school, or if she'd ever married Sheriff Lee Gaines. Her emotions were erratic, rising and sinking like the tide. Her moments of lucidity were brief and jarring—bitter reminders of what June couldn't have. It made Gaines physically sick.

But he hadn't missed a visit. Not one day.

It wasn't because he was expected to make pilgrimages, as the long-suffering, dedicated husband. Sure, Gaines was a public figure. He had endured, stayed strong in the face of tragedy. Kept the people's confidence.

That was his job. This was his wife and he loved her.

"Privacy, please." He'd wink at the aides. "I need time alone with June," he'd add, and they'd scurry away to count meds or make notes in charts, closing the door behind them.

Gaines's emotions, grief, sorrow, bitter disappointment—the enduring anger at the man who'd robbed these years with June—emerged only in the safety of his wife's presence. And she wouldn't tell a soul.

"How are you, sweetheart?" Gaines would ask, taking her limp, soft hand. Chief, who at first would sit and cock his head expectantly, didn't bother now, choosing to lay under Gaines's feet and doze.

After remarking about his morning run, the weather, or potential weekend fishing plans, he'd kiss his wife's cool cheek and duck out the back door, swallowing back the pain.

Everyone had a cross to bear. His was just heavier than most.

Gaines entered the station, a low brick building marked with an American flag and the bright red and blue of the state flag beside it. His entrance caused a flurry of activity, and, as usual, a chorus of greetings and acknowledgments rang from his deputies, the secretaries, and a couple of attorneys. Even when the sugar-sweet smell of doughnuts hit his nostrils, he didn't stop. He headed, unsmiling, straight for the glass door to his office.

"Boss?" Dwayne Johnston, his most senior officer, followed a step behind. They'd worked together since Johnston came on the force, wet behind the ears. Now, a dozen years later, though he'd never say it, he often thought of the deputy as a son. June, tragically, had never been able to bear them any children.

Pushing aside the thought, Gaines turned and gazed at Johnston, who wore a worried expression, eyebrows furrowed.

"This better be good," Gaines growled. "I haven't had my coffee yet." He opened his office, stepped inside, and motioned for Johnston to sit.

"She's out," Johnston replied in a hushed voice. "The Marshall girl. What do we do?" The deputy plucked a notebook from his back pocket, poised to take down any directive.

The temperature in the room dropped twenty degrees.

Gaines's grip tightened on the desk, but he kept his face devoid of any expression. Instinctively, his eyes shot to his secretary's desk. She'd know. She'd confirm it in less than ten seconds, but her chair was empty.

Gaines swung his attention back to Johnston. "Allison Marshall?" He already knew the answer.

"The one," his deputy said.

Tension pooled in his neck and shoulders. The information could be wrong. It could be a rumor, idle gossip, something that held no weight. But Johnston wasn't that kind of deputy. He was solid, a go-to man, one of the few who didn't vomit at the sight of his first dead body or call in sick after pulling a double shift.

Gaines scratched out a few notes, the graphite marking the

memo with short, dark letters. His arm stiffened as he marked the end of the last sentence, pressing so hard the tip broke in two, sending shards flying. Without waiting a beat, he tossed the pencil in the trash, making the slender piece of wood clang against the metal can.

His jaw tightened. He should have been told. What in the world had happened? Some screw-up at the state level? Gaines straightened in his chair. He didn't need to pretend with Johnston, but with the rest of the staff—with anyone else—he couldn't give the impression he didn't know what was going on in his own jurisdiction. Gaines tightened his fist under the desk.

"Time and date stamps from late Friday night." Johnston glanced back at the assistant's area. "I found it on her desk. Just sitting there."

Gaines held up a finger—his signal for silence at all costs. Someone had put the fax down; some idiot who'd grabbed it off the machine, assuming the news would filter into the right channel. Namely his.

The light on his assistant's phone blinked with a message. The warden had probably called her too. He'd bet a fortune on it—if he had one—and then some.

"Anything else, boss?"

Gaines shook his head.

Johnston shifted in his work boots, inching back toward the door.

With a curt nod, Gaines dismissed him. "Thanks, that'll be all."

The door slammed, leaving him alone with his thoughts.

Gaines pressed his roughened fingers to his temples, squeezing hard.

Allison Marshall was out. It was one heck of a way to start his week.

FIVE

ALLIE

2016

The same everything remained, Allie marveled, as the ocean breeze caught strands of her hair. They'd driven the highway hugging the Georgia coast into Brunswick, taking Newcastle Street along the train tracks as soft light trickled through the trees, bathing the afternoon in muted shades of forest green and amber. Allie gazed out the window, resting her chin on one hand. She caught a glimpse of Selden Park, and then Brunswick Landing Marina, where the white masts of dozens of sailboats bobbed through the trees. The sight made her heart swell. How she had missed the unspoiled beauty of the area, the maritime forests and pristine shoreline. She could almost taste the salt air.

Allie searched for something to fill the silence. "So, still lots of tourists here for spring break?"

Emma slid her sister a sideways look. "I don't know if they can fit another golfer on Sea Island. I was lucky enough to have dinner in the Georgian Room at The Cloister last week. Oh my goodness, I never wanted to leave."

Allie sat up straighter. She could have fresh shrimp again.

Oysters, scallops, and red snapper. All of it, straight from the ocean, caught off the barrier islands around Brunswick. Sea Island, Jekyll Island, St. Simons Island, and Little St. Simons Island made up the four Golden Isles, named for the gold-seeking Spanish explorers who arrived in the territory four centuries earlier.

In town, she and Emma passed the three-story Ritz Theater, with a new neon sign hanging from the front façade. At night, her sister said, the letters glowed gold and could be seen from blocks away. They turned left on Gloucester, continuing past the downtown shops and restaurants. She strained to see more of what she'd missed, reading signs and looking into store windows.

Allie drew in a breath at the sight of a Wolverines poster. Football fever was always in season. In Georgia, the sport was like blood and oxygen, sustenance for living. It was all anyone talked about.

For a stranger, a quick drive through downtown would prove Brunswick's devotion to the gridiron. Banners hung on every corner, each proclaiming "Home of the Mighty Wolverines" or "Wolverine Spoken Here." Spirit signs appeared in front lawns every August, each bearing a player's name, position, and jersey number. Most cars and trucks sported at least one black-and-silver football sticker.

For Allie, it was a reminder of the past. Of the man who was responsible for putting her in Arrendale, the man whose face filled her nightmares. She shivered, thinking about the sheriff.

To the best of her knowledge, he was still involved in Mansfield Academy—still hanging out on the football fields during practice and on the sidelines during Friday night games. Every time he was on the school's campus, he had access to Caroline.

Until now, there had been absolutely nothing she could do about it.

Her sister rolled to a gentle stop and parked, the hum of the idle engine blending with the pulse of the fading day. They had stopped in front of a tiny little house on a quiet street, just a short walk from the Marshes of Glynn Park and Fancy Bluff Creek. Allie imagined walking near the marshes again, fragrant with sea air, watching egrets and herons fly about the rustling tall cordgrass and needlerush.

Emma interrupted her daydream.

"Mom and Dad said to go ahead in," her sister said, handing her the key from the glove box. "They said they'd be here in a bit, since they didn't exactly know what time we'd get back. No way to predict, right?"

"Right." Allie swallowed, folding her fingers around the metal edges.

"Good luck," Emma said with a half smile, casting her eyes toward the house. Her fingers tapped at her knee. "With everything."

"Thanks," Allie replied. She pulled the car door handle, swung her legs to the ground, and stood up. She stretched, feeling her spine pop and her neck loosen.

"So, let's do dinner—maybe tomorrow or the next night? To celebrate." Emma brightened and then hesitated.

"Sure." Allie couldn't think about dinner. Or eating. Or later this week.

She was home.

Her parents would be here soon. With or without her daughter.

Allie closed the car door, backed away, and waved. *Make sure Caroline knows.* She wanted to call out the words, making them echo down the street. *Make sure she knows I'm home.*

But all that Allie could hear and see was Caroline's anguish the day she'd received her verdict. Her daughter's face crumpling. The tears. And the promise she'd made Caroline.

January 2007

As the jury foreman announced the decision, Allie went numb.
Guilty.

Allie imagined herself slipping into a coma, unable to move or protect herself from harm. Unable to cry or beg for mercy.

Behind Allie, her mother gasped and cried out while her father murmured words of comfort. Caroline began to sob.

On the opposite side of the courtroom, speculation rattled through the aisles. The courtroom doors opened as people raced out with the news. One of Allie's lawyers patted her hand. "We'll appeal it," he said.

The judge banged his gavel. "Quiet!" he demanded. Sentencing would take place the following week. The rest of his directives were lost to Allie.

She felt a touch on her forearm. Her parents stood so close their bodies seemed melded together. Her mother cried openly, her face awash with grief. Her father's shoulders sagged, his eyes dulled with pain and disbelief.

On either side of Allie, officers took her by the elbows and pulled her to her feet. She wobbled like a newborn calf, legs shaking, hands trembling.

An anguished cry pierced the air. *Caroline.*

Allie turned. Her daughter wrestled her way out of Emma's grasp and ran up the center aisle. Her dark hair flew out like a cape behind her. She was calling, "Mommy!"

With the force of a comet hitting the earth, Caroline launched herself at Allie, throwing her thin arms around her waist, pressing her head to her mother's chest.

"Don't leave me," Caroline shrieked. "Come home, Mommy. Home. I'll do anything."

Officers moved in to pull her away. She flicked a desperate glance in their direction. "Please. One minute," she pleaded. Miraculously, the uniformed men stepped back.

"Caroline, sweetheart." Allie knelt down eye level with Caroline. "I want to come home. More than anything. Don't you believe me?"

Her daughter's crying slowed to hiccupping sobs.

"I am going to do my best to get back to you," Allie murmured. "As soon as I can."

Caroline eased back to look at Allie's face. She glanced up at her grandparents, then to Emma. "They're saying bad things. They say you did bad things."

Allie felt her heart collapse in on itself, the chambers deflating, the arteries bursting. The only thing more agonizing than leaving Caroline was disappointing her.

"It's not true. We're going to find out who really did this."

"Miss Marshall." One of the officers nudged Allie's arm and motioned for the door. "It's time." He stepped closer, ready to move Allie back to her holding cell.

Caroline stood motionless, her body slack and lifeless.

Allie grasped at the remaining seconds. She needed time to stop, for the earth to quit rotating. "I love you. No matter what— you're in my heart." Allie held her daughter's gaze.

"P-promise?" Caroline asked, choking back a sob.

"I promise."

2016

Allie wiped a tear from her eye with the bottom of one sleeve. It was the first day of her new life, and she was determined to make the most of it, starting with this moment.

With a deep, cleansing breath, Allie straightened her shoulders and walked toward the house. She examined the exterior of the little cottage her parents had picked out. It was small and tidy, unobtrusive, painted gray with white trim. The house was flanked with trees of all shapes and sizes—hickory, water oak, and sweetgum with its red-brown bark. A small porch held two wicker chairs and a tiny table. Empty flower boxes sat at each windowsill, waiting to be filled.

Home.

Allie rolled the word around in her mouth. It was strange, even thinking it. A place of her own. Somewhere without bars. Or guards. A space she could stretch out in and not touch cement wall.

Allie's breath quickened.

Home was the ability to walk down a street and still be able to pick out the house where your first-grade teacher lived. Home was the knowledge that the local library still held that musty smell and books stacked to the ceiling. Home meant that when you went for a drive, every single person you passed waved.

Allie loved Brunswick, always had. She'd grown up here, and had planned on coming back to practice after going to med school and completing her residency.

Now, though, she was in many ways a female version of Robinson Crusoe. Shipwrecked, sea-salt brined, and beaten from the surf. Left to her own devices. A stranger in a strange land, empty-handed, wishing to God she had a compass and a radio to signal for help.

She was starting over in Brunswick, but she was a survivor.

After all, she'd lived through Arrendale, a jungle in its own right. A place so treacherous, so full of predators, many women didn't make it out. She'd existed, however, relying on her own wits, her instincts. Tamping down fear and pushing away despair.

Allie *would* prove her innocence. She would find the clues that linked Sheriff Gaines to Coach Boyd Thomas's murder, if it was the last thing she did.

And then, only then, Allie would be truly free.

SIX

CAROLINE

2016

After splashing her face with water, Caroline pressed her forehead against the cold tile in the girls' restroom.

She didn't need to go to an assembly, or any school event, for that matter. And Caroline certainly didn't need to attend Mansfield Academy's Career Day, with its parade of smiling working professionals in uniform, telling her about the great future available as an airline pilot or an Army Ranger. Or listen to someone's uncle who spent the last thirty years working as a boat captain. Or, God forbid, listening to some all-knowing healer with his bright white doctor's coat and shiny stethoscope. If someone announced that a lawyer or judge was talking today, she might actually scream.

She couldn't think about the future.

Life as she knew it was over. Caroline needed an escape plan—now. A one-way ticket out of Brunswick, Georgia. A legitimate excuse to move to Switzerland. Or join the Peace Corps in Tanzania.

Anywhere but here.

The bell rang. She couldn't procrastinate any longer. Caroline glanced in the long mirror to smooth her dark hair and made her way into the hallway, through the throng of jostling students, out the doors, toward the auditorium building.

She followed the brick-lined walkways dusted with golden sand. The powdery crystals were everywhere—on the edges of the road, in sparse patches of grass on the middle school playground, and, on a windy day, in her hair and shoes.

Inside the double doors, standing on tiptoes, she scanned the room for Maddie's blonde head. Someone had waxed the floor to a dull shine, making everything smell of lemon. But the space was also dark and stuffy, like someone had flipped off the air-conditioning hours ago. It figured, when cramming together four or five hundred kids.

Fanning her face, Caroline dodged a group of girls. With a glance at the rear of the room, she noticed Maddie's hand in the air, waving. Gotcha. Third row back, fifth seat in. Relieved, Caroline quickened her pace. Stepping over book bags and easing past knees, she made her way down the aisle, finally sinking into the seat that had been saved for her.

Caroline exhaled, leaning toward Maddie. "I really have to talk to you—"

On stage, someone tapped a microphone. The dull sound reverberated around her. Teachers nearby clapped their hands and shushed students. The principal's voice asked for quiet.

As the room settled, Maddie tilted her head closer, lifted an eyebrow. "What's up?"

As she opened her mouth to speak, Caroline's neck prickled. She turned her head. From the middle of the room, one of the history instructors glowered in their direction.

Swinging her eyes back to Maddie, Caroline pursed her lips and tilted her head ever so slightly. Sharing it now wasn't worth the attention.

Scooting down in her seat and folding her arms across her chest, Maddie shrugged, looking briefly annoyed, then smothered a yawn. Stretching her arms out in front of her, Caroline feigned an equal amount of boredom.

They'd talk later. She'd tell Maddie everything.

Forcing thoughts of her mother from her mind, Caroline attempted to concentrate on the brawny FBI agent behind the podium. His deep voice echoed as he spoke about his training, and his story seemed to resonate with a few people sitting near the stage.

When a professional wedding photographer took the microphone next, Maddie wriggled in her seat and made a gagging motion around her neck. Risking detention, she snorted.

"As if," Maddie muttered. Their friends nearby tittered.

After smothering her own giggle, Caroline checked her watch. Almost done.

Maddie leaned in close. "So, Saturday night Will and some of the guys are having a bonfire out at his dad's place on St. Simons. It's right near Ocean Forest Golf Club, off Sea Island Drive. Want to come?"

"I'll ask." Caroline loved St. Simons. She loved the wind in her hair, the pale gold sand beneath her feet, how there was water as far as she could see. The sunsets on Brunswick were beautiful, but from St. Simons, they were breathtaking. The sky exploded in deep blues and purples, with streaks of blood orange and red below, turning the ocean shades of silver as the sun dipped low on the horizon.

As Caroline prepared to close her eyes and try to daydream through the next fifteen minutes, imagining sandpipers dancing on the shores of the Atlantic, a clear, crisp voice interrupted.

"Have you ever felt alone?"

A murmur traveled through the auditorium. There were a few scoffs. A cough or two. And then awkward silence.

"Really alone?" the woman continued, emphasizing both words.

Caroline opened one eye suspiciously. She felt alone all the time. Whether she was around Maddie or Jake, or a hundred people, she would never fit in. Never be normal.

Behind the woman on the stage, the screen dropped from the ceiling. An instant later, the image of an elderly woman appeared on the background. It wasn't any image. The lady looked destitute. Homeless. Obviously living on the street.

Caroline's stomach contracted. She actually *liked* old people. They weren't scary or weird.

Another picture. This time a man under a bridge. He was old too. Dressed in rags.

"These are real people. And they need your help."

This statement got murmured protest from a few students. Even Maddie rolled her eyes. But Caroline listened.

The speaker ran a place—a home—for the elderly. Not just some place. A nice one, with gardens and pets and birds. She showed photos of that too. And explained that they didn't turn anyone away. Some dude in town had donated a gazillion dollars to make sure everyone in Brunswick had a safe, nice place to live.

Caroline stared at the photos, locked in, while the woman talked. Students could work with nursing home residents a few days a week.

". . . especially those who are wheelchair-bound," the woman explained. "Many don't have family or friends who visit."

The nursing home lady rattled off more details. Students wouldn't be paid, but they could earn volunteer hours. Valuable for college applications and résumés. Flexible schedule. After school. Weekends. As much time as you wanted to give.

An escape plan. And she could help people. People who were alone too.

When the presentation finished, rousing applause shook the room, most of it mock approval for the sake of making noise. Students whistled and catcalled. Paper airplanes flew across the seats, and teachers yelled for single-file lines. Thankful for the chaos, Caroline slipped out the side door and made her way through the crowd to the school office, the idea still forming in her head.

Back at her aunt's house, Emma's reaction was about as tepid as she'd expected. "The nursing home?" Her aunt wrinkled her nose like she'd sniffed burnt toast, shuffling through the mail with perfectly manicured seashell-pink nails. "Wait." She glanced up with a raised brow, gesturing with the envelopes. "Did Maddie talk you into this?"

Emma loved Maddie. With her family's status in the community—practically the first settlers on Brunswick—her friend could do no wrong.

"Um, sure," Caroline replied, her throat swallowing the lie like dry bread. "It's good for college. Volunteering and stuff." She laid the paper in her aunt's waiting hand.

"In that case, you can do it together," Emma said with a hint of a smile. She whipped the sheet around, scribbled her name at the bottom in large, looping letters, and handed it back. "What did Jake say?"

"He's fine with it," Caroline lied. She hadn't actually decided what she'd tell him.

"Good." Emma turned back to the bills and colorful flyers. As she ripped open the next mailer, a grin spread across her face. She stopped suddenly. "It's great what you're doing, this volunteering," her aunt said, pausing for emphasis as she locked eyes with Caroline. "I love you so much. More than *anything*."

"Thanks," Caroline mumbled, though her voice stumbled over

the acknowledgment. Feeling her face grow warm, she folded the paper, creasing each end. Her aunt was always saying over-the-top, gushy things like that to Caroline, even in front of her friends.

Emma cleared her throat. "So, I have something to tell you . . . about your mom."

Caroline's head jerked back up. She glanced over her shoulder, as if someone might be standing behind her.

"Um. Well. What I need to tell you . . ." Emma hesitated and reached out her fingertips to graze Caroline's cheek. ". . . is that your mother actually came home today."

Her aunt's touch burned her skin. Feeling her knees lock, Caroline's throat closed tight while she waited for Emma to suggest she go and see her. A visit, to get to know each other again. Forgive and forget. The past in the past and all of that.

But Emma just drew Caroline in and hugged her close, rocking her back and forth and stroking her hair softly. After a few moments, Emma murmured, "It's going to be okay. I'm here. I always will be, sweetheart. I promise."

Head swirling, Caroline finally pulled away. She'd heard that years before. With clumsy, shaking fingers, she stuck the now-crumpled paper in her backpack. Eyes glazing with tears, she pulled the zipper hard and tight, watching its silver teeth knit together across the khaki canvas, wishing she could tuck herself inside.

SEVEN

ALLIE

2016

Forcing her feet forward, Allie walked up the smooth driveway, her feet soundless on the pavement. The key slid in the lock. Twisted with a click. Allie turned the knob and pressed gently.

The door swung wide open to reveal hardwood floors and a cozy interior. She inhaled the faint scent of pine cleaner. Her mother had definitely been here. While she felt for a light, Allie heard the quiet rumble of wheels on gravel behind her. One car door opened, then another.

Allie swallowed hard. She couldn't make herself move. Through a couple of jagged breaths, she heard footsteps on the porch. A low murmur. A woman's voice, unmistakably her mother's. Slowly, she turned and lifted her eyes to the doorway.

Like in a dream, her parents stood waiting. Her father, with his salt-and-pepper hair more pronounced than nine months ago when they last saw her at Arrendale. Her mother, with her short, dark hair swept behind her ears. Worried eyes, lips pressed in a line. As usual, her clothes and haircut were impeccable. She wore a slim-fitting, dark red dress, sensible pumps, and tasteful jewelry.

"Hi, Mom," Allie murmured, tears immediately springing into her eyes.

"Darling," her mother answered, her voice breaking. She opened her arms and wrapped Allie in a tight embrace. The light scent of honeysuckle wafted from her mother's skin, transporting Allie to her childhood. With careful hands, she held Allie back at arm's length.

"You're so thin." She blinked and glanced at Allie's father.

He had closed the door and was leaning against it, watching them with red-rimmed eyes. He took a heavy step toward Allie, but slowed to a stop, as if an invisible barrier held his body back.

"Allie."

Her voice caught. "Dad," she whispered.

And they stared at each other. Strangers, yet family.

Of her two parents, her prison time had been more difficult on her father. He'd aged what seemed like twenty-five years in ten. The arrest and trial had broken his heart. His face, still handsome, was lined with years of worry. He was painfully slender.

There was no way to close the distance between them. Though she'd sworn her innocence years ago, her father's doubt lingered. He didn't say as much, but Allie knew. She could see it in the way he looked at her—even now.

It killed Allie inside. The bond they'd shared was gone. The taste of it was bitter on her tongue. *I'm your daughter. Your own flesh and blood. Why can't you believe me?*

Her mother slipped an arm around her elbow and pulled her close. "Let me show you around."

Clearly thankful for the distraction, her father disappeared back into the foyer.

"There's a grocery store within walking distance," her mother continued. "A new Walgreens and a few restaurants close by. Of course, you're close to Gloucester and all of the downtown shops."

"And Dad's office," Allie added, tilting her head north. "I remember that much."

Her mother flashed an uncomfortable smile. "There's a bed in the back, and we brought over your old dresser and nightstand. I picked up some new clothes and put them in the closet. And Emma found you a refurbished computer, in case you want to get started job searching—or whatever." Her mother paused, winded from spouting all of the information in one breath.

"That's . . . so amazing," Allie said, feeling her cheeks grow warm. "Thank you."

"It's the least we could do . . ." Her mother's voice trailed off.

The small house was furnished simply and tastefully. Gauzy white panels, pressed and smelling of starch, hung from curtain rods. Her mother had selected a few paintings to grace the bare walls, along with a large silver-and-white clock.

It wouldn't be her parents' house, a grand old wooden structure, graced with a huge front porch and pillars. As a girl, she'd loved watching the ocean from her second-story window. It changed colors with the seasons, it seemed. Deep turquoise in spring, crystal blue for summer, the time for crab legs and oysters on the half shell. In the fall and winter, the surface changed by the hour from eggplant purple to cider gold.

Allie glanced around at the walls, the lone clock on the wall. The coast couldn't be seen from here, even if she climbed on the roof of the little house. But she was happy to have four walls and would sleep on the floor, if necessary. She ran a hand along a window frame, lifted the linen covering, and looked out to the street, in time to see the tail end of a police cruiser turn the corner.

In an instant, Allie's frame tensed, her face flash frozen. She listened for a buzzer, a lock closing tight.

2011

During her first five years as an inmate, Allie believed torture was being bounced from three different locations within the Georgia Department of Corrections. Each place, its own slice of hell, required months of readjustment and acclimation.

Allie hadn't counted on Arrendale.

Until 2004, the facility was men only and known as the most violent in the state system. Blood spilled daily. The body count was staggering. The news eventually trickled to the right ears.

In a campaign to quell public outcry about unsafe conditions, Arrendale transitioned into an all-women's prison the next year. But despite all efforts to sanitize its reputation, Arrendale's toxic atmosphere remained, as if a sickening disease had been pressed into the mortar or Anthrax piped in through the air vents.

From the first moments inside, Allie sensed it.

She was attacked the first week after being approached by a gang of malevolent, tattooed women. She'd ignored the overtures at first. Pretended she didn't hear them. Then the requests became more insistent. A shove. A yank on her hair. Threats.

Allie kept her head down and waited for the attack.

They jumped her at suppertime. A burly, muscled woman yanked her down to the floor and cut her face with a chip of brick, just above her eyebrow. She straddled Allie while her friends held down her arms and legs. Blood trickled into Allie's scalp. Instead of struggling, she lay still.

"Still think you're better than us?" the woman sneered, spittle dotting the edges of her cracked lips. "I'll fix that pretty face for good. Then we'll see—"

Guards yelled, attempting to press and wrestle their way through the crowd. Other catfights broke out, each officer fending off dozens of angry women surrounding Allie and her assailants.

Allie stared at the inmate crushing her ribs. "Go ahead."

The woman scowled in frustration. "You're too stupid to be scared."

As her attacker's hand came down to cut a second time, Allie channeled all of her focus and energy. She grabbed the woman's wrist, imagining it belonged to Sheriff Lee Gaines, and turned the bones until they snapped. The inmate yowled in pain and twisted away, allowing Allie an escape. Shifting her weight, Allie rolled upright, pinning the woman facedown on the concrete with one knee.

"Don't ever touch me again," Allie breathed close to her ear, then let the woman's limbs drop. She had everyone's attention and wasn't about to let the moment pass. Seconds later, Allie was yanked to her feet by a group of guards, the other woman dragged away by her elbows.

In the safety of the infirmary, after being cleaned and stitched, Allie collapsed into shivering convulsions on her gurney. No one had won. She was sickened at having to harm anyone, but she had been in the fight of her life. Allie had never been so frightened—not even in the courtroom on the day of her sentencing.

The warden ordered forty-eight hours in the SMU, the special management unit, or lockdown, for fighting. Allie used the time to put the day's events in perspective. Her limited knowledge of human anatomy and show of false bravado had saved her. She wondered if it was enough to keep her alive the next time.

It seemed a good time as any to pray, though Allie had never been particularly religious. Saying the words—talking to the air above her head—somehow comforted her. Her breathing slowed. Allie closed her eyes tight. There'd be proof soon enough if anyone up there actually listened.

Lord, help me survive this. Keep Caroline safe until I get home. I'll do anything.

The mantra became like a heartbeat. It kept her sane. Human.

One wish. One promise.

Every moment. Every day.

One step closer to Caroline.

2016

"Allie?" Her mother touched her arm. "Everything okay?"

Swallowing hard, Allie bobbed her head.

"Well, what do you think?" her mother asked.

Overwhelmed with gratitude, Allie faced her parents. "This is all . . . so much." Her voice cracked. She couldn't finish talking and pressed the back of her hand to her mouth. The little place was sparse, but it was hers. And she would be here tonight, alone. For the first time in ten years, a human or computer wouldn't monitor her every move.

"Thank you. It's wonderful."

"I'm so glad you like it." Her mother smiled.

"How in the world did you have time?" Allie asked, wide-eyed.

Her mother hesitated, her eyelashes fluttering in her husband's direction. Her father, face reddened, shifted from one foot to the other. "We sold the office," her father admitted.

Smothering a small cry, Allie covered her mouth with one hand. She couldn't speak. Sold? Just like that?

"To a young vet and her husband," he continued. "They have a son who's seventeen."

Allie's head swam. The vet office was an integral part of their lives, or so she had thought. For as long as she could remember, it was where her father worked—it was how people knew him, and his office was the place she spent summers and every day after school. Had her return to Brunswick caused this?

"It's a lot to take in, dear." Her mother clasped her hands together, trying desperately to look upbeat and cheerful. "But it was time to hand over the reins."

Allie's eyes met her father's. Even being away from the business for years, she knew the sale and transfer of a large animal vet office wasn't simple. Letting it go, giving it up, had to be like cutting off a limb.

Her father shrugged and gazed at the floor. "It was time," he echoed, as if he'd rehearsed the lines to himself until he believed them.

Allie's lips parted, but she couldn't think of a single thing to say.

"Get some rest," her father added gruffly. "I'm sure you're exhausted. From the drive. And everything . . ."

Allie blinked. They were leaving. It had been all of forty-five minutes. Maybe less. And still, no Caroline. Her heart thudded against her chest well.

"What about Caroline?" Allie asked slowly. "I-I thought she'd be here by now."

At the mention of her daughter's name, her father set his jaw.

Her mother stiffened and avoided Allie's gaze. "She had to stay after school. Homework—or something? She's so busy." Her mother's voice tightened, trying to sound light.

"You know teenagers," her father added, then stopped himself. A thin sheen of perspiration appeared across his hairline.

The words stabbed at Allie.

No, she thought. She did not know teenagers. She did not know anyone anymore. She didn't have friends, or a bank account, or a vase for fresh-cut flowers. Allie hadn't had a long, hot shower in what seemed a million years. She never slept through the night, and couldn't remember when she'd felt the sun on her skin without a barbed-wire shadow falling across it.

Her mother squeezed Allie's hand. "Just give her some time. She'll come around."

Allie tried to smile. She nodded as her eyes filled with tears.

She had to believe it. Believe she could prove what had really happened that night. And that Caroline would give her a second chance.

It was all she had lived for.

EIGHT

EMMA

2016

"Caroline," Emma repeated. She knocked again, beginning to lose her patience.

The music cranked louder.

Emma raised her voice. "Caroline, answer me!"

A second later, her niece jerked the door open three inches. Music blared at Emma's face, pushing her back. Startled, Emma gripped the door frame and caught her balance.

Caroline was a beautiful girl, dark hair and long eyelashes— but when angered, her face vacillated somewhere between fury and pain. Her creamy skin was pale and blotchy, eyes red-rimmed. She'd showered and changed, traded her school uniform for shorts and a faded Ramones T-shirt that smelled of baby powder.

Body prickling with concern for her niece, Emma motioned for her to turn off the song.

After a beat, Caroline pursed her lips and pressed the volume on her phone. When the room was silent, she twisted an earring, unable to meet her aunt's gaze.

"I know you're upset," Emma said, keeping her voice calm. She

43

reached out, pushed the door open farther, and tucked a strand of loose hair behind one of Caroline's ears. "But we need to talk about your mom, and you might as well eat while we're doing it."

There was a long pause before Caroline answered. "I'm not hungry."

"Honey." Emma sighed. She knew what was best for Caroline. She'd raised her since she wore smocked dresses and matching hair bows. "You have to eat. We've talked about this." Emma wouldn't allow Caroline to turn into one of those anorexic girls who ate only lettuce and thought skin and bones looked beautiful.

"I can't. I'll be sick," Caroline protested, crinkling her forehead and punctuating the last two words with emphasis.

Emma swallowed back another reproach. She would jot it down in Caroline's food diary, the one she began when her niece hit puberty. Though Caroline didn't know it, Emma kept track of everything. What she ate, her moods, her menstrual cycles. There was nothing that escaped her. It was for Caroline's own good.

"And I've got homework." Caroline gestured to the large stack of books on her bed.

After a beat, Emma nodded. It did look like a lot of homework, and Caroline had eaten breakfast. Skipping one meal was okay. She would allow it.

Caroline murmured a "thank you" as Emma backed away and shut the door. The lock clicked into place. Seconds later, music started playing, blaring from her speakers. Emma stood still, one hand pressed on the wooden edge of the door frame, as if it were a connection and not a barrier to her niece. Emma would figure out another way of coaxing her out tomorrow.

For now, Caroline's unhappiness was apparently going to include a tribute to Druery, a band out of Athens, Georgia, that sounded like a millennial version of The Doors. The homework excuse was doubtful. Caroline was a good student and had likely finished any assignments at school.

When the song started over, seemingly louder, Emma gripped the door frame and pressed her ear to the center of the smooth polished wood, where a peephole might be, imagining she heard her crying. Emma thought about her niece staring at the wall. Rocking on the bed with her arms wrapped around her knees.

Emma stilled the breath in her lungs, almost willing her own heartbeat to stop. She strained to listen, but there was no sound, other than the lyrics.

The world, in all its bitterness, sighs. It's the end of everything we tried to hide. You'd rather run; I'd rather die.

Emma hugged her arms tight to her chest, squeezing her rib cage, her fingers pinching her own skin. She hoped it would leave a mark. A reminder of how much she loved Caroline. How much she had sacrificed for the girl.

They'd been through hell and back with Allie's trial. She could live through a few days of this—both of them could. If it got much worse, she'd talk to Caroline's school counselors or an adolescent psychiatrist.

It was a fact: there wasn't any *good* time to reacquaint with a mother who'd been gone for a decade. No feel-better poem or Hallmark card saying. There wasn't any advice that would make a bit of difference.

Caroline needed stability. The sort of stability only Emma could provide.

In the kitchen, Emma uncorked and poured a Merlot-Syrah blend that boasted hints of cherry and chocolate on the tongue. Then, as she'd done more than a hundred times before, she logged on to the Internet and typed the URL she knew by heart and stared at the screen.

Emma took a long sip of the wine, allowing the velvety liquid to slide down her throat. She swallowed and examined the screen. Even in her mug shot, Allie was beautiful. Sea-glass eyes staring serene and cool at the camera. Sleek blonde hair grazing the tan collar of her prison-issued uniform. A face that belonged in a Rembrandt painting.

The exterior existed for everyone to examine, like taking turns with a science lab microscope. Allie was like a drop of blood between two slides. Something to be coded, checked, and recorded. Anyone could do the research, find the Lee Arrendale State Prison home page, and enter her name or inmate number. Allie's color photo would appear, along with her height, weight, birth date, information about her incarceration, and current sentence.

Emma scanned the details she knew by heart. Nothing had changed, except the release date had been verified. Added. And made official.

Allie was home. Allie, who used to be perfect in every way. Allie, the A student. Allie, the great mother. The favorite daughter.

But in the ten years Allie had been behind bars, Emma had become the good daughter, the one everyone counted on and respected for her sacrifices. She'd taken care of Caroline as if she were her own. She'd worked hard, done everything she was supposed to. She was now the shining star, the example to follow.

And Emma wasn't about to let that change.

No one—not Allie, not her parents, not the people in Brunswick—would ever make her feel inadequate again.

March 2006

Allie and Ben were lying in the backyard hammock, heads on opposite ends, swaying to make any breeze in the still, Georgia afternoon. For a Saturday in late March, the unseasonably warm weather, above eighty degrees, had drawn everyone in Brunswick outside to enjoy the weekend. Allie's small black lab, Molly, still just a puppy, with her shiny coat, dark eyes, and large paws she'd grow into, lay under the knotted ropes, dozing and shaded from the sun while Emma flipped through the latest issues of *Vogue* and *Cosmo*.

"Your MCAT scores are stellar. You're going to get in," Ben said to Allie. He waved a hand as if to dismiss her question. "We could pack a lunch and go to Driftwood Beach. Forget about medical school, for a few hours at least."

Allie smiled. "Thanks. Wish you were on the admissions committee."

"What are you worried about?" Emma asked, raising her head an inch to look at her sister. She propped herself up in the chaise lounge on one elbow, grabbed the bottle of sunscreen, and squeezed a creamy dollop onto her open palm. As she rubbed it into her skin, warmed by the sun, the lotion scented the air with coconut. "You just mailed off the applications yesterday."

"I know." Allie wrinkled her nose. "Even applying this early, replies can take a year. I might get a call in September for an interview to join next year's class."

Emma finished coating her skin with sunscreen and dropped back into the lounge chair. She stared up at the canopy of leaves, tracing the shelter of thick branches and gnarled trunk. Why couldn't her sister just be normal? Couldn't she relax for one day?

"What are the numbers for a first-year med school class at Emory?" Ben asked.

"Five thousand students apply, more or less." Allie paused. "They interview seven hundred, give or take. From there, they pick one hundred and forty, half of them women. Not exactly a slam dunk."

"If anyone can do it twice, you can," Ben argued. "Besides,

you've got the single mom thing going. You're twenty-six years old, you're smart, you're a hard worker."

Emma twisted her lips in frustration. Did her sister have to have validation all of the time?

"I was twenty when I applied the first time." Allie lowered her voice. "A lot of things have changed since then. More competition—"

"They accepted you before." Ben brushed away her excuse with a wave of his hand.

"Even if you don't get in," Emma interrupted, "Mom can keep Caroline and you can still work at Dad's office." She huffed a sigh, then went back to flipping through the magazine, smoothing down the shiny pages. She examined the lithe models, imagining how one of the gauzy dresses and strappy sandals might look against her skin and thinking it would surely attract some attention at one of the parties on St. Simons.

From the corner of her eye, Emma could see Allie frown and exchange a quick look with Ben. Her sister was such a goody-goody. Such a worrier and, what was worse, upholder of a strict moral compass—a girl who expected everyone else to live by the same impossibly high standards.

And her sister, of course, was too smart to stay in Brunswick. She would get out of this town and would leave everything, including Emma, behind.

A rustling sounded near the shrubs, interrupted the resentment bubbling up in her chest. Emma sat up and ran a hand through her hair as Morgan Hicks stepped between the azaleas, carrying an open bottle of wine. Another girl, a freckled, strawberry blonde, and two guys trailed behind, each making their way through the narrow opening in the landscaping.

"Um, how about using the front door?" Emma asked under her breath.

Allie sat up. "Aw, Em. It's okay, right?"

Morgan kissed Allie's cheek, said hello to Ben, then slid a glance at Emma. "Sorry, we'll call next time." She winked at one of the guys, who raised a six-pack of beer in response.

"It's fine." Emma shrugged and heaved up into a sitting position, wiggling her legs so that her feet dangled close to the ground.

"This is Kira." Morgan slung an arm around the girl's shoulders. "Jack is her boyfriend, this is Alec, and . . ." Her voice slurred and trailed off. She paused, then snapped her fingers. "Chase!" she exclaimed.

"When'd she meet them, five minutes ago?" Emma whispered under her breath. Morgan *did* spend her time shopping and dating Atlanta's most eligible bachelors. Her family made tons of money. She never could decide whether to loathe Morgan or emulate everything she did. Morgan blew hot and cold with Allie as well. She was occasionally overtly cruel to her sister, a trait her sister refused to acknowledge, but one Emma found slightly amusing, especially when Allie was on her last nerve.

"Please be nice?" Allie leaned over to nudge her sister. "Morgan likes you." She gave Emma's hand a quick squeeze.

Morgan clapped to get everyone's attention. "So, Alec's mom and dad have a place on St. Simons," she said, arching an eyebrow. "They've bought a new yacht and are docking it this morning."

Emma pressed her lips tight as Morgan continued her story. There was *always* a story or drama flaunting someone's wealth. Allie and Emma's own father had money, but not that kind.

"So we decided to avoid the commotion and drama and swing through town to see you first." Morgan struck a pose, hip out, a grin on her red lips, as if she'd just announced an unexpected space shuttle landing in the waves off Sea Island.

"Great," Allie exclaimed, nodding. "I'm so glad. Mom and Dad are out at the movies with Caroline. Ben, can you grab some extra chairs? Check the back porch."

Ben unfolded himself from the hammock and headed for the garage.

Morgan plopped down in a chair and made a wry face. "I haven't seen you in forever!" she exclaimed to Allie, then turned back to the group and smoothed a stray hair from her face. "So, I should make the formal introductions. Kira and Alec are attorneys at my firm. Jack's at the DA's office in Atlanta," Morgan said with a sly smile. "And my friend, Allie, is going to be a doctor." She raised her cup in a tipsy salute.

Chase twisted off the cap of a beer bottle. "Just finished my MBA." He turned to Allie as Ben returned with folding chairs. "So, med school, eh?"

"Hopefully." Allie suppressed a grin.

Jack tapped his chin, finished off his beer, and pointed at Ben. "What about you? What's your claim to fame?"

Ben hesitated, glancing at the bottle in Jack's hand. "Political advisor."

Jack sputtered, then laughed. "No way, man. Really?"

"Really." Ben sat on the hammock next to Allie and began rubbing her arm. He winked over at her. "If Sonny Perdue wins his second term as governor, there's a good chance I'll be tapped to join his staff."

Allie pulled him close and kissed him. "It's going to be great. And Perdue's going to win."

Emma pursed her lips and rolled her eyes. If Ben wasn't so darn devoted to her sister, she would have made a move a long time ago. After all, Ben was hot, in a boy-next-door sort of way. But he was different. He had strict ethics, like Allie. He was a straight shooter. And had been positively smitten with Allie since they were little.

Sighing, Emma tried to focus on the conversation around her.

"So, a couple of lawyers, an MBA, one doctor," Jack was saying, ticking off the careers on his fingers. "That's a pretty good showing." He paused and swung around to look at Emma, who jumped. "All right, young lady!" Jack stood up and lunged suddenly, pointing in her direction as if he were thrusting a sword at an opponent.

Emma reddened and jerked back, almost falling off her seat. Everyone except Ben and Allie let out a giggle.

After stalking back and forth, rubbing his chin, Jack stopped. "You're a model?" He winked and gave her a long look. "Sure pretty enough to be one."

Emma softened a bit but rolled her eyes for effect anyway.

Jack tipped his head and pretended to adjust his glasses. "A psychologist? Psychiatrist?"

"She's twenty-one, Jack, not thirty-five," Allie interjected.

Emma's stomach twisted, and her skin prickled hot. *Stop. Stop. Stop.* She wanted to clap her hand over this guy's mouth. She hated Allie for not telling them to leave right then. Goose bumps rose on her skin. Inside, her sister was probably enjoying it.

"Come on, this is fun," Jack retorted. He unscrewed another beer bottle and took a long swallow. "How about a pilot? That's it. An airline pilot." Jack wavered, waiting for applause or confirmation. "Right?"

"Don't," Ben said, shooting Jack a warning look. "Quit, man. It's not a game."

Emma sent Jack an icy glare. "Just a lowly office manager at a vet office. Guess you crashed and burned on that one, smart guy."

NINE

CAROLINE

2016

Like walking a tightrope on roller skates, everything in Caroline's life felt off-kilter. At any second, she'd swing to one side, lose her balance, and *splat!* on the pavement.

Maybe that would be better, because in the past forty-eight hours, she'd spiraled out of control. Lost all sense of bravery, shut herself up in the house, and managed to lie to everyone she knew.

Caroline lay back on the bed, arms stretched over her head. She stared at the ceiling, connecting specks of dust and dimples in the paint. Trying to make sense of what wasn't making any sense. She was usually logical. And thoughtful. And a good friend.

But when Maddie tried to drag her to the mall, Caroline made up an excuse about doing a favor for her aunt. When her grandparents called and asked her to dinner, suggesting her favorite she-crab soup, she invented a movie get-together with Emma. When her aunt suggested a drive to Jekyll Island to check out the Sea Turtle Center, which she usually loved, Caroline feigned a headache. She'd even refused an afternoon Starbucks run with Jake.

She'd stayed in her room, window cracked, listening to the

rain, the warm air thick and sweet with earthy foliage from the salt marshes. All because she couldn't find the right words. The right time. A proper, reasonable explanation.

Because nothing said "awesome" like your mother getting out of prison.

Interlacing her fingers, Caroline covered her eyes, pressing her thumbs tight into her temples.

Sure, everybody—all of her friends—had awful stuff happen. Maddie's mom was addicted to sleeping pills and painkillers. Another one of her friends had a dad who blew his family's fortune at the dog tracks. The bank foreclosed on their McMansion. They took the cars, her mom's jewelry, even the beds. Jake's dad was an alcoholic and hit him. There were times, according to Jake, his dad would get so wasted he wouldn't remember smashing plates or breaking the TV. One time he ran the family car into a tree.

Caroline decided she'd rather have any one of those problems. Any day. In fact, she'd take all of it—combined—over a mother who'd spent the last ten years as an inmate. A parent convicted of killing someone.

She pulled her sleeves past her fingertips and wiped at her damp cheeks.

There would be no tender reunion.

The best she could, she would stay away.

Ignore her. And be invisible.

There was a knock on her bedroom door. Firm. Insistent.

"Caro?" Emma's voice floated through the wooden barrier. "You okay? Can I come in?"

Caroline took a deep breath and adjusted the messy ponytail on top of her head. "Sure."

Her aunt cracked the door, wide enough that Caroline could see half of her face. Her aunt was her mirror image. The same chocolate-brown eyes. The same shiny dark hair. "Hey there, sweet-heart. Feeling better?"

"Sure. Good enough to do my shift at the nursing home."

The door opened a few more inches.

"You're positive?" Emma scanned her face. "Want to talk about anything?"

"No, it's okay." Caroline glanced at the clock, then pushed herself up into a seated position, crossing her legs on the bed.

"If you change your mind . . ." There was a pause, and Emma tried to smile.

"Thanks." Caroline shifted uncomfortably. She knew her aunt was making every effort to help, and she loved her for it. She would do better tomorrow, she promised herself.

Emma cleared her throat. "And I know you have to go soon, but I brought you a little something." Her aunt held a small object from behind her back. She stepped forward and placed a gray velvet jewelry box on Caroline's bed.

"Oh, wow." Pangs of guilt ricocheted through Caroline's body. The room seemed to spike twenty degrees. With Emma watching every move, Caroline carefully picked up the gift, placed it in the center of her open palm, and slowly lifted the top. "Oh, wow," she repeated, sucking in a breath.

Inside lay a platinum necklace with half a heart edged in tiny dia-monds. Her finger traced the delicate chain. For a half moment, she thought it was a mistake. This was for best friends. Or a married couple on those jewelry commercials. Caroline's eyes rose to meet Emma's.

As if sensing the question on Caroline's mind, Emma patted the center of her own chest, where the matching platinum and dia-mond pendant rested.

Caroline had been so distracted, so focused on her own worry that she hadn't even noticed the new jewelry.

Emma smiled broadly. "See? This way we'll never be apart."

"Thank you." Caroline lifted the necklace from the box and secured it around her neck, expecting that her aunt would give her a small lecture about love, trust, and family, but instead, she just hugged her close.

Caroline allowed herself to melt a little in the embrace.

"Have a great first day, sweetheart," Emma whispered into her ear. She released her and brushed a stray hair from Caroline's cheek. "I'll let you finish getting ready."

The door closed behind her aunt with a click.

With a final glance at the clock, Caroline reached for her backpack, gathered her belongings, and slung the bag over one shoulder. It was time to go. Time for her first real shift at the nursing home.

Caroline paused to look in the mirror. Her reflection gazed back, so pale and serious that it made her shiver. Maybe, just maybe, if people could see through her skin, they wouldn't like what they saw underneath.

Someone flawed. Someone scared. Not the perfect niece Emma wanted her to be.

She was a girl who smiled on the outside while she died a little on the inside.

A daughter running away to avoid the past.

Caroline's steps made a *slop-slop* sound on the pavement.

The last raindrops dripped from the sky, like someone had squeezed a cloth tight, then let go. The clouds broke apart, torn balls of cotton, and were floating away.

As she walked farther from home, the tension in her neck and back lifted. She could breathe and inhaled deeply, clearing her lungs. It felt better to be outside.

She was needed, she reminded herself. She had a job. Yesterday's orientation had been less than exciting, but everyone was so welcoming and enthusiastic. It almost made Caroline feel as if she belonged.

Water lay in scattered puddles. Caroline picked her way around them, even jumping over the biggest one she could find. Leaping across it made her feel five years old again, and she twirled her umbrella behind her back, stirring the breeze. She liked the way the air smelled after a storm, clean and fresh, unspoiled.

The nursing home doors swished wide, opening a world of entirely different scents. On the first floor, sharp sanitizer filled her nostrils. On the second, baby powder and soap mixed with the dinner menu. *Pot roast tonight*, Caroline thought as she stepped off the elevator and sniffed the air carefully. The aroma of green beans and baked potatoes floated through as she passed the kitchen and headed for the volunteer office to check in. Ten minutes later, Caroline had filled out consent forms and pinned on her volunteer badge.

As Caroline stepped into the hallway and waited for a supervising employee to swing by and pick her up, she watched as a parade of elderly ladies and a few men hobbled to the dining room. A rail, for gripping and steadying, lined the walls. It was all in slow motion, as if someone had taken the minutes and stretched them like rubber bands, taut and thin. Because there was nowhere to go. No one to see.

When a tiny, wizened woman seemed to stumble and sway, Caroline rushed forward, offering a hand to help. She grasped the resident's frail frame, guiding her to a seat at one of the tables.

"Thank you, dear." The woman smiled up at Caroline with watery blue eyes as she drew a white cloth napkin across her lap.

"Of course." Caroline flushed with pleasure. She liked helping.

And the people here didn't care at all what brand of shoes she wore or the last names of her best friends. They probably didn't know—or couldn't remember—about her mother.

Maybe, *for once*, she could simply be.

After pushing in another resident's chair, she spent the next hour shadowing one of the more experienced aides, waiting and listening patiently until she was given a task or two to complete on her own.

Finally, she had her chance.

"Take this plate to room 204, sugar?" the aide asked, handing over a warm, covered dish on a plastic tray. "Just warning you, this one won't leave her room. Won't come into the hallway. Can't do much with her." The aide shook her head, black curls bouncing against each other. "But we have to try."

Caroline straightened and smiled, balancing the dish and platter. "Of course."

She repeated the room number to herself as she walked out of the dining room into the hallway. Caroline hurried her steps, glancing at the tiny numbers at the corner of each doorway. "204, 204," she reminded herself.

The door was opened, but she knocked twice anyway. A boy, not much older than she was, swiveled his head at the sound. His eyes, warm and brown as a thoroughbred's coat, were bright and inquisitive. He wore scrubs the color of ripe apples in the fall, setting off his tanned skin and squared jaw.

"Um, I'm . . ." Caroline's voice drifted off. Stay or go? Where was she needed?

"We're almost finished," he said with a grin and turned back to his patient, expertly manipulating her arm, stretching and bending the joints. "Hey, I'm Russell. I volunteer in PT." His smile was huge, showing a row of perfect white teeth. "Physical Therapy," he added quickly. A lock of dark hair fell over his eye as he gestured for Caroline to set down the tray.

"Hey," Caroline said, a slight tickle creeping up her neck.

When she put down the dinner tray, she noticed that the woman was staring at her and smiling. Like she recognized her. But that wasn't possible. Caroline had never seen her before.

"Hello, dear!"

In response, Caroline offered a small wave. "Hi."

"Oh goodness, I couldn't tell at first," the woman squinted. "My eyes seem to play tricks on me these days. But it is you." She waved at Caroline to come closer. "Now, come over here so that I can see you." In her navy-blue dress, pearl earrings, and sensible shoes, she could have been one of the ladies from church who drove a big Cadillac. *What is she doing here?*

"It's been such a long time," the lady continued, smiling as if they were friends, reunited after years apart. "How are you, dear?"

Caroline gulped and shrank away. This was too weird.

Russell raised an eyebrow at the resident and moved his body between Caroline and the woman. "I'll have your friend come back and visit later," Russell said to the woman and motioned for Caroline to leave the room. "There are some other folks waiting on their supper."

Grateful, Caroline backed out the door, one foot behind the other. "Let's finish up here. Just a few more minutes." Russell's voice carried into the hallway.

Caroline leaned her head against the nubby plastic wallpaper, listening. He was so very patient. The woman began mumbling, strings of words Caroline couldn't quite put together.

"Patients . . . Surgery, three o'clock. Pitocin drip . . . Stat."

Knuckles resting on her lips, she couldn't resist taking another peek. Between bursts of speech, Russell patiently answered or commented. She'd never seen a person take as much time and care with another human being.

When he finished, Russell came out into the hallway and closed the door behind him. "You did fine," he told Caroline. "She's a tough one, stubborn to the core."

Caroline hesitated, trying to find the right words. She didn't want to seem scared, or uncaring. "What's wrong . . . I mean, what happened to her?"

"Head trauma ten years ago. She was in an accident." He sighed. "Her memory—the short-term part—is really piecey. She has some good days and some bad. This wasn't one of the better ones."

"She thinks she knows me," Caroline said, pressing a hand to her heart. The muscles below her fingers seemed to ache with the woman's loss of memory. "Why? How could she?"

Russell leaned against the wall. "Well, she could call me George Washington, for all I care." He gave Caroline a kind smile. "You can't be afraid of her. Or any of the patients here. If anything, they're afraid of you. Imagine waking up every day and not being able to remember who you are. How terrified you'd be."

Caroline looked at her shoes, absorbing the advice. "It would be okay with me."

Russell blinked his eyes and tilted his head.

"No kidding. You'd trade what you've got to be in this place?" He rubbed his stubbled jaw with one hand. "You've got to have a whole lot of baggage you're carrying around with you for . . . what? All of fifteen years old?" Russell smiled.

"Almost sixteen," Caroline lied, her face reddening. Why had she said that? It was months until her next birthday.

"I'm seventeen and a senior at Brunswick." He peered at her closely. "You go to school there?"

"Mansfield Academy," she murmured, dropping her eyes to her

shoes, then letting them travel back up to his face. He was still looking right at her.

"Ah, the elite school." He winked. "Now I'm sure I've got more skeletons in the closet." Russell winked again and challenged. He tapped his chin. "Let's wager on some ice cream in the cafeteria. Loser pays."

"I'll win," Caroline responded under her breath. "I'm a freak."

Russell wrinkled his forehead and extended a hand. "You're pretty sure of yourself." They shook on it. His grip was warm and reassuring.

No wonder the residents liked him. There was something there, behind the nice face and features, that made her want to open up and confess everything.

Caroline looked up at him. When Russell squeezed and let go, she felt a jolt down to her toes. After a moment, she regained her balance and stepped back. "Um, I have to check in with the nurses. It's my first day, besides orientation. I'm here until seven tonight."

"Okay, so that's about thirty minutes." Russell checked his watch. "I have one more person to check on, and then I'm finished. That should work out about right. You have time for that ice cream?"

"Okay." Caroline ducked her head, unable to look at him square in the face. She had all of the time in the world, but she wasn't certain she wanted to spend it talking about her screwed-up family. She'd said too much already. She needed to be paying attention to the residents, making sure she was doing her job.

"Give me your number?"

Caroline stopped. "Excuse me?"

"So I can call you and tell you where I'm sitting," he said, his eyes twinkling.

"You won't remember it."

"Try me." Russell smiled broadly.

Flattered, and against her better judgment, Caroline rattled off seven numbers. Fast. And blushed.

"Nice. Meet you in the cafeteria then?" He jabbed his thumb at the elevator. "I have to run. A lovely ninety-year-old in room 307 is waiting for me."

Caroline nodded and let out the breath she'd been holding, relieved Russell was heading to another floor. It would give her time to decide what to do. Should she really meet him later?

She blinked her eyes and turned one shoulder. One of the aides had drifted back to the nurses' station, holding a chart in one hand. Caroline headed in her direction.

"Hi," Caroline said softly. "Is there anything else you need? Anything I can do? I'm here another half hour."

The aide looked up and pursed her lips. "Oh, you go on home, sugar. Thanks for your help. Just sign out on that sheet for me, all right?"

Swallowing back a pang of regret, Caroline picked up the ballpoint pen and poised it over the volunteer sheet. She'd come here to hide, but they were already telling her to head home. Where was left? Where would she go? Caroline scribbled her name, pressing so hard the tip ripped the page. She took off her badge, hung it on the wall. "Good night," she murmured.

"Have a good evening," the aide said with a smile, opening a drawer and searching.

"Thank you." Caroline turned and walked toward the exit, hugging her arms around her rib cage. She could go to the cafeteria and wait. But then, there would be questions. She pressed a hand to her chest. What if he found out about her mother?

She heard the elevator doors chime and begin to open. She moved even faster, hoping it wasn't Russell, done early. Six more steps. Toward the door, toward outside, where no one would look at her or ask questions, or pretend to care.

Two more steps. The doors opened, and the space was full of carts and trays and people. No room for another body. Even if she squeezed.

"I think I'll take the stairs," she called back to the nurses' station.

"Okay," the woman replied. "I'll buzz you out."

"Thank you."

Moments after Caroline reached the end of the hallway, the sensor flashed red and the lock clicked open. The door swung into a wide, yawning stairwell. It was dingy and gray and smelled of burnt rubber.

At the bottom, below the Exit sign, she pushed hard on the door's metal bar. Outside, despite the afternoon rainstorm, early evening had turned humid, almost suffocating. Steam rose from the pavement under barely glowing streetlights as the sky turned brilliant shades of poppy red and gold.

Barely noticing any of it, Caroline drew a ragged breath and began to run. After weaving through the parking lot and dodging cars, she pushed her body harder, forcing her legs to move faster.

But every ounce of effort she expended seemed wasted. She might as well be running in quicksand. The air, thick and sticky, clung to her like guilt.

TEN

ALLIE

2016

Allie's parole officer, Gladys Williams, was a serene-faced, long-limbed woman with skin the color of rich mocha. She wore a trim, bright red suit, the color setting off her brown doe eyes and glossy black hair. Her voice, low and musical, reminded Allie of jazz vocalists in New Orleans.

Her office wasn't far, but Allie had asked to borrow her mother's car to make the drive. The first meeting consisted mostly of a lecture, which Allie supposed wasn't at all out of the ordinary.

"Never had a parolee sent back," Gladys explained, leaning back in her chair and studying her with a grim expression. "Don't plan on you being the first." She ran through potential offenses—obvious ones like missing parole meetings or phone check-ins, avoiding known offenders, and getting arrested again.

"I understand," Allie replied. She wasn't the same person as she'd been ten years ago. Nine years earlier, she'd been vulnerable, naïve, and full of grief. Quick to anger. Fast to defend herself. There was so much she didn't know and had to learn. There were no how-to manuals for prison life. No tips that taught you how to survive.

In the end, it all came down to a will to live. Wanting freedom more than wanting to give up. Wanting justice, and a real life with Caroline.

"Don't go looking for trouble," Gladys warned. She stared at Allie for a moment, not allowing Allie's gaze to fall away. "People aren't going to always be accepting about you moving back to Brunswick. There might be a tendency for you to want to set people straight. Even do a little investigative work of your own."

Clearly, Gladys was an intelligent woman, fully aware of small-town politics. Under duress, off the record, she might even agree that some cases were far from fair, that evidence was overlooked or buried. Her job, though, wasn't to defend Allie's guilt or innocence. It wasn't to make things right or hold anyone's hand. It was to keep her parolees safe.

As Gladys continued to talk, Allie suppressed the urge to defend herself, to explain that—if given time—she was sure she could connect Sheriff Gaines to the coach's death. The two men, who'd worked together to create a championship football team, must have come to blows over something huge, Allie thought. With the worst of timing, she'd stumbled into a storm like no other, getting sucked into the vortex, everything she'd ever known to be true ripped from her grasp.

"Are we clear?" Gladys finally asked. "No drama. No gossip. No editorials in the paper. And no talking to anyone about the coach, his football team, or how much you still believe those players were being abused or coerced into bulking up with steroids."

"I understand." Allie dropped her chin; her eyes flooded with tears. She'd been naïve and reckless, so bent on exposing the truth, only to find out that no one wanted to hear about it. Allie wiped at her cheeks. If she even breathed a word of her suspicions, Gladys would likely tell Allie—ever so politely—that she was due for an IV full of psychiatric medicine to flush the idea out of her system.

Gladys softened her voice. "I know this is hard. But I want you to have a real chance at a new life. A second chance." She paused. "So let's start by looking for a job. Something that will keep you busy, out of the public eye if possible. Let things settle down."

Allie nodded. She had held a job at the prison library and had loved the calm. She enjoyed being around the books and often helped the other inmates who were taking classes or pursuing a GED. While the library was a possibility, she imagined that well-heeled local moms probably wouldn't relish the idea of Allie even being in the same building during children's story time.

"Where'd you work in high school?" Gladys asked, reaching for her Coke and finishing the bottle in a few swallows.

"I was a vet tech in my father's office," Allie answered, her fingers toying with the edge of her shirt. She looked up at Gladys. "He just sold it. I don't know the people who bought it. They're new in town."

Gladys considered this, swiveling back and forth in her chair. She made a pyramid with her hands and rested her chin on her fingertips. "Put in applications everywhere you can, but try the new vet too. Sometimes people will surprise you."

After another ten minutes of lecture and advice, Allie shook hands with Gladys, left the office, and slipped into her mother's car. She slid behind the wheel, but instead of heading home, she drove south, taking Ocean Highway, crossing Fancy Bluff Creek, and turning on Jekyll Island Road, then South Beach View Drive. She needed solitude and time to think.

Allie drove the narrow streets until she reached St. Andrews Beach overlooking Jekyll Sound. It was just as she'd remembered it, with its walking trail, a nature overlook, and areas for bird watching. It was a short walk to the ocean's edge, and Allie slipped off her shoes after crossing the deserted wooden boardwalk.

Not caring that she'd dirty her pants, or if anyone saw her, Allie sat cross-legged on the sand, gazing out at the waves. The sound and motion were magical. Her pulse slowed; Allie's brain quieted.

Allie thought again about Gladys and her advice. She said a silent thank-you and counted this as an unexpected blessing. It was a nod toward hope, faith, and a bright future. Encouragement. Something Allie so desperately needed after so much heartbreak.

2000

Sixteen years ago, the night she'd met Caroline's father, Allie was celebrating. Earlier that day, she'd finished the MCAT exam with dozens of other medical school prospects. The assessment was grueling. Hours later, chemical equations and compounds still swam in Allie's head, iridescent minnows in a fish bowl, darting like the haphazard patterns she'd left on the answer sheets.

Indulgence seemed the proper reward. She was spending the night in Atlanta, and Allie allowed herself to veer off the path of reason for a few short hours. The other students—a few acquaintances from near Brunswick, the rest, new faces—swept her off to dinner, laughing, swapping stories. Afterward, they'd all headed to an upscale bar and restaurant, planning to keep celebrating late into the night.

A mile from the bar, Allie admitted that she was still twenty and underage.

"What?" One of the girls from Dahlonega smiled as if she hadn't heard her correctly.

"How?" The guy who lived in Buckhead wrinkled his brow.

The chatter in the car silenced.

"Um, I finished high school in three years," she protested, feeling her cheeks flush pink. It had always been a bit of consternation between her and Emma, who'd accused her of doing it to show off. Her sister didn't understand. Allie was ready to break out of Brunswick, ready to tackle medical school and start her career. "Hey, you can just drop me back at the hotel," she added, squirming down in her seat.

But in the end, she'd been overruled. And during the evening, after being slipped a few martinis and dancing under the lights, Allie caught the attention of a dark, handsome foreign exchange student.

A half hour later, Antonio had sidled over, introduced himself, and whispered in her ear. Minutes later, he kissed her full on the lips. When his hand slipped under her shirt, resting on the small of her back, Allie shivered with delight. Dizzy with anticipation, giddy with attraction to the dark and exciting student from Italy, she let him take her home.

He was engaged, a fact Allie discovered eight hours too late. The morning after, on the back of the bathroom door, triangles of white tied with bits of string caught her eye. A woman's bathing suit.

Antonio had smiled and explained, his expression unwavering, matter-of-fact.

It was as if Allie had found a lost key or a missing piece of cheap jewelry. His fiancée had left for Rome only days before. He'd join her when the semester ended—for their wedding—in December in Milan.

Allie left his apartment building, half dressed, oxygen like fire in her lungs as she choked on the knowledge. She didn't want this anyway—she convinced herself—the complications of a relationship, especially one that involved another country, another culture. Certainly not one that involved a wife.

By the time Allie realized she was pregnant, the handsome Italian exchange student had already flown back to Tuscany. She'd never contacted him. And wouldn't.

The mistake was hers alone.

As the months passed, Allie hid her burgeoning belly in her parents' backyard while everyone in Brunswick buzzed about the identity of the baby's father. Her friends had rallied, planned a baby shower, and her parents had eventually accepted the idea after initial shock and disappointment.

Ben, the boy next door, came to her rescue. They'd grown up together, scraped their knees together, lost their front teeth at the same time. There were pictures of them together in her backyard, splashing in a blue plastic pool.

In the months before Caroline's birth, and almost every day after, Ben was there. He'd bring a funny book on parenting or a small baby gift, Allie's favorite cookies or a new magazine.

Little by little, Allie began to sense what was obvious to everyone else. The day after Caroline's first birthday party, when her daughter was down for a nap, Ben confessed.

"Ben," Allie said, shaking her head, thinking she heard him wrong. "You . . . what?"

"I love you. I've always loved you," Ben said, his face breaking into a wide grin at her reaction. "Since you were in diapers."

Allie blinked back tears as Ben took her in his arms and kissed her. When she caught her breath and met his steady gaze, one question burned in her mind. "But what about—"

Ben put a finger to her lips. "I love Caroline like my own daughter. Don't you know that?"

All at once, Allie melted, sobs of joy wracking her body.

"You don't have to worry. I'll take care of you and Caroline," Ben whispered, lifting her face in his hands. "I will spend every day, every waking moment, making you happy. I don't care about the past. I love you, and that's for always."

2016

Allie woke with a start, clutching her pillow. For a moment, she couldn't breathe. She clicked on the lamp next to her bed, willing the light to chase away the nightmare that had haunted her for the last decade.

He was there, pale and motionless. Lying on his back, arms and legs sprawled out like he'd fallen from three stories up. There was blood, a cut on his head. He blinked at Allie and opened his mouth to speak. There was a gurgle, low and wet, deep inside his chest.

Screaming, Allie sank to the floor and checked for his pulse. Tilted his head back and started compressions, rescue breaths. Too late. It was all too late.

Heart thudding inside her chest, Allie rubbed at her eyes with her fists, blinking into the darkness, trying to shake the panic. It was midnight—she had fallen asleep hours ago.

After spending the afternoon in downtown Brunswick looking for a job—and being met with a very chilly reception—Allie was so exhausted that she didn't even bother to undress.

Kneading her temples, Allie let her eyes adjust to the darkness, taking steady breaths to slow her racing pulse. She reached for her phone on the nightstand, scrolled through her contacts, and dialed the number of the only person she trusted in the world.

"Allie?" Emma's sleepy voice came through, punctuated with a wide yawn. "It's midnight. What's wrong?"

Allie hunched her shoulders and wrapped her arms around her knees. "Everything. Nothing. I don't know." She started crying.

"Hey. Whoa. What happened?" Emma asked.

After choking back more tears, Allie cleared her throat. "I don't think..."

Emma waited. "What, Allie?"

"I don't know if I can do this. Be here." The words tumbled out of Allie's mouth faster than she could catch them.

"What happened?"

Allie swallowed and wiped at her forehead. "First parole meeting." She inhaled deeply, put a hand on her chest.

Emma didn't answer right away.

"Then I put in job applications. Like, a dozen, all over town. Some of them I did online at the library. A few I had to do in person. One restaurant, a tackle shop down by the pier," she added. "There was one job for a cleaning technician, which is a nice way of saying janitor. That lady snatched the application out of my hand and told me they'd filled the position."

"Listen," Emma said. "That's a lot of stress. Give yourself a break."

In her brain, Allie knew her sister was right. But in her heart, she was frightened. That she couldn't handle it. She couldn't do this. Any of it. Allie eased her way to the floor and stretched out on a small rug. She stared into the black of the ceiling. Lying close to the ground felt better, sheltered. There was only the sound of her sister's breath in her ear.

"And Caroline never came by the house," Allie admitted. "Not all week. And I'm really hurt."

This wouldn't be news to Emma, but Allie needed to say it out loud. The words made it true. Without telling someone, without sharing her feelings, staying in her fantasy world was possible. Her daughter might have forgotten, she was late, or she had a valid excuse.

"I know," Emma replied. There was silence, and then her sister let out a deep, long sigh.

As Allie turned her face to the window, the moon, shimmering and silver, peeked out behind a cloud. The sudden light washed over her arms and legs, found its way across the room, where a photo of Caroline sat in a white frame. Sitting up and reaching for the picture, phone still in the crook of her neck, Allie took it in both hands as if somehow she still had a thread connecting her daughter. Her breathing slowed. Deepened.

"Hey, you still there?" Emma said.

Allie readjusted the phone on her shoulder. "Yes. And I'm a little better. Thanks for listening to me go on like a crazy person."

"Get some sleep," Emma answered, punctuating the command with a yawn. "It's late. You'll feel better in the morning."

"Are we still on for dinner tomorrow?" Allie paused, staring at the night sky beyond her daughter's picture.

"Sure," Emma murmured into the phone. "See you then, okay?"

ELEVEN

EMMA

2016

Almost without breathing, Emma watched Caroline sleep. The spill of her lush, dark hair over the pillow, one slender arm flung over her head. There was a steady rise and fall of her chest under a lavender camisole. The pendant she'd given her lay on Caroline's chest, the tiny diamonds glinting in the light from the hallway.

It was early morning, before the dawn broke over the city, and Emma had been up for hours, her mind full of questions about what the future might hold with Allie back in Brunswick. She couldn't lose Caroline. She wouldn't let it happen.

Unable to fall back to sleep, she'd tiptoed into Caroline's room. Slipping Caroline's cell phone from its charger, Emma entered the password and checked Caroline's social media accounts and e-mail. She searched for anything out of the ordinary, but after coming up with only the usual teenager banter, and a few benign messages from Maddie and Jake, Emma breathed relief and returned the phone to the exact place Caroline had left it.

Checking on her—watching over her like this—was a habit for her. Though Caroline shared much of what happened in her life,

Emma needed to know everything. And anyone who hurt Caroline would have hell to pay. Especially Emma's sister.

Deciding that an early-morning walk might help clear her mind, Emma inched from the room and closed the door. She scribbled a quick note for Caroline, set the alarm, and locked the door.

Outside, all of the windows in the row of well-kept houses were still dark. There were no children playing, no rumble of mommy SUVs, and no avid bicyclists to avoid. Misty morning rain fell from the clouds, and a slight breeze caused the nearby hibiscus and bougainvillea to bend and sway, heavy with moisture.

As the rain intensified, like the *rat-tat-tat* of a snare drum, Emma turned toward home, picking her way around the growing puddles. She frowned up at the slate-gray sky.

How many times had she considered leaving Brunswick, just catching a bus, taking a train, or buying a plane ticket, after hearing endless stories about her wonderful sister?

After high school, she was given the chance.

When Armstrong State in Savannah offered her an athletic scholarship, Emma snatched up the opportunity. Volleyball was the one thing she was really good at, other than earning an A in her computer science class.

At Armstrong, though, Emma partied more than she'd studied, chased boys, slept with professors, and cut classes. Despite a natural affinity for computer programming and excelling in those classes, at the end of two semesters, she was rewarded with a 2.5 GPA, numbers that, to Emma, evidenced that she would never measure up to her sister. Despite protests from her academic counselor and pleas from her coach to get a tutor, Emma spiraled into a fog of lethargy, quit college, and came home.

Back in Brunswick, her father, tight-lipped, held the door open while she dragged in her only suitcase. Her mother, ever the peacemaker, insisted Emma be given a position at the veterinary clinic. After a week of negotiations, she got her way. Emma spent her first week updating the network, installing software, and designing a simple website. Upgrading, improving, streamlining. Proving her worth, which was no small task.

She was only twenty, and to make her parents happy, she tried community college at the College of Coastal Georgia, finally cobbling together enough credits for an associate's degree in computer science. Her sister, of course, had finished her bachelor's degree, had a toddler, and was busy making grand plans to go to med school.

It was all so easy for Allie. Even as a single mother, Allie made it all look effortless.

Before Arrendale, it was still true.

1994

Towels tucked under their arms, Emma and Allie wandered behind their parents down the familiar squares of sidewalk. Her mother carried a luscious fruit salad in a chilled silver bowl. Her father swung a small cooler as he walked.

The neighborhood party at the Hicks's home was well underway when the Marshalls arrived, the scent of barbeque sauce and charcoal briquettes wafting through the warm air. Her parents immediately struck up a conversation with the hosts. Allie ran over to talk to Morgan and the other teenagers, while ten-year-old Emma hung back, taking it all in. A pool sparkled at the far corner of the expansive yard. It was long and curved like a tropical oasis, with pink oleander trees edging the water.

Emma glanced around. Her parents were still talking. Morgan was giggling with Allie. Her sister was smiling and laughing. Emma wandered closer to the pool, over the manicured lawn, onto the Pennsylvania blue stone deck. She plopped down on her towel, stuck her feet in the water, and kicked, watching the droplets arc and fall.

"You're not supposed to be by the pool, Emma," Morgan Hicks announced.

Startled, Emma jumped and whirled.

Allie stood next to Morgan, looking uncomfortable.

It *was* Morgan's house. Emma glanced over to where the adults were standing. None of them looked the least bit concerned. They had drinks in their hands and were laughing at something Morgan Hicks's father had just said.

"Come on," Allie pleaded, waving her hand back toward the house.

Morgan glared and took a menacing step forward.

"Why should I?" Emma argued back.

"Because my mom said." Morgan reached down and grabbed for Emma's hand.

The motion threw both girls off balance, sending Emma straight into the deep end.

For the longest ten seconds of her short life, Emma thrashed and pulled to get to the surface, making no headway. She paused and looked up, seeing Allie's face distorted above the ripples of the water. Staring. Motionless. Waiting.

Fear swallowed Emma. Allie was going to let her drown. She was Morgan's friend. She would take her side. Pretend it was an accident.

Like air bubbles to the surface, a million awful ideas floated skyward and burst.

With a splash, her sister and Morgan jumped in. Their feet hit the bottom of the pool. Each girl took one of Emma's elbows and pushed off from the pool floor, kicking up hard, dragging Emma to the side. Coughing and sputtering, Emma clung to the edge. Her shoes, tiny and yellow, remained at the bottom.

There was a rush of frenzied activity, shouts, and panic. Legs and arms, hands reaching. Her parents pulled her out, dried her face and hair, hugged and kissed her a hundred times. Someone brought dry clothes. A drink of water.

Emma dozed on her father's shoulder on the way home. Sometime while she slept, the owner of the local newspaper called.

Emma found out later that a reporter came to her parents' house and interviewed Allie. The writer called Allie and Morgan heroes; they'd saved Emma's life. It was front-page news the next morning.

The article, Emma noted, explained nothing about what happened in the seconds before she'd plunged into the pool. That her sister had tried to coax her away, that Morgan Hicks had grabbed her hand. How Morgan had deliberately pushed Emma off balance and watched, expressionless, as she'd sunk to the bottom.

Emma was small and helpless. She was ten years old. And she could have died.

Her own parents, oblivious, rallied around popular opinion. Didn't question. Enjoyed the snippet of publicity. Counted their blessings, and went on with life.

It was then Emma knew.

One small voice, speaking the truth, wouldn't make a difference.

People accepted the stories they were told.

The community believed what it wanted to believe.

Allie might have forgotten the incident, but Emma never did. And she vowed that one day the tables would be turned, only she wouldn't be the one to jump in the pool to save her sister. In fact, she might be the one to give her a little push.

TWELVE

SHERIFF GAINES

2016

"Sheriff?" Gladys Williams peered up at Lee Gaines through her bejeweled spectacles. She was dressed in a bright purple suit, accented with gold piping. Her hands were poised over the keyboard, a phone tucked between her chin and shoulder.

The space was small, poorly lit, and smelled like French vanilla coffee creamer, the kind June had liked so much. Thick files covered Gladys's desk next to an ancient PC. The far wall was covered with photographs, family pictures, and pinned with sayings like "God is Good" and "Trust in Him."

"Come on in," Gladys said. She replaced the phone on the receiver, swiveled in her chair, and motioned for him to sit.

Leading Chief by his leash, Gaines moved forward and removed his hat. "Thank you." The sheriff perched awkwardly on the edge of the fabric-covered seat. Chief took his place next to his shined boots, long tongue lolling.

Gaines didn't pay unexpected visits to parole officers. He didn't like stirring up trouble, creating problems where there were none.

But Allie Marshall, if curiosity got the best of her, could cause all sorts of problems. Problems that needed to stay buried.

"I take it this isn't a social call? Something going on that I might want to know about?" Gladys adjusted her glasses and reached for a pen and pad of paper. Her lips, painted in a shade of fire-engine red, pursed tightly.

"Perhaps," Gaines replied acidly. Chief's ears perked.

"All right," Gladys answered, keeping her tone light, but her body remained on alert. She'd been in the business for twenty years; she had heard and seen it all.

"Has the Marshall girl been in?"

Gladys met Gaines's gaze. "Right on time. Her parents found her a place in town. She's looking for a job."

A flicker of a frown crossed the sheriff's face. "How'd she seem?"

Gladys pushed back in her chair and crossed her long legs. "How they all seem. Shell-shocked, on edge, trying their best to appear normal when they're dropped back into the real world with a 'felon' label pasted on them the size of Atlanta."

With a shrug of his broad shoulders, Gaines brushed off her prickly answer. "Hazard of the occupation."

"She did her time," Gladys answered evenly. "The state decided to release her early. She's free to live her life."

"Free with some stipulations of parole."

Gladys didn't flinch. She held his gaze, unblinking. "Of course," Gladys answered, her voice matter-of-fact. "That's where I come in." Her voice took on a bit of an edge. "And, again, so far Marshall's been fine. No red flags. No attitude. She's smarter than most, you know."

"Not smart enough to avoid getting caught," Gaines jabbed back. His arms tensed and his neck prickled. He was getting personal, letting Allie Marshall's release worry him. Not a thing had happened. Yet.

"Look." Gladys took off her glasses, folded them, and placed them to the side of her keyboard. "I know you and Coach Thomas were friends. Tight, like brothers. A lot of people in this town mourned his passing."

"At least one didn't." The words slipped out of Gaines's mouth before he could stop them.

Gladys kept her face serene, her hands clasped in her lap. "Sheriff, I've seen Allie Marshall's file. By all accounts, she verbally alleged to more than one person that Coach Thomas was abusing players. Then she wrote that editorial to the *Brunswick News*, and all hell broke loose." She paused. "It's not for me to say, but despite all of that, something about what went down doesn't quite fit."

Gaines stiffened. "I wouldn't be sharing those opinions around town. You won't be too popular."

"I'm not in this job for the popularity," Gladys said flatly.

Touché, Gaines thought.

"All I am saying is that launching a public campaign, like the Marshall girl did, and asking for an investigation of a football coach don't jive with planning to kill someone in cold blood," she added.

"When a person breaks from reality, it doesn't matter," Gaines shot back. "Bundy was brilliant. Kaczynski too."

"Serial killers?" Gladys said slowly, as if it was the first time she'd ever spoken the words.

"Who's to say—" Gaines stopped himself and began to sweat. He was taking this too far. And Gladys Williams, despite her professional demeanor, was getting suspicious.

"Well then, Sheriff, that would be for you and your men to investigate." Gladys examined his face. "Is that what this visit is about? Has something happened?"

"Not yet." Gaines stood quickly and slid the hat back on his head. Chief bounded to his feet. "Just keep a close eye," he added gruffly.

Gladys nodded. "It's what I do."

THIRTEEN

EMMA

2016

In a bizarre way, to Emma, dinner out with Allie felt more like an awkward first date. A little weird. And very public.

They'd driven to a small restaurant with a view of the long wooden pier that stretched from the shore of St. Simons into the ocean. It was a perfect night for dining on the restaurant's porch, sipping sweet tea, and watching the fireflies dance across the grass.

As the hostess led them to their table, Emma kept her eyes forward as much as possible, hoping they'd make it through relatively unscathed. At first, there were a few unkind stares, some murmured comments and startled glances. Then a group of chattering, well-dressed, older women fell silent. Emma moved quickly, motioning for Allie to follow.

As Emma eased past the large gathering, she felt a nudge on the crook of her elbow. Out of habit, she turned her head.

Morgan Hicks's mother stood up, hands on her hips, a morose look of displeasure on her face. She'd aged twenty years or more in the last decade, with deep smoker's lines etched around her downturned lips. Her throat jiggled with loose skin when she started to speak.

"Allie Marshall, you have no right to be here," Morgan's mother began. The women's group watched with rapt attention. At nearby tables, other patrons shifted uncomfortably.

"Mrs. Hicks," Allie replied quietly. "I'm sorry you feel that way—"

"After what you did to that poor man," she scolded, raising her voice. "You dare to come back here?"

The dining area fell silent.

Allie opened her mouth to retort when Emma stalked back, grabbed Allie's arm, and half dragged her over to their table. "Are you crazy?" Emma breathed, pulling out her own seat and collapsing with a glare at her sister.

Allie sat down, red-faced. "What was I supposed to do?"

"Not talk. Try to ignore them." Emma snatched the linen napkin from the table and shook it out. A server took their order, poured water, and disappeared. Emma glanced over Allie's shoulder at the table of women. "They're leaving anyway. Thank goodness." She opened her menu and scanned the entrées. "I can't stand that woman. Or her daughter."

"Morgan." Allie stirred her ice water with a straw and then poked at the lemon slice.

"Yeah, that friendship didn't work out so well for you," answered Emma with an arch of her brow.

Allie gazed at the horizon as the sky turned brilliant shades of magenta and crimson. "She did cut and run pretty fast."

"Listen," Emma said, waving over the server. "Forget Morgan. Let's try to enjoy dinner. Want to order?" She glanced at the menu and selected the first entrée she laid eyes on, shrimp fajitas with mango-lime slaw. Allie chose the pan-seared scallops with bacon, edamame, and grits.

"That sounds amazing." Emma smiled at the server as she handed over her menu. After he disappeared into the kitchen, she shifted the conversation back to Allie. "So, should I ask how the job search is going?"

Allie shrugged and smiled. "Slow."

"Any calls at all?"

"Nope. I tried at the flower shop, a bakery. Applied for every housekeeping, server, and restaurant job I could find in Brunswick," she replied with a wry smile. "There was one position at a wedding dress shop, but I didn't even bother there."

Emma wrinkled her nose.

"I always expected you'd get married." Allie gave her sister a lopsided grin. "I'd hoped that one of us would."

Emma shrugged. "It still could happen . . ."

"Come on," Allie said. "That summer before I was supposed to leave for school? There was someone you really liked. You snuck out all of the time. I remember." She gave Emma a knowing look.

"Oh, that?" Emma smiled. "It was nothing. Puppy love." She offered a forced laugh.

"What about that former fiancé of yours?"

Emma glanced away and then back at her sister, who was watching her every move. "Former. Key word. After I broke it off, Mom was so freaked out, so disappointed, that she'd practically run away if I brought it up."

Allie tucked her legs under her chair and leaned in. "I'm sorry."

"Don't be. It was five years ago." Emma wrinkled her nose and swirled the liquid inside her glass, creating a tornado of sweet tea and ice.

Her sister toyed with her napkin and settled it into her lap. "So, do you ever hear from him? Your ex?" She played with her salad, rolling the tomato slices over, piercing Bibb lettuce and strands of unwieldy arugula with her fork.

"No. It was a pretty tough breakup." Emma sighed.

"You grew apart? Or was it about something else?"

"He wanted kids." Emma shrugged. "I didn't."

Allie's forehead creased. "You know? I don't get it. You're so good with . . . Caroline." Her voice faltered.

Emma hemmed, examining her salad plate. "I didn't feel like I could handle a baby. Caroline was at such a tender age." She looked up at her sister pointedly. "We were all so worried about her. Dividing my attention wouldn't have been fair."

Allie's face lost color.

"And . . ." Emma said the next words softly and carefully, knowing they'd cut deep and fast. "And you were . . . gone. For so long from Caroline. From all of us."

Allie inhaled sharply and winced. "I know." She hesitated. "I'm so grateful she had you. I-I never meant for her to be a burden."

"Never," Emma said as something fierce and raw tugged at her heart. "I love her. I always will. She's blood. There's nothing that will come between that."

"Of course," Allie murmured, her words barely audible.

Emma took a sip of water, gathering her thoughts. Nothing would come between her and Caroline. Ever. But Allie, Allie had let her down. The tie was broken; the blood was tainted.

"Anyway, it just didn't work out," Emma added. "I'd rushed into it, thrown myself into the wedding planning. Mom was reviewing catering menus like her life depended on it." She ran a finger around the rim of the glass. "I think I loved the idea of being married. But then it seemed like we were being Barbie and Ken in one of those pink plastic playhouses."

The truth was that none of it—and no guy, no matter how perfect and kind—would ever compare to the only man she had ever truly loved.

April 2006

The headline stirred the already-hungry Brunswick fans into a feeding frenzy. *Star Coach Lands in Wolverine Country.* A small crowd had already gathered for the first day of spring training, everyone eager to catch a glimpse of the new hire.

Allie's dog, Molly, stopped in her tracks, sniffing the air. "Come on, girl," Emma urged, shivering as Allie guided her puppy back toward the football stadium.

Rain drizzled as gray clouds hung low over the playing field, scraped raw in places, more clay than grass. Every cleat was caked in red brown; spatters of dirt patterned every shin. Between plays, the ball was wiped clean and handed back.

While Allie made the social rounds, Emma surveyed the crowd. Most notably, Sheriff Lee Gaines stood on the edge of the field. He'd been a school booster since the beginning of time, with a passion for the game said to rival the University of Alabama's Bear Bryant.

The whistle blew again; players gulped water from plastic cups. Two hulking linebackers took turns drinking from a Gatorade jug, swapping trash talk between mouthfuls.

The new coach, Boyd Thomas, stalked to the end zone. His staff, in matching windbreakers, parted as if a jetliner had taxied onto the field. The coach stopped and spoke to the quarterback, emphasizing the conversation with crisp gestures. He grabbed at the headphones around his neck and spun a finger in the air, signaling the players to resume the drill.

He was a University of Georgia graduate, Emma had noted

from the article in the newspaper. And below a long section, the story noted that Thomas had risen from a foster kid to a head coach with one of the winningest records in the state. The last paragraph mentioned his family would be taking over the pharmacy and old-fashioned soda shop downtown. The coach's wife was a pharmacist, and the current owner was retiring and happy to leave the place in capable hands.

As Emma watched, the players huddled, clapped hard, and got into formation. The quarterback called his play, leaning in to catch the snap. Feet shuffled, bodies collided.

Coach Thomas caught the edge of his ball cap and pulled it out straight, peering toward his players. A perfect spiral landed into the arms of a waiting wide receiver.

After several more plays, another whistle blew. Practice was over, and Emma felt a tug on her arm. Her sister was ready to leave. She ignored Allie and stared, lips parted, as the new coach ambled over and shook hands with Sheriff Gaines and the athletic director.

As a sudden breeze cut across the field, Molly began to bounce and tugged at her leash. At a sharp yelp, Allie shushed her pet, causing Emma to glance up, expecting annoyed glances at the commotion.

But Coach Boyd Thomas was walking straight toward her, a brilliant smile on his face, causing Emma to go weak all over. He was rugged and handsome, broad-shouldered and strong. His eyes, though, dealt the final blow. Dark. Passionate. More than a little dangerous.

Emma didn't believe in love at first sight. Sure, she'd kissed her share of guys; she'd had brief crushes. But the spark never tripped like this, fireworks didn't explode, the earth and trees never melted away.

Now it was all happening at once.

"Wolverine fan already, eh?" he said, walking over and bending to scratch the puppy's head behind her ears. His college ring—gold signet—glinted against the dark parts of Molly's thick coat. "We're looking for a mascot." He grinned. "I think she'd be perfect."

It was the start and end of everything.

2016

"I know you aren't telling me the whole story." Allie frowned.

Emma waved a hand, glad the restaurant's noise and clatter drowned out her sister's words to anyone farther than one foot from their table. She heaved a sigh. The reaction was typical Allie, always the bleeding heart. Her sister still wanted to save the world, even when she couldn't save herself.

"Don't shut me out." Allie leaned in, bending her head to get Emma's attention. "What happened?"

Frowning, Emma looked away, pretending to study the dozens of lights strung along the pier. Allie's persistence, all of this concerned questioning, was grating on her nerves.

Emma's breath caught. She realized what was happening. Why Allie agreed so quickly to come to dinner. Her sister was trying to soften her up, get Emma to drop her guard. And at just the right moment, Allie would try to steal her daughter away.

Emma tightened her fists under the table. She took a deep breath. Emma would give Allie a taste of how hard she would fight to keep Caroline.

"That night . . . the night I went into the hospital." Emma lowered her chin and made herself sniff. "Th-they had to do surgery."

"Surgery?" Allie echoed.

Emma plucked the napkin from her lap and wiped at her eyes. "I should have told you. I just couldn't . . . before. But I-I can't have children. Not my own."

An incredulous look washed over Allie's face. "What? Oh, Emma . . ."

A sudden breeze ruffled the palm trees nearby, and the waves crashed harder in the distance. The sun had all but disappeared, causing the horizon to darken to a midnight blue.

The sky had been that exact shade the evening Emma tearfully told the police about a drifter passing through town, a grungy man in a Rolling Stones T-shirt who'd jumped in her car at the corner of Parkwood and Kemble. She said the man had pressed what she thought was a gun to her head, dragged her to Goodyear Park, and tried to rape her across from the Lutheran church. She'd fought him off until someone had driven by, scared him, and the man had taken off into the sparse woods.

The police officers nodded grimly as Emma told them she was barely able to get herself to the ER, only a block away. A day later, she sat with a sketch artist and reimagined the drifter's face. The police had searched Brunswick and St. Simons Island, coming up empty.

Allie shivered and broke the silence. "Emma . . . I-I don't know what to say. That's awful. I'm so sorry."

"It's been—" Emma brushed away an imaginary tear and sniffed, reaching for her napkin. "Difficult, to say the least."

"I can't believe you didn't tell me," Allie said. "You've always been better than I am at keeping secrets."

"I made Mom and Dad promise. It would have only made you worry." Emma lowered her voice until it was barely audible, thinking quickly to make up a story that would play on Allie's sympathy. "They found a mass in my uterus and did a hysterectomy before I could blink." Emma sipped her water, straightened, and cleared her throat. "It's all messed up down there. And I wanted my own baby, not someone else's."

"Did you tell him?"

"Of course," Emma replied in a soft voice and rubbed her temples. "And he suggested adopting. He brought me brochures he'd collected, showed me websites."

"And?" Allie raised a brow.

"I knew it wouldn't make me happy." Emma drew in a deep breath.

Allie seemed to absorb this. "At least you had a choice. And you didn't jump in and get stuck in a bad situation for years and years."

"A bad situation?" Emma shifted and wrinkled her brow.

"An unhappy one." Allie corrected herself. "I know that marriage is not the same as what I went through. You walked away . . . I lost a whole decade. It's just wasted and I can't get it back." Allie looked out at the ocean and then back at Emma, her voice soft.

"Of course."

"I've had so much time to think," Allie continued. "And I have some ideas . . . some theories about everything that happened."

Wrinkling her brow, Emma leaned forward to get a better look at her sister's face. She recognized that expression, the stubborn and determined one. "What do you mean?" Emma asked. "Theories?"

Allie licked her lips. "I know that we couldn't ever talk about it, back at Arrendale," she murmured, "but I've always thought that Sheriff Gaines had *everything* to do with the coach's death."

Blinking at her sister, Emma's jaw fell open. "What?"

"I'm serious."

"Stop," Emma hissed, glancing around. Now that the restaurant had filled up, no one, thank goodness, was paying them any attention. "Do you realize what you're saying?"

"I do."

"This isn't the time or the place." Emma frowned, keeping her voice low. "Don't you want to put the past in the past? Let it go?" She paused and held her sister's gaze. "You're finally free."

Allie blinked, bit her lip, and looked away.

Managing to conjure a sympathetic look, Emma continued, "I'm so sorry. I know it's been hard for you. But you are out of that awful place. And that's a blessing."

Her sister didn't reply.

Emma unfolded the napkin over her lap. "Listen, good comes out of bad sometimes. Like all of these years—all of this time having Caroline—it's been a blessing to me." She watched as her sister stiffened.

As Allie stared out at the waves crashing on the shore, Emma's lips curved into a smile. She pressed her fingertips to the center of her chest, setting her jaw as if daring her sister to look up and defy her. "I love her so much. Caroline is my whole world."

FOURTEEN

ALLIE

2016

Emma's words sent a jolt through Allie's body, like a rush of adrenaline after a lightning strike. The words hung in the evening air, daring, almost taunting her, as if Allie were somehow a threat.

Allie bristled, ready to defend her rightful place as her daughter's mother. But when she opened her mouth to argue, Emma withdrew from her, crossing her arms across her chest. This was the Emma she knew. Oversensitive, quick to react. The first to have hurt feelings.

Perhaps, Allie thought, up until that minute, she hadn't realized the depth of Emma's love for Caroline. Her ten years behind bars had sheltered her from real life. In the few moments during those very first years when Allie let herself dwell on everything she was missing, the regret only hollowed out her soul.

Inhaling deeply, Allie thought long and hard as the silence built between them. As a gust of wind made the napkins flutter, she bit her lip. Emma was her flesh and blood. Family. Allie could—and would—take the high road, soothing Emma's feelings until her sister accepted that things were going to change.

And change, they would.

"I owe you so much," Allie said, swallowing her pride. "Thank you for taking care of my daughter."

Emma raised a brow, ready to mount a challenge.

"Really. Thank you for everything," Allie repeated. "I mean it."

"You're welcome," her sister said softly, the tension melting away from her face.

Allie blinked back tears. "I used to think I had everything all figured out, that my life was pretty close to perfect." She caught her breath, swallowed hard. "I was so stupid. I buried myself in books, studied all the time, even after Caroline was born, like I had something to prove to the world. And all for what?" Allie said. "No one at Arrendale cared that I had a college education, that I was going to med school or wanted to be a surgeon."

Emma hesitated. "Why?"

"Inside that place? It didn't matter. I was nothing. Nobody." Allie cut her hands through the air with a slashing motion. "The end." Her words weren't hollow. The statement was solid and true, full of regret, as if she had only a day more to live and Dr. Jack Kevorkian were waiting in the hallway, syringe in hand.

The server appeared, refilled their water glasses, and lit the candle in the middle of the table. Allie watched as the wick caught fire, staring into the red-orange flame.

If time travel existed, she would go back. In half a second, she'd climb in the contraption, however rickety, plug in the year, the month, the day. Allie would send the machine back to the precise place and moment everything changed. She'd memorized the time, the smell of the air, the sound of her dog, Molly, panting in the backseat. She could picture the open door of the pharmacy, the light spilling out onto the pavement.

Allie would erase it all, rewind, stay home. It was a snapshot, a flash, and a heartbeat like any other. A tiny moment that sent Allie's life—and everyone else's—hurtling in an entirely unexpected direction.

No wonder Emma was angry.

"I can't vote, can't carry a gun, can't run for public office. No alcohol, no drugs, no travel overseas, and no associating with other felons. If my parole officer thinks I'm screwing up, it's over." Allie pressed a napkin to her face, choking back tears.

Emma frowned, putting both hands flat on the table. "This was a mistake, coming out here to dinner. Pretending everything was fine."

The server appeared, carting a huge circular tray. Steam rose in buttery wisps from the plates. He swiveled the platter, his hand ready to serve the entrées.

"I'm sorry," Emma said, turning to face the server. "Can you box it up?"

The man frowned, but nodded and slipped away.

Allie leaned forward, searching her sister's eyes. She realized then that Emma was the only one who could help her reach her daughter. "So . . . will you help me talk to Caroline?"

With a frown, Emma played with her fork. "She's scared, Allie. She hasn't seen you in years."

Allie's heart raced. She pressed her fist to her lips. "But I miss her. I want her to be a part of my life again—even if it's a very small part at first."

Emma pursed her lips. "It's quite a shock for everyone. Having you back here."

Allie blinked, cut to the core. She pushed away from the table and stood up.

Emma shifted her eyes to her lap. "I didn't—"

"Don't." Allie winced and held up a hand. It hurt too much,

even coming from her own sister. The one person who'd stuck by her. Who was supposed to be in her corner. What Allie did know—at that moment—was one true thing: her daughter didn't want to see her. And whatever the reason, fear, anger, sadness, it didn't really matter.

Looking at Emma now, it was obvious. So transparent it made Allie want to scream and pound against the heart-pine floor until her palms bled or the beams buckled. She had tricked herself, bent reality into a fairy tale. It was how she'd existed the past decade, clinging to hope like a sailor in a nor'easter. Now, instead of reaching shore, Allie was a sinking ship, taking on water, not a paddle in sight.

FIFTEEN

CAROLINE

2016

Caroline's head thudded with irritation. She didn't know which was more frustrating: worrying about her mother messing up her life or tackling complicated geometry theorems at seven fifty-five in the morning.

As her teacher droned on near the whiteboard, Caroline did her best to shut out the world. She sat in the back of the classroom, the very last row, mercifully out of her instructor's line of sight. It was a coveted position, a seat used to pass notes, work on overdue assignments, or study for the next test.

Maddie, unfortunately, was absent. The rest of her friends had elected out of honors math. Today, for all intents and purposes, she was alone.

For a moment, Caroline thought that maybe if she concentrated hard enough, she could make the room disappear, and the students around her with it. She closed her eyes, leaned her elbow on the desk, and covered one ear with her palm, hoping to muffle the scratch of pencils and the shuffle of notebook pages.

It didn't work. The noises seemed to burrow under her skin,

making their way up her neck and scalp, settling in her brain. The sounds prickled, causing Caroline to fidget and scratch like she'd rolled in a bed of poison ivy.

"Miss Marshall, is there a question?" the teacher chirped expectantly in her direction.

Caroline started to say no, then changed her mind.

"Yes, ma'am. May I go to the nurses' office?" She pressed a hand to her forehead for emphasis and drew her lips into a frown. Caroline felt everyone's eyes swivel to the back of the room; she could feel her neck flush and tingle, the way it did when she was excited or embarrassed. Caroline just hoped she looked sick.

The math instructor waited a beat, then dismissed her with a wave of her wrist. Head down, Caroline grabbed her backpack and slung it over one shoulder. She picked up her books, clutched them to her chest, and edged out of her seat.

Girls close by bent their fair heads together and whispered. Caroline resisted the urge to jerk her head around and look. She slipped to the front of the classroom, ducked out the door, and started breathing again when her shoes hit the hallway floor. Morning light streaked through the windows, making patterns on the tiles. As she walked, her fingers traced the rows of lockers.

She was in no hurry to get to the office, which meant facing school workers with their inquiring, concerned faces. The questions would start. "Poor thing," they'd cluck and take her temperature, maybe even call Emma. Emma, who would ask a million questions and not want her to work at the nursing home this afternoon.

Caroline stalled, scuffing the toe of her shoe as she bent over the drinking fountain and gulped at the arc of water. Refreshing, icy drops splashed her cheeks and chin. Caroline wished she had an entire pool, the size of a football field. She would dive in, sink to the bottom, and grow so cold she wouldn't have to think, feel, or move ever again.

Her outside would be as thick and frozen as her heart and soul.

"Caro," a voice called out from behind her.

She whirled, catching her books before they slid from her grasp. It was Jake.

He looked amazing, his face already sun-kissed, his hair wind-blown, wearing a faded T-shirt and jeans that fit him just right. His skin, even from a distance, smelled warm and spicy. Caroline caught her breath.

With her mother back in town, she'd done her best to avoid him the past few days. He'd left a few voice mails. Texted.

Caroline hadn't responded. She didn't know what to say. Or how to feel. Shame about her mother being back had consumed her.

"Hey, stranger." He looked quizzical, glancing her up and down. "You lost?"

Jake waited for her reply, watching her face. He didn't realize how right he was.

Caroline tried her best to smile, but only managed to tuck her arms closer in to her body and shrink back against the brick wall. She wanted to ask what *he* was doing in the hallway during classes, but she couldn't make her lips move.

Shoulders hunched, adjusting his backpack, Jake swallowed. "So, I'm glad I caught you, actually." He shifted from side to side and darted his eyes down the hallway. He opened his palms like he was cupping their air, then let them drop. "I've been trying to call you. About next month," he began. "The dance . . ."

Caroline drew in her breath.

She knew before he said it. There wouldn't be a dance. Or movies. Or a boyfriend.

It had happened already. The news was out about Caroline's mother, bits and pieces of gossip scattered like dandelion seeds in the wind.

"I think it's better if we—" Jake stammered and hesitated, his forehead wrinkling. He smoothed his brown hair across his forehead, patting it down, a gesture that meant he was nervous.

Caroline stopped him. "Really?" she interrupted, fighting to keep her chin up. Inside, she was crumbling.

"It's just that . . ." He stopped again, staring down at his shoes.

"It's fine," Caroline said, her voice barely audible.

Jake raised his eyes to hers.

In a stab of defiance, an effort to defend her family, Caroline stood straight and looked Jake full on.

"I know what you're doing," she added. "And I know why." Her bottom lip trembled the slightest bit. She bit down to make it stop. Caroline wasn't going to cry, not over Jake or a stupid dance, or her mother's criminal record. "Just go. Leave me alone."

"Okay," he muttered.

Caroline raised her voice. She wasn't yelling, but it felt like the effort took every ounce of her strength. Deep down, she knew it wouldn't make much difference. In fact, it might make things worse. But Caroline couldn't seem to stop herself.

"I'm not her, you know," she insisted and poked at her own chest. "I didn't do it. I didn't do anything. I was *five* years old."

The color drained from Jake's face, leaving the surface marbled and smooth.

He backed away, slamming his shoulder and books into the row of lockers. When he moved again, his backpack zippers clanked against the metal.

A teacher opened a door into the hallway and poked her head out. "Is there a problem?" she asked, looking from Jake to Caroline. "Perhaps you two need to visit the office?"

"No, ma'am." Jake turned on his heel and stalked off as the teacher closed the door with a quiet click.

Caroline knew full well Jake wouldn't go to the office or his next class. Most likely he'd disappear into the bowels of the boys' locker room, the gym, or weight room. He could do what he wanted.

Jake was untouchable. A mythical god. Royalty with a black Mercedes convertible. Like King Charles VII in *Joan of Arc*, the book they were reading for history class. Caroline could see the words on the page. Joan led Charles's army into victory, securing his crown. Later, she was captured by the enemy. When the king made no effort to rescue her, Joan was burned at the stake.

Caroline shuddered, pretending to fumble with her backpack while she wiped away tears. Just like Charles and Joan, in the hour she needed him most, Jake had left her too.

SIXTEEN

EMMA

2016

Emma had worked six hours straight, tweaking and adjusting a new website for a client. Despite working her way through a bowl of stale popcorn earlier that afternoon, her stomach still rumbled, empty and protesting at nearly six o'clock.

The screen door slammed, announcing Caroline's arrival.

"How was your day?" Emma called out, still typing.

No answer, which meant something, or nothing. There was no teenage instruction book for roller-coaster hormones, raw emotions, and accompanying mood swings.

"Caro? Is that you?"

The house echoed with the words.

Emma checked the kitchen first, where her niece liked to stand, refrigerator door wide open. She wasn't there. The bathroom was empty, as was the back porch. Her heart began to thud against her rib cage.

Then, on cue, music floated from Caroline's room into the hallway. Today's selection—Killer Blue, another band out of Athens—and just as dark as Druery.

I'll see you on the edge of never. Good-bye, good-bye, good-bye forever.

Rounding the corner, Emma found Caroline in her bedroom, lying flat on her back, shoes still on. She hadn't bothered to even start changing out of her nursing home scrubs. Instead, she was staring at the ceiling, as if something fascinating lay hidden among the tiny bumps and ridges.

You always said we'd be together. Good-bye, good-bye, good-bye forever.

"A little morose, isn't it, Caro?" Emma asked. When Caroline didn't answer, Emma turned down the volume on the speakers. She stepped closer and realized Caroline's eyes were shining with tears. "Hey, want to talk about it?" She walked over to Caroline's mattress and sat down on the edge.

When the bed settled, Caroline blinked, which sent a lone tear down the side of her face into her hairline. Emma fought the urge to reach out and brush it away.

"What happened? Something at school? Did someone hurt you?" Emma threw questions at Caroline like a homeland security officer interrogating a terrorist suspect.

Her niece only buried her head.

Emma set her jaw and pushed herself off the mattress. "I'm here if you need me," she said, shaking her head. She hadn't taken three steps when a bitter sob escaped from Caroline's body.

"I want things to be normal," Caroline said in a small voice. She draped the crook of her elbow across her forehead. "She should leave."

"Who?" Emma turned and asked. "Allie?"

Caroline nodded. "I don't want her here. It's messing everything up." She sniffed back tears. "Jake broke up with me," Caroline murmured. "I mean, he started to," she continued. "He was going to say it. He just stood there looking sick."

A spark of fury lit in Emma's chest. "Oh, Caro. I'm so sorry," she said, dropping down beside the bed, gripping the duvet cover. Jake didn't know it yet, but he would pay dearly for this.

"I told him that I'm not her," Caroline added. "That it wasn't my fault. I didn't have anything to do with it." After a deep breath, she continued. "I ended up telling Jake to go away," Caroline added with a catch in her voice. "And he did. It's like he never, ever cared about me at all."

"I'm sorry," Emma replied, stroking her niece's arm, vowing to make Jake understand what he'd done. Emma didn't forgive or forget.

Caroline shrugged, and her eyes welled up with tears. "But it's like I'm guilty too."

"No, sweetheart. You're not," Emma said firmly.

"And a lot of my friends are acting weird. Like, if I come down the hallway or into a room, they all stay ten feet from me and whisper."

Nodding, Emma plucked a few Kleenex from a nearby box and held them out. Teenage girls were awful and mean. So insensitive. "Even Maddie?"

Her niece shrugged and took them, wiping at her nose. "Not yet."

The fire burning inside Emma reached a full-blown blaze. She reached a hand toward her niece, let her fingertips graze her shoulder. Emma would fix this. "You know that I love you like my own daughter. And nothing will change that, right?"

Clutching her pillow, Caroline leaned back against the wall. "Right." Her gaze drifted from Emma to the window. "I was thinking . . ." She exhaled. "Um, never mind. It's silly. There's no way."

"Just ask," Emma said. "What can I do to help?"

Caroline grimaced. "Don't make me go back to my mom. I don't want to. I hate her."

Emma drew in a sharp breath. "Well." She thought quickly. "I promise you don't have to do anything, not right now," Emma replied, inhaling through her nose, trying to keep calm. She forced herself not to smile. "It's been a rough week for everybody. I just want you to be happy."

"Thank you." Caroline sniffed and dabbed at her eyes with the back of her hand. "But is there a deadline for when I have to go and live with her?"

"I don't think so, but I don't know for sure," Emma replied. "Let's not worry about that right now." She hoped Caroline didn't see how tightly she was balling her fists, her nails digging into the skin. When she looked down, forcing her hands to relax, the little half-moon marks had almost drawn blood.

Caroline's questions were valid. When would she have to move? Would someone force her? Who would make that decision? And how?

Emma patted Caroline's leg. "No one's rushing you. No one's made any decisions."

"Okay," Caroline said. She shut her eyes and tucked her knees in close to her body, like a terrified little girl. "What if I didn't have to go? Ever. What if I stayed here and you . . . adopt me?"

Pulse throbbing in her temples, Emma resisted jumping up to celebrate. This was more than she'd ever dreamed about. *Of course* Caroline belonged with her. *Of course* they should stay together.

"I'm serious. You could." Caroline shrugged, blinking her brown eyes wide and spreading her palms to the ceiling. "Why not? You're already my guardian."

"Sweetheart, I'll look into it," Emma said, smiling. "I promise."

Caroline threw her arms around her aunt and squeezed tight. "I love you."

"I love you too."

For a long time, Emma held her. Finally, Caroline's breathing slowed. She yawned and rubbed her eyes.

"We can talk about all of this later. Sleep well." Emma settled her niece on the bed, drew up the covers, and kissed her head before leaving the room.

Maybe Killer Blue was right. Caroline might be on the edge of never. But that was right now. It wasn't permanent. Allie couldn't come back and assume her daughter would want her back, or that anyone else did either. Life didn't work that way.

No matter what, she couldn't allow Allie to ruin Caroline, to twist her heart and mind, to turn her against her own family. She wouldn't let it happen.

She'd adopt Caroline and the talk in the town would settle down; Allie's parole would become old news; there'd be something else to gossip about. Football, the county fair, church suppers. It didn't matter. Eventually, families would return to their routines. The Marshalls would too.

And then Caroline's broken heart would heal. Caroline would get stronger. Caroline would be happy again. She'd turn out all right . . . but only if Emma helped get her through it.

And maybe everyone else, including Allie, needed a gentle nudge to get out of the way.

Emma tapped her fingers on the sofa. She eyed the newspaper, with the real estate section on top. There was a short article about a Dr. Natalie Harper buying her father's building and taking over the veterinary practice. Some other business deals followed.

Pushing herself off the sofa, Emma retrieved a small but very sharp pocketknife from the kitchen, cut out the article, and slipped both into her jeans.

It was proof. Things changed. Life went on. She didn't have to wait or wonder. And Emma could right some wrongs now. She *could* help move things forward.

No good ever came from looking back anyway.

SEVENTEEN

ALLIE

August 2006

The screen door slammed hard. "Game time," her father called out, seat cushions tucked under one arm.

Caroline popped out the door next, pompons in hand. "Ready, Mommy?" she asked, shaking the shiny streamers.

"Ready." Allie grinned, gathering Molly's leash and latching the clip onto her collar. Her dog, still a puppy, had been handpicked by Coach Thomas to serve as the school's mascot. At first Allie had politely declined the coach's request, stating the obvious—Molly was a Lab, not a wolverine; she was a puppy; she might not react well to the crowd. In the end, after much cajoling by her sister, Allie relented and allowed a trial run. To her surprise, Molly enjoyed the spotlight, sitting on the sidelines next to the line of players during practice, watching the ball travel up and down the field. They would see what happened during a real game.

As Molly pulled to walk faster, Allie heard the strains of the marching band warming up in the distance. The drums beat out a rhythm; trumpets sounded, preparing for the rush of players on the field. Caroline climbed onto her grandfather's back. Allie grabbed

Emma's hand, pulling her forward and laughing. Her mother trailed behind, stopping to chat with a neighbor over a hedge.

The stadium was less than a mile away.

After dropping Molly off with one of the water boys who promised to watch her every moment of the game, Allie and Caroline stopped at the concession booth, peering up into the stands to find the rest of the family seated in an upper row.

After climbing the concrete stops, Allie handed Emma her Coke. "Stop pouting. We're here, right?"

Emma grimaced, shifting over to make room for her sister just as the players ran onto the field, a rush of silver and black. Minutes later, the opposing team joined the Wolverines under the goalposts, their sea of red helmets and jerseys bobbing and weaving like matadors readying for a bullfight in Pamplona. A whistle and the longest second of silence. A single coin tossed in the air. Twirling, arcing, falling.

Allie's eyes searched the sidelines after kickoff, roaming over helmets and athletic staff in Wolverine visors. After several plays, Coach Thomas called time. He frowned, his eyes glinting in the stadium lights. He yanked a team member to his feet, grabbed a piece of jersey, pulling the player inches from his face. Allie squinted for the number on his back. It was Ben's brother. After an impassioned speech, the coach released him to the field for the next play.

In the next sixty seconds, it was third down, fourth down, do or die. Then an arced pass flew through the air forty yards. Touchdown! The crowd jumped to its feet, the noise deafening. Her parents hugged Caroline.

Allie was still watching the field. Instead of celebrating, like everyone in the stands, Coach Thomas was ranting and angry. He'd drawn three players into a huddle and was shouting, slapping helmets. Grabbing jerseys and face masks. Though he was half a head shorter, he put his hand on the chest of the tallest player and pushed hard, knocking him off balance. When the player hit the ground, Allie could swear Thomas stepped on his forearm before stalking away.

Wincing in pain for the player, Allie turned her head. Her father had seen it too.

Her father crossed his arms and frowned. "Not the way a man should lead."

"Maybe they're coming down off a binge—crashing after a major sugar and caffeine high," Allie murmured, half joking.

"Well, I know they're eating. A lot. They seem a lot bigger this year," her father added. "The team's always in the weight room. Most all of the players were told to gain twenty pounds. I heard the coach has them on this special diet with supplements and protein shakes."

Allie stopped. "Really?" She'd seen rows of muscle-building drinks at the health food store, tanned men with ripped abs and enormous biceps on the labels.

Her father nodded. "More than one parent has said so."

Allie ran her eyes along the sideline, mentally taking measurements of shoulder pads and helmets. Her father was right. *Big* was an understatement. Some of these guys were huge. She leaned closer to her father and lowered her voice. "Wow. Um, would protein shakes do all of that?"

For a moment, her father didn't answer. Then he turned and murmured into her ear. "Doubt it. These kids are getting something, though."

Something. Allie licked her lips. "Like medicine?" She looked at her father.

His jaw tightened. "Maybe."

What did that mean? Her father looked worried. Allie's mind

spun a dozen different scenarios. Did he mean something . . . illegal? All of a sudden, she felt hot. There were too many people, too many elbows and legs. She fanned herself, desperate for some air, thinking about her friends on the field, Ben's brother in particular.

2016

Allie sat at her desk, kneading her temples, trying to erase the memory.

No one else had wanted to see the coach's temper. How he handled his players. As long as the team was winning, the people of Brunswick would overlook almost anything. Allie knew that now.

She'd been so bold, actually going so far as to accuse the man of giving his players steroids to bulk up. They'd become a powerhouse team almost overnight, and the change in players, the attitudes, the aggression on the field, had been obvious.

After a moment's hesitation, Allie clicked off the job search website. She Googled the DEA website and navigated to the Office of Diversion Control, where the public could report suspected illicit pharmaceutical activities.

There, she went back to the year 2000, searching for investigations on pharmacists in Georgia, specifically, Coach Thomas's wife, searching for anything her attorneys might have overlooked.

Surely, if Thomas had been bold enough—even in the past—to order supplies through their family's pharmacy, the DEA would have noticed. But there was nothing. No mention of his wife, or their pharmacy.

Allie tried the Georgia Bureau of Investigation, but found that only offenders could search for their own criminal history records. Head thudding from staring at the computer screen, Allie clicked off the website and closed the laptop.

She paced the house, trying to shake off the feeling of hopelessness. She passed the calendar hanging on the wall, her next parole appointment with Gladys Williams circled in red. The woman's warning burned in her ears. *Don't go looking for trouble.*

She'd intended to job search on the laptop Emma had given her—and she started out the day doing so, even jotted down a few leads. One, strangely enough, being offered with the new veterinarian in town.

An hour later, Allie found herself outside her father's old office, staring at a crumpled Help Wanted sign beneath the arms of two spiky, sprawling sego palms. Swallowing hard, she squatted down, picked up the paper with two fingers. The paper was bent, a little dirty, with tape still hanging off the edges.

Allie's heart stilled. It wasn't a great omen, but she tucked it under her arm anyway and headed for the office. The knob turned easily, and Allie stepped inside. A petite brunette with a pixie cut sat behind the counter surrounded by files and paperwork. Beside her, a tiny candle flickered, emitting the fragrance of grapefruit and tangerine.

"We're not quite open." The woman smiled and gestured to the mountains of mail. "It'll be Monday, if you'd like to make an appointment."

"Thank you," Allie said.

"I'm Dr. Harper, but you can call me Natalie," she said, extending her hand across the counter to shake Allie's. The woman's palm was soft, the grip firm. "Do you have a dog or cat?"

"Neither," Allie answered, releasing Natalie's hand and stepping back. "I saw the sign about the job." She held up the paper. "It must have fallen off the door. I wondered if you were still looking for someone."

Natalie started to laugh. "They say word travels fast in a small town, but that's amazing." She was perky and energetic, all of forty years old, Allie guessed.

Allie flushed. "I'm Paul Marshall's daughter," she explained.

A surprised expression crossed Natalie's face. She quickly replaced it with a pleasant smile. "Dr. Marshall said he had two daughters, correct? So you must be . . ."

"Allie."

Natalie cocked her head and thought for a moment, pressing her fist under her chin.

Allie braced herself. She expected to be turned away, or worse, kicked out. It was possible Natalie Harper might ban her from the office altogether, even if she had a team of horses and a truckload of cash to pay veterinarian expenses.

"Did your father tell you to talk to me?" Natalie's expression remained pleasant. If she was worried or uncomfortable, her face didn't reveal a thing.

Allie bit her lip. "He doesn't know I'm here." She paused. "I just thought . . . Well, I'm qualified to do just about everything here. I might be a little rusty, but I've kept up with the medical advancements, medications—" Allie stopped. "Sorry, I'm nervous."

"It's fine."

Allie reached into her back pocket and withdrew a folded résumé. She slid it across the counter to Natalie. "I know I'm not your ideal candidate. But I do have experience."

Natalie opened the creamy parchment paper. With one finger, she traced the lines.

Allie knew each by heart. She had listed her acceptance to medical school, college honor societies, and charity work. Her last place of employment was the business in which the two women were standing.

Allie's breathing became shallow. She forced herself to slow her pulse, inhaling deeply through her nose, exhaling out her mouth. She needed to give Gladys an update on her job status and couldn't do that if she passed out.

Natalie looked up from the résumé. "It took some bravery to walk into this office," she said. "Even bigger cojones to ask for a job. My son got himself into a scrape a couple of years back."

Allie stiffened.

"A DUI." Natalie cocked her head. "He didn't even have a driver's license. After arguing with the officer who arrested him, the judge read him the riot act. He got a hefty fine, community service, and went to rehab."

Allie gulped. "I had no idea." Emma had been wild as well, but her antics had never gotten her arrested and into a courtroom. In high school, her sister would have positively wasted away from mortification, despite her don't-care attitude.

Natalie shrugged. "It's no secret, but we don't go around promoting it either. We came here—and bought your dad's business—to get away from the kids he was messed up with." She pressed her palms together. "When this all went down with Russell, and we sat in the courtroom, I prayed, 'Please, please, please. I'll do anything. I'll give up wine and chocolate, be less grouchy, stop cussing so much.'" She grinned wryly. "I told God, if my son was able to do this—really change—I'd look out for other kids like him. People who'd lost their way too."

Allie's throat tightened. She wasn't about to correct Natalie, but she hadn't lost her way. She was in the wrong place at the wrong time. And the killer was still out there.

After another beat, Natalie took one last look at the résumé and put it down on the counter. "I'm only going to say this once. I run a tight ship. I'm demanding. I need you to be on time and not call in sick, if at all possible."

"Of course."

"We offer a three-month probation. At the end, you can walk away, or we can let you go. No questions asked. No hard feelings."

"Sounds more than fair," Allie said.

Natalie crossed her arms. "It's a tech position. Doesn't pay much. Two dollars over minimum wage, with two weeks' vacation. If you work over forty hours, you'll get overtime. We take most holidays off. The office is closed the week of Christmas except for emergencies."

A tiny surge of hope bubbled up in Allie's chest.

"I have one last question for you," Natalie asked, giving her a long, hard look.

Allie didn't flinch or look away.

Natalie paused for a beat. "Did you do it?"

"No." Allie held her gaze as long as she could.

"Good," Natalie replied, her face softening. "Then I guess all that's left is to decide one thing. When can you start?"

"Yesterday," Allie said quickly.

"Excellent." Natalie jerked her thumb toward the back of the building. "If you're not busy now, I have all of these boxes to move. Of course, my husband and son have disappeared," she added. "I'd like them out of here before Monday morning. I was thinking the storage shed out back?"

Allie grinned. "Say no more."

EIGHTEEN

CAROLINE

2016

Caroline's days were playing out like a Stephen King movie. Everywhere she went, tension built. It was the anticipation, the beats leading up to the moment when tragedy struck the main character. It didn't matter how many times she'd seen *The Shining* with Emma, the scary parts still made her jump.

In gym class, no one looked in her direction. In the hallway, her classmates stopped laughing and talking when she walked past. In class, the heat of people's stares singed the back of her neck like sparks from a brush fire.

She'd finally confessed to Maddie right there in homeroom, amid the dull roar of rustling papers, the scrape of chair legs on the floor, and the endless chatter. When a substitute teacher walked in and set her briefcase down on the front table, her arrival did little to dissipate the noise. For that, Caroline was grateful.

"I'm sorry I didn't tell you sooner about my mom," Caroline answered. "I should have, right away." She glanced across the aisle to Maddie, gauging her reaction.

"Did you think I hadn't heard?" Maddie knit her brow and

almost sputtered the sentence, her voice just an octave above a whisper. Her face reddened and she rolled her eyes.

Caroline sucked in a breath. She'd expected disappointment from Maddie, but not necessarily anger.

"We're supposed to be friends. *Best* friends. And you let me go on thinking I'd done something wrong?" Maddie stared at Caroline as if she were a specimen under a microscope. Bacteria. Something contagious.

"You have to believe me. It wasn't what I'd meant to happen," Caroline struggled to explain. "I couldn't talk to anyone."

"You don't trust me." Maddie traced the line of the desk with one finger.

Caroline shifted closer, trying to get Maddie to look at her. "I didn't know how to tell you. I've been sick about it. *Every* day. I haven't talked to anyone."

But Maddie ignored that she'd said anything. Her eyes were icy blue, frozen over. "After all this time I've had your back," she hissed and finally glared in Caroline's direction.

Stung by Maddie's reaction, Caroline slid back in her seat and jerked her eyes away, willing herself not to break down.

She swallowed hard with the realization that—right or wrong—she'd crossed the line with Maddie. Maddie, who lived to be the first to know everything, who prided herself on creating and controlling gossip with their circle of friends, and the entire school, for that matter. She operated, more than a bit, through fear and intimidation.

"I'm sorry," Caroline apologized, knowing it wasn't enough.

Maddie turned her head slowly and gave Caroline a sidelong glance. "It's too late." She paused. "And what you did to Jake's Mercedes after he broke up with you? Cutting up the leather seats? Tearing up the ragtop? That's not just juvenile . . . You destroyed his car."

Blood rushed to Caroline's cheeks. "What? I-I didn't!" Heads turned all around them at her exclamation.

But instead of making things better, the denial only served to fuel Maddie's fiery mood. She set her jaw and crossed her arms. "Really? So I suppose you don't know anything about keying the sides of the car or the slashed tires either?"

"I would never," Caroline sputtered.

"I'm beginning to think you were never really my friend." Maddie scrunched up her shoulders and narrowed her eyes.

"That's not true," Caroline pleaded.

Maddie sniffed and turned her head away.

Caroline shrunk down in her seat, trying desperately to hold back tears. She dug her fingernails into the soft part of her arm, focusing on the pain. She started shaking. She wouldn't lose it. She couldn't. Not in front of Maddie, God, and everyone at school.

With all of the strength left inside her body, Caroline focused on breathing in and out. She stared at a mark on her desk and tried not to think about anything other than existing. Surviving.

When the bell rang, Maddie stalked off.

Caroline sat still and let everyone in the room file out first. When every seat was empty, she got to her feet. For a split second, her thoughts flitted to her mother. Was this how she felt? Alone? In a corner? Like everyone hated her?

In a fog, Caroline pushed the thoughts away and stumbled to her locker. She put her hand on the lock and dialed the combination. Her fingers fumbled with the numbers on the dial. She couldn't make them work. Finally, on the fourth try, the lock released and swung free.

Breathe, Caroline reminded herself. *Just get through the day.*

Maddie and all of her friends didn't understand the kind of pressure she was under. Neither did Jake. How could they? If anyone else's parents screwed up, they did it behind closed doors. Drinking, affairs, gambling. None of them were arrested and thrown in prison. Those names weren't splashed in huge letters all over the local newspaper. Their parents weren't on TV being shouted at by reporters. They weren't ignored and ridiculed.

And despite being upset, even angry, Caroline would never destroy someone's car.

As she yanked open the locker, rattling the thin metal door, the bell rang. Caroline would be late for class. The hallway emptied, doors closing like dominoes falling in a row. Another locker door slammed. Shoes clicked, staccato, on the tile. Caroline grabbed her textbook and hugged the weight to her chest, trying to slow her racing heart. Eyes drilled forward, she ducked into Spanish class and slid into her seat.

At the disruption, her teacher grimaced, clapped her hands, and called the class back to order. Caroline flipped open her textbook, turning page after page. She clenched and unclenched her fists, picked up her pen, then glanced at the clock. *Faster*, she urged silently. *Tick, tock. Tick, tock.*

She sunk down in her chair, forced her fingers to write. *Muchas gracias.* Thank you very much. *Socorro!* Help!

Caroline bent her head and concentrated. *No entiendo.* I don't understand.

That was for sure.

Caroline jumped when her cell buzzed in her pocket. She shifted in her chair, and as quickly as she could, drew out the phone, silencing the vibration. But as Caroline started to slip her phone into her backpack, she couldn't help herself. After a moment, she looked at the screen and the text from a number she didn't recognize.

You missed our ice-cream date. Want to try for Saturday?

It was Russell.

He'd remembered.

NINETEEN

EMMA

2016

For ten minutes that morning, Caroline had hovered around the sink, rearranging cups and emptying the dishwasher. When the clinking and banging didn't stop, Emma wandered into the kitchen, set down her coffee, and interrupted. "Hey, sweetie. What's up?"

At the sound of her aunt's voice, Caroline jumped. After catching her breath, she turned around and leaned against the counter. "Hey, did you hear someone messed with Jake's car?"

Emma frowned, tamping down her internal satisfaction. "I had, as a matter of fact. His was one of a row of them in their neighborhood. The cops think some kids came through and vandalized them around three o'clock in the morning."

"Oh." Caroline's eyes had grown wide. "I had . . . no idea."

"Yeah, crazy, right?" Emma added, picking up her mug to take a sip and hide her smile of satisfaction.

Caroline frowned. "I-I'll bet he's furious."

"Some people get what's coming to them," Emma added sharply, stirring sugar into her cup.

"Well, Maddie actually thought I had something to do with it." Caroline gulped, her eyes misting.

Nearly choking, Emma sloshed her coffee on the table, spots of liquid splattering like dark raindrops. "What in the world?" She narrowed her eyes as she reached for a napkin to catch the drips.

"Yeah." Caroline shrugged. "She's not really talking to me."

Emma hesitated, steadying her anger. Now she would have to set Maddie straight. The girl wouldn't bother Caroline again when she was through with her. "I have a feeling that Maddie has found out by now that you didn't have anything to do with it, Caro."

"Really?" Caroline's forehead crinkled, but her pale face brightened. She leaned against the countertop, playing with the edges of her shirt. "I hope so."

"Let me know, all right?" Emma asked, ducking her head to catch Caroline's eyes.

"Okay." Her niece tried to smile. "Um, and so, anyway, I need to go to the library for a little while, to work on a project for school. After that, I wanted to meet a new friend at the coffee shop. Can I go?"

Emma reached for the newspaper, glanced at the headline, and pushed it to one side. Her eyes flickered to Caroline. "A new friend?" The corners of her lips edged up.

Her niece flushed. "His name's Russell."

"And who is this Russell?"

"Just a boy I volunteer with at the nursing home." Caroline's face grew hot.

"What? I need to know." Emma grinned. "And I *am* allowed to ask. I want to make sure you're safe," Emma said, playing at defending herself. "It's my job."

Caroline ducked back, smiling, then scuffed the floor with the toe of her shoe.

"Does he go to Mansfield?" Emma searched her brain, trying to remember if Caroline had ever mentioned him.

"Brunswick. He's a senior. He just moved here with his parents. He doesn't know many people yet." Caroline looked up at the ceiling and attempted a casual shrug.

Emma tapped her fingertips on the countertop, gazing out the kitchen window. Inside, she turned cartwheels. This meant Caroline wouldn't be moping around over Jake. "Blood type? Social security number?"

Her niece folded her arms across her chest.

"You know I'm teasing," Emma said with a laugh.

"It's not really a date either."

"I wasn't asking," Emma replied, smoothing out the curve of her lips. She was desperate for the girl to get outside, see other people. Of course, she'd hunt down the new guy, too, if he even thought about wounding Caroline's fragile heart.

"All right."

Caroline grinned and slung her bag over one shoulder.

"Have your cell phone?"

"Yes."

Emma reached for her purse and pulled out a few twenties. She folded them in half and handed them to Caroline, whose eyes widened at the gift.

"Thank you." She flung her arms around Emma, giving her a quick squeeze.

"In case you decide to go to the bookstore. Or whatever." Emma winked.

Caroline grinned and picked up her keys. She flew out the door a few minutes later, shutting it so quickly that the table quivered.

Emma sighed and smiled to herself. She could hear Caroline's steps across the porch. A few minutes later, with Caroline almost out of sight, her cell buzzed with a text from Allie.

Need a needle and some thread. Have any?

What in the world? Emma reread the message and sighed. She was tempted to ignore the text, but after thinking about it, now was an excellent time to find out what her sister was up to.

Emma saved her work, shut down the computer, and headed for the storage closet inside her small garage. It was a small mess, as she'd never unpacked many of the boxes since they'd moved to the house five years earlier. After rummaging through a half-dozen containers, after moving Caroline's roller skates and paint cans, she found her sewing box.

On her way out the door, Emma grabbed a sheet of scrap paper, dashed off a note to Caroline. She added Allie's address and phone number. Not that it was likely anything could drag her niece away from her coffee date, but in the event of a freak tornado or global crisis, at least Caroline would know where to find her.

Emma tucked the small plastic container on her hip. Walking took less than five minutes, down the sidewalk, around the corner, and into the humid morning, the salty sea air tickling her nose.

The yard looked freshly mowed and edged. Allie had put out potted plants—perky red geraniums—on the steps. Her sister yanked the door open before Emma raised her fist to knock.

"Hey. Thank you," Allie said, looking genuinely grateful. She held out her hands to take the sewing box. "I thought you might have one of these."

"No problem," Emma replied, glancing around the small space. "I actually needed a break from work."

"It's not what you think," Allie scoffed and started to smile. "Stop looking so nervous. Nothing's wrong." She held up a dark pink scrub top with a ripped seam. "I got a job yesterday." She waved Emma inside the house.

"What?" Emma's jaw fell open.

"Yep." Allie tapped her lip. "The vet who bought Dad's office hired me." She looked up at her sister and shrugged. "She had an ad online, so I went in and talked to her."

"Natalie Harper?" Emma tried not to squeak.

"Oh, do you know her?" Allie perked up, smiling. "I guess it makes sense, considering Dad would have told you all about it."

A little shiver ran up Emma's back. Her father had actually shared very little about letting go of the business. She tucked a stray hair behind her ear. She'd been so busy taking care of Caroline that she didn't think about how strange it was . . . until now.

"Emma?" Allie was staring at her.

"Um, no," she replied quickly. "He didn't give me any of the details, other than it was sold," Emma added. The truth was, her father had practically disappeared when he found out Allie was being released. But it was nothing her sister needed to know. Why would it matter? Emma shoved the thoughts out of her head and mustered as much enthusiasm as she could. "That's great, though, about the job."

"Thanks, I'm pretty happy about it." Allie's cheeks flushed pink, the way they always did when she was particularly pleased about something. "I hear Caroline's working . . . or volunteering."

"Yep." Emma bobbed her head, glancing past Allie at the wall. She should have left right away. *Such a mistake.*

"What's she up to this morning?"

"Having coffee. With a new guy," Emma said, keeping her voice nonchalant. "He's a physical therapy volunteer and works at the nursing home. And a senior at Brunswick."

Allie stiffened visibly. "So, have you met him?"

Emma wrinkled her nose. She had it under control. "No. But,

um, it's just coffee. And it's a Saturday morning. What do you think is going to happen? I know where she is, and Caroline has her cell phone. I made sure."

"Fine," Allie muttered, opening the sewing box and examining the contents.

"She'll be home soon." Emma glanced at her watch. "And, by the way, keep the sewing stuff. I don't need it right now."

"Thanks."

A thudding silence filled the room before Emma could move to the door.

"How is Caroline? I mean, how is she holding up? Emotionally."

Emma cleared her throat. "She's okay. She's good." She wasn't about to mention Jake or Maddie. She was going to be positive and chipper.

Allie was suddenly a few shades paler.

"Like you said, she's doing volunteer work. She's at the nursing home, building up her service hours," Emma added. "I'm so proud of her."

Allie didn't answer and struggled with a smile. The words had pierced her. She knew her sister felt like she should be the one saying those words. But Emma didn't regret saying it. She had raised Caroline. She could and *should* take the credit.

"I'll tell her you asked about her," Emma said, moving toward the door. She wanted to leave. She couldn't stand the sad look, the pitiful expression.

"Whatever she says . . . let me know," Allie said, her voice low and tremulous.

Emma nodded. "I really need to get going." On the front steps, Emma waved and turned away. She headed in the direction of home, leaving Allie behind.

Her sister was clinging to a thread of hope. She didn't realize that her life now was like a maze with no exit, leading her only in circles. Pushing Allie and Caroline apart was for her sister's own good. Caroline's too.

Really, Allie shouldn't need it spelled out. All of the signs were there: Caroline wasn't speaking to her, old friends ignored her, and her own parents were keeping a safe distance.

With a few final steps, Emma flung open the door to her own house and closed it tight behind her, breathing hard and starting to perspire. Emotion she'd tamped down for so long—hurt, loss, anger, and heartbreak—rose in her throat, threatening to spill out. Her sister was a reminder. Now, here in Brunswick, she felt like a weight around Emma's neck. Pulling her down. Suffocating everything.

Sooner rather than later, Emma needed Allie gone.

TWENTY

NATALIE

2016

"You hired her?"

Natalie watched Nick cough into his hand, eyes wide, as if he'd been told his home was burning to the ground. He paced back and forth, occasionally turning to glance at her. Nick was usually a go-along, get-along kind of guy, always comfortable with a prerogative to change one's mind.

"Really?" he asked again.

"It's temporary. We'll see how it works out." Natalie inhaled and blew out a big breath. "She's qualified. She's overqualified, actually." She locked eyes with her husband. "And when it comes time, when it really matters, I want someone like me to give Russell a second chance."

"He's doing all right," Nick defended him.

"He's still living with us," Natalie said. "What about when we're not around? What if he starts hanging out with the wrong crowd again? Who'll help him get away then?"

"Maybe he's learned his lesson."

A rap on the door interrupted them.

Nick jerked his head toward the noise. "What the—"

"Calm down and stop arguing, babe. It's the sheriff," Natalie said, bending sideways a few inches so she could wave for the man to come in. Her pulse ramped into overdrive. *Please don't let it be about Russell.* He couldn't be in trouble already. He'd promised.

"On a Sunday?" Nick muttered.

With the metallic scrape of old hinges and a groan of wooden floorboards under his boots, Lee Gaines removed his hat and lumbered into the office with a German shepherd panting at his side. "Hey, folks."

"Sheriff," Nick replied, glancing at the dog and then back at Natalie.

"Hello," she added warily, her eyes just grazing his face. "Hey, boy," she cooed to the dog, reaching out the back of her hand for him to sniff.

"This is Chief." Gaines released the German shepherd from his leash and fell silent, watching the canine. The dog proceeded to cautiously sniff at Natalie's fingertips, followed by Nick's knuckles. Once relaxed, the dog ran his nose along every inch and corner of the room.

When he was finished, Chief came straight back to Natalie, who leaned down and scratched behind his ears through the thick, wiry fur.

Sheriff Gaines stiffened and furrowed his brow. "Normally, Chief doesn't take much to women." He frowned at the dog.

"So, what can we do for you, Sheriff?" Nick stepped forward to interrupt and offered a chair. "Have a seat?"

"No thanks, I won't stay long." Gaines hooked both thumbs into his belt and let his eyes rove across the newly refurbished waiting area and reception desk. "Looks like you've been hard at work."

Natalie watched Nick trying his best to tamp down his

annoyance with the drawn-out niceties. She cleared her throat, shooting her husband her best cease-and-desist look.

"Thank you, Sheriff. We're glad you approve."

Gaines rubbed one hand under his chin. "It would be a shame if anything got in the way of your new enterprise here. Folks do talk, you know. They see things."

"I'm sorry," Natalie said, standing up and throwing back her shoulders. "I'm really not following you. Is something wrong?" Her voice quivered the slightest bit. She was clinging to the edge of the table, her knuckles bone white.

"Simple." Sheriff Gaines ran his palm through his brush cut and then snapped his fingers for Chief to heel. The dog, ever obedient, trotted swiftly across the room and sat next to his master. "What I'm speaking of, in friendly terms, is allowing people of questionable background and morals to get involved in the day-to-day operation of your business."

"It would be easier—" Nick started.

Natalie held up a hand and smiled as sweetly as she could manage. How dare he call her judgment into question? But she didn't need to make enemies. She could play this better.

"Sheriff Gaines." She lowered her voice and blinked up at him, eyes wide. "Now, whatever are you talking about?"

"Ma'am. All I wanted to do was remind you to be careful."

Natalie lifted an eyebrow and waited.

Gaines rocked on his heels and gripped his holster, his eyes turning dark with frustration. "There was some history, here in Brunswick. Involving Allie Marshall. I heard that she stopped by."

Natalie saw Nick eye Gaines's hand. She thought it probably twitched a little too much for his liking.

"That's right, Sheriff," Natalie said. "She did." She slid a glance at her husband.

"Mind if I ask why?"

"She needed a job. We have an opening." Natalie corrected herself, "Well, we *had* an opening."

Gaines visibly relaxed. "You filled the position with someone else. Good." He grinned.

"Um, no. We thought we'd give her a chance." Natalie squinted at her husband. "See how she fit into things. She's qualified. Right, babe?"

"Honey, that's your call." Nick managed a weak grin.

The sheriff's jaw flinched as he moved his eyes toward the back of the building. Chief sensed the movement and began to sniff the ground, his nose edging the cabinets.

"I see," Gaines finally said.

"Nick and I believe that it's our civic duty to help others in need," Natalie explained, lowering her eyes to the German shepherd. The fur around his neck bristled. His ears pricked up. Animals could sense tension and discord, and in this moment, the room was supersaturated.

"She's a felon," Sheriff Gaines said with force. "I thought you should have all of the facts."

Chief whined a little, tugged at his collar, looked up at his master, paws touching and lifting from the floor.

Natalie leveled her gaze. "Of course, we don't know everything, but we did buy the business from her parents. They shared some of the . . . story . . . about the trouble she's had."

"Trouble? Is that what she's calling it?" Gaines stared at Natalie as if he'd been told Allie had broken her leg dancing with the New York City Ballet instead of sitting inside Arrendale State Prison.

"Sheriff." Natalie spoke slowly. "We found she had the necessary qualifications and experience. What more could a veterinarian ask than an employee guided and educated by a man as fine as Dr. Paul

Marshall?" It was a sound argument, Natalie told herself, unless you believed that Allie Marshall actually killed a man in cold blood and watched him die.

When Gaines simply held her gaze, she continued, feeling the muscles in her neck tighten. "We need to be in business and stay in business. Miss Marshall—Allie—can help us. We need a seamless transition from her father's office to my office," she added shakily.

"It may be the worst decision you ever made," Gaines said. "She's fresh out of prison, with a history of violence. Who knows what other tricks she may have picked up on the inside." He rubbed at his smooth-shaven chin. "Bad things can happen, Dr. Harper. Assault, robbery. I've seen it time and time again."

Natalie's throat went dry. "Well, Sheriff, you'll be the first to know if and when anything goes wrong." On wobbly legs, she moved around the counter to the lobby area.

There was a beat of silence, and Gaines shifted in place. "I'll be on my way, then."

"Thank you for stopping by, Sheriff." Natalie stuck out her hand to shake and offered him a bright smile. "Now, if you'll excuse us, Nick and I have so much to do before we can open the doors tomorrow."

Gaines's hand chilled Natalie to the bone, his skin the temperature of a raging river in spring. His fingers closed over Natalie's and squeezed hard. *Argh!* Was the man trying to break every bone? When she looked up, wincing in his grip, the sheriff's eyes glinted dark as the night sky.

"All right, Natalie," Nick said as he hurried over. "Want to get those files in order?" At the sounds of his voice, Gaines dropped Natalie's hand and turned to her husband.

As Nick escorted Gaines and the dog outside, he made an effort at small talk. "How 'bout those Wolverines this year? Is that quarterback ready to go?" He held the door wide open, with a worried glance back at his wife.

As Natalie massaged her hand, the warm afternoon breeze flooded the room, ruffling papers and sending Post-its fluttering to the ground. She didn't move or stoop to pick anything up. All Natalie could think about was getting this man out the door.

As if reading her thoughts, Sheriff Gaines paused before sliding on his hat and stepping onto the concrete steps.

He glanced back. "Dr. Harper." He tipped his hat. "Nick. Call me if you need anything. Don't hesitate."

Nick stood in the doorway and nodded. "Yes, sir. Have a good day."

With a snap of Gaines's fingers, Chief strained at his collar and followed. When the sheriff opened the doors of his squad car and motioned, the dog barked in response and jumped into the backseat.

From the window, Natalie watched Gaines slide into the patrol car and crank the engine, but what she really saw was the sheriff staring down at her. His image was now burned in her mind. It was hatred on his face, pure and unadulterated. Hatred, bordering on obsession.

Surely no sheriff or lawman liked a convicted felon returning to town, but Allie didn't fit the description of a hardened criminal. At least not the ones Natalie had seen on television. She chewed her bottom lip. Her experience, admittedly, was limited.

She put a hand on her heart and exhaled as the vehicle backed up. The wheels crunched on the gravel as the car turned and crept down the driveway, leaving puffs of dust behind.

As Nick came back inside, brushing off his khaki pants, he didn't have to stop or ask what Natalie needed.

This time he locked the deadbolt and set the alarm.

TWENTY-ONE

CAROLINE

2016

"You know, I thought you'd stand me up again," Russell said, rising out of his seat to give her a half hug across the café table.

Inhaling his masculine scent and feeling his stubble brush her cheek, Caroline allowed herself to be wrapped up in the embrace. When she withdrew and stepped back to sit down, Russell was staring at her as if she were an exotic jewel on display at a museum.

Her skin warmed as she met his gaze.

"I ordered you a latte—hope you don't mind. You look great," he said, casting an admiring glance at her hair and bare shoulders under the thin straps of her yellow sundress.

Caroline bit her lip but smiled. "Thanks. I'm not sure how. It's been a rough week."

"Well, the week's over. And I'm glad you said yes," Russell said and grinned. "Impressed that I remembered your number?" He tapped his head and winked.

"I am." Caroline laughed. She couldn't help herself. She smiled back and took a sip from her mug. *Coffee*, she reminded herself. They were just meeting for coffee.

They were sitting outside, under a patio umbrella, watching the birds perch nearby. Overhead, streams of white clouds cut ribbons through the sky. A jet pierced the blue with its silver body. Caroline wished she were on it, going anywhere.

What she was doing now was a close second to getting away from her hometown—sharing a table with a new boy in town. He was cute, friendly, and hadn't grown up in a big mansion in Brunswick, or down the street from Grandpa Paul and Grandma Lily, or around the corner from her high school. He was, as she'd discovered earlier, the new veterinarian's son.

His family had just moved here from the Atlanta suburbs, and Caroline liked that he came from outside Brunswick and St. Simons Island. He had lived somewhere different. In a really big city, one with skyscrapers. He knew that there was a whole wide world outside this little corner of Georgia.

"So tell me about Caroline Marshall," Russell said, sitting up straighter. He leaned forward and brushed a stray lock of hair out of his eye.

"You haven't finished telling me about you," Caroline insisted, raising her chin and feeling flirtatious.

Russell rubbed the hint of stubble on his chin and settled back against his chair. He motioned for her to begin, a lazy smile playing across his face. "Fine. Shoot. Ask me anything."

A swirl of emotions welled up in Caroline. Relief from any scrutiny or a need to measure up. Admiration for Russell's confidence. Appreciation for his good sense of humor. It was refreshing and honest.

They smiled across the table at each other.

"So, you really seem to like volunteering at the nursing home," Caroline said, breaking the moment. She took a sip of her latte, letting the sweet milk and foam tickle her lips. Her plan was to keep the conversation about Russell, away from the potholes that made up her own life. She watched as he grabbed his napkin, folding it into quarters.

"I like working with people who've seen so much and have all of these stories to tell," Russell said. "The exercise and rehab part can really help people perk up and respond, but there's something about spending time with someone—one-on-one—that's just as important. A person has to want to try to move or try to lift his leg a little higher. Without a little incentive, it doesn't matter. People waste away and wait to die."

"Wow." Caroline let the word escape in a rushed exhale. The explanation was more than she'd expected, deep, honest, and profound. Caroline felt goose bumps prickle her arms. She shivered, despite the warm breeze, and looked off in the distance, thinking about the people in the nursing home where they worked.

"Aw, I didn't mean to get on a soapbox and talk your ear off." Russell reddened through his cheeks to the tips of his ears.

Caroline dropped her eyes for a moment, then looked back up. "I think it's great." She toyed with her mug. "It sounds like how my Grandpa Paul used to talk before he retired." She tilted her head to one side. "It's so weird. Your parents buying my grandpa's office. It's kind of surreal." She frowned.

"Yeah. My parents told me about your grandpa. They've heard he's a good doctor and a really good guy." He looked at Caroline intently. "Can I—"

"I don't really want to talk about it," Caroline cut him off, panicking. He was going to ask her about her mother and prison. Or whether she really killed the man she found in the pharmacy that night. How it felt. So many people had asked. She squeezed her hands together to keep them from shaking.

Russell frowned. "I was going to—"

"Don't, please." Caroline winced.

A bird alighted on the table, chirping and fluttering over the crumbs. Russell shooed it away with a gentle sweep of his arm.

"Whoa. Hold on here." Russell paused and looked at Caroline. "All right. Let me guess." He leaned back and spread his arms wide. "You're having a meltdown about something. Fight with your best friend? Or school is awful?"

Caroline moved her fingers away from her eyes. She was silent for a moment. Maybe she could trust him. Maybe she'd feel better if she talked about it.

"Well," she began, "something like that. Some stuff happened."

Russell watched her, listening.

"A lot of days I want to be invisible. I've tried pretending everything's fine, but nothing's the same. Even my teachers act weird." Caroline stopped herself, afraid she'd spilled too much already.

Russell frowned. "It won't be like that forever. You'll get out of high school, go to college."

Caroline lowered her gaze. "I can't even think about tomorrow..."

A light gust of wind rustled through the hanging baskets, each dripping with ivy and trailing cones of blues and purple blossoms. The motion lifted the corners of the napkins on the table, sent the check flying. Russell leaped up and grabbed it after several steps.

"Got it," he exclaimed, beaming as he turned back toward the table.

"Nice catch." Caroline forced a bright look, trying to shake the angst bubbling up in her chest.

Russell sat back down and squinted over his mug, watching her.

"So, school sucks, you're stressed out, and everyone's acting weird." He tapped his chin, then met her eyes. "Are your mom and dad splitting up?"

"Not even close." Caroline was surprised and relieved that he didn't know. "I've never even met my dad."

Across from her, Russell wrinkled his forehead. "All right. Go ahead and tell me."

"You really haven't heard?" Caroline said, suspicious.

He shrugged. "Let me hear it from you."

Caroline sucked in her breath and unloaded. "My mom's a-a convicted felon." She bit her lip. "She went to prison ten years ago for supposedly killing a man—the man who used to be the coach of the high school football team."

Without flinching, Russell kept his eyes on Caroline's face.

"No one actually saw it happen, and there wasn't much for the cops to go on. A tiny bit of forensic stuff. A 9-1-1 call that put her at the scene." Caroline swallowed. "They fought it, my mom and my family did. But the jury convicted her. She was sentenced to sixteen years, but was paroled early and got home, like, last week."

"Okay," Russell said. He didn't look away.

"While she was away, I lived with my grandparents at first, and then moved in with my aunt." Caroline traced the handle of her mug. "Emma, my aunt, she's pretty chill. Like she worries and everything, but it's not awful."

With a smile, Russell nodded for her to go on.

"Now my mom's out and wants to see me." She chewed her lip and hesitated. "And I just can't do it."

Russell put his elbows on the table and leaned in. "Things may look different in another month or two. Once things settle down. I know you don't think so, but you'll get through this."

Caroline picked up her cup, swirled the caramel-colored liquid. "I thought volunteering at the nursing home would keep me busy and get my mind off things."

"And?" Russell asked.

She shrugged.

He waited a beat or two. "Are you doing it just to avoid your mom?"

Caroline offered a guilty look, wrinkled her nose. "Maybe at first. Now I really like it."

"Good." Russell ran a hand through his hair. "I'm not saying don't volunteer. I think everyone should do it. When I go in that place, I am always so grateful that I can walk and run, that I'm not in a wheelchair." Russell picked up his bagel and took a bite.

"I know," she answered.

Russell looked at Caroline as he chewed. When he finished, he squinted at her. "The stuff about your mom, that's messed up," he said. "But what do they say? There are two sides to every story? And I'm sure she cares about you and wants to make things right."

"You think so?" Caroline swallowed hard. The hairs on the back of her neck stood on end.

"It's a guess."

Caroline considered this. "Well, I'm not sure. And a lot of times I don't want to be thankful," she said, raising her voice. "I'm so mad at her and the world that I want to scream sometimes. When she was gone, it was better. I could just pretend that Emma was my mom, that nothing happened."

Russell wrinkled his brow.

"I don't know if I ever can forgive her. For doing it. For leaving me." Caroline squeezed her eyes shut and rubbed her forehead.

Russell was silent for a moment. "Pretending helps for a while. But you get to a point when it's easier to face it and go on. Take it from someone who has been on the other side; it's pretty lonely and awful there too."

Caroline frowned, half listening. "You have no idea." This wasn't how she wanted to spend her day. She'd trusted him, and he'd turned on her already, telling her what to do. She stood up, sloshing her coffee. "Look, I really need to get back. Homework. I have a paper due."

Russell tilted his head and locked eyes with Caroline. "Are you sure?"

She felt herself starting to melt, just a little, until she reminded herself that he'd probably do the same thing Jake had done. Drop her and walk away. And Russell wasn't even her boyfriend.

"Come on," Caroline said softly. "Just forget it." They stared at each other in silence until she lowered her eyes to the ground. She stayed focused on a crack in the sidewalk until Russell spoke.

"It's okay."

Caroline looked up as Russell pulled out his wallet and held up the check. "I'll take care of this. You go do what you need to do." He paused, forehead creased, and put a hand on the table. "If you change your mind, Caroline, and need to talk, just give me a call. I understand a lot more than you think."

A stab of panic hit Caroline. Maybe Russell was different from Jake. Maybe he understood. Maybe he actually *got* her and wanted to listen. And she'd hurt him. It was all over his face. The moment she opened her mouth to try to apologize, another couple wandered up and sat down at a table nearby as Russell pushed back his chair, stood up, and walked away.

Heart pained, Caroline watched him go around the corner, into the restaurant. Tears blurring her eyes, she sat back down outside, alone. Russell wasn't going to plead with her or beg. He didn't play games. She told him she had to go and he listened.

The sun moved across the sky, a burst of amber and gold. The rays warmed her shoulders, hit the surface of the table and her water glass. The ice melted into slivers, then disappeared.

She reached a hand into her bag, feeling for her cell and

earphones. She slipped them on, and for a few moments, she allowed herself to drift.

Nowhere to go and no way out. We're underground, no voice to shout. Buried beneath our own demise. You left, left, left. You left me. Good-bye.

The lyrics reverberated in her ears; the strains of music played.

Caroline shifted her eyes back up, blinking against the sun. It was hard to see the couple nearby, talking behind their menu. The woman laughed, threw back her head, then leaned over and kissed her date—maybe her husband—whoever he was. Shielding herself, Caroline put her back to the couple. She curled up in the chair, hugging her knees to her chest while she breathed in the music. *You left, left, left.*

Everyone did. Despite what they said or promised. Her father. Her mother. Jake and Maddie. Now Russell.

You left me. Good-bye.

TWENTY-TWO

EMMA

2016

At home, after finishing the final tweaks on a client's website, Emma's mind turned to Allie and Caroline. Her niece was so stressed, so upset, and barely eating. She had to think hard—come up with a new solution to drive her sister out of their lives for good. As for Caroline's ex-friend Maddie . . . Emma's hands curled into fists . . . Well, that could be handled later. She would deal with Allie first.

Emma got up and paced the room, glancing at the magazine and newspaper clippings she'd tacked to the wall. Feature stories on clients, interviews with local business owners she worked with, and an article about her mother's garden club.

Sometimes it took looking at the situation in reverse, doing the opposite of what she expected might work. Emma stopped and zeroed in on the newsprint, an idea forming in her head.

With a burst of inspiration, Emma sat down and did a quick Internet search. It took all of ten seconds to find the article she wanted. As she hit print and watched the paper slide from the machine, Emma reached for the page, brought it down to her lap.

She read and reread. Gripping the paper, her mind whirred with possibilities. This one thing, this reminder from the past, could help Emma make things right. Instead of shielding everyone from her sister, perhaps she should force Caroline and Allie together.

The discomfort would be temporary, and certainly everyone, including Caroline, would manage to get through it. The theory was well worth testing.

Then, from the corner of her eye, Emma noticed the screen of her cell light up. She'd had the ringer off for the past few hours, concentrating on her deadline. She grasped the phone and tapped at the call history. Emma had missed four calls from her mother in the last thirty minutes. Her skin prickled. Was something wrong? What had happened?

Taking a breath, Emma listened to the voice mail. Her father was out to dinner with friends, her mother explained. He'd been golfing all day, and she felt lonely. Did Emma want to get together?

Relief flooded Emma's body. There was no crisis. No drama. For once.

When Emma called back, her mother picked up on the first ring. Emma suggested a drive to St. Simons, where they might catch a glimpse of dolphins playing in the waves along the shore and watch the sun set in the horizon over the Atlantic. They could spend the hours, she added, under the shade of a covered restaurant patio, sipping frozen drinks.

But her mother had opted for privacy and asked that they spend a quiet evening in the comfort of Emma's backyard. It was a lovely evening to be outside, Emma thought, under the canopy of her magnolia trees, with their curved branches, creamy-white blossoms, and glossy green leaves. And she could keep an eye on Caroline, who'd been quiet and pensive since her date with Russell.

It wasn't a complete surprise—her mother's sudden interest in solace and privacy. Since Allie's release, her mother had postponed all social activities for the near future, pleading that she needed to tend her garden or had "projects" at home. Emma understood, however, that avoiding everyone in a thirty-mile radius shielded her mother from most public scrutiny and gossip.

Both of her parents had always dealt with uncomfortable situations this way. Emma had half expected her mother to flee the country, but perhaps she was trying—this time—to handle things differently.

"How is everything?" her mother asked after a sip of wine, watching a pair of industrious bees. They buzzed in unison, hovering and ducking in and out of deep red hibiscus blossoms.

Emma raised her glass, swirling the liquid. "Caroline's still freaked out about Allie being home. She's already had a tough week with Jake breaking up with her. And one of her best friends—you know Maddie, right? She's been ignoring her."

"Bless her heart," her mother said. "The poor girl. It's the last thing she needs."

With a frown, Emma crossed her arms over her chest, hugging them to her body. She'd been thinking about Maddie, dwelling on the girl's cruelty. How could she drop Caroline like this? It was time Maddie was taught a lesson.

"So, what about her trying to spend some time with Allie?"

"I've talked to her a lot about this. Almost every night." Emma pursed her lips. "Caroline is freaked out. Her life's all upside down, and I know she blames a lot of it on her mom getting out of prison. Right now she just wants to stay away from Allie."

Her mother drew a breath. She blinked and looked away. "Oh dear," she murmured, pursing her lips. "Allie—well, she won't be happy."

"I know," Emma sighed. "I'm taking it day by day. Caroline is fragile right now, she needs time, and some stability. It's all so new, with Allie back. It has to feel like she's been dropped onto another planet."

"Well, I'll let you handle it, dear," her mother said. "No one's spent more time with Caroline. You know best."

"Thank you," Emma said, the words swelling her heart a full size larger. Her parents had never lauded her with much praise in high school and her college years. She was going to soak up every minute now. She deserved it, after all. She'd earned it.

"I know that you'll help her make the right decisions."

"I will." And she would. About Caroline. Allie. Emma gritted her teeth. Even that Maddie. She stretched her arms overhead, releasing some of the tension in her shoulders as her mother took another sip of wine.

"So, let me tell you what I'm planning with the landscaping at the house." Her mother smiled and set down her glass. "I've decided that we need to plant some hydrangeas . . ."

Listening to her mother change the subject without missing a beat, Emma realized they were done talking about anything personal. Anything difficult. It was a "wave the flag" visit. A show of concern. Something to check off the list.

It was fine. Emma could play the game too.

She'd done it her whole life, and it had finally paid off, as far as her parents were concerned. Now she was the good girl. The one who made her father and mother proud. The stars had finally aligned, but in her favor this time.

"Don't you think so, dear?"

Her mother's question snapped Emma out of her thoughts.

"Yes, definitely," Emma said, mustering some enthusiasm and hoping it was the right answer.

Her mother's face dissolved from concern into a slow smile. "Good, I thought so too."

And her mother kept right on talking.

After another hour, Emma kissed her mother good night. It had been a pleasant evening, but one that had taken effort. Emma was drained from smiling politely, from nodding and paying close attention to her mother's talk about shoes and people from church.

As her mother drove away, taillights getting smaller in the dark night, Emma allowed her shoulders to relax. Overhead, the moon grew brighter, shining like a pearl against black velvet. Stars dotted the sky, winking as cicadas and crickets chirped in unison.

It was nights like these that made her love Brunswick. She felt safe. After her mother's visit, she felt loved. She'd prayed for so long for her parents to see her as the favorite daughter. Finally, this dream had come true.

With a final glance around the yard, Emma climbed the front steps, let herself inside the house. She wandered by Caroline's room; the door was cracked an inch. Her niece had fallen asleep, a novel on her chest. Tonight she looked at peace. What she wouldn't give to see that every day on Caroline's face.

Her eyes fell on the picture frame that housed a photo of a smiling Maddie and Caroline, arm in arm at a school football game. Her skin prickled as she walked over and picked it up. She needed to take care of this little problem—once and for all. Once she was finished, Maddie would come crawling back to Caroline, whether she wanted to or not.

Emma tucked the frame under her arm and plucked two other small snapshots of Maddie that had been tacked to a board filled with movie ticket stubs, bumper stickers, and high school memorabilia.

She examined all three on the way to her office, deciding on the one she liked best. After dumping the two others in the trash, frame and all, Emma opened her scanner and inserted the photo of Maddie. While the machine whirred to life, Emma clicked a few icons on her computer screen, bringing up the program she used to edit images.

Tomorrow, everyone, like it or not, would focus on Maddie Anderson.

TWENTY-THREE

ALLIE

2016

When her alarm burst into trills Monday morning, Allie tapped the button to silence the noise and rolled out of bed to stretch. For the first time in forever, the day didn't loom ahead with a sense of shadowy dread. She had a job. A purpose. One step closer to a normal life.

Allie brewed herself a pot of coffee, inhaling the rich, nutty fragrance as the machine bubbled and percolated. After pouring herself a cup and doctoring it with creamer, Allie took a sip, letting the sweet liquid soothe her throat, still scratchy from sleep. Holding the steaming mug with both hands, she stepped into her front room and glanced outside.

In typical fashion, many of the houses on her street and around town were in full swing, decorated for the football season. Banners streamed from windows, flags flew from posts. In many yards, large wooden placards were painted with players' jersey numbers and the "Go Wolverines!" slogan.

She moved to the next window, reached for the cord to open the blinds and allow the morning sunshine to warm the room. As she tugged gently, the shade rose, folding neatly in place. From the corner of her eye, Allie noticed a bright red rectangle among the sea of black and silver, erected in her own yard on a sturdy wooden post. A sign.

A For Sale sign.

With a lump wedged deep in her throat, Allie flung open the front door and raced down the steps in her nightshirt and shorts. Despite the warmth of the morning air, goose bumps raised on her bare arms and ankles. She shivered and surveyed the huge white letters on the display.

Then she smelled something rank and awful. Her eyes began to water and sting. Allie covered her nose and mouth with one hand and backed away. Someone—whoever had taken the time to place the For Sale sign in her front yard, maybe someone else—had also deposited animal waste across the freshly cut grass.

The brown piles lay in clumps, spaced every few feet.

Allie's stomach contracted with disgust. She held her breath and tried not to vomit, pressing with her free hand on her abdomen.

The sound of a car door slamming jolted Allie from her state of shock. She looked up in time to see the neighbors staring at her and the mess on her lawn. The couple, a young woman and her husband, bent their heads together to talk. They both looked away when they caught Allie's glance.

Meanwhile, the owner of the house next door had shuffled to the front sidewalk to retrieve the morning paper. Allie swung her head to glance in her direction. The older woman bent down to pick up the plastic sleeve and its contents. When she straightened, she noticed Allie and the sign. She frowned at Allie, then scowled to herself.

Allie didn't wait to see more. She sprinted back into her house, pulled on sweatpants, a jacket, and hat and then gathered a shovel, plastic gloves, and two large trash bags. She willed herself to ignore everything else and keep focused on the task at hand. With the best invisible barrier she could muster between herself and the world, Allie stepped back outside.

Though she was hurt, the prank only served to fuel Allie's determination to prove her innocence and protect herself and her daughter. The killer was still out there. Who else would go to such lengths to publically shame and scare her?

As she entered her bathroom and stripped off her clothes, only one name, one face, came to mind.

Sheriff Lee Gaines.

Allie stepped into the shower, scrubbing and rinsing as if she could wash away the hurt. After thirty minutes of hot water, steam, and plenty of soap, Allie felt semi-human again. She pulled on a pair of navy scrubs, gathered her hair up in a loose ponytail, and arrived fifteen minutes early for her first day of work, determined to shake off the lingering unease over this morning's incident.

Natalie drove up and parked at the office moments after Allie arrived. She jumped out of her car, juggling a stack of magazines and steaming hot coffee. "Hey there. Right on time. I like that."

"I'm ready to go," Allie replied with a nervous smile. "Can I help?"

Natalie handed over veterinary journals and a few books. "My office," she told Allie. "Thanks. Give me just a sec. Want to grab the blue bag out of the trunk?"

Allie walked around to the back of the car while Natalie punched in a code.

"Anything else?" she asked, shaking off the tightening in her throat. It would be odd, working here, strange at first. Allie had known everything before. Every code, lock, and key. It was a matter of trust, she told herself, and she hadn't done a thing to earn it. Not yet.

Natalie flicked on the lights. Allie followed her down the hallway. The walls and floors had been scrubbed clean and smelled of lemon.

"We've got an easy schedule today. Just a few patients. Later in the week, things get busier. We'll have some boarders this weekend."

"Wonderful," Allie replied. "That's really good to hear."

Natalie paused at the doorway to her office. "I've been doing a lot of thinking about your role here, Allie." She took the blue bag from Allie and set it on a chair. "How we should work things."

"All right," Allie answered, a pang of nervous energy in her chest.

"Let's keep it simple. I'll handle the patients, for the most part. My husband will be here to answer the phone this morning," Natalie said. "The delivery truck should be here in thirty minutes. You can organize that, check the exam rooms, and fill in what's needed."

Allie nodded.

"By the way, none of this is a punishment," Natalie added. "Let people get used to me, first, and the new office. Then we can let them know you're here too. One step at a time."

"I understand," Allie replied. "Thank you so much for giving me this opportunity."

Natalie opened her mouth, but hesitated when a beep sounded, signaling someone opening the back door. A rangy man with dark, close-cut hair, loaded down with delivery boxes, met them halfway. He wore work clothes, a flannel shirt, and beige Carhart pants torn at the knees.

"Special delivery," he said and winked at Natalie.

"What, no flowers?" Natalie grinned and turned to Allie. "This is my husband. Office manager, construction worker, jack-of-all-trades."

"Good to meet you," Nick said with a quick, broad smile.

"You too," Allie replied with a smile.

Nick glanced back to Natalie and then down at the packages.

"So, my dear, to answer your question, no flowers today. We have amoxicillin, Depo-Medrol, dexamethasone, and equipoise."

Allie stopped breathing as Natalie and Nick continued bantering. The last two were steroids. Her mind raced to the football players, the coach, and Sheriff Gaines. By the time she snapped back to the present, Nick had set the boxes on the counter and was making another trip. The door closed behind him with a bang.

"Hey. You okay?" Natalie asked, ducking her head at Allie and waving a hand back and forth.

"Um, sure. I mean, yes," Allie said, trying to shake off the chill that had crept into her spine. "I'm just . . ."

Natalie waited.

"Never mind," Allie said, mustering up a something she hoped came close to brushing off a momentary distraction. "Let's get to work."

At the end of the day, Allie's body ached, sore from bending and stretching. But it was okay. She'd accomplished something, been part of a greater whole. Allie smiled to herself as she stuffed her scrubs into a bag and changed into street clothes.

She had managed to get through an entire day without thinking about Arrendale. She had thought about Caroline a dozen times instead of the usual hundred.

Busy was good.

The phone rang. *Emma.* Her sister sounded bright and cheery, and talked so quickly that Allie couldn't interrupt.

"Hey, listen. I was thinking, with it being your first day of work and all . . . why don't you come over tonight? For dinner. You can see Caroline."

Allie hesitated, her heart thumping in her chest.

Of course she wanted to see Caroline, but felt equally afraid of what might happen if she did. "Didn't you say she needed more time?"

"I know what I said." Emma sounded impatient. "Look. I've been thinking. Maybe I was wrong. The sooner she gets over it, the better. Which includes her being uncomfortable."

"Are you sure?"

"Come on. Have dinner with us."

Allie's anticipation, hope, and fear lodged in her chest. Lifting her chin, she swallowed back any trepidation and focused on the positive. Finally, after ten long years, she would look into her daughter's eyes. It was what she'd lived for. Nothing would stop her from going to see Caroline.

"I'll be there," she said. "See you tonight." With a trembling hand and a full heart, Allie hung up the phone.

TWENTY-FOUR

CAROLINE

2016

In the past week, Caroline's social life had come to an abrupt standstill. No one text messaged or called. Not Maddie. Certainly not Jake. Not even Russell. She'd seen to that.

There were no Snapchats or Instagram shares; even the stupid jokes that a few friends usually sent on e-mail had ground to a standstill. No invites to St. Simons Island or anyone's beach house.

Even though she'd been starving the night before, the peanut butter and jelly sandwich she'd made herself still sat untouched. Even the sour cream and onion potato chips, piled high on her plate, held no appeal. Instead, Caroline had sat for an hour on her laptop, refreshing the screen until her vision got blurry.

Not one of her girlfriends had stopped by the house. She'd waited for the usual knock on the door, even finished her homework early. She could tell her aunt wanted to ask, but Caroline had buried herself in a book, held the cover so that it shielded her face. It hadn't done much good. The lines on the page swam together.

Caroline had tried to remember if she'd heard anyone mention a party or trips out of town. She realized then that she, too, had disappeared the previous week, avoided talking and skipped lunch.

If this was isolation, the way Eskimos lived in Alaska, she didn't think she could take it.

Being alone. With no one her own age to talk to. Caroline swallowed. Did her own mother feel the same way this very same minute? Who did she talk to? Did anyone visit? And what was she thinking about Caroline?

A sudden coldness hit her core.

It wasn't her fault. None of this was her fault, Caroline told herself.

Today, this Monday morning, would be better. She'd force herself to act perky. She was scheduled to work at the nursing home later in the week. Maybe Russell would be there, and they could talk. She needed to apologize, if she had any chance of them being friends, let alone anything else.

Caroline glanced in the mirror one last time. She ran her fingers through her hair and smoothed down her shirt. Today, at least, her eyes weren't so bloodshot and tired.

After stalling until the last possible moment, Caroline took the stairs. Emma was waiting at the bottom landing.

"I'm late." Caroline edged closer to the front door and tried to duck around her.

Her aunt pulled Caroline into a quick hug. "You've got a minute, don't you? For me?" Emma murmured into her hair. She let go, held her out at arm's distance, and gave Caroline's elbow one final squeeze.

Caroline stepped back farther, took a deep breath, and waited.

Emma smiled. "Listen, I know you've been upset. I was thinking . . . and just hear me out, okay? Maybe you're going about this whole situation with your mother the wrong way. Maybe staying away from your mom isn't helping—"

As the words penetrated her ears, Caroline jumped back as if she'd been jolted by a Taser. "What?" She pulled away. "I'm not doing anything wrong."

"Just listen, please."

"No." Caroline tried to edge past Emma. Her head started to pound. Why was Emma doing this?

Her aunt blocked her path with one arm. "I'd like you to give her a chance."

Fists tight at her sides, Caroline stopped. Her voice was thick. "Why should I? I thought you weren't going to make me. You're supposed to be on my side."

Emma exhaled deeply. "I've been thinking it over, Caro. Not just about how you feel. But how she must feel too. And I have to believe that she does love you," Emma rattled off in one breath. "Surely she never, ever expected any bad things were going to happen."

Caroline glared at the ceiling, arms folded.

Emma stepped out of the way. "Will you at least consider it?"

"Why can't we move away?" Caroline asked, cheeks flushed berry pink. "I hate it here."

"Caroline, it's not so easy," Emma replied.

"Then you should go and talk to her," Caroline pleaded. "Tell her she's the reason all this bad stuff is happening to me. Tell her to move. And that no one wants her here."

Emma folded her arms and frowned. "That's not my place."

Furious, Caroline locked eyes on her aunt. She'd never thought Emma would turn on her. Betray her like this. It hurt so much that Caroline almost thought she wouldn't be able to breathe. She was suffocating in this room, in this house.

"I've got to go." Caroline slipped past.

"Try to have a good day," her aunt said as Caroline slung her backpack over one shoulder. "If you need anything—"

Fighting tears, Caroline bent her head and rushed out the door. Any other day she would have paused to admire the candy-pink camellias bursting open along her walk to school. She would have paused to inhale the perfume of the Confederate jasmine blossoms on vines that wound their way around neighbors' mailboxes. Most of all, she would have inhaled the scent of the ocean, the salt air that reached her aunt's front yard when the wind shifted just right.

Caroline, though, ignored it all. Eyes forward, she walked without really seeing her surroundings, kept moving by rote memory, by sheer force of forward motion. If she didn't care about failing and the mortification of enduring summer school, she would have skipped every day for the rest of the semester.

As the first bell rang, loud and shrill, Caroline slipped into homeroom. Tittering erupted behind her, and her instructor glared at whoever was making the noise. With a crackle, announcements began over the intercom.

A sidelong glance confirmed that everyone around her was on their tablet or cell, clicking through social media feeds and giggling about new posts. A sharp cry broke through the murmuring chatter. Caroline swiveled her head. It was Maddie now, one hand over her mouth, staring at a phone screen. Some of their friends—former friends, she guessed—gasped and raised eyebrows as Maddie stuffed the cell in her pocket and dashed from the room. Even more noise erupted when the door slammed behind her. As the teacher shouted for quiet, Caroline furrowed her brow and reached for her phone.

She had just enough time to pull up SnapdIt, the new app everyone at Mansfield used to send video messages and pictures—all of which vanished after viewing unless you remembered to take a screenshot. The message waiting for Caroline almost made her drop her phone. She blinked and rubbed her eyes to make sure she wasn't seeing things.

But the picture was of Maddie. Caroline sucked in a breath as the bell for first period sounded overhead. She couldn't move. The photo was burned into her brain: Maddie in tight jeans, smiling provocatively, hands crossed over her bare chest. The picture left little to the imagination.

A few students bumped Caroline's arm on the way out of the classroom, laughing and pointing at the image on their own phones. As quickly as she could, she tucked her cell in the deepest pocket of her backpack, as if it might hide Maddie altogether. Caroline pushed herself out of her seat and made her way into the hallway, where every single person was looking toward Maddie's locker. Of course, the girl wasn't anywhere to be found.

Caroline endured history class, dutifully attempting to take notes while everyone around her talked in hushed tones. Some texted, some still showing off the photo of Maddie. When the next bell rang, everyone vaulted to their feet. A din of talk and laughter swelled around Caroline. The instructor opened the door. Like the bursting of a dam, students gushed into the hallways, spilling in every direction. Caroline clung to the edge of her table and let the noise and rushing subside.

During the three-minute break, Caroline glanced for Maddie through the crowd. She stopped, raising her heels, not really expecting to catch a glimpse of her. If Caroline knew Maddie, she was long gone.

At lunch, everyone was strangely intent on a few red flyers sitting in the middle of their table—probably touting the evils of Internet pornography and warning of penalties for spreading filth, especially in a school. As Caroline tried to take a bite of her sandwich, she turned her back to face the wall and caught a glimpse of one of Sheriff Gaines's deputies entering the school office. It was likely the whole universe had seen the photo, including Maddie's parents, who would try to sue whoever was behind the scheme.

Caroline glanced at the clock, desperate for school to end. Despite how ugly Maddie had been about her mom coming home, Caroline still ached for her friend. She couldn't imagine the ridicule, the embarrassment, a situation almost worse than her own mother coming home from prison. She reached for her cell, pulling it out of her pocket. She flipped over the phone, found her list of contacts, and before she could stop herself, sent a text to Maddie.

I'm here if you need me, she typed. *Text me if you want to talk.*

Despite willing her phone to buzz with a message, the cell remained silent. Caroline's heart dropped with every minute that passed. When the lunch break was almost over, she headed for her locker, twirled the combination with three fingers. It unlocked and the door swung open. Shoulders hunched, Caroline stood back and took the backpack off her shoulder, preparing to stuff it in the hollow between her bookshelf and gym shoes.

A sheet of the same red paper floated to the floor, landing between her shoes. Caroline glanced around and scanned the hallway. Now there were red rectangles taped everywhere, down the school's hallway, like the pep rally flyers cheering on the football team before a game.

She picked the paper off the ground and shoved it inside one of her books. Caroline closed the locker, twisted the combination, and headed for class. When she was safely in the back of the room, Caroline withdrew the crinkled page from her book, unfolded the paper, and held it in her lap.

When she scanned the fuzzy print, Caroline gasped and smothered her mouth with one hand. Heads turned, but soon went back to the lecture. Glancing up to make sure the teacher wasn't staring directly at her, Caroline examined the page a second time. It was laid out in columns, like a newspaper, and the date was 2006. A photo showing a high school football player tackling another was placed at the bottom.

Like a tourniquet had been wrapped around her throat, Caroline struggled to breathe. The column wasn't a story; it was an editorial. Written by her own mother. She read the name again to make sure she wasn't seeing things. Caroline shrunk down in her seat, curling her head down and away from the class while she studied the sentences. A cold sweat broke out on the back of her neck as the words sunk in.

The editorial talked in detail about a player who had gone into a rage after an opposing team's touchdown. The player punched and kicked the other quarterback, injuring him. The player was given a penalty and removed from the game. He was then suspended from the team pending an investigation.

Her mother—Caroline still couldn't believe she had written such a thing to the paper—went on to say that the blame should fall on Coach Boyd Thomas. She alluded that some of the football team members were being given steroids to enhance strength and speed on the field. Steroids that caused mood swings, rage, and suicidal behavior.

A second paragraph alleged that Thomas and his staff were hazing players—beating the new teammates after practice or at midnight meetings—as a rite of initiation. Her mother, according to the letter, had witnessed the coach rough up a player after a game and had talked to at least one team member—a boy who wouldn't deny the beatings were happening but refused to share his name.

The editorial called for an investigation into Coach Thomas, his staff, and drug testing for all of the players.

Caroline stopped reading. Why would someone make enough copies of this to string down a school hallway?

"Pop quiz," her teacher announced, a stack of papers cradled in her arms. She walked down the aisle, handing out one to each student. "Put your books away," she reminded and paused by Caroline's desk. "Something the matter, Miss Marshall?"

A few classmates exchanged murmurs.

"No, ma'am," she muttered, taking her copy and centering it on the desk. Caroline reached for her pencil and squinted at the page. She couldn't focus or think. She folded the red paper tight and stuffed it into her pocket.

Caroline closed her eyes and exhaled, gripping her pencil. Her neck prickled; her skin felt hot. Someone had taken the time to find the editorial. Copy it. And distribute it to the entire school, teachers included. It was a cruel, mean trick, meant to embarrass her, to bring attention to the not-so-secret fact that Caroline's mother was home from prison.

"Thirty minutes, people. Let's get started," her teacher called.

Every sound in the room amplified. Her teacher's heels clicking on the tile floor. The scratch of pencils and the creak of desks. When it all came to a crescendo in her head, Caroline suppressed a moan, causing her instructor and all of the students around her to look. It was all too much, too many people, too many noises. She leaped up, grabbed her backpack, and ran from the room as a low murmur of questions followed.

"Caroline, wait!" the teacher called after her. But she didn't stop. She had to be alone. Somewhere she could quiet the voices in her head and make sense of this. Away from all of the eyes and the staring and the voices. Caroline reached for the long silver bar on the school's double doors, slamming into it with her palms and right hip.

A half mile away from the brick buildings on campus, chest heaving, lungs burning for more oxygen, Caroline nearly tripped over a heaving crack in the sidewalk. After another block, she dropped to her knees behind the thick trunk of an oak tree, hugging her arms to her chest. As she raised one shaking hand to wipe her forehead, Caroline realized that her cheeks were slick with tears. She was weeping, the drops splattering her shirt and jeans.

Then Caroline heard the anguished sound. Guttural, like a wounded animal. After a moment, she realized it was coming from her own lips.

TWENTY-FIVE

EMMA

2016

Just before five o'clock, Emma poured two glasses of wine and waited for Allie to arrive. She sipped, the liquid warming her throat and her belly, as her thoughts turned to Caroline. She wondered how her day had unfolded, what stories she would bring home.

Emma wouldn't have long to wait now. She drained the glass, feeling a rush of dizziness as the effects of the alcohol spread throughout her body.

It would be a telling evening. Like watching a movie unfold, waiting for the cliffhanger. She'd felt that same anticipation, so many years ago.

August 2006

Emma had lingered after Coach Thomas's second home game, offering her parents an excuse about forgetting her wallet at the concession stand. She promised she'd be home soon, kissed her niece on the head, and told her sister good night.

As soon as Allie disappeared into the crowd with Caroline,

Emma made her way outside the locker room area and positioned herself near the doors. She walked back and forth, holding her cell phone to her ear, making occasional murmurs into the phone.

Her timing was excellent. Moments later, Thomas walked out, deep in conversation with one of his key players. He looked up. They locked eyes.

Emma kept up the imaginary dialogue, offered a small nod in the coach's direction. He finished talking to the player, patted him on the shoulder, and told him to head home. With flourish, Emma hung up the phone and tucked it into her purse. "Good game. I think you have some happy fans."

"We aim to please," the coach answered with an ounce of swagger.

Summoning moxie she didn't think she possessed, Emma pressed a slip of paper and a business card from her father's office into his hand. "I brought that number you were wanting."

Coach Thomas raised an eyebrow.

Emma leaned in near his cheek. "Have a good night."

With trembling legs, she walked away, pacing her steps so that she appeared to be taking her time. Around the corner, a block past the stadium, Emma stopped and gripped her heart. Her breath came in short bursts, her fingers tingled, her entire body throbbed.

What was she thinking? Was the note a mistake? Would he come?

On the paper, Emma had written four numbers—the security code to her father's office. She'd added three other words: *Back door. Tonight.*

If he were intrigued, he would put the clues together. If he wanted more, he would meet her there. If ... if ... if ...

It took him less than an hour.

The rear entrance to the building was private and blocked with rows of thick shrubbery. The parking lot wasn't visible from the street.

At ten thirty, Emma heard truck tires roll down the driveway and stop. A door opened and shut. The alarm code was entered. She met him in the hallway, wrapped only in a white sheet over her bra and panties.

He didn't speak as the door closed behind him, covering the two of them in darkness. Emma backed against the wall, pulling him toward her. His lips found hers. His fingers brushed her skin. His breath was thick and hot.

She unbuttoned his shirt, reached down for his belt.

With one hand, he grabbed her wrists, pressing her arms against the wall over her head. Before she could cry out, he ripped the delicate lace from her skin.

With sudden force, he swept her into his arms and carried her into the first open door. He laid her on the floor's thin carpeting and knelt down, bruising and marking her body with his hands, lips, and teeth. The act left her breathless, a little frightened, and wanting more.

Every Friday night it became their meeting place. She'd wait for him there, until midnight or into the early morning. Sometimes, when the team traveled away, he didn't visit at all. His absence only fueled Emma's determination to have him.

Each time they were together, they played games of their own. He'd tear at her clothes, desperate and hungry. She'd put him off, tease until he tingled from head to foot with desire. They made love on chilled exam tables, on chairs, next to volumes of veterinary books. When he was finished and spent, he'd trace the bruises he left on her delicate skin and kiss the marks, as if to say she was his. He owned her completely.

She opened her heart wide, poured herself into him. His lips burned and scorched hers, a passion Emma couldn't imagine.

There was nothing she wouldn't do to see him. She shed every bit of herself. She went willingly, carrying secrets and dreams.

2016

When Allie rang the bell, Emma jumped, checked the clock on the wall, and calculated how long it would take for Caroline to show up.

Tick. Tock.

"Right on time," Emma said, balancing plates with one hand as she opened the door wide. She tilted her head in the direction of the living room. "Come on in. I made up some chicken salad."

Allie shrugged off her jacket, draped it over the edge of the sofa, and collapsed into a chair. "Sounds great."

"I can't take the credit. Mom's creation." Emma stepped into the kitchen and retrieved the bowl from the refrigerator. As she lifted the lid, she glanced at her sister. Beneath the cheery exterior, her sister was nervous.

Allie pursed her lips and glanced at the clock, kneading her hands.

"Um, and so, by the way, did you know that Ben's back in town?" Emma asked, a smile playing on her lips. "I ran into him at the grocery store about an hour ago."

Allie stopped rubbing her hands, frozen as if she'd seen a ghost. "Ben?"

"He's been back for a while, actually, maybe a couple weeks," Emma added. "His parents moved to Florida, so he's living in their old house. The word around town is that he's disillusioned with the whole political scene and quit whatever campaign he was working on."

Allie nodded and blinked rapidly, shell-shocked at the announcement.

Ben, ever the knight in shining armor, had pledged to wait for her sister. Emma curled her lip in satisfaction as Allie glanced away. Her sister had returned Ben's loyalty by breaking off their engagement and breaking his heart.

Emma knew that just the thought of Ben so close would add another heavy layer to Allie's already-substantial stress.

Sure, Emma knew it was logical for Allie to let Ben go. Allie had agonized afterward for more than a year, confiding several times in Emma that it was one of the most awful decisions she'd had to make. But Allie had sworn, too, that she wouldn't have forgiven herself for making him put his life on hold.

Tamping down a flare of jealousy at the depth of Ben's love, Emma had comforted her and listened, agreeing emphatically that her sister had, indeed, done the right thing.

Back in the present, Emma capitalized on her sister's silence and continued. "He's doing freelance reporting for a few newspapers and writes for a couple of blogs."

Before Allie could remark or reply, Emma heard the familiar creak of the front door opening. Footsteps pounded toward the kitchen. "Hello?" Caroline called, her voice scratchy. "Where are you?"

"In here." Emma swiveled her head to look at Allie. "At the table—"

Caroline skidded to a stop, momentarily thrown off balance at seeing her mother. Her dark hair lay in thick, tangled waves around her shoulders. Thick lashes framed her wide, chocolate-brown eyes. Below, her lips were glossed the color of raspberries. Smudges of dirt marked the knees of her jeans, and there was a place just below her elbow beginning to bruise. And she was furious.

Emma squinted at the mark. "What happened?"

"Nothing," Caroline snapped. "I'm fine."

"All right. Well, why don't you come in and say hello?" Emma said, keeping her tone even.

Caroline ignored the polite request. She threw her backpack to the floor, bent over to unzip it, and shuffled through folders and notebooks. After a few tense moments, she yanked out a red piece of paper and waved it around.

Emma reminded herself to act surprised. "What is it?"

"Did someone think this was funny? A joke?" Caroline shook the page, making it rattle.

Emma wrinkled her forehead. "I'm not sure what you're talking about." She glanced at Allie, whose skin looked bleached white. "What is that? Where did you find it?"

"It was in my locker," Caroline said through clenched teeth. "There were more copies, though. In the lunchroom. In the hallways." Her eyebrows arched, framing her face.

Thrusting out her hand, Emma beckoned her niece to give her the paper.

"It's an editorial from the newspaper. From, like, ten years ago," Caroline spat out, and then swiveled and glared at Allie. "You wrote it. You started the whole thing."

The room vibrated with the accusation.

Emma hoped, in some small way, that Caroline lashing out at Allie would bring her niece some relief. She knew, only too well, that ridding that sort of emotional poison was necessary and cathartic. Once a person betrayed you, they couldn't be forgiven.

Caroline needed to put up walls, blocking out Allie once and for all. This, what was happening tonight, was the start.

Allie didn't deserve Caroline. She wasn't worthy. Emma, after all, had done the work of raising a child, spent the time parenting her, guiding her, and loving her. Emma would take care of her. She always would. She wouldn't allow Allie to take Caroline away.

Allie didn't reply, but kept her gaze level. Her eyes said everything, with Caroline stomping around like a wild animal, gnashing her teeth and behaving like a three-year-old.

"Calm down," Emma said. She grabbed the red paper from Caroline's hands and skimmed the type.

As if she could tell her aunt was scrutinizing every move, Caroline inched away and stood by the window. When Caroline spoke, her voice was softer. "Do you know . . . Do you realize how many copies they made of this?" She stared at the red paper.

Allie didn't answer.

"Hundreds! Probably a th-thousand," Caroline said, looking up at Emma, her words getting caught in her throat. "They were in the basement, in the teachers' lounge, in the locker rooms." She swallowed. "I ran out of school. I stayed in the park until everyone went home."

Emma gave her niece a moment to breathe. Caroline's eyes were puffy from crying. Caroline trembled, shivering like she'd been locked in a subzero freezer. She shut her eyes and covered her face, pressing her fingertips to her temples.

"Did you have to put it in writing?" Caroline finally murmured. "Because you were going to med school and you were 'so smart'?" She made quotation marks with her fingers. "That's why everyone thinks you killed him. You probably did."

Allie rose out of her seat shakily. "That might be what everyone thinks, Caroline. But that's not what happened—"

"Let's not do this now," Emma said, putting both hands up.

Allie ignored her. As did her niece.

"Then why did you go to jail?" Caroline demanded. "You ruined everything! I hate you. I hate everyone." She began to sob and sunk down against the wall, knees splayed.

Emma rushed to Caroline, one arm circling her shoulders, her hand stroking her cheek and wiping away tears. As Caroline's sobs slowed, Emma heard footsteps. She looked up to see her sister standing by the front door. She was leaving. *Thank God.*

"I am innocent, no matter what anyone says about that night," Allie said, her voice husky, as if she'd inhaled smoke from a wildfire.

Caroline jerked her head up, wiping her tears on her sleeve. She sucked air in gulps, her chest rising and falling. Emma started to soothe her, patting and rubbing her back, but her niece pulled away. Caroline studied her mother, unblinking. She seemed shocked at first, then perplexed, as if it were necessary to consider the statement.

"I am. I'm innocent," Allie repeated, standing still, unwavering.

Caroline drew herself up and lifted her chin. "Then prove it."

TWENTY-SIX

EMMA

2016

Allie left without saying good-bye. The editorial had disappeared along with her. Emma didn't really care, though it wasn't going to do her sister any good destroying one copy when a thousand were floating around Brunswick.

Emma didn't hurry closing up the house, locking the doors, and shutting off lights. She knew that Caroline was still awake. Every so often she heard her moving. She would check on her in a little while, reassure her that everything would be all right. For now, allowing the evening's drama to settle was best.

It took effort to guide Caroline in the right direction without pushing her too hard. So many decisions. All of the worry. But the sacrifices were necessary. Caroline needed Emma's protection.

Fortunately, tonight her sister had come to the house willingly; she trusted her, no doubt hoping that Emma would help pave the way for a peaceful, civilized reunion.

And as predicted, Caroline's bottled-up outrage and anger spewed into the open within seconds of seeing her mother. Caroline channeled all of the blame and hurt she'd stored and hurled it at

Allie like a grenade. Ten years of worry and wondering had taken a heavy toll.

Emma placed both hands on the counter, took a deep breath, and glanced at the clock. She needed to talk with Caroline, make sure she was holding up as best as she could.

There was one thing gnawing at the back of Emma's mind. Caroline, surprisingly, didn't entirely dismiss Allie. Emma had wanted Caroline to stand up and shout, scream at her mother for being a liar and a fake, and accuse her of awful things.

But she hadn't.

Somehow, a sliver of doubt about Allie's guilt had pierced Caroline's heart.

Prove it.

The words didn't come with a dose of hatred or disdain. In fact, the opposite seemed true. Had she imagined it, or had Caroline really inched away from her? Nudged her away, moved apart, while she listened to Allie plead for mercy?

Caroline had been surprised, or shocked, and had involuntarily twitched as a response. There could be no other explanation. Emma would have to double her efforts to widen the divide between them. Prove to Caroline what a terrible choice it would be to believe in Allie, even for a moment.

With a soft knock on the bedroom door, Emma peeked inside Caroline's room.

"I wanted to say good night."

Emma made out the outline of a shape in the dim light. When her eyes adjusted, she saw Caroline's face. Anxious, a little terrified, confused. Emma made her way over to the bed and knelt down. "Oh, sweetie. I'm so sorry. I know you're hurting."

Caroline shook her head.

"Can I talk to you about it? Just a little?"

Another nod.

"Whoever put up copies of that article—that editorial—was cruel. It was hurtful and deliberate. There's no reason for anyone to bring up the past. It's done." Emma sighed. "Just so you know, I'm going to call the principal and the superintendent and get to the bottom of this mess."

"All right," Caroline murmured.

"And since someone shoved this back into our lives, at the very least I can tell you what I know about it, okay?"

Caroline's shoulders tensed, like she wasn't sure she wanted to know any more. Finally, she nodded.

"So, one thing you have to understand about Allie is that she has always been very driven. She's never been shy about sharing her opinion," Emma said. "It got her into trouble with teachers when she'd try to correct them, and it upset Grandma, because she doesn't like any type of controversy. But Allie would get an idea into her head sometimes, and she wouldn't let it go."

"So what made her write it?"

Emma shifted her eyes. "There was this really talented player, a big guy who wasn't getting along very well with his teammates."

Wide-eyed, Caroline tucked the pillow closer.

"So, during one of the games, near the end of the season, this same kid punched the other team's quarterback—a cheap shot, no question. Really hurt the guy; took him out of the game. The referees gave our guy a penalty, of course. Everyone was talking about it."

Her niece sat up straight, eager to hear the story. "And then what?"

Emma hesitated. She had Caroline's full attention, but she had to tread carefully and choose her words wisely. She wouldn't criticize Allie, not outright. She would be the better sister. The wiser, more caring sister. And from now on, she would make sure to say

Allie's name instead of "your mother." So Caroline would think of her that way too.

"Somehow, Allie decided it was Coach Thomas's responsibility. She said the coach needed to watch out for the players better, teach them right from wrong. If they were out of control, he had to stop them."

"So that's when she wrote that article for the newspaper?"

"Yes. She did a little investigation work. Talked to some players," Emma said. "Her boyfriend at the time had a brother who was playing for the team. I think it must have been him she talked to. One week after practice he showed up to school with cracked ribs and bruises."

Caroline bit her lip. "The article said she saw something happen."

"I don't know. Maybe she did. Maybe she didn't," Emma said. "It's her word against his."

"What do you think?"

Emma ran her hand along her leg, deciding how to answer. "I didn't agree with what Allie wrote. I didn't *think* he would do those things."

"But if she did see something, that must have made my mom pretty mad." Caroline frowned.

"Yes, it did. Grandpa Paul and Grandma Lily were really upset at Allie. Everyone was upset. She'd made such poor choices. Embarrassed the family." Emma lowered her voice. Here was an opportunity to drive home her point. "Allie proved that she wasn't exactly the golden girl that everyone believed her to be. It broke all of our hearts." She sat back and looked at her niece, who'd cast her eyes down at the fingers that lay laced in her lap. "About two weeks after that, the coach was murdered and your mom got arrested."

Caroline rolled over on her stomach, hugged the pillow under her chin. "Did you know him? Coach Thomas?"

"I did." Emma felt her voice catch. Inside, she was dying, recalling it. She smiled brightly to cover it up. "Everyone liked him. His family owned a pharmacy in town. He was very nice to me. One time when you were sick, he made sure I had the right medicine for you. And he asked about you, remembered your name. I thought he was very caring."

"Wow. I guess so," Caroline said, widening her eyes.

Emma reached over and squeezed her hand.

"She did it, though, didn't she?" Caroline's voice was muffled.

After a pause, Emma lowered her voice. "I think there's a lot we don't know about that night. But when the court was presented with all the facts and witnesses . . . well, they agreed that Allie was guilty."

When Caroline didn't respond, Emma stood up and pushed the chair back under the desk. She had made her point about Allie, planting key questions without insisting she had murdered anyone.

"Emma?" Caroline said.

"What is it, honey?" She leaned on the chair and smiled down at her niece.

"Um, something bad happened to Maddie today. Like, really awful."

Though she kept her face awash with concern, a shiver of delight coursed through Emma's body. "What happened?"

Flipping on her side, Caroline hugged her pillow. "There's a bad picture going around of her. On SnapdIt."

"What's SnapdIt?" Emma asked, playing innocent. Caroline, at fifteen, didn't realize the extent of her aunt's tech skills. Emma wasn't simply a web design geek. In her spare time, she honed her knowledge of computer hacking and breaking down cyber security measures.

"A phone app. You share pictures and stuff. Messages," Caroline said. She ducked her head. "Someone sent out this photo of Maddie. Without . . . without many clothes on."

Emma forced her jaw to drop open. "Oh no."

Caroline flushed. "Maddie left school right after someone sent it out. One of the sheriff's deputies came to the school. I don't know what else happened."

"They'll take it down, sweetheart. They'll get to the bottom of it." Emma reached down and patted Caroline's hand.

"Okay." Caroline frowned and stared off into space. "I still feel . . . well, really bad for her. She doesn't deserve it." Her niece's eyes filled with tears.

"Even though she's been so awful to you, you're still worried about Maddie?" Emma said, raising her brow. "I know you care about her. I know you'd like to still be friends, but if she really posed for a photo like that . . ."

"I know," Caroline whispered, wiping at her cheeks.

"Just be careful, honey. Sometimes people get what they deserve." Emma allowed the words to hang in the space between them. She wanted Caroline to think about that. Digest it and remember it.

Her niece winced and frowned.

"Oh. Shoot. And there's something else," Emma added, trying to inject an air of nonchalance. "I was going to tell you earlier, but . . ."

"What is it?" Caroline tilted her head back to face Emma.

"Allie got a job," Emma said. "With the vet who bought Grandpa Paul's office."

Caroline sat straight up. "What? Why?"

Emma shrugged. "It was news to me too."

"W-won't people stop going there?"

"Well, they'll either leave or stay. Simple as that. Grandma and Grandpa know. I called them earlier. They were just as surprised."

Caroline rubbed her forehead and sniffed.

Emma tipped her head to see her niece's face. "What is it?"

Tears began dripping down Caroline's cheeks again. "I know what this means," she said, her voice small.

Emma put a soft hand on Caroline's back and bent down to listen.

"It means she's not leaving."

TWENTY-SEVEN

SHERIFF GAINES

2016

Like an airborne virus or poison, rumors in Brunswick floated through town easily, spreading their way across the school, every store and business, eventually making it inside the sheriff's office.

Gaines had already spent the majority of yesterday afternoon out of the office, dealing with the aftermath of the Maddie Anderson debacle—he'd have the state and feds to deal with for quite some time as they investigated the child pornography angle. The school officials were outraged; the media was calling nonstop. Her parents were understandably hysterical, and the girl was out of school, and rightly so, with a therapist this morning.

The sheriff reached for his coffee, now cold, when one of his deputies brought in a copy of a bright red flyer. "Boss, hate to do this to you, on top of the Anderson case. My daughter brought this home last night after cheerleading practice," he explained as he handed over the sheet. "These were sent in text messages to a lot of the students and papered all over the school."

After a glance down the page, Gaines wanted to smash his fist through the wall. This was getting out of hand. It was one thing to stick a For Sale sign in her yard just to scare the girl away. But someone was determined to fuel the fire about Allison Marshall, get her to ask questions, think harder, and dig around in the past. The sheriff, white-knuckled, gripped his desk. Those secrets needed to stay buried.

He dismissed the deputy with a curt nod, simmering about his next move. After letting his blood pressure cool, he called the assistant principal of Mansfield Academy, who confirmed the story. "We're doing what we can to quash this mess," she said. "So far, no one's come forward and admitted to distributing them."

And no one would, Gaines thought as he slammed the phone back on the receiver. Kids were smarter than that, and tricky. They lied right to your face. Then again, so did adults. After decades in his career, Gaines didn't know which was harder to accept.

Gaines got up from behind his desk and closed his office door. The blare of the scanner and the constant churn of noise from dispatch had given him a vicious headache. Most of the time he channeled the power and prestige of his job, soaking it up like rays of the sun on the Georgia coastline. But on days like this, Gaines felt like an overpaid babysitter, chasing after toddlers who didn't want to go to bed on time. It was human nature, though, which he had to admit kept his office busy and his staff employed. Of course, if everyone behaved, he might as well retire.

He sat back down, eased into his chair, opened the piece of paper, and reread the editorial. The day it came out in the newspaper, a decade ago, there was so much uproar a person from outside would have thought the city council had decided to begin public hangings in the downtown square.

When he finally talked to the person who should have been most upset and affected by the article, he remembered what struck him most was that person's remarkable indifference. It had been years ago, yet he still remembered every detail with acute clarity.

September 2006

He'd decided to make a trip to the athletic department. He found Coach Thomas and his assistants out on the field, setting up drills for practice. Gaines didn't want to draw more attention to the mess than already existed, but he needed more details, and might as well start with the source.

"Coach." Gaines stuck out a hand and gripped the one offered. "Got a minute?" He could feel eyes drilling into his back. The staff kept working, offering the pretense that the sheriff's presence wasn't unusual. They all knew why he was there.

"Let's walk," Thomas suggested and brushed off his shirt, straightened his ball cap.

They ambled for a few hundred yards, away from the sound of the assistant coach's voice and his whistle. A slight breeze carried the fragrance of freshly cut grass.

The sheriff stopped when he felt they were far enough away from curious spectators. "I hate to have to ask, but there are some serious allegations being tossed around," he began. "I'd like to get to the bottom of this—I'm sure the school does too."

"That joke of an article in the paper?" the coach said, taking off his ball cap, wiping his brow, and settling the hat back on his head. "Don't give it another thought. I've got that handled." He smothered a smirk behind his fist.

"Handled?" Gaines asked. "How so?"

"Let's just say I've made some inroads with the family." Coach Thomas winked.

The sheriff narrowed his eyes, unsure of what the man was saying. "As in, a personal connection?"

Thomas offered a sly smile.

Gaines's mind spun, gripping at the possibilities. The older sister had dated the same guy for years. She'd also written the editorial.

Now, the younger Marshall girl? She was known for being on the wild side and dating older men. She would likely see the coach as a conquest—a prize to be won. Add in a little jealousy, and there was no telling what drama an affair with a married man could spark.

Gaines's stomach plunged. "Well, I hope to God that y'all kiss and make up, because there's a whole lot more at stake than some spat over who-knows-what." A chill settled under his collar, despite the humid day.

"Let me tell you, Sheriff." Coach Thomas wiped his mouth with the fingers on one hand and paused. "There ain't nothin' coming between me and my boys. I love them, I love football, and I love this high school." He spoke slowly and in a calm voice. "I've done nothing wrong—nothing but care for those boys, bring this program up to one of respect, worked with the players to turn them into the finest athletes they can be."

"And—"

"And you brought me here, Sheriff." The coach sauntered closer, sticking the brim of his hat dangerously close to Gaines's face. "You handpicked me." He widened his arms to both sides, palms turned toward the ceiling. "You, the other boosters, the assistant coaches."

"We did," Gaines agreed, trying to remain affable. Gaines frowned. He'd expected a solid defense, not an attitude of nonchalance. He didn't like it, not one bit.

He hadn't even asked the question that was eating at his heart and soul. Was it true what the Marshall girl wrote?

"There are things the community doesn't need to know," Coach Thomas offered with a wave of one hand. "Should never know."

The sheriff's gut twisted. "Such as?"

"Like I said, Sheriff, I take care of these boys and I know what's best for them. Everyone else needs to stay out." Thomas put both hands on his hips. "Between me and you, a little help now and then is not out of order. Do you get what I'm saying?"

Despite the warning lights flashing like crazy in his brain, Gaines kept his gaze steady, flexed his arms, crossing them across his broad chest. "Why don't you explain?"

"It's safe. I've made some of it myself, and tried it too," Coach Thomas said, beaming. Like he was curing disease or creating clean drinking water for people in third-world countries. "The boys, they're calling it Wolverine Juice." He chuckled.

The breeze off the Atlantic caught at the edges of Gaines's jacket. He blinked as grit flew into his eye. "You're making it now?"

"Only if I have to."

The sheriff considered this carefully. "Where?"

"Ah, don't worry. Little place, it's *quite* a ways from here, buried in the woods. Inherited the ramshackle old cabin years ago—the trust pays the property taxes. Wife hates the place, refused to go after the first visit." Coach Thomas chuckled and adjusted the brim of his ball cap. "But I think I've found a better source. Some pure product," he added and smiled.

The sheriff's body tensed. *Cabin. Pure product.*

"These are guaranteed wins, there, Sheriff. You've seen the numbers. Our record. And D'Shawn—he was one little blip on the radar, a mistake. The kid just got sucked into wanting more and more." The coach's face lost the amused expression. "But I saw what that did to him. It was too much. It pushed him over the edge, cost us the game. It won't happen again. We can't afford it, not if we want to go to state. Listen here—"

Gaines pressed his knuckles into one palm. He was done listening. "No. Hear me out, Coach. They are going to investigate D'Shawn, and maybe a few more of the hotshots you've got out on the field. That doesn't worry you?"

"Sheriff, you know better than I do there are ways to outsmart the system. I have contingency plans for all of that. And hey, you can help." He pulled on the brim of his hat.

Gaines exhaled heavily. He'd come out here hoping for a denial. Even a weak explanation—the kid had gotten some gear from Atlanta, a friend gave him some. It was a one-time thing. A mistake. The last thing he expected was enthusiasm about a homebrew operation.

The sheriff stood stock-still, a choice in front of him. His duty was to report it. The call would ruin the season, taint the program, cost Coach Thomas his job. It would make the news, and not just the paper; the television stations would carry a story like this. Players might lose scholarships. It was a nightmare with fallout worse than a nuclear explosion. The sheriff's mind whirled.

Mansfield Academy had a proud tradition. Careers began here. The football program brought in the money that kept the school alive through ticket sales, alumni support, and donations. Parents sacrificed monthly to send their aspiring football players to the program, often working two jobs during Brunswick's summer tourist season to afford brand-new uniforms every season, the best training equipment, and a new scoreboard that was reputed to be almost as large as the size of the University of Georgia's.

If the football program was discredited, Mansfield Academy might not be able to survive. That, in turn, might ruin the town. At first, a few people would move away. Then entire families. The economy would go belly up . . . with the weight of it all squarely on his shoulders.

No, he couldn't let this massive failure come to light. As a former player, a school booster, and sheriff, it was his duty to protect the school and all those associated with it. He narrowed his eyes, his decision clear.

"I want you to shut it down, Coach." Gaines took a hold of the man's shirtsleeve, jerked him to attention. "All of it. Clean it up. Now. Are we clear?"

"This is the thanks I get? For a winning season? For a locked-down, one-way ticket to state?" Coach Thomas shrugged off the sheriff's grip. "I'm delivering exactly what you and the other boosters wanted." He licked his lips. "I'd call this conversation ungrateful and uncalled for."

The sky blackened. A few drops of rain hit the sheriff's shoulders. "Coach. Everyone loves to win. That's not the point. You need to be clean. Your players need to be clean. They'll sanction the school if they find anything. They'll have your job." Even worse, they might come after him. His job. His retirement and pension. He was a part of this now, too, and he felt the weight of it come to rest on his shoulders.

"They won't." Thomas leveled his gaze across the field, past the bleachers. "No one has any faith. Don't you think I have some experience with this? That I've thought it through?"

"And I'm telling you to take care of it," Gaines growled. "Get it cleaned up. All of it. Stop making it, acquiring it. And we'll just pretend you never told me about any of this. We clear?"

The coach stared at the ground, studying blades of grass. "Sure, Sheriff."

Gaines gritted his teeth. "You *make* sure of it."

TWENTY-EIGHT

ALLIE

2016

As uncomfortable and awful as it was, Allie could manage being snubbed by childhood friends and their family members. She could handle the For Sale sign. She could deal with piles of dog or cow excrement.

But this new attack—this assault on Caroline—was different. Someone took the time to find a decade-old editorial. They'd copied it and distributed it everywhere, knowing the hurt and harm it would cause.

Maybe worst of all, when Caroline challenged Allie's innocence, Emma—who knew the truth, who said all along that she believed Allie—didn't rush to defend her. In fact, Emma didn't defend her at all.

Allie bit her lip. The truth was this: She'd written the letter about the coach. She'd had a drink or two. But anyone could have found the man. Anyone. And it would have been Coach Thomas's blood on someone else's hands.

The person who spread copies of the editorial through the high school had a score to settle. And Allie was an easy target. In her mind's eye, she saw the sheriff aiming his gun—with Allie right in the crosshairs.

At the time, she'd tried to convince herself that her attorneys were making every effort to prove her innocence. But as she thought back to her hours on the witness stand, at her brutal cross-examination, Allie's stomach clenched. There were so many accusations, so many attacks on her character, her faith, and values.

Allie wasn't at all proud of what had happened with Caroline's biological father, but it was an impossible situation—a mistake she could never rectify—as she'd been so young and foolish.

At her lawyer's urging, Allie had finally confessed the story to them in private. Antonio, Italy, his fiancée. Her attorney was silent after she'd explained, digesting the situation, one hand clenched in a fist. He had been unable to reassure her that the judge would be at all sympathetic. As an unwed mother in the Deep South, with the father of her child nowhere to be found, the lawyer explained what she already knew. Allie's character—right or wrong—was unmistakably tainted.

The prosecution hammered away at her values so emphatically that Allie herself began to doubt the decisions she'd made so carefully more than six years ago. She forgot about being an A-student, a girl accepted to medical school, a woman who had a bright and shining future ahead of her. The words, with edges sharp as steel, cut her to the core.

Now, she was older and wiser. And despite her attorney's stated intentions, had he really done the best he could with her case? Hired the best experts and investigators? What had he overlooked about Sheriff Gaines? About the coach?

She powered up the laptop Emma had lent her and moved a stack of papers to the ground. Allie typed in the sheriff's full name, took a deep breath, and hit the return key.

Her first attempt brought up his bio on the sheriff's department website. She double-clicked on an image of Lee Gaines and made it full screen, then studied his face. The slope of his mouth, the jut of his jaw. Chest out, shoulders back, badge gleaming.

She scanned his bio, touting his "tough on crime" stance, his awards, and his campaigns and reelections. There were articles detailing his arrest records, video of him giving press conferences, and a few mentions of his community service work. Allie slowed to read the story detailing his wife's accident, called "a tragedy beyond measure" by the local newspaper.

It was too difficult to read; it hit too close to home. Gaines should have been attending to his June, who was clinging to life. Instead, he'd acted as judge and jury before he'd even read Allie her rights.

A paragraph in, she clicked out of the page. She gulped back a sob, deciding instead to focus on searching for any information that might have been overlooked on Coach Thomas. Allie found posts touting the coach's experience. A few that included a mention of Thomas's hometown and high school football career. His business, and his wife's and children's names.

She scanned a long story about the coach, his funeral, and the memorial service. Donations to a scholarship fund in lieu of gifts. A note about where they'd moved; the survivors, the reporter called them. Allie's stomach flip-flopped. The wife and children left after the trial ended, moving near family in North Carolina.

And, then, there were the articles about Allie. The trial. The verdict.

Though her eyes began to burn, Allie searched for hours, jotting down dates and comments in a small notebook. After a while, the dead ends, twists, and turns that led to nowhere made her dizzy. She leaned back and rubbed her temples. This was how it felt to be dropped into a huge concrete maze in the dark. Find your way out, inch by inch. Go on intuition, some trial and error, and sheer determination.

She worked on making a timeline, starting with his years in foster care and his adoption at age five by a family who was unable to have children. She added his high school years, his college time at the University of Georgia, followed by where he'd started coaching. Allie noted each season's record, any championships. She read recaps of games, reviews of big matchups. Each school went from losing to winning. The players signed with good college teams.

The pattern: impeccable record, proven success, every decision measured and focused. Improving the community's morale bettered his career. He was a gifted leader. On the surface, there was nothing to dislike. He was good-looking and a family guy. Many articles made mention of his church involvement, Rotary membership, and civic clubs, the generous donations to adoption agencies and children's charities.

She paused, glancing back over the page. Her eyes fell on his major in college. *Chemistry.* Allie stiffened and sucked in a breath. This made it entirely possible—and plausible—that the coach possessed the background and knowledge to manufacture steroids.

Of course, at the time of the trial, all that mattered was the man's unwavering commitment to football, his team, and the people of Brunswick.

But none of it explained why Gaines would want the coach dead.

Then it hit her. The article Caroline brought home. Maybe she'd been looking in the wrong places, assumed each new job was a step up: better school, bigger salary, more prestige. But what if it was more than that?

What if the moves followed some kind of controversy or trouble? A scandal, sexual harassment, underage drinking? Issues with players, parents, or boosters? Or his own family?

Allie rubbed the back of her neck. Her fingers fumbled over the keyboard, trembling—worried she might find something, frightened that she wouldn't.

What can I prove?

Her shoulders ached from sitting. Allie straightened, glancing once more at her notes. She wasn't a detective. She needed help. She was drowning in details, going in circles, and getting hopelessly frustrated. Allie got up from her desk and stumbled toward the bed. As she lay down, easing her body between the cool sheets, she allowed herself to drift off. After hours of restless slumber, tossing and turning, she woke with one thought: *Ben*.

Ben was the only person who might give her a chance to explain. She'd tried to push the thoughts of him out of her head. He was back. He was here. Ben had made a huge career change, one that allowed objectivity.

He'd make an excellent journalist, Allie thought. And now he wouldn't be bound anymore to one particular party or candidate. Ben might be able to help her. It was the longest of long shots, an almost-guaranteed slam of a door in her face.

Ben, after all, had left town right after she'd broken it off. It made sense. She'd ended their relationship. She shivered. Allie had broken his heart, but why *had* he disappeared so quickly? Because she'd ended it? To put distance between them as soon as possible? To try and forget her? Or was there something more?

Allie sat up. Ben's brother had protected Coach Thomas. Did Ben know something she didn't? She pressed her fingers to her forehead, propping her elbows on her knees. He might tell her to go to hell.

If Ben did, at least one thing was certain. Hell didn't frighten her. Not that much.

Allie had already been there.

TWENTY-NINE

CAROLINE

2016

Caroline hadn't seen Russell in days. The hours seemed to pass in slow motion, measured in songs she memorized. Her current favorite was Druery's "Deliver Me."

Tell me about the freedom you crave. We can't get out today. The streets, they all head one way.

The rhythm and words gave her something to focus on, a way for her brain to disconnect from all of the worry. Unfortunately, Emma didn't see it that way. Every few hours she'd open Caroline's door. It was the same question every time.

"You okay?"

Caroline would nod and shift her body away, put her back to the door. When Emma offered to make homemade strawberry ice cream, one of Caroline's all-time favorite recipes, she offered a polite no.

"Not hungry," she told Emma. "Thank you anyway."

As for school, she existed by slipping into the girls' restroom and locking herself in the last stall between classes. She skipped lunch, choosing to hide out in the musty basement near the custodian's supply room, which smelled of bleach and cleaning supplies.

No one bothered her there. Caroline pretended to cram for a test if anyone walked by. It had worked so far.

There was still buzz about Maddie's photograph, and she'd returned to school a different person, reserved and quiet, slipping from class to class with her head down. Caroline noticed that Maddie, now more pale and drawn than when she had the flu last year, quit wearing makeup. She was dressing in slouchy clothes that covered her slim figure. There were rumors of Maddie being put on Xanax and antidepressants, of Maddie not leaving her house on weekends.

That morning their eyes had met across the hallway between classes. For a moment, Caroline felt a surge of hope. But Maddie's eyes were swollen, with dark circles underneath. She looked haunted, and turned and walked away before Caroline could even react.

In the swirl of students rushing around her, Caroline stood still, watching the girl who had been her best friend disappear into the crowd. As hard as she could, Caroline wished she could erase it all and start over. She'd give anything for a fresh start from the past few weeks.

With thoughts of Maddie still heavy on her mind, Caroline headed home to get ready for her volunteer shift at the nursing home. She remembered how they'd laughed and joked on career day. How Maddie had rolled her eyes and poked fun at the speakers. Her always-up-to-no-good grin that made Caroline laugh.

She winced at the memory.

Caroline called out to Emma that she was home and went straight to her room, where she brushed her hair into a long, tight ponytail. She washed her face, scrubbing until it glowed, then ran some ChapStick over her lips. Caroline bent over to tie her tennis shoes, straightened her waistband, and pulled her backpack over one shoulder.

"Emma, I'm leaving, okay?" Caroline headed for the front door, double-checking to make sure she had her keys.

"Already? Want a ride?" Emma said, leaning out of her office door.

"No thanks," Caroline replied, waving to her aunt. Today was about standing on her own two feet. She would show Russell that her volunteer work was more than running away from her problems. That she wasn't really that shallow and selfish. And she would give him the apology that was way overdue.

The walk did Caroline some good. The air was clear and crisp. Her freshly washed skin tingled. A few of the residents lifted a hand to wave as she walked up the curved driveway.

"Hello," she said and smiled as she walked past. Through the doors, up the elevator, to the nurses' station.

"Caroline," one of the aides greeted her. "How are you, honey?" She smiled widely, showing a gold tooth on one side.

"Good."

"Glad to hear it. We sure need an extra pair of hands tonight." She reached across the counter for a list, then handed it to Caroline. "Here are the folks who need dinner brought to their rooms. You don't have to do anything other than set the trays down and make sure they're comfortable. If anyone needs something else, come and find me."

It would be fine, Caroline told herself. She'd duck in, duck out. Caroline busied herself with the trays, her stomach growling as the scent of roast beef and gravy drifted from the cart. On her way out of the corner suite, she thought she'd caught a glimpse of Russell. His shoulder and arm around a tiny, bird-like lady, helping her walk. Other residents and staff congregated nearby.

She backed away and turned her cart. Caroline didn't need an audience. She'd save seeing Russell for last. The cart's wheels squeaked across the floor as she pushed, trying not to appear flustered or rushed.

Russell had offered to listen. He wasn't trying to be smart or condescending. He seemed to understand, like something bad had happened to him or a friend.

Caroline had just reacted, switched herself on the defensive, and fired back.

She was immature and emotional, and he'd probably also added hysterical pain in the butt to that list. Someone to avoid. Psycho, even.

He deserved an "I'm sorry," even if he decided never to talk to her again.

She'd find him today, say what she needed to say before he told her off, and hope for the best.

Caroline stopped and scanned the names and room numbers on the list. There was at least one new resident; most of the rest she knew by sight. And there was a Dr. Gaines. Room 204. The woman who thought she knew her.

Gaines. She wondered if it was a cousin or a sister to the sheriff. Checking the number, she rolled her cart in the direction of Dr. Gaines's room. She bent down, easing the tray off the rack into the crook of her elbow. With her free hand, she rapped twice on the door. Hearing nothing, she held her breath and pushed down on the handle, letting herself in the room.

It was dark, the curtains drawn, and smelled faintly of Windex, as if someone had just been in to clean. Dr. Gaines sat facing the television, though nothing was on. Maybe she was dozing. Or thinking. If so, Caroline didn't want to disturb her. She tiptoed across the carpeting and set her dinner on a small table near the bed.

As she turned to leave, Dr. Gaines spoke. "Hello? Who's there?"

Caroline stood still, caught. She made herself swivel around and smile. "Hi, Dr. Gaines. I brought you some dinner." She pointed toward the tray.

"Thank you." Dr. Gaines strained to sit up taller and waved her closer. "Emma, dear. I've been wanting to talk to you." Slowly she lowered her gnarled hand, resting it, waiting.

Her throat went dry, but Caroline forced herself to take a step forward. "I'm Paul and Lily's granddaughter," she added, making her voice louder, pressing her palm to her chest.

"Yes, yes. They've been so worried about you," Dr. Gaines mused. "They don't know what's wrong." She sighed and folded her hands on her lap. "I understand that you don't want to tell them. That's your decision. But someday you should let them know. They love you and they're worried about you."

"I-I don't understand."

Dr. Gaines continued, "It's so disappointing, after all the expectation and excitement." Her eyes bore into Caroline's. She wasn't being unkind; it was like she knew something. A secret. Dr. Gaines exhaled a ragged breath. "Even with your situation."

Situation?

"I'm just worried about you needing someone to talk to. Have you been back for a checkup or spoken to the grief counselor I recommended?" Dr. Gaines blinked at Caroline, expectant.

"No," Caroline answered, stuttering. "I-I think—"

"Emma," Dr. Gaines cut in. "This is not the end. You can adopt. You have options. We'll find you some help. There are children who need loving parents . . ."

Emma. Grief counselor. Adopt. Situation?

Dr. Gaines had to be insane or plain out of her mind.

Caroline didn't need to be frightened. It was Dr. Gaines who was confused, not her. The whole thing was just a silly mistake. Sure, she looked like her aunt, everyone said so. But Emma had never been pregnant.

"Um, excuse me. I forgot something." Caroline backed out of

the room, into the hallway. She closed the door with a click, turned, and bumped straight into Russell's chest.

"Oh." She jumped.

"Hey." He touched her shoulder. "Where you going so fast?"

Caroline flushed pink. "I needed to grab something." She paused. "And . . . I was going to find you after my shift. Later. I needed to apologize. To you."

With a lopsided smile, Russell stepped closer. "Thanks."

"I mean it, really," Caroline said. "I'm so sorry. I acted like a baby. All defensive. It wasn't right. You were trying to be sweet and listen. I just freaked out."

"Apology accepted, okay? I know you're under some pressure," Russell replied, gesturing with his hand. "You've got a lot to handle with your mom and stuff at school."

Caroline grimaced.

"So, tell me, what just happened?"

Caroline sighed. "That lady. Dr. Gaines. She weirded me out a little."

"She's really harmless," he said. "Gets a little irritated sometimes. Hey, did you know she's married to Sheriff Gaines?"

Caroline balked at the thought. Sheriff Gaines always seemed proper and buttoned-up. Rigid. Cold, almost.

"He comes in every day." Russell shrugged. "If that's not love, I don't know what is. It's crazy, what happened." He paused. "Tractor trailer hit her. She should have died."

"Oh, wow," Caroline sputtered. "No wonder she's messed up. She thinks I'm Emma. And she was talking crazy . . . about my 'situation,' and 'there are children who need loving parents.'"

"Wait, who's Emma?" Russell wrinkled his forehead.

"Oh, sorry. My aunt. I live with her."

"Well, do you look alike?"

"Um, sure. We do," Caroline agreed.

"Hey." Russell rubbed at his chin. "Dr. Gaines could have been your aunt's doctor," he added, raising an eyebrow.

"Hmm. Maybe," Caroline said, scrunching up her forehead. She couldn't imagine Emma picking Dr. Gaines, though. "What kind of doctor was she?"

"An ob-gyn. She delivered babies."

Caroline wrinkled her nose and started to laugh. "Oh, I don't think so—"

The look on Russell's face, serious and contemplative, stopped her.

She felt the hairs on her neck stand at attention when she remembered what Dr. Gaines had said. *This is not the end. You can adopt. You have options.*

THIRTY

ALLIE

2016

All day at work, Allie thought of nothing but Caroline's challenge and talking to Ben. She ran everything through her mind several times, planning out what she might say and how she should approach him.

Allie's distraction caught up with her in the afternoon. At Natalie's office, she'd knocked over a tray of instruments, dropped a vial of medicine on the floor, and in her haste to clean up the mess, splashed cleaning fluid on the dog's owner. The man, less than pleased, didn't hesitate to complain to Dr. Harper immediately.

He wasn't the first person to express distaste at having Allie in the office. Most of the time there was no basis for the person's unhappiness, other than personal feelings. Allie was aware that her status as a felon made it difficult for some owners to be comfortable, but she worked hard, kept to herself, and did her job. When someone complained, Natalie excused Allie from the room, wrote a note in the chart for future reference, and made sure to explain the circumstances.

Natalie's pat answer was that the office needed an experienced tech, she hired who was available, and the state of Georgia approved the work as part of her rehabilitation. Generally, the person who complained didn't say anything else after that.

Today, however, Allie's carelessness had cost her. Natalie was a good employer who'd taken a big chance on a convicted felon. Allie needed to worry about doing her job well and making herself useful. Chasing ghosts from the past didn't have any place in a vet clinic.

Despite telling herself that, Allie couldn't help but think back to when her life was so different. A pang of regret hit her square in the heart. Ten years earlier, she'd put in a shift with her father at the vet office, go home to Caroline, and spend the evening with Ben, or reading journals like the *Lancet* and the *Harvard Health Journal*. It wasn't exactly normal. No one else she knew was quite that focused.

Of course, Emma had called it "obsessed." Ben, though, always understood.

Pressing a fist to her lips, Allie swallowed a sob. Why hadn't Ben fought harder? Why hadn't he demanded another chance? Why?

Allie closed her eyes and lowered her chin to her chest.

No. It was all her fault. Such a huge mistake—thinking that she knew exactly what Ben needed, what he wanted, and what he could handle. If she had to do it all again, she would have just let him love her.

October 2006

When the last patient, a feisty border collie, and his owner made their way to the vet clinic's lobby, Allie smiled and headed for the employee break room. Her father had sewn up a small gash on a golden retriever, they'd performed surgery on a Labrador with a bowel obstruction, and she'd given shots to a half-dozen squirming corgi puppies. The litter, an adorable mess of clumsy bodies and legs, made Allie grin. The dogs' collective yelping drowned out every other sound in the office.

Allie shed her soiled scrub top, balling it up and tossing it into the mouth of her open canvas bag. She pulled the thick band from around her ponytail and shook out her hair, feeling the heaviness settle against the back of her neck. With a glance at the clock, Allie scrubbed her hands at the sink, watching the suds and water swirl to the drain below her fingertips. Thank goodness her mother loved watching Caroline. As a favor, Ben would be picking up Caroline in a few minutes.

When she bent to slip off her shoes and set them on the bottom shelf, Allie ran a hand along the smooth wood, wondering how many times she'd touched this same spot. The break room, cramped and windowless, held only lockers, a small stove, and a noisy yellow refrigerator. But Allie wondered if she would miss it. The office, the animals, even the ugly break room with its outdated appliances.

She'd interviewed with Emory in September, sat through a day of grueling scrutiny from white-coated physicians. Allie had managed to maintain her composure, express her love of medicine, and profess that the school had been, and still was, her first choice. She would arrange schooling and after-hours care for Caroline. Her family wasn't far, she added, and could help on weekends.

Allie reached for the envelope inside her bag. She drew it out carefully, set it in her lap, and ran a finger across the black letters. Her name, stamped onto the smooth white paper. When she broke the news last night at dinner, her father had been ecstatic and talked nonstop, repeating at least five times he was glad she wasn't leaving right away. Ben had hugged her and kissed her head. When her grandmother began clapping, a bewildered Caroline clapped along and began singing "Happy Birthday," making Allie grin and shake her head.

Even twenty-four hours later, the acceptance hadn't fully sunk in yet. She'd probably sleep with the envelope under her pillow to make sure she hadn't dreamt the delivery. Right now, medical school still seemed like a foreign country, a place to visit where she didn't know the customs and didn't speak the language. Allie straightened her shoulders. *This is silly.* She knew a lot about wounds and injuries; she'd sewn up plenty of lacerations, and she'd helped tend to the sick.

Allie connected with animals, sensed illness or pain. People, though, were different. People were complicated, with millions of questions and lists of ailments. Would she freeze up, forget everything she'd learned, not trust her intuition?

Ben, on more than one occasion, assured her that these anxieties were normal. In fact, he'd planned a picnic for this evening—just Allie, Caroline, and him—to get her mind off medical school and help her enjoy the remainder of her soon-to-disappear free time.

Allie changed quickly and drove to Neptune Park on the southernmost tip of St. Simons Island. Nestled between the towering white lighthouse and the red brick library, the park offered sturdy concrete picnic tables and wooden benches overlooking the ocean. There was a massive wooden playground that Caroline adored and a huge shade tree that offered respite from the late-afternoon heat.

As promised, Ben and Caroline were waiting. She found them easily—her daughter on the swing set, her dark hair flying behind her as her feet sailed into the air. Ben talked and laughed with each push, no doubt entertaining her with the jokes and light teasing that her daughter adored. Behind them, the sun, tinged with orange, dipped lower on the horizon, causing the sky to glow electric blue.

She stood there, watching, her bag tucked on her shoulder.

They even looked like father and daughter; everyone remarked on it. Both dark-eyed, with dark hair and high cheekbones. Caroline was delicate and bird-like, while Ben towered above her, broad-shouldered and square-jawed. Her daughter's giggle floated through the air—contagious, almost magnetic—and Allie found herself practically jogging toward Ben and Caroline.

"Mommy!" Caroline shrieked, jumping off the swing in delight. She ran to Allie, arms wide open for a hug and kisses.

Ben hovered nearby, waiting, as Allie stroked Caroline's hair and asked about her day. "It was good? I'm so glad. Where did Grandma Lily take you?"

Her daughter chattered away, bouncing and skipping as they made their way to a table near the playground. Ben spread a blanket over the table, set out a picnic basket, and checked on the pile of chilled drinks in a small red cooler next to the bench seat. He handed Allie a bottled water and offered Caroline pink lemonade.

"My favorite," she said, taking the drink. "Thank you."

Ben bent at the waist in a slight bow, making Caroline laugh. "My pleasure, madam."

Allie smiled and swelled with pride. He was amazing. And adorable. How could anyone resist him? She sometimes forgot that Ben was a highly connected and well-thought-of political consultant with high hopes to help to run Sonny Perdue's second gubernatorial term. The job that would make or break Ben's career. It was all he'd ever dreamed of—and he was so close to having that brass ring in his hand.

Caroline and her friend's giggles interrupted her daydream. As they ran up to the table, Ben grinned and raised an eyebrow as the girls whispered back and forth, then looked up at Allie with hopeful faces.

"Can we stay another twenty minutes?" Caroline pleaded, wringing her tiny hands.

Laughing, Allie nodded. "Go ahead, and stay where we can see you, okay?" She waved her hands as they squealed in delight and scampered off, back to the swing sets and monkey bars.

"So much for the big date," Ben teased and sat down on the bench.

"Oh, that's what this is?" Allie fluttered her eyelashes.

"Hey, I wrangled the night off and drove back from Atlanta—just for you. I spent hours slaving over this sumptuous meal. Only the finest egg salad sandwiches and sour cream and onion potato chips," Ben said, puffing up his chest with pride. "Oh, and your mom made chocolate cake."

"Aha! You did have help," Allie said, elbowing him in the ribs.

Ben crossed his arms and looked serious. "Of course I had help. You don't want any old chocolate cake. This had to be perfect."

"Oh . . ." Allie blushed, unable to find words.

"Sometimes I can't believe it's been four years." Ben rubbed his chin, tilted his head, and smiled, brushing an imaginary piece of lint from his khaki pants. "I can still see you, that day after Caroline's first birthday party. She was down for a nap—"

"And I was crying," Allie said. Her eyes filled, flooding her vision. She fumbled to wipe both cheeks, smiling at the memory.

"When I found you, do you remember what I said?" Ben asked.

Of course Allie knew the answer. It was etched in her memory. She leaned closer to him, burying her face in his shoulder. He smelled like fresh air and sunshine.

"That I didn't have to worry. You would take care of me. And Caroline," Allie murmured.

"And that I would spend every day, every waking moment, making you happy. I didn't care about the past. I love you, and that's for always."

Allie snuggled closer. "I remember."

Ben shifted away, peeling his body away from hers. He turned to face Allie.

With a jolt of realization at what he might be planning to ask, Allie trembled. Her hands began to shake.

"We've been together for four years." Ben swallowed. "And I'm so happy that you've been accepted to medical school, but I also know that we have some decisions to make."

The sun dipped below the tree branches, painting the sky in crimson and orange. Leaves fluttered to the ground, crisp and dry. Parents were gathering diaper bags and sleepy children.

Ben's words tumbled, end over end, in Allie's mind. But he was smiling. And fumbling in his pocket.

"Will you—" Ben's voice cut through the noise in her head. Ben who loved her. *Always*.

Allie's breath quickened. Her heart thudded against her rib cage.

"Will you marry me, Allie?" Ben said, taking her hand and getting down on one knee.

Around the two of them, the world could have melted away. All Allie could see was Ben's face and the sound of her daughter's laughter.

"Yes," she breathed. "Absolutely, yes."

2016

Natalie was adjusting her white Crocs and reheating a cup of coffee when Allie found her at the end of the day. "Before you run, let's chat for a minute."

Allie nodded and sat down. She couldn't look at the clock. The seconds ticked loudly, reminding her that she wasn't finding any answers.

"So, how's everything going?"

"Today, not so well," Allie said, owning up to the mistakes. She wouldn't, she couldn't, mention the conversation with Caroline. Her sister's dismissal of Allie's innocence. How much it had cut her to the quick.

Instead, Allie drew a breath. "Natalie, I'm so sorry. My mind just wasn't where it needed to be. It won't happen again."

Natalie leaned back and looked Allie up and down. "You had a bad afternoon. We all do. How are you holding up otherwise?"

Allie fingered the edge of her scrubs. "It's been a little strange. Most people look at me like I have the plague. Or some fatal disease, like if they get too close, they'll catch it." Allie sighed. "A few people are decent." Her eyes welled up. "The rest just ignore me."

"Okay, I'm sorry. Don't cry." Natalie winced. "I just want you to know that I'm not upset. I'm happy with your work. And I'm sorry for whatever you've been through."

"I love this job. And the other . . . Whatever people think, it's fine," Allie said, wiping at her cheeks with the back of her hand. "I just care about my family."

Natalie waited.

"The worst part is that my daughter isn't talking to me. She doesn't know what to think. She was so young when everything happened," Allie said.

Natalie nodded. "That's pretty normal. Kids think you're the enemy, put on earth for the sole purpose of making their lives miserable." She pressed a fist to her chin and leaned closer to Allie. "Took our son a long time to realize we were really on his side."

"I'm sorry," Allie said.

"Hey." Natalie shrugged. "There's no perfect family here. Or anywhere. We all have our baggage," Natalie confided. "Russell has a new chance at life. A fresh start. Now that he's out of that mess back in Atlanta."

Allie swallowed. Natalie understood the situation.

"I'm glad Russell has you." Allie didn't want to bring up the editorial, but forced herself to ask, "Did you hear about what happened at Mansfield Academy?"

"The thing from the paper?" She shrugged. "Sure, the gossip reaches this office too. Someone's trying to scare you off, Allie, and stir up trouble. And they're using Caroline to get to you."

"I'm sick about it." Allie pressed a hand to her stomach. "Emma finally got to talk to both the principal and the superintendent. They say they're handling it, but I'm not sure what that means. We'll see."

"Well, keep me posted. And take time off if you need to. Just let me know." Natalie swept her arm in a shooing motion and stood up. "Go on home. And try to have a good evening." She smiled.

"Thanks," Allie answered. "I've got a few stops to make."

Natalie paused and gave her a curious look. "Good night, then." She bent down and picked up her Crocs. "Hope you find what you're looking for."

Allie watched Natalie leave the room.

Me too.

The truth.

THIRTY-ONE

EMMA

The tighter Emma held on to Caroline, the more everything spun out of control.

With Allie home, all of the protection she thought she had built up now seemed made of sand and salt water. Enough time in the sun, and with enough wind, the walls would crumble to the ground. Now, grain by grain, it was happening, and Emma didn't know how to stop it.

Dinner with Caroline was equally frustrating. She'd spent the afternoon preparing her niece's favorite gumbo, a recipe that involved creating a thick, buttery roux and chopping piles of celery, tomato, onion, okra, and bell peppers.

"So, you've been spending a lot of time at the nursing home," Emma said as she handed over a steaming bowl. "See anything of your friend?" A hint of a smile began sneaking across her face.

"Yes. He helped me out the other day," Caroline said, wrinkling her nose. "I was having a little bit of trouble with one of the residents."

"What happened?" Emma took a sip of water, her eyes never leaving her niece. "Something bad?"

"No, nothing like that," Caroline said. "Just a lady who had a bad accident and some brain damage—she kind of freaked me out. Her day-to-day memory isn't very good, but sometimes she remembers stuff further back."

"That's got to be awful," Emma said, shaking her head.

"Yeah, she's really confused sometimes. I feel bad for her, to never get to leave that place," Caroline replied. She lifted her chin to look at Emma. "Have you ever been to the nursing home? Like, inside?"

Emma pondered for a minute. "A long time ago. I can't think of anyone I know who lives there now."

"Do you know Dr. Gaines?" Caroline asked.

Emma, mid-sip, almost inhaled her drink. "What?"

"A lady, her name is June Gaines." Caroline focused on her bowl, stirring the thick broth. "She's a doctor. Or she used to be."

After taking a second to compose her thoughts, Emma continued. "It must be the same person. I guess I didn't realize she was there." She crumpled her napkin in her hand. "I haven't thought about her in forever."

"It's just weird because everyone else is like ninety years old," added Caroline.

Emma allowed herself a small smile. "I'm sure there are some lovely ninety-year-olds," she chided her niece playfully.

"Oh, there are," Caroline said, smiling at the joke. "But she's younger and has nicer clothes, and her hair is always done. She doesn't fit in there. That's why it's weird."

"What did she say, exactly, to freak you out?" Emma's throat went dry. She reached for her water and downed half the glass.

"Nothing. Just rambling. It was just a little weird." Caroline picked up her roll and pulled it apart, watched the steam escape. "She thought I was someone else."

"Like a celebrity or something?" Emma asked lightly, forcing a giggle.

"No, nothing like that." Caroline frowned. "But I think she delivered babies."

Emma's chest began to tighten. "From what I remember, a lot of babies. For a while, she was the county's only female ob-gyn. So she was busy, worked long hours, took call, and went in for emergencies."

Her niece sat up at full attention, wrinkled her forehead, and leaned in to hear the rest. "Will she ever get better?"

Emma wrinkled her forehead. "I don't know. That's one for the specialists. Anything else, Miss Twenty Questions?" She smiled and winked at her niece.

"Well, if she delivered a lot of babies, did she deliver me?" Caroline asked.

Emma considered this. "I don't think so," she said. "Allie had a male doctor." She picked up her water glass and sipped.

"Why not?" Caroline lowered her eyes to the table. "She didn't want anyone to know?"

Trying not to choke, Emma picked up her napkin, dabbing it to her lips. "Caro, I'm not exactly sure."

But Emma was sure. She knew Allie was figuring out what to do about medical school, deciding whether she could get her enrollment postponed, and worrying about how to tell their parents.

"We didn't even know she was pregnant for a long time," Emma added softly. It was a harsh reality for her niece to absorb, and not entirely true. Allie had told Emma right away; she'd shared the whole story.

Caroline sniffed. "So she didn't tell anyone, and then it was too late to get rid of me?" Her cheeks flushed bright pink. She pushed back her chair, ready to stand up and leave the table.

"Honey, wait," Emma said, motioning for Caroline to stay.

"Please, don't go. Talk to me." She waited until her niece settled back in her seat before starting to speak again. Emma licked her lips and formed a story in her head. This was her opportunity, a moment she could use to drive Caroline away from Allie for good.

"She really couldn't take care of you, Caroline," Emma began. "She was so focused on medical school, so intent on leaving town, that I think when she found out she was carrying you, she didn't want to believe it at first."

Caroline's lips parted. "Like, she was in denial? Or in shock?"

"Exactly."

"So, then what?"

Emma thought carefully. "She was distraught, especially after she told your grandmother and grandfather. They were pretty upset. Allie said more than a few times that she didn't know what to do."

"About me?"

Emma nodded.

"Oh," Caroline gasped. "She didn't want me. My own mother didn't want me." She clapped her palm over her mouth. After a few seconds, Caroline's hand slid down below the base of her neck. She pressed and held it there, eyes closed tight, as if she were having chest pain.

"It wasn't exactly that simple," Emma whispered. But she wasn't going to try hard to defend her sister. By all rights, she should be Caroline's legal parent, since Allie had made her choice a long time ago. "Sweetheart, I'm sure she thought a lot about her options."

Her niece's eyelids fluttered open. "Like giving me up for adoption? Instead of an abortion?" Caroline's voice hit a shrill tone.

"She probably did think about that," Emma replied, keeping her tone low and even.

"Why didn't she just give me away? Let some strangers have

me?" When Emma didn't reply, Caroline moved her silverware to her plate, picked up her cup, and stalked into the kitchen.

Emma closed her eyes and took a breath. This, however unpleasant for the moment, was exactly what she needed to encourage. Thinking about what to say next, Emma cleared her own dishes and walked to the counter to stand next to Caroline. She turned on the faucet, squirted some dish soap, and began to rinse her plate.

Caroline stared at the suds, jaw set, stone-faced.

"The sooner you get over this stuff with your mom and move on, the better it will be for everyone," Emma said gently. "Why don't I set up an appointment for you to meet with a counselor? That way you can talk it through. Make some decisions."

"And how will that fix things? See a therapist and then what? He'll tell me I'm as crazy as my mother and that I'll probably kill someone when I turn twenty-five?" She sniffed and then tears began to stream down Caroline's face.

Emma put her hand over Caroline's. "No one can fix it. But a professional might be able to help you deal with the situation. Give you ways to figure out how to let all of it go." She squeezed Caroline's fingers.

"I'll think about it." Caroline ran her fingertips along her cheeks, catching the tears.

"That sounds good. And that's a really grown-up decision to make. Because what happens with Allie affects all of us. Everyone in the family. It's not been easy on Grandma and Grandpa. They're so upset about what she's done. And Grandpa had to retire . . ."

Emma watched Caroline's expression. It was a lot for a teenager to take in, but she wasn't capable of making choices by herself. Not about this.

"My head hurts," Caroline whispered. She pressed a hand to her forehead and bent over the counter. "I'm going to go lie down."

"Okay, sweetheart. Come get me if you need me." Emma kissed her niece's forehead and watched her pad down the hallway. With soft steps, Emma retreated to her own room, turned down the sheets, and slid into bed. As she settled in, she thought about the past, when she thought everything in her life was perfect. She had love. She had big plans and a future.

And like with Caroline, it had all come crashing down.

Emma wiped at her cheeks before a tear dripped onto her pillow, and she tried to remember all of the good she'd had in her life. Before he was taken away, the man she loved had given her hope. Made her feel beautiful. And adored. She remembered all of the little moments they'd shared. Her favorite was the night they'd made their baby.

September 2006

With a spark and a whoosh, Emma lit a match. She held the flame over several candles, lighting each wick in turn. The glow softened the four walls, stacked with sterile instruments and drawers of medical equipment. She brought in soft pillows and blankets, arranged them into a cozy nest on the floor. There was little more she could do for ambiance.

She checked her hair for the fifth time, rubbed her lips together, and took a sip of water. On tiptoes, she raised up to glance out at the back parking lot. Empty.

Emma listened for his truck. No hum of an engine, no crunch of tires on gravel. She turned away from the window and slumped down, sliding against the painted cement block wall.

He was ready to leave his wife, he'd told Emma.

Just a few more days. Just another week. Before she knew it, they'd been together an entire month. The relationship consumed her, like an addiction.

Emma stopped eating, couldn't sleep, and began to make mistakes at her father's office. The occasional morning she missed work or forgot to place an order for paper towels, exhausted from midnight phone calls, hurried liaisons in back parking lots, and daydreaming about the future.

Best—or worst—of all, there was no cure, no antidote, no test to run or medicine to take. Time was the release. Only being together would set her free. She couldn't believe her life could change so completely in just a month.

The security keypad beeped four times, numbers punched into the system. Another ding signaled the code was correct, and Emma heard the sound of metal, the back door, scraping against the linoleum floor.

"Hey, babe." He clutched his ball cap in one hand. "You missed the best part of the game." He pulled off his windbreaker and laid it over the closest chair. "Two-point conversion in the last fifteen seconds of the quarter. Put us up by one . . ." His eyes were expectant, excited, and more alive than she'd ever seen.

It was her cue.

"And you won?" Emma squealed and jumped to her feet.

He hugged her to his chest and brought a hand under her chin so he could tilt her face to his. "We officially have a winning season."

Emma's lips met his then, their hands and faces melting into each other. It was times like these, she thought, that it was hard to tell where she left off and he began. They were meant for each other, soul mates. She knew it.

He bent in front of her, kneeled down, and she caught her breath. Was this it? A proposal? But he began to nuzzle her bare legs, sliding his hands under Emma's skirt. "We have to celebrate," he murmured and kissed her thigh. "Right now."

As dizzy and light-headed as she felt, Emma forced both hands onto his muscled chest and pushed him back with as much effort as she could muster. "Wait a second," she cautioned. "Did you talk to her? You promised." She jutted out her lip.

If he was frustrated, Emma couldn't tell.

"I can't tonight, not with the win and all. All the positive attention the team's finally getting, the momentum." He paused. "Breaking that news would kill the team's spirit. You can't have that on your conscience."

Emma didn't answer; she knew there was more than some accuracy in what he was saying. Football in Georgia mattered more than academics and grades; the sport was leagues above the arts and community service. It was all anyone ever talked about from July through January, and then spring training began.

"I miss you," she tried, and ran a finger down his collar, to the embroidery on his chest. She traced the letters. "I want to be with you every day," she murmured into his shoulder, laying her cheek against his shirt.

Strong hands gripped Emma's shoulders, held her out at arm's length. He held up a finger for her to stay quiet, then reached into his pocket. Emma watched his hand, which he withdrew, fist tight. He stretched his arm until his hand reached below her nose. He flipped over his palm, opened his fingers, one by one.

"The game coin," Emma breathed. She couldn't pull her eyes away from the glinting disk cradled in his hand. It was a symbol of what he loved most in the world.

"For you," he said and pressed it into her palm. "You're everything to me. Know that."

Emma curled her fingers around the gift.

"Give me just a little more time. And we have to be extra careful." He reached out, drawing her close. "I promise I'm leaving her." His breath, hot and sweet, caressed her face. "Say you'll wait?"

"All right," Emma murmured.

His eyes locked on hers and his voice grew darker. "And there's one more thing. I need your help."

At the request, Emma sat up, fighting a twinge of worry. She brushed a stray hair from her eyes. "Anything. What is it?"

Coach Thomas pushed himself up on one elbow. In a few solemn sentences, he explained. It would change everything. It would mean a better future. For Mansfield Academy. For them.

Emma clasped her arms around her knees, pulling them close, while her head and heart dueled over the request. "It's just for now? For a little while?"

His forehead crinkled. "I think so."

In the end, she couldn't deny him. "Then, yes."

Thomas broke into a wide grin. "Emma, I love you."

She stopped breathing. Her hand released the coin; it slipped through her fingers, clinked on the floor, and rolled away.

"Get it later," he told her and pulled her close. He tore at her clothing, desperate, wild.

Emma allowed herself to be swept away, carried on a raging river, dangerous and uncontrollable.

When they lay on the floor, legs entwined, his fingers tangled in her hair, he drifted off to sleep. Emma watched the pulse in his neck, the regular rise and fall of his chest.

She wanted to believe him.

I love you. Emma played the words over in her head. *I love you.*

Everything was in place. All he needed was a little incentive.

She was looking out for him. She knew what was best. She'd put the plan in motion nearly four weeks earlier, when she stopped taking her birth control pills, began eating better and walking more. Three days ago, Emma had even stocked up on prenatal vitamins. She reached out and stroked his hair.

Now, it was up to Mother Nature to do the rest.

THIRTY-TWO

ALLIE

2016

Allie hurried her steps, tucking her hair into a ponytail and clutching her bag to her side. Below a row of gray storm clouds, the sun hung low on the horizon, turning the sky shades of burnt umber and orange.

As she turned on Ben's street, a crack of thunder echoed in the distance. This time of year, afternoon storms cropped up off the Atlantic in what seemed like minutes, sending torrents of rain across St. Simons Island and into Brunswick.

Frowning, Allie cast a glance at the sky. For now, the rain was holding off. She prayed it would stay away at least until she reached Ben's door. But when she reached the sidewalk in front of his parents' house, the small white structure looked dark and closed up. Even the Live Oaks looked dark and intimidating, with their huge, gnarled branches dripping with Spanish moss.

Allie ran her eyes over the windows of Ben's house, searching for a sign of life, a flicker of movement. She walked to the edge of the yard, looking for a clue that his family still owned the property. His car wasn't there, and the mailbox wasn't marked with a name.

She wondered again why Ben had given up the political life he'd been so passionate about. What had happened to change that?

Behind her, Allie heard the rumble of a car engine, smelled the faint, acrid odor of exhaust. If a neighbor was pulling up and parking, she couldn't just stand here in front of Ben's house.

She felt like sprinting, or at least breaking into a jog. The last thing Allie needed was the driver of the car reporting her to the police for loitering. She shielded her eyes, pretending to block out the setting sun, and slowly ambled away.

"Allie?"

She whirled around in surprise.

"Hey, what are you doing here?" Ben said, talking to her through the open window of his car. His forehead was wrinkled, but he didn't look angry. He pulled over to the curb and parked.

Allie bit her lip. *Calm down. Just explain.* She watched as he stepped out of the vehicle. "I'm sorry. Hi."

Ben watched her thoughtfully, his expression guarded and serious. He probably pitied Allie, felt sorry for her, and was just trying to be nice before telling her to leave.

He finally answered. "I heard that you were back," Ben said slowly, as if the words were difficult to pronounce. "How are you?"

"I wish I knew," Allie said. She tried to smile, but the corners of her mouth wouldn't move. She could almost touch Ben. He looked the same, other than a few gray flecks in his short, thick dark hair, tiny wrinkles around his blue eyes. "I just found out that you were back too. Emma said you've been back for a few weeks, I guess?" She hesitated. "I hear you're doing some freelancing."

Ben nodded. "You heard right. I've been writing and reporting for about two years on the side. It's been really good. About a year ago, I realized that since I was working from home, 'home' didn't have to be Atlanta. I could come back here."

"That's great," Allie said, looking up at him. He was still so handsome it made her catch her breath. And he did look happy.

"How's Caroline?" Ben asked, shifting his weight from one side to the other. "I've seen her around a little. From a distance."

Allie thought about this. It wasn't a secret that Ben used to be her boyfriend, but maybe no one had reminded Caroline. And why would they? It would only dredge up bad memories.

"She's angry. Her world's been turned upside down again."

"Of course." Ben stiffened, then looked toward the house.

"I won't keep you," Allie said. "But I didn't just happen to be wandering by."

"I didn't think you were." Ben crossed his arms.

Allie sensed the abrupt change in attitude, the slight edge to his tone of voice. As if to emphasize his displeasure, thunder rumbled, still miles away. "You know, I shouldn't be here. This was a mistake." She started backing away, nearly falling over the curb.

"Whoa." Ben jumped forward to catch her arm.

His touch, warm and steady, sent waves of emotion through Allie's body. Breathing hard, pulse thudding, she glanced up into Ben's eyes. "Thank you."

After another beat, Ben let go of her, almost regretfully. "What do you need, Allie? I assume you walked all this way?"

"I did. It's not that far." Allie began to explain, and the rest came out like the rush of a waterfall. "I'm here because of Caroline. Ben, I saw her for the first time in ten years." Allie's voice caught. "She'd been avoiding me, so Emma invited me over, but then someone made copies of that editorial—you know, the one from ten years ago—and put them all over the school—"

"Slow down," Ben said, holding up a hand. "Why don't you come and sit down for a minute?"

As they approached the house, she gathered her thoughts.

"So Caroline's not too happy you're back?" Ben asked. "Is that it?"

"More or less. I don't know." Allie's shoulders sagged as they sat, side by side, on the top porch step. "She doesn't believe me, Ben. I told her . . . I told her I'm innocent."

"I'm sorry." Ben's eyes flickered. Was it pity? Pain? Regret?

"I appreciate that," Allie replied softly, turning her head to look at him. "I really thought that if . . . if you could talk to your brother . . ." She closed her eyes. She'd never forget walking in the woods on the path behind the stadium. And then stumbling on Ben's brother, Coach Thomas, and two players.

"And what would that prove, Allie?" Ben asked, his voice hushed. "Would it change anything?"

"You saw what the coach did," Allie whispered.

Ben stared at the ground, jaw tight.

"If he could talk to Caroline. Explain what happened. Even for a few minutes . . ." Her voice trailed off.

Ben raised both hands, as if to press the words away. "No. He has a wife. They're about to have a baby girl. I can't upset them. Ask him to reopen that wound."

Allie was quiet. *What about my wounds?* "There were other guys on the team," she added. "What about them?" A flicker of hope caught fire inside her. She paused and caught his eyes, locking onto his gaze. "And you're a journalist. You could write a story. Pressure someone to reopen the case."

This time Ben hesitated.

"I think . . . I've always thought that the sheriff might have had something to do with Coach's death."

Ben's head swung around. "Wait, what?"

"I do," Allie said, this time with more conviction.

"How? Exactly how would you know that?" Ben asked, frowning.

A bolt of lightning cut across the darkening sky as the words slapped at her, cold and hard. A surge of anger broke through. "He hates me. He fast-tracked my case and didn't even look for another witness."

"That's not a reason."

Pursing her lips, Allie tamped down her frustration. She had to stay calm if Ben was going to listen. "I think it was hard for him to be objective—he was too close to the coach. Gaines knew bad stuff was going down." She swallowed. "Gaines is the county sheriff and he did nothing. He looked the other way."

"You're right," Ben mused, wrinkling his brow. "But that doesn't make him a killer."

Allie pulled her knees in close, wrapping her arms around them. "Ben, if the coach was giving those kids steroids . . . and if Gaines knew his career was about to get blown apart, he might have snapped."

"He is a bit of an egomaniac about the whole sheriff thing," Ben said and raked a hand through his hair.

"A bit?" Allie closed her eyes. Leave it to Ben to sugarcoat a rat, long tail and all. She didn't know how he'd survived the cutthroat world of politics for so long.

"Listen, I'm trying to hear what you're saying." Ben sighed. "But I'm worried about you. Why are you deliberately trying to jeopardize your parole? Aren't you thinking about that?" He tilted his head to look straight at Allie. "What will that do to Caroline? How will that help?"

"But—"

"Don't say any more, please. I can't do this, Allie." He shifted his gaze to the ground. "I have to go. I'm sorry I can't help. Really. Good luck."

As her eyes welled with tears, Allie realized she'd been reckless and stupid to come here and ask for a favor. He'd pledged everything a decade ago, and she'd forced him away; he wasn't going to sweep in and save her now.

A gust of wind rustled the trees above their heads while Ben stood up.

"Caroline—she's all I have," Allie cried out. She couldn't stop the words from jumping from her lips, from reaching out and attempting to catch him.

As thunder rumbled in the distance, Ben pivoted back to face Allie, his face pained and full of sympathy. "I know."

As the first raindrops began to fall, he turned and walked away. Allie's heart plummeted.

This time Ben was the one saying good-bye.

January 2007

Ben hadn't been called as a witness, though opposing counsel spent a full two days interrogating him before the trial. During his deposition, he'd stated that Allie had never been violent. That she'd been focused on medical school, her daughter, and her family.

At the start of the new year, Ben had taken a top post in Governor Sonny Perdue's administration and couldn't visit Brunswick more than a day or two because of his new duties. It exonerated him, and Allie was glad. If she was forced to sit and look into Ben's eyes, seeing his disappointment, his bewilderment, she thought she might die a little more each day.

It was awful enough that each hour they sat inside the courtroom, her mother and father appeared more stricken, their skin and faces becoming almost translucent. It seemed, by the end of the testimony, one or both of them might vanish into the atmosphere.

Allie suffered gut-wrenching anxiety when the prosecutor held up photos of the dead coach and close-ups of the man's bloodied head. He talked about fingerprints, Coach Thomas's skin under her fingernails, and hair fibers. The attorney talked about the murder weapon authorities had found near the coach's body—a wooden chair leg with no identifiable prints. To emphasize the brutality of the crime, the prosecutor passed around photos of the coach's family with their smiling, happy, sunlit faces.

Next, a recording of the anonymous 9-1-1 call punctuated the courtroom. The jury sat transfixed as a muffled female voice, breathy and anxious, told authorities she'd seen a blonde woman outside the pharmacy. She described shouting and the sound of something being broken. When the wail of an ambulance pierced the room, the call ended abruptly.

When the lead lawyer for the prosecution stepped forward, members of the jury began to shift and stir, readying themselves for a reading of Allie's newspaper editorial.

After enduring a traumatic line-by-line dissection of her own words, Allie tightened her fists as a self-assured and arrogant Sheriff Lee Gaines took the stand. Even without a word, Gaines commanded authority in his dark, pressed uniform, reminding everyone that his very presence was law.

The sheriff remained polite and patient while he responded to questions about his life in Brunswick, winning election after election, and his wife's accident. Next, Gaines took nearly sixty minutes describing the horror of finding his friend, the coach he loved like a son, dead. His voice cracked as he told of his disbelief at finding Allie Marshall hovering over his body at the crime scene with blood on her hands.

A loud gasp escaped from the back of the room, causing the judge to bang his gavel and lecture the crowd before Allie's team could begin their cross-examination. When the room came to order, the sheriff leveled his gaze, unblinking at the lawyer as he approached the bench.

Allie's attorney posed two questions after reminding the jury that Gaines's own wife had almost died that night. Could he have remained focused? Why wasn't he at the hospital with June?

But as he asked, the man's voice wavered. His confidence faltered as the broad-shouldered sheriff on the stand stared him down. In her seat, Allie shivered as if the blood in her veins had been turned to ice.

Gaines lifted his chin and gazed out into the audience packed into the small courtroom. His voice, confident and deep, resounded in the small space. "My wife was being cared for by the finest team of professionals in Georgia. Every minute I wasn't with her, I worked the case and led my team," he replied. He leaned forward, willing everyone to listen. "I'm not a doctor. I couldn't do a thing for June other than pray and hold her hand. She loved Coach Thomas too. June would have insisted, had she been able to, that I bring the perpetrator to justice," Gaines replied, his eyes swiveling to Allie. "That's the knowledge that kept me focused."

Under the table, Allie pressed her fingernails into the skin on her palm. The prosecution fast-forwarded through the remaining questions, looking smug. Any following objections were overruled.

The next witness was a medical doctor, an expert who testified in DUI cases across the southeast. For the next hour, prosecutors hammered Allie's blood alcohol measurement of .04 into each jury member's psyche. The state's legal limit for intoxication was .08, but the lawyers pressed that impairment of safe driving and sound judgment began after one drink.

When it was the defense's turn to argue for Allie's innocence, the team made a valiant effort. A first-time offender, Allie's stellar academic record was noted, as was her recent acceptance to medical school and her work in her father's veterinary office. Allie estimated that her lawyer made his fatal error when he postulated that someone else visited the pharmacy earlier on the night of the coach's murder. Her attorney speculated about a break-in, a robbery in progress. Coach Thomas had surprised the intruder, he hypothesized.

This statement brought a short, sharp harrumph from the judge, who promptly asked for cross-examination, then closing arguments. Allie's attorney whispered to his paralegal what everyone already knew: the superior court judge wanted a verdict, and fast. Rumor had it the judge hoped he'd be tapped to fill a vacancy on the Georgia Supreme Court. A conviction would underscore his "tough on crime" motto and might cement the governor's appointment.

At the end of the day, the jurors were given instructions, sent away, and sequestered. They'd taken only thirty-six hours to deliberate. Now they were due back in five minutes.

Inside the courtroom, Allie's palms were wet with sweat. She hadn't slept in days. Her parents sat behind her, stiff and pale. Her mother's eyes had been red-rimmed for weeks. Her father lost twenty pounds. Caroline waited in the hallway with Emma.

After talking to her mother about her daughter's tender emotional state several weeks before, Allie insisted Caroline not visit the jail—and be kept away from most, if not all, of the courtroom drama and mudslinging.

Today, though, the verdict would be read. Caroline needed to be close by, Emma argued. Today Allie might go home. And in the end, Allie acquiesced. Caroline could wait outside.

Allie didn't say the rest. Today she might also face years in prison.

Inside the courtroom, Allie focused her gaze on the rich, dark wood grain of the jury box, following the swirls and knots. She reminded herself to breathe as her fingers twisted together under the table. Her lawyer, equally nervous, shuffled papers and cleared his throat.

A door opened and the judge walked in. With a collective shuffle, everyone pushed back chairs and stood up. He motioned "be seated," and gestured for the jury to enter the room.

As the jurors filed in, taking their seats one by one, an uncomfortable silence ballooned around the room, filling it with hot, still air.

Allie swallowed, trying desperately to read faces and minds. No one looked at her. She was invisible.

"Have you reached a verdict?" the judge asked.

"We have, Your Honor," answered the first juror, who stood up. He held a folded piece of paper, which he spread with his fingers. "We the jury, find the defendant, Allison Marshall . . ."

Allie closed her eyes.

". . . guilty on all counts."

THIRTY-THREE

EMMA

2016

After Allie's trial and sentencing, Emma had done everything possible to keep her life quiet. She'd created a nice little web design business for herself, built up a solid client list, saw her parents every day. Emma took care of her niece without fail.

Her life was normal. No complications. No real relationships, save the one broken engagement. Everything adhered to a schedule and was planned out, until Allie came home. Now her life felt like the loose stitches in the hem of a dress. One pull on the right thread, and everything was going to fall apart.

Emma rubbed her lip and sat up straight. She had been staring at the same web page for an hour, the piping-hot cup of peppermint tea she'd made an hour ago now ice cold and untouched. The client had her on a tight deadline, and she couldn't manage to get anything done. Photos appeared grainy and uneven, graphics refused to load, and the suggested font for the website had somehow escaped her, like runaway insects fleeing certain destruction.

With a gentle movement, she pushed away from her desk and slid her keyboard away, the power button almost out of reach.

Emma's thoughts gnawed at her mind like tiny, jagged teeth. She rubbed her temples and pressed fingers under her arched brows.

Questions pounded her brain, hammering away at the security and anonymity she'd cherished for so long. What were the odds that her niece would end up meeting Dr. June Gaines? Out of the entire nursing home, Caroline got assigned to this particular floor?

She listened for any sounds from her niece's room.

Tonight Caroline had gone to bed early and didn't even play one of those depressing Druery songs. Not one. All of the talking, the discussion about June Gaines and her mother especially, had likely worn her out.

Emma poured a generous glass of red wine, eased the back door open, and settled into the nearest lounge chair. She put the rim to her lips and took a long drink. After a few minutes, Emma felt the warmth of the alcohol spread through her chest.

Caroline extrapolated all ideas about her mother to the negative, decided to jump to conclusions after Emma had begun talking about Allie's pregnancy. The abortion, the adoption—none of it was close to being true, but if those were Caroline's perceptions, she wasn't about to correct them.

Emma sipped her wine, propping up her head on the palm of her hand. She glanced toward Caroline's room. All of this was necessary. The questions. The tears, the doubt.

Otherwise, without the barriers in place, her niece might open a window, give an inch, and allow Allie to slip back into her life. Emma resolved, then and there, to double her efforts to ensure Caroline's affection. They would plan a girls' spa day; she'd suggest a trip to the Florida Keys, a place Caroline had mentioned she'd always wanted to visit. Emma would buy Caroline the new tablet she'd been eyeing and take her clothes shopping. All things Allie couldn't do.

Buoyed with confidence in her new plan, Emma smiled, rose from her seat, and walked back inside the house. She poured a second glass of wine and drank deeply, letting the sweet flavor rest on her tongue. She tiptoed up to Caroline's room, plastered with posters and haphazard drawings from last year's art class. She slowed by the open door and breathed in the scent of coconut lotion her niece liked to use. Caroline lay snuggled under the thick white chenille duvet, pillows surrounding her dark hair.

Without making a sound, she slipped out her phone, tapped the screen, and pressed the record button as she scanned the room. This recording, and many others, were proof that Caroline was content and adjusted. She slept like a baby; her room was lovely and filled with nice things. She'd heard horror stories of children being carted off to the Georgia Department of Child Protective Services for neglect and abuse. A neighbor, a family member, anyone could make the call to investigate. But with the recordings, Emma felt that no caseworker could ever prove that Caroline wasn't well taken care of and happy.

And Emma didn't only take videos at night—she had started the video collection using bulky cameras to capture Caroline's dance recitals, her first loose tooth, and her first class play. Then Emma worked with smaller devices that fit in the palm of her hand—recording first days of school, soccer games, and field trips.

Her collection spanned more than two hundred recordings over the past ten years of Caroline's life. On evenings that Caroline spent the night with a friend, Emma would start at the beginning, watching every single moment since Caroline was five years old. She knew every laugh, every smile, and every moment on-screen.

Emma smiled to herself, pressed the phone screen to end the recording, and quietly pulled the door closed. She would transfer the file to her computer and watch it tonight. But when Emma reached the office, she went past it to the back room, where she hesitated at the doorway, her hand gripping the edge of the trim.

Though it was the least-used room in the house, Emma had fashioned it into an eclectic reading area with a slouchy couch, two rounded chairs, several tall bookshelves, and a thick braided rug. Emma had framed Caroline's finger paintings, a few crayon drawings, and a watercolor of the town square's massive fountain. On the shelves, cut-glass bowls sat next to hand-painted china from England. Emma's parents had brought the set back from their honeymoon. Her mother had asked her to keep them, citing the need to downsize, though she and Emma's father hadn't done the first thing to look at a smaller house.

There were black-and-white photos in an art deco collage on the left wall. The center frame held her parents; the most recent were snapshots of Caroline at the beach. She inhaled when she glanced at the outermost rings. Almost every one contained a photograph of Allie and Emma. In high school, on the beach at St. Simons, at a high school basketball game. As she gazed at the images, her lip curled back, her eyes narrowed, and her pulse began to thud loudly, like the urgency of a summer rainstorm beating out a rhythm on a rooftop.

Rising up on her toes, she reached for the frame from the wall. Emma lifted the collage off the wall; it was heavy and unwieldy, and the wire didn't want to release from the hook.

She tugged. Still stuck. She tried tilting the frame. No use. The blood in her hands rushed to her shoulders, making her arms throb and ache. With one last attempt, Emma tugged harder.

The collage came loose and slipped from her fingers, bouncing against the floor and breaking in two. Emma wrinkled her brow and knelt down, listening for sounds of Caroline, now possibly awake from the noise. But the house remained silent.

With careful fingers, she turned over one half of the collage and then the other. The glass was shattered in most of the frames. It was a sign. She should get rid of the entire thing. Emma's stomach twisted, bubbling with anxiety. She glanced around the room. Emma hadn't really noticed it before, but there were reminders of Allie everywhere. Not just the photo on the wall.

There were books they'd shared as children, a jewelry box Allie gave her on her sixteenth birthday, and trinkets from trips they'd taken as teenagers. Seashells from the beach in Hilton Head, "gold" nuggets from Nevada, and an ornate Mardi Gras mask they'd picked out together in New Orleans after Allie's high school graduation.

Why did she hang on to any of it? It gave Caroline the wrong impression. Caroline had already said she wanted Emma to adopt her. The keepsakes conveyed that Allie was still important in their lives, when exactly the opposite was true.

Emma touched the mask, running her finger along the lace edge and over the plume of feathers. She drew in a deep breath, picked it up, and crushed it between her hands. With a soft cry, she ripped at the satin and intricate lace trim.

She would destroy it, and every single reminder of Allie in her house.

THIRTY-FOUR

ALLIE

2016

It had been a week since Allie had paid a visit to Ben's house, and the rejection still stung. She hadn't tried to talk to Caroline again, though she thought about their conversation, and her daughter's challenge, every minute of every day. *Prove it.*

Though painful, she could make sense of Ben's reaction and Caroline's distance. Emma's behavior, though, was the strangest. Her sister remained distant and irritable, making excuses to get off the phone or pleading that she was too busy to talk.

Allie unlocked her front door and let her keys drop into a dish on a table in the small foyer. She set down her bag, flicked on the overhead lights, and pulled off her jacket. The house was starting to feel more like home. She lit a cinnamon candle, letting the spicy scent fill the air with warmth.

She leaned down to scoop the mail off the floor. Allie noticed one additional letter, stuck in the delivery slot. She grabbed it, tossed the junk mail into the recycling, and examined the envelope. No stamp, no address, no postal markings.

Allie glanced back toward the front door. A hand-delivered

note. Who had left it? With her thumb and forefinger, she picked up the letter by the corner and held it over the trash. Whatever it was—hate mail, a nasty note, junk—she didn't want it.

Then, on instinct, she changed her mind. She drew her arm back, flipped over the envelope, and tore it open. She withdrew the paper inside, unfolded it slowly, and read the first line.

"The Lockland Law Firm of Aiken, South Carolina, is representing the parents of Lamar Childree, a rising senior at Feld Ren High School, who died a day after collapsing at football practice."

Allie shivered. It was a press release, dated more than twelve years ago. Childree couldn't have been more than seventeen or eighteen. Poor kid. She bit her lip and read the next few lines.

"The voluntary football practice was held on a sweltering summer afternoon. The players were required to participate in two-hundred-yard sprints, finishing in less than forty-five seconds. Failure yielded additional, more extreme exercises, or being cut from the team.

"While Childree showed signs of heat exhaustion, heatstroke, and dehydration, he was forced to continue running. The coaches did not halt practice. When Childree collapsed, he was rushed to a nearby hospital with a body temperature of 108 degrees. He died the next day."

What did any of this have to do with Brunswick? Coach Thomas? Or her? It was possible that someone had slipped the letter through her mail slot by accident. Except no one made mistakes like this.

Allie read the press release again, more slowly the second time. Press releases were sent to newspapers. TV stations. Journalists. She tapped a finger to her bottom lip and stared out the window. *Was Ben trying to help?*

The doorbell rang and Allie jumped, folding up the paper and sliding it into the nearest drawer. Allie peeked out the window, seeing a familiar figure on the front steps.

"Mom?" Allie opened the door wide, trying not to appear stunned.

Her mother held up a colorful tote bag, looking cheerful, as if a dinner date had been planned for the last three months. "I didn't think you'd mind a visitor. You've been working so much, so I decided to bring you some supper."

The scent of fried chicken wafted toward her as Allie opened the door wide for her mother to step past. "Where's Dad?"

"On the golf course, dear." Her mother made a face as she handed over the bag. "Your father hasn't talked about anything lately but picking out a new five iron."

They both laughed, then her mother's smile fell away.

Allie wrinkled her forehead. "Mom? What is it?"

"I'm sorry I haven't been over here to see you more." Her mother paused. "This has all been so difficult, especially with your dad deciding to retire and sell the practice."

An uneasy quiet settled over the room. "It was pretty quick," Allie agreed. She hesitated. "I was wondering about that," she added, playing with a loose thread on her shirt. "Why all of a sudden?"

Her mother dropped her eyes to her lap. "Oh, honey. With you coming home . . ."

Allie's cheeks flamed red, even though she'd anticipated the answer. If she hadn't grown up watching her parents do everything possible to avoid confrontation and conflict, she might actually be hurt.

Years in Arrendale had prepared her as well. Not seeing her parents on holidays. Never seeing Caroline. No one but Emma visiting month after month. In the pit of her soul, in the deepest recesses of her mind, their absence felt like an admission of her culpability.

Right now it was a thought she couldn't afford to entertain. Not for a moment, if she was going to survive and prove her innocence to Caroline.

"Since you've been back, our friends don't know what to say. Some people aren't even speaking to your father." Her mother sighed. "And you know how that makes him feel."

"Yes," she added in a whisper. Guilt tangled inside Allie, like skeins of silk thread blowing wild in a breeze. She watched as her mother rose and walked to the kitchen. A few moments later, Allie heard a cabinet door open, then water running from the faucet.

Alone in the room, her thoughts wandered back to her father. He had to know that selling the practice would generate gossip. It was almost as if he shared Allie's guilt. Avoiding her only served to stoke the fire, like there was something to hide.

Allie glanced around the room. Was there something to hide? Was he connected to the coach or the sheriff in some way? She rubbed her temples, trying to ease the tension. Her father was a good man, wasn't he? Friendly, helpful. Almost too helpful to people.

"It's going to get better," her mother said, walking back toward the sofa, fresh lipstick on. "You're home, you're okay, you have a job, and that's all that matters," she insisted brightly. "People are going to talk no matter what, right? Next week it'll be something else."

"Let's hope so," Allie said, attempting a smile.

Her mother stopped and glanced out the front window. She swiveled her gaze back to Allie. "I do have to ask . . . and it's just me worrying . . . but are you in trouble?"

"What?" Here was the real reason her mother had stopped over. Dinner served, with an ulterior motive on the side. She wanted information. Allie quit looking over the piles and turned to face her mother. "Why would you say that?"

"Well, it's not me. I heard about that editorial and how Caroline was so upset, bless her heart. Emma said—"

"Mom, I'm fine." Allie cut her off, then softened. "Thank you for asking, though. It means a lot to me."

Her mother shrugged and let her hands fall. "We haven't really talked about it much." Her voice quavered. "But I've always hoped the police would find a clue."

Allie's breath caught. Her lips parted as tears sprang to her eyes. How many years had she waited to hear someone say this?

"I prayed that someone would find proof of what really happened that night." Her mother's voice cracked. "That someone else was responsible—" Her mother broke off, struggling to maintain her composure. Her hand found Allie's and squeezed.

The gesture was comforting, but her mother's words were gold. Allie thought she might die before she heard them.

"Mom, there's nothing I want more."

THIRTY-FIVE

EMMA

2016

Could people go from normal to nervous breakdown status in the span of a few weeks? Without checking scientific studies, Emma's face in the mirror confirmed it. Clumps of her hair fell out in the shower, she wasn't sleeping, and the dark circles under her eyes appeared tattooed in place. She had lost her appetite. Not even the scent of grilled coconut shrimp from her favorite Brunswick restaurant enticed her to stop and eat.

This morning, though it was still early, Emma was bleary-eyed from researching adoption. According to the state of Georgia, Caroline fell into the "Special Needs" adoption category. Special needs children were those who had been in the care of a public or private agency or individual other than the legal or biological parent for more than twenty-four consecutive months.

Emma clicked on the policy and forms, as well as the Division of Family and Children Services contact information, sending each file to the printer. As the white sheets appeared in the machine's tray, Emma reached for an envelope, folded the pages, and slid them inside. She had to do something about this. And soon.

Just thirty minutes before, her sister had called, immediately spiking Emma's anxiety levels.

"Can I help with something?" Emma offered, struggling to keep her tone casual.

"Would you mind if I borrowed your car?"

Emma gripped the phone, her whole body drawing back as if Allie had offered to bring poison as payment. "Want me to drive you somewhere?" she forced out.

"Thanks. No," Allie replied slowly. "It's something I need to take care of myself."

Emma paced the floor.

Allie might be looking for another place to live. Perhaps she was already thinking of moving away. Emma hoped so, but why wouldn't her sister tell her? Emma rubbed her chin absentmindedly. Allie's parole meetings were during the week, so that wasn't it.

Emma thought quickly. She could say no, but didn't want Allie to catch the smallest hint that she was plotting against her. And this little excursion of her sister's ensured time away from Caroline. Better to keep her sister happy and unsuspecting. "So . . . driving is not against the rules?"

"You mean, like a parole violation?" Allie laughed. "No. It's not. I'm sure of it."

"And . . . you don't have to check in with anyone?"

"I check in every week with Gladys. I go in and meet with her next Wednesday. It's not like I'm going to Mexico," she answered. "Gladys cares that I'm working. Not calling in sick. That's what's most important right now."

"If you say so," Emma said, doubtful.

"Are you sure you don't need the car?" Allie asked finally.

Emma drew a breath, mind whirling until it settled on the perfect white lie. "No, it's fine, really," she replied, her voice fighting not to strain. "Caroline and I are walking downtown to grab breakfast and get our nails done," Emma added, picturing Allie's face crumple as she delivered the plan. "You know, the last time we went there, the owners thought Caroline was my daughter. They're so funny."

There was a beat of silence on the phone.

"Well, have a good time," Allie finally replied. Her voice, stretched thin, betrayed the hurt.

"We're just locking the front door behind us," Emma cut in. "I'll leave my extra set of car keys under the flowerpot on the back patio."

Emma hung up and immediately called for Caroline, on edge that Allie would head over any minute. "Ready to go? Get your purse. We'll be late."

Her niece replied with a muffled shout through her bedroom door. She'd be right there, Emma translated. A minute later, there was the sound of footsteps, the smell of baby powder, and finally, the sight of long dark hair piled on top of her niece's head.

They set off walking, with Emma setting the pace double time until they put enough distance between them and the house. Caroline, in flip-flops, struggled to keep up with her aunt's long stride. "Where's the fire?" she quipped breathlessly.

Emma slowed when they rounded the first corner, her own heart beating against her chest. "Oh, you know me. I like to be on time."

Though that was true, Emma's worry stemmed from one place—and one place only. Allie had been different since Caroline's "prove it" challenge had been issued. The determination was back, the slight edge, the focus her sister summoned when honing in on an important task. There'd been an uptick in her energy and how much she reached out to Emma.

Just like the shimmering surface of a serene lake, hiding a hive of activity just below the surface, there was more to this trip. Emma knew it. Allie just wouldn't say.

THIRTY-SIX

ALLIE

2016

Hours later, Allie edged the car into the first little town, along a deserted street. Homes in varying conditions lined the road. She squinted and looked for numbers, then checked her sheet. Twenty-nine.

After a peach house with green trim, and next to a cottage that looked like it hadn't been painted in years, Allie found it. A charming little two-story, blue with white shutters and a narrow front porch. The sidewalk leading to the home was old and worn, like the neighborhood.

She'd done an Internet search the night before and read more about Lamar Childree. There were dozens of articles. The last one mentioned the football staff and the very same Coach Boyd Thomas who had died as she tried to save him.

The first stair creaked under Allie's foot. She jumped at the noise and then laughed at her own nerves. Allie took the remaining steps two at a time.

The mailbox, battered and worn, bore the name Childree in small black plastic letters. This was the place. Allie drew in a deep breath and raised her arm to knock on the door. She hesitated, weighing the privacy of a family who'd lost a son against her own personal void: a daughter who didn't believe in her, a girl forced to grow up without a mother.

Allie almost ran from the porch. But she'd driven this far, done this much. She needed to talk to the boy's parents. Clenching her teeth, Allie rapped her knuckles three times and backed away from the screen door.

The lock clicked a few moments later. The door swung open an inch and a female voice called out, "Who's there?"

"Allison Marshall."

"You selling something?" she demanded. "'Cause we ain't buying." A woman peeked out, dressed in a long terrycloth robe. "We don't have no money. Can't a family have any peace?"

The pain in her voice pierced Allie's rib cage, dangerously close to her heart. She didn't want to dredge up the past, but her need for the truth made her bolder, perhaps a bit reckless. "I'm not selling anything. I wanted to ask a few questions about your son."

Her answer was a door slam, which sent a *whoosh* of warm air at Allie's face. In the distance, the sun glowed huge and orange. The light cast a neon glow on the cars and houses. Allie turned to leave, making her way down the steps to Emma's car.

The woman didn't want reminders. She couldn't get her son back. And she'd be insane to take on the burden of someone else's problem. It would require reliving the tragedy—too much to ask of a mother who would never stop grieving for her child.

"Ma'am." There were footsteps behind her, running, heavy. A hand grabbed her arm.

Allie stopped and turned her head to look at the dark, stocky man who held her. She pulled, stretched, and wiggled against his grip. He didn't release her.

"Tell me why you're here and I'll let you go," he said. Childree's father—it had to be—was weathered, with sinewy arm muscles, and clearly was not taking no for an answer.

"The coach . . . ," Allie began and then choked on her own words. "Your son's coach."

The man released her. He squared his body between Allie and her sister's car. "What's that man got to do with anything? Praise sweet Jesus, he's long dead."

The edges of his face blurred in the fading light. His eyes, charred black, red at the edges, were bottomless. He'd lost as much as Allie. No, more. Childree's son was gone. Buried. They'd had a funeral and said good-byes as best as any parent could to a child. Her soul ached for this father, a man who had expected to grow old enjoying his son by his side. Perhaps he'd dreamed of sipping sweet tea on his porch, his wife by his side, watching his grandbabies play.

Now, she imagined that the future stretched out in front of this man, cold and dark. Empty. A road to nowhere.

Allie pressed a hand to her stomach, steadying her resolve. She might have a chance with Childree if she was honest. If she appealed to him as a parent who had lost so very much. Maybe, just maybe, she could make him understand. "I'm the one who found Coach Thomas," she began, her voice shaky. "That night."

The man's dark face went slack. Disbelief? Pain? Fear?

"I didn't kill him."

Childree stared past her, jaw tightening as she uttered the words. "You have children, miss?"

"I do. A daughter." Allie lowered her voice to a whisper. "She's fifteen and doesn't speak to me. I'll lose her forever if I don't find out what really happened."

The dead boy's father absorbed this, his fists clenched tight together. "Then you know what it's like." Childree's head dropped. "Missing a child."

Allie's eyes stung with tears. "I lost my daughter too." Allie lowered her voice. "It's not the same. Caroline—she's still alive. But she doesn't know me. I'm afraid she might never want to." Her voice broke.

The man drew his gaze back to Allie, taking his time to look her up and down. "And you think the coach had something to do with what happened to my boy?"

"Yes," Allie whispered.

Childree pursed his lips and squinted at the ground. "Tell you what," he said, scuffing his foot on the wooden slats. "Meet me at the corner of Fifth and Wade. Coffee shop there."

"Thank you." Allie nodded and backed away as quickly as she could, practically running to the car. From the corner of her eye, she saw one white curtain move back an inch. His wife watched as she opened the door, slid behind the wheel, and cranked the engine.

"On your way, now," Childree raised his voice. "Go on, go."

Allie found the coffee shop easily, a seventies-style diner with wide Formica tables trimmed in stainless steel and loud, orange décor. She was nursing her second cup when Childree finally arrived. He entered slowly and raised his chin to the man behind the counter. The only other customers, two men in the back, didn't look up.

Childree eased into the booth. "I don't have long," he told Allie. "How do I know you don't want to scam me or my family?"

"Look, Mr. Childree, I'm not trying to cause trouble. I've done my time and don't want to violate my parole," Allie whispered.

Childree motioned for coffee.

"I have a few questions and I'll leave you alone. Please."

The man fell silent when the waitress sidled over and poured the dark liquid from a glass pot, eyeballing Allie the entire time.

When she walked away, Childree placed both elbows on the table and leaned forward.

"What you share with me . . . ," Allie continued. "It could answer questions for other families. Families of other players who might have not suffered like your son, but who have physical injuries or problems that prevented them from ever playing ball again."

Childree nodded. "He was no good. That coach."

Allie blew on her steaming-hot coffee. "There are no words for me to express how awful this must have been for you. I read the articles. Everything I could find. I'm so very sorry."

"Obliged," the man muttered. He reached for his coffee, grasping the handle tight. "I told my son to be careful."

"Why?" Allie asked. "What made you think he needed to be?"

The wiry man tapped his temple. "Watchin'. Listenin'."

"I see."

"He rode those boys at practice. Like dogs."

"Did he . . . hurt them?" Allie asked, her voice barely audible, even to herself.

Childree held up his hand, thick fingers spread toward the ceiling. "I suspect he did. I suspect it more now. There's so much I didn't do. Shoulda seen."

Allie clutched her coffee mug, barely feeling the heat sear her fingertips. This man had been through hell.

"They told me it was heatstroke," Childree said. "And maybe that was part of it. They practiced some insane hours. I told my son a dozen times, 'Boy, you don't have to do this. You can quit.' But, he never listened. And now he's gone. It ain't right, a mother and father burying their child." The muscles in his face twisted with grief, a portrait of loss, of unanswered questions, of agony and helplessness.

Allie heart pounded. "It sounds like, Mr. Childree, you didn't raise your son to be a quitter."

Childree grimaced. "That's right. I taught my son too well. And he died for it."

Allie reflected on the man's version of the story. "What had been happening with him? Anything out of the ordinary?"

"He changed. His mood, his sleep, his activity. Went from a straight-A student to failing exams, getting into fights—"

"Really?" Allie sucked in her breath. Fights, aggression, just like the Wolverine players. Her mind raced with questions and possibilities. "A few fights? How many?"

"I lost count. Every day, bruises on him. I saw his back one day—he'd taken off his shirt after mowing the yard. It looked like someone'd taken a bat to my boy. When I confronted him, he tol' me it was none of my concern, not to worry myself."

Just like Ben's brother.

"He was so angry. And he was bigger, taller. Stronger too. Lamar worked out all the time with the coach's team of trainers. Volunteers he brought in for special clinics. Conditioning, strength training, they even did a self-defense class one time. He was obsessed with doing anything the coach said, like his life depended on it." Childree wiped his forehead.

Allie held her breath, trying to process all of it. "Mr. Childree, you said self-defense? Like with a police officer?"

Childree nodded. "Yeah. You know, Coach Thomas worried about someone jumping them or pulling a knife." His reddened eyes darted from Allie to the front of the diner. "The neighborhoods can be a rough place."

Following his gaze to the rundown building across the street, Allie took in its broken window and peeling paint. "I see." She turned back to face him, clasping both hands on the table. "You don't happen to remember the guy's name? The self-defense class trainer?"

"Nah." Childree took a sip of coffee.

Allie's shoulders sagged as she fought to get her mind back on track. "And how did things go from there?"

"There was one day he was so nervous. Shaky. Knocked over a few things in the kitchen. Could hardly look me in the eye."

"I accused him of taking something. Drugs, pills, something to build up his muscle and speed. He denied it, and then punched a dent in my pickup just to get back at me. He apologized later, but I knew he was hiding something."

Just like the player who'd hit the quarterback. Outright rage, uncontrollable. And no one in the community wanting to look for reasons. Everyone turning the other way.

"Did you say anything to the doctors at the hospital? To the school?"

"Sure." Childree laughed, hollow and bitter. "You know what they told me?"

"No, sir."

"Same thing as Lamar did. My son's coaching was none of my business. The staff said it was my son's fault." Childree pressed a hand to his chest. "They said he didn't drink enough water, that Lamar didn't tell the coaches that he needed a break. As if a child should know better than grown men who are supposed to be looking out for him. My boy wanted to do his best."

Allie swallowed. "I'm sure he did."

Childree covered his face with his hands. "I miss him. Every day. Every single day." He composed himself, brushing away tears with tight fists, one still gripping a napkin. "My son, when he died, he was not the same person. Someone, something, messed with his mind."

"I'm so very sorry," Allie whispered.

"Were there drugs?" Childree looked at the ceiling. "God knows his mother would never admit it. It would kill her to know for sure." He looked at Allie. "But something was wrong. Something was different. He changed, and it started with that man."

THIRTY-SEVEN

EMMA

2016

On her tiptoes, Emma reached for the top shelf. Her fingers brushed against a small, silk-covered box, tied up with yellow ribbon. With a careful grasp, she pulled the container from its resting place and cradled it between her two hands.

All that she had left of her baby.

Emma glanced behind her, as if someone had called out or made a creak in the hallway. There was nothing but the sound of her own uneven breathing. Her palms were damp. She sank into the nearest seat.

With a shaking hand, Emma reached for the ribbon. She tugged and the bow came apart. Emma lifted at the edge of the box. Under layers of tissue paper, her fingers found a small black velvet satchel. With a deft motion, she pulled the cinched edges apart and dropped the contents into her open palm.

Coach's college ring. And the game coin. Emma closed her hand around the cool metal.

He'd confided that his wife thought the ring was ostentatious and gaudy; she'd bothered him about it so much that he'd finally, begrudgingly, put it away for safekeeping years earlier.

Emma, aghast at the confession, had treasured the University of Georgia ring. He'd given it to her two months after they'd begun meeting. She'd worn it on a chain—hidden inside her shirt—until the sight of it made her burst into tears.

One by one, Emma opened her fingers. She released the ring and the coin, setting them on top of the velvet bag. She shifted her gaze back to the box.

A rustle outside startled Emma. She tensed and twisted toward the window. A sturdy branch, choked with green leaves, brushed against the glass. The wind had picked up, and the sky was the color of marble, gray swirled with creamy white and black.

Emma shivered and sucked in a breath, then lifted the rest of the tissue paper away. The porcelain cherub was smaller than she'd remembered, delicate, with details etched and hand painted. The figure was really an angel, Emma decided, and all she had left of her unborn child.

Fate didn't play favorites. Everyone lost someone. Her parents lost Allie, Allie lost Caroline, Caroline lost her mother. Emma had lost twice as much. Her baby and the man she loved. The last time Emma saw him, he was alive.

What had happened in those final moments? What had he said? Was he thinking of her?

Emma could never ask. She could never say.

But with Allie home, every day was more difficult. Her sister wanted answers. Caroline wanted the truth. But the truth was complicated, ugly, and painful. And people were interfering.

Like water in a whirlpool, memories and meaning began spinning, turning faster, until everything and every person seemed sucked into the vortex. It was killing her, one neuron and one cell at a time, like a fast-growing cancer out of control.

Somehow she'd stop it. She had to. And her next target would never even see it coming.

THIRTY-EIGHT

ALLIE

2016

"What's our Friday look like?" Natalie breezed into the office, pulling off her sunglasses and tossing her keys on the desk.

"Pretty busy," Allie answered, holding a copy of the schedule. "The usual suspects—a wound check, routine exams with immunizations, a tumor we need to biopsy. One of our owners called and said her pug's having seizures, the last one thirty minutes ago. I advised her to bring him in—"

"She didn't want to?"

"Not at first. She wanted meds, but I convinced her to come in."

"Okay, good. What about this afternoon?" Natalie asked, pulling a scrub top over her head.

She watched as her boss smoothed her top and ran a hand through her short hair. Natalie's pixie cut was adorable, a look that would cause most people to underestimate how solid and tough the woman was from the inside out.

"This afternoon we're supposed to head out to a few farms," Allie said. "Most are about twenty miles out. It's a nice day. We can tour the stables."

Natalie bobbed her head, tied her scrub pants. "Okay."

Nick popped his head in the door. "Ready to go? Phones are on."

"Thanks, honey," Natalie called after him. It was almost a bellow, Allie decided, looking in amazement at the small woman beside her.

"Impressive," Allie said.

"It's all in the delivery." Natalie winked. "But I've been told I lack subtlety. By more than one person."

"If it isn't broken, don't fix it, right?" Allie replied with a grin.

"Exactly. I like the way you think." Natalie pulled on her lab coat, wrapped the stethoscope around her neck.

As they walked toward the first exam room, Allie hesitated, thinking back to what Lamar Childree's father had said. *Someone, something, messed with his mind.* Allie had been up since dawn mulling over the comment. What had happened at Childree's school also happened at Mansfield Academy. Coach Thomas had lead teams at both places.

But where would the coach get the drugs? His own pharmacy? Was it possible to fold in occasional orders for steroids with all of the other legitimate ones in ways the DEA wouldn't have noticed?

It would be much easier, much safer for his reputation and family, if he had alternate sources. She had a fleeting, terrible thought—a quick glimpse of the coach and Gaines teaming up on her father after hours, threatening to put her dad out of business unless he complied with their demands. Of course it was a long shot, but would it be so crazy?

"Hello?" Natalie waved a hand.

Allie jumped at the sight of fingers two inches from her face. "Sorry." She coughed and reddened. "My mind was somewhere else. I'm back now."

"Well, good." Natalie wrinkled her nose. "Because we need to chat a minute about something."

From down the hallway, Nick's voice interrupted. "Hey, Natalie?" The sound of his footsteps followed, coming closer.

Natalie held up one finger and put it to her lips. "Hey, babe," she replied as her husband rounded the corner and stuck his head into the room.

"The rooms are full," Nick said, glancing from Allie to Natalie. "Anything I can do?"

"Thanks." Natalie smiled at her husband lovingly. "We're just finishing up, okay? Be right there."

"Good deal."

As soon as Nick disappeared, Natalie looked up at Allie. "So, I didn't want to say anything, but Emma stopped by last night."

At the mention of her sister, Allie stiffened. "What? Was she looking for me?"

"No," Natalie replied. "It was odd. Russell and Nick were gone, and I was doing paperwork." She licked her lips. "When I went to lock up, she was standing at the front door."

Mind spinning, Allie folded her arms across her chest, hugging herself tightly. "And?"

"She introduced herself. And said she wanted to talk about you," Natalie said, raising an eyebrow. "She said she was concerned. That you had been acting erratically. That I should be on guard."

The sentences hit Allie like a sucker punch. "Whoa. What?"

"Oh, there's more." Natalie grimaced. She pressed her fingertips to her chin. "I probably shouldn't even tell you."

Despite the sickness growing in her chest, Allie shook her head. "Please do."

"She was talking about adopting Caroline."

Allie's vision went gray, as if a sudden, thick fog descended over Natalie's office. Had she heard right? *Adopting Caroline?* Try as she might, the words would not make sense.

"I didn't know how to respond," Natalie added. "I told her that everything was fine here. Everything." She paused and crinkled her brow. "I also told her that if she was worried about you, she needed to talk to you directly."

All of the air Allie had been holding in her lungs expelled in a rush. What in the hell was her sister thinking? What was she doing?

"I feel awful telling you," Natalie added, "but I felt like you should know."

"No. Really. Thank you for telling me." But it was everything Allie could do not to completely lose it. Her face flushed hot. She wanted to cry, scream, and shake her sister. Instead, she swallowed the defensiveness and anger, struggling not to break down. "I-I'm not a bad person. I—"

"Allie," Natalie interrupted. "I would let you go if I thought otherwise." She cocked her head and scanned Allie's face. "You do, however, need to set that sister of yours straight." Natalie heaved a big sigh and tapped her short nails on the countertop.

A cold sweat settled over Allie's body. "Believe me, I will."

Natalie nodded. "Well, if you're still up for it, we've got a whole day ahead of us."

Allie steadied herself. She could do this. Focus, work. Caroline was in school. She would deal with Emma this afternoon. "Sure. I'm fine."

"Good." Natalie smiled encouragingly. "Let's get to work."

As best she could, Allie pushed aside the shock of Natalie's news and focused on her job. Knowing Emma, she would have some justification, but this went beyond any boundaries of concern.

Natalie and Allie spent the morning in the office and the afternoon visiting three local farms. They admired horses and checked out stables, getting to know the owners and listening to concerns. Allie held back and listened, ball cap and sunglasses on. Natalie hadn't introduced her, just let people make the connection and ask questions if they wanted to.

Allie, happily, didn't get much more than a passing glance. These were families who kept to themselves, who worked hard and wanted good, quality care for their animals. The less said, the better, Natalie decided. And Allie was okay with that.

At the end of the day, Allie didn't bother to change at the office. She slung her backpack over one shoulder and called out a goodbye to Natalie.

During the short walk to her tiny house, she called Emma, only to have her call go straight to voice mail. Allie hesitated and then decided not to leave a message. She needed to cool off. Her sister would answer the phone eventually.

In the meantime, Allie needed to think more about Lamar Childree. She unlocked the door and closed it behind her, dropped the bag on the floor. Allie decided that the next step would have to be talking to someone who'd played at Mansfield. A big star who'd had a bright future, someone who's career might have crashed and burned.

Sliding down the wall, Allie buried her face in her hands. But first she needed to have a good cry.

THIRTY-NINE

CAROLINE

2016

Every day Caroline disappeared into herself a little more. If she could figure out a way to become the Fantastic Four's Invisible Woman, she would have done it weeks ago.

Now, instead of classmates acting like she was a freak, almost everyone ignored her altogether. Jake avoided her, and Maddie was barely ever in school.

What was worse, and underscored it all, was every single instructor acted like she was made of glass. Of course, they meant well, but the pitying looks and glances over her head were enough to drive her crazy. If she heard one more "How are you?" from an adult at the school, she might start screaming.

To blend in even further, every day, Caroline wore the same uniform—a dark skirt and blouse. She kept her hair tied back in a simple ponytail and tucked Emma's platinum heart necklace away in the bottom of her top dresser drawer. She didn't want a single thing getting her noticed or making her stand out.

Today Caroline had been sent to the guidance counselor's office during homeroom. Now, outside the office, head tucked into her chin, she waited as the world moved around her. Phones jingled, students walked in with excuses, and the bell rang while the copy machine whirred, spitting out paper every five seconds.

"Caroline Marshall," someone called for her. "Miss Bell can see you now."

With a small sigh, Caroline got to her feet and slunk into the room. Miss Bell was a light-skinned and very pretty Latino counselor with a musical voice. She was popular with the students, but even her reputation did little to buoy Catherine's enthusiasm.

"Good morning, Miss Marshall. Just so you know, as guidance counselors at Mansfield, we're required to check in with all of our students at least twice a semester," Miss Bell said, opening a file on her desk.

Relief flooded Caroline's system. Maybe this wasn't about Emma calling the school and raising Cain about the red flyers. She lowered herself even farther in the seat.

"So, how are things going?"

Caroline shrugged and looked away. "Oh, okay." She focused on her socks, straightening each one, then fiddled with the laces on her saddle shoes.

"I see that you're taking a full load. All honors courses," Miss Bell added with a megawatt smile. When Caroline looked up and met her eyes, the smile faded. "My dear, some of your instructors have mentioned that your grades have dropped recently." The counselor flipped over a page. "Did you realize that you are close to failing science and English?"

This caused Caroline to flinch. She bit her lip. With the drama at her house, anyone would fail two classes.

Miss Bell cleared her throat. "I'm here to help. What can I do? Would you like the name of a tutor? I can pass a few names on to your aunt."

Caroline tugged at the edge of her sleeve. "All right."

The counselor ran a red nail down a typed list.

Goose bumps rose on Caroline's arms and legs. Emma would not be happy about the failing grades. It would be worse if Caroline didn't tell her first.

"So?" The woman read off a seven-digit combination, Emma's number. "Is this the correct number?"

"No, ma'am." Caroline hated to lie, but the words slipped out before she could swallow them back. She transposed the last four numbers in her head and rattled them off.

"All right, thank you." The counselor jotted the number down. "Will she be home this afternoon?"

"Oh, I don't think so. No, ma'am." Caroline blinked up at her. "Maybe Monday." Another lie. "And I'll let her know to expect your call." Another fib. The lies were starting to add up.

"Monday it is." Miss Bell cupped her chin in one hand. "Caroline, I know things have been hard, but I can't imagine what your life must be like now. All of the scrutiny."

It was all Caroline could do not to race from the room. She prayed the woman would stop talking. "Yes, ma'am."

Miss Bell smiled and patted the desk, smoothing away a particle of dust. "Well, there's one thing I know for sure. And that's when life throws us something really tough, it doesn't last. It'll get better. Really. You have to believe that."

Ugh. *Please let this be over.* It was all Caroline could do to sit with her hands folded and nod every few minutes.

"... suicide." The woman stared at Caroline through her glasses. Caroline only caught the last word of the sentence.

"Pardon me?"

The woman adjusted her chair and inched closer to the desk. "If you're having thoughts about hurting yourself, you need to call me." She handed her card across the desk.

Caroline took it and stuffed it in her pocket. That would make things worse, not better. Did everyone think she was nuts? Did they think she was going to bring a gun to school and shoot up the cafeteria, Columbine style? Then off herself? Drown herself in the nearest river or the bathtub?

She was just sad and confused and a little depressed maybe. Wasn't that expected when someone's mother got out of jail? Then again, it didn't happen every day. Not in Brunswick.

So they were worried about Caroline killing herself. Suicide. Caroline shuddered. She hadn't even given it a thought until this lady brought it up.

"Day or night. My cell phone number is on there. If you start feeling bad, you should also let your aunt know. She can call a psychologist or psychiatrist, someone who specializes in that. You don't have to go this alone."

The bell rang, signaling four minutes until the next class.

"May I go?" Caroline edged out of her chair and turned her head, expectant that she'd be set free.

"I hope this has been helpful for you, dear."

"Very," Caroline lied again and grabbed for the door. "Thank you," she added.

She glanced at the clock and bit her lip. Another eight hours and she'd be at the nursing home. Caroline was going straight to talk to June Gaines. This time she hoped she'd get some answers.

FORTY

CAROLINE

2016

After several hours of carrying trays, helping file charts, and folding blankets, Caroline earned a ten-minute break. With a shaking hand, she poured a glass of orange juice. It was her backup—an excuse—in case anyone asked what she was doing in the room. If Dr. Gaines denied it, Caroline would say that the older woman was the one who was confused.

Ever so carefully, making sure the hallway was clear, she crept across to Dr. Gaines's room and put one hand on the knob. With her heart lodged in her throat, she pushed open the door and stepped into the dark space. The only light came from a lamp behind June's shoulder.

"Someone there?" June's voice was thick and rubbery.

"Just me," Caroline said. "I brought you some juice."

June motioned with one wizened hand for Caroline to come closer.

Sliding one foot toward June, Caroline's knees buckled. She slopped a bit of juice onto her hand, barely feeling the cold liquid. Another step. She was close enough to touch Dr. Gaines. As her eyes adjusted, she realized that someone had taken her to the nursing home's beauty parlor. Her hair looked freshly coiffed, and she smelled of lotion and powder.

The woman tilted her head, examining Caroline. "Emma."

"Y-yes," Caroline stammered. "It's me."

Dr. Gaines's hand shook as she took the glass of juice and brought it to rest in her lap. "How are you, my dear?"

"I'm a little confused," Caroline began. "I'd like to ask you a question."

The older woman straightened at the request, extending her free hand for Caroline to sit close to her. "Please."

Caroline slipped into a nearby chair. "Could you tell me about the night you took care of me?" she asked. "What happened to me? I-I don't remember."

June Gaines slowly closed her eyes. A painful look crossed her face.

"Can you tell me?" Caroline pressed, shifting her eyes to the door. Her heart was hammering so loud she thought the aides at the nurses' station might hear her.

"Poor, poor girl," June Gaines murmured. "He'd hurt you."

Caroline sucked in a breath. "How? Who—"

Outside the room and around the corner, she heard a man's voice. Gruff, distinct. And close by. The voice came closer. *Sheriff Gaines.*

"I have to go," Caroline said, jumping from her seat. "I'm sorry. They need me at the desk." Glancing around, she picked up a spare lunch tray and headed out of the room, only to come face-to-face with Sheriff Gaines and his giant German shepherd in the hallway.

She couldn't turn away.

"Everything all right this evening?" The sheriff's voice, low and gravelly, seemed to penetrate her skin.

"Yes, sir," she squeaked out, glancing up so quickly that she only registered a blur of uniform and dog.

Gaines eased the German shepherd back to let her pass.

"Thank you." Caroline hurried away, keeping her head down. She couldn't help but smell the canine's damp fur and a hint of sea air still lingering on the sheriff's clothes.

As she headed for the nurses' station, she could hear June getting agitated, mumbling nonsense about medical issues. Caroline slowed her steps, listening.

"Now, June, what's wrong?" Gaines said gruffly.

"It's too late, can't save her," June cried out, her next few words incoherent.

Caroline backed up to the wall, hugging the tray tighter to her chest.

"Stop," Gaines insisted, the agitation rising in his voice. "Pull yourself together."

"He'll hurt her again. There's no telling what he might do."

"Shh. Junie, hey now. It's okay," Gaines added softly. "She'll be fine. Don't you worry."

As Gaines's room door closed with a click, a lone tear slid down Caroline's cheek.

There was no doubt now. Ten years ago, someone had really hurt Emma. What had happened? And why wouldn't Emma tell Caroline the truth?

FORTY-ONE

SHERIFF GAINES

2016

The last real conversation Gaines had with his wife had been ten years ago.

It wasn't even a conversation. More like an exchange, short, curt, to the point. He'd blown her off, sent another officer to check on the hospital case when the call came in about Coach Thomas.

Guilt crept up his neck. It happened every time he thought about that night. He wished he could reverse time, go back, and slow it down. Tell her to be careful driving home. Tell her he loved her.

The truth was this: That night, that particular hour, Gaines cared more about his job. He was in a bad mood, and he didn't want to talk about labor, epidurals, or babies. They were both workaholics; they didn't have children—June couldn't, which was fine with him. So she buried herself in her career, which left him as her only friend and confidant. She couldn't talk with the other nurses or staff.

So that part landed with him.

She could go on forever. Her list of tasks and favors was endless because June always wanted to save everyone. She was altruistic and good.

He loved her for it and at the same time it drove him crazy, because it wasn't the real world. Not his world. People got themselves into messes; he could help, but in the end, it was their job to get themselves out.

Especially on nights when there wasn't enough manpower in Georgia to handle all of the crises. Gaines felt a migraine coming on. He craved an icy Coke, a bag of chips, and a fried shrimp po'boy. What he needed was a good night's sleep, an air-conditioned bedroom, and no interruptions.

November 2006

"Lee, I need to talk to you." June's voice was halting, the way she got when she was upset and deciding the best course of action to pursue.

Her voice mail came on the heels of three other emergency calls that had the department in a small uproar. After downing a barbeque sandwich in three bites, Gaines forced himself to take thirty seconds and call his wife. "We're really busy," he told her, his scanner blaring in the background. He cupped his hand over the receiver and motioned for one of the deputies to turn the volume down. "What's up?"

June gave him the details. "I have a patient . . . I think she's in an abusive relationship. She was pregnant. She's all beaten and bruised. Gave the city PD some story about a drifter who attacked her and tried to rape her at gunpoint, but the story doesn't add up. The gal who handled the rape kit said she really didn't find anything—of course it will take awhile for the tests to come back. What concerns me is that she has older injuries, and when I pressed her about them, she stopped talking."

That was his cue to come up with an answer. "Did you give her the number for the women's shelter?" Gaines asked.

"Lee," she sighed. "She won't even admit what's going on."

He cleared his throat. "Anyone who can help out?"

"She has a solid family, but won't let me call them. As an adult, she doesn't need consent for anything."

Gaines took a swig of cold coffee. This was way out of his jurisdiction, but June liked to run cases like this one by him. The women whose lives she couldn't fix.

"Lee, she lost her baby as a result of the attack."

"Oh, bless her heart," Gaines exhaled. "Does the father— whoever he is—know that?"

"I don't think so. No one's shown up here identifying himself as the daddy, but I have my suspicions."

Gaines pulled at his collar. "Do I know the kid?"

June paused. "The man," she corrected firmly. "And, yes, I believe you do."

"Great. Just great." It was all he needed. One of his cronies knocking up some twenty-one-year-old debutante.

As a new 9-1-1 call came over the scanner, the station exploded with electricity. Gaines covered the phone. "Hang on, June." He couldn't listen to his wife and dispatch at the same time. "What's going on?" the sheriff called out to the closest deputy.

One of the men looked up. "Distress call. Someone's collapsed at a pharmacy downtown. Weak pulse, nonresponsive."

"What's the address?"

The scanner blatted the address again. His officer looked to him for direction.

"Sweetheart, listen," Gaines snapped. "I have an emergency. I'll get by there later."

June was silent for a moment.

The sheriff swallowed and gritted his teeth, expecting her to reprimand him sharply.

But his wife replied softly, calling him by his full and given name. "Boyd Lee Gaines . . . it's important to me that *you* look into it," June replied softly. "Now, promise me you'll talk to the girl later tonight. I'll give you her name when you call me back."

The sheriff closed his eyes. "I promise."

2016

Gaines remembered hanging up, swearing under his breath, and grabbing his gear. He'd promised. He'd broken that promise. And it was the last time they'd ever spoken.

June—the living, breathing, full-of-life woman he once knew—was gone forever.

In his office, alone, Gaines sat at his computer, head in his hands. It wasn't often that the grief got to him, but June was so out of control, so agitated today, that he could barely reach her. And for what?

After they'd gotten June sedated, he'd quizzed the nurse about visitors. Who was her regular nurse? Who else had contact with his wife? What about the cleaning people or the dining room staff? Someone, he insisted, was upsetting June.

Finally, one of the aides stopped and inquired about the commotion.

She cocked her head. "There's a high school volunteer assigned to her. She was in earlier and saw Dr. Gaines."

Everyone stopped talking.

Gaines edged closer. "You have a name?"

The aide grabbed a clipboard and shuffled through paperwork. "Christie, Carol . . ." She ran a finger down the page. "Caroline," she chirped. "Caroline Marshall."

Marshall. The sheriff's throat went dry, but Gaines showed no reaction. "Thank you," he forced himself to say, though his jaw was so tight he could barely speak the words. "That'll be all." He nodded his thanks, leaving a bewildered staff in his wake. Outside the nursing home, he'd walked, not rushed, back to his squad car and gotten inside.

Below his calm exterior, the blood in his veins pulsed hard. He grabbed his cell and dialed while pulling out of the parking lot. At the sound of a familiar voice, Gaines barked for the deputy to find an old Mansfield yearbook. By all miracles, a few dusty copies had been located. They were waiting on his desk when he arrived.

After thumbing through the first two impatiently, in the third he located a photograph of one Caroline Marshall, sixth grade. Gaines scratched his head. She didn't look a thing like her mother.

Gaines closed the book and pushed it to one side. With a sharp intake of breath, he pulled his keyboard closer and began typing for any and all records on Allie's sister.

One popped up—a website business run by none other than Emma Marshall. He clicked through the bio page and waited for her information to load. The sheriff blinked at the image and compared the yearbook photo. Caroline Marshall was the spitting image of her aunt.

His fingers hovered over the keyboard before entering the login for the local hospital records. One of his part-time deputies worked several shifts a month in medical records and had passed on access to the system more than a year ago.

Gaines typed in the Marshall sister's name and waited as letters and numbers populated the screen. Emma Marshall had been an emergency room and obstetrics patient. The same night the coach had died.

This had been the girl June was talking about.

Gaines fell back against his office chair, chin in his hand. He rocked back and forth. Marital status: Single. Address: Brunswick.

Place of employment: Her father's veterinary office. He'd thought about the coach having an affair with the younger sister but then assumed, for all of these years, that the coach had seduced Allie Marshall. It made some sense that they'd had a lover's spat, and she'd retaliated with that stupid editorial in the paper. The editorial that could have blown his career to hell.

The sheriff sank farther into his chair. Was it possible he'd had the wrong woman all this time?

Gaines replayed the decade-old conversation with June. After that night, all of the tragedy, the guilt wouldn't let him forget it.

"Do I know the kid?"

June paused. "The man," she corrected firmly. "And, yes, I believe you do."

"Great. Just great."

But oh, it was a stretch.

But it meant that Allie Marshall had an entirely different score to settle. She'd witnessed at least one of Coach Thomas's infamous discipline sessions. And that meant she'd guessed correctly about the steroids—on her own.

Gaines groaned out loud, shaking his head. The older Marshall girl had been set to go to Emory. Medical school. She'd worked in the vet clinic for years, done surgery alongside her father. Handled emergencies.

The sheriff felt the room start to spin.

There was only one way to know for sure.

FORTY-TWO

ALLIE

2016

After borrowing her mother's car, Allie mapped out the route to D'Shawn Montgomery's house. Montgomery was the player who'd lost the big game for the Wolverines in 2006. Allie remembered, because it was the same night Coach Thomas had beaten Ben's brother.

To the best of her knowledge, after getting a scholarship to Clemson, Montgomery played for the Tigers for three years and went pro. Picked up in the NFL draft, Montgomery signed a contract, received a million-dollar signing bonus, and promptly fractured his leg during the first preseason workout. Montgomery came back to Brunswick.

At one time, the living space must have been impressive, mammoth among the smaller cottages that dotted the rural road. But the yard had grown tall, full of straggling weeds and dandelions. On closer inspection, paint peeled from shutters, at least two windows were broken, and the mailbox appeared to have been used for target practice. It lay crumpled, shot full of holes, next to the front concrete steps.

Allie raised a fist to knock on the door. When her knuckles made contact, the sound was hollow and tinny. Music played inside, a television blared. She rapped again, harder this time.

The door opened a few inches, then several more. A tiny woman eyed Allie with suspicion. "You with collections?"

"No, ma'am."

"Good, my husband had to chase a man off with a shotgun last week," she snapped and wiped moisture from her mouth with the back of one hand.

"Is D'Shawn here?"

"What do you want with my son?" The woman narrowed her eyes. "My boy can't leave the house these days. He's on disability."

Allie gulped back her surprise. "Ma'am, I just wanted to talk about his football career."

D'Shawn's mother smiled then, flashing a gold tooth. "Ah, you're a reporter," she guessed. "Must be a slow news day, but that's all right." She beckoned inside. "Don't know if he's up to talking much. He ain't been feeling right lately." The woman shuffled along in her slippers. "But now, a news story, that might put a little spark back in him, yes it might."

Allie thought about correcting her, but decided it would be less trouble to explain later than ask first. Once they realized the connection, it wasn't likely she'd have another chance, considering the mailbox and the husband who chased away unwanted visitors with a shotgun.

She had to ask D'Shawn face-to-face. Watch for his reaction. Caught off guard, he wouldn't have time to lie or make up an elaborate story.

"So, he's had some health problems? I'm so sorry," Allie said, hoping she might explain.

"Health problems. Yeah, you could say that," D'Shawn's mother answered with a sniff and a roll of her dark eyes. "High blood pressure, depression, heart all clogged up. Now the doctor says he got these cysts on his liver."

Allie's brain raced. It all could be related to genetics—unlucky family history—environmental factors, or drug use. His doctor would know, but those records were HIPAA protected. Her best chance was simply to ask.

They walked down a dark hallway and around a corner. The back of the house was brighter. Windows lined the far wall. Allie blinked and let her eyes adjust. They fell on an inground pool, the water's surface smeared with a film of green algae. Overturned plastic chairs and crumpled beer cans littered the yard.

"Here's my boy," the woman exclaimed. "And his daddy. D'Shawn, this here girl wants to talk to you about football. She's a reporter."

D'Shawn, covered with a sheet and a tattered cotton throw, appeared to have been sleeping. He looked smaller and much thinner than in his photos. His dark face had a yellowed cast. There were empty pill bottles and open containers scattered on the tray beside his elbow. The room smelled of mildew and cat urine.

"Where you work at?" The father peered up at Allie through smudged spectacles.

Allie yanked her gaze away to answer the question. "Well, you see, that's—"

"His Clemson days, now that's the story there. You should have seen him on the field." D'Shawn's mother closed one eye to look up at Allie.

"Yes, ma'am," Allie agreed and glanced around for a place to sit. The sofa and chairs were covered with ratty, threadbare blankets. Food containers were stacked on most of the tables. Allie decided she'd stand.

Mrs. Montgomery launched into a speech about D'Shawn's rise to fame, his NFL draft, and the resulting injury that ended his career.

"Mama, stop." D'Shawn's weak voice filtered through the woman's chatter.

Allie turned with a small smile and clasped her hands at her waist. "Would you mind giving us a minute?" She looked at the father first. The man didn't move a fingertip. Apparently he spent most of his waking hours in the same chair.

D'Shawn's mother clicked her tongue and rocked her head back and forth, still mumbling about the Clemson Tigers and her boy. His parents weren't leaving. She needed a crane to burst through the ceiling and pick them up.

It was about to get ugly. Allie needed to take her best shot, grab for information, and go.

"What I wanted to ask, and my question may seem a bit unusual," Allie began. "It involves the high school here."

D'Shawn frowned and looked at his father. "What?" He narrowed his eyes at his mother, still swaying back and forth. "You said Clemson, Mama. What this about high school?"

"More specifically, D'Shawn, your coach in high school," Allie said and decided to dive in. "Did he encourage you or any other players to use anything to make you stronger and faster?"

Silence filled the room.

Allie swore she could hear her own rib cage expanding and contracting. She forced herself to say the word. "Steroids?"

"What you say to my boy?" D'Shawn's mother launched her small frame out of her chair and came at Allie, one wizened arm drawn back to slap her face. "You want me to call the police? What kinda reporter are you?"

Her husband jumped up and held her back.

"Wait a minute." Allie backed up and put both hands up to ward off an attack in case she wriggled free. "I don't want to get anyone in trouble. I was only asking about the coach. Boyd Thomas."

"The same man who got hisself killed?" the father asked. His wife stopped struggling.

Allie nodded.

"He got a scholarship for my boy, full ride to college," the man added. "All them boys woulda done anything for him. Ain't that right?" He looked over at his son for agreement.

D'Shawn stared at his hands. He hadn't moved or said a word.

"Son, answer your father. He asked you a question," the mother said in frustration.

Allie tensed and scanned the former player's face for clues. He was holding back, she thought. He knew something. But his parents weren't helping.

"A player from another school died," Allie explained. "Same coach. Different high school. It was before he came to Brunswick. The boy's father thinks he was given steroids."

D'Shawn's chin lifted, defiant. "I don't know about no kid dying. Could be true, maybe not. What I do know is about me. I used to be a star. I used to run the forty in 4.6 seconds. The NFL drafted me. I was on my way." He pounded his chest with one fist and then let his hand drop. "Now all I got is a disability check and doctor bills. What do anyone care now?"

D'Shawn's mother murmured under her breath. Her husband rubbed his chin.

"I care," Allie said.

A look of realization came over the father. "You there, what your name? You're not from the paper." He released his wife from his grasp and came toward Allie, his face angry.

"D'Shawn, please," Allie said and threw a hopeful glance at him. "Can we talk, just the two of us? I can explain everything."

"You're the one who killed him," the father accused.

"I did not," Allie said, keeping her voice steady.

The husband jabbed a finger at the front door. "Get out, right now, and take your trouble. We—my son—he been through enough."

Allie stared at D'Shawn. "Please."

The former football star averted his eyes but moved his jaw side to side, thinking.

"D'Shawn—" Allie took a step backward, then another. "What did he give you?"

"He had a cabin where he kept stuff," he muttered.

Allie's heart nearly jumped out of her chest.

"What?" D'Shawn's mother exclaimed. "That's nonsense. We would have known about that." His mother rushed to his side and sank down, clinging to his arm. "Don't say another word, baby. Your mind's not remembering right. She's just trying to twist this all around, put ideas in your head."

D'Shawn's voice sharpened. "Coach Thomas? He made up Wolverine Juice. That's what we called it, anyway," he added. "Then . . . he got better stuff. Serious gear." His head fell back against the cushion.

"Sweetheart," his mother pleaded.

Better stuff. Serious gear. Allie's skin tingled as if someone had dumped a handful of ice down the back of her shirt. "Mrs. Montgomery," she tried to get her attention. "Please let him tell me. I really need to know where it came from."

D'Shawn's father took her elbow. "You leave or we're calling the police." He motioned at his wife. "Call that 9-1-1 anyway."

At the threat, D'Shawn began to laugh. "Yeah, a lot of good that'll do." He chortled and covered his face with his hands, then started coughing. His body vibrated with the force.

Why was he laughing? What else did he know? His mother rushed from the room.

"You see what you've done?" The father wrapped his huge hand around Allie's arm and dragged her toward the front of the house.

"I'm sorry," Allie tried to murmur.

He yanked open the door and shoved her outside. "Get out."

In the dark, Allie almost lost her balance on the steps but managed to stumble away. D'Shawn Montgomery's father stood in the open doorway, looming. "Don't you come back, you hear?"

FORTY-THREE

SHERIFF GAINES

2016

Though his mind was on Coach Thomas and the Marshall family, when the call came in from D'Shawn Montgomery's father, Sheriff Gaines grabbed it on the first ring. The families of current and former players had precedence and required personal attention.

Deputies knew the drill. They had strict instructions to run all calls by Gaines, whether it was a lost dog, a speeding ticket, or a noise ordinance violation. Whether he could make the issues disappear or not, his involvement mattered. It was the appearance of his concern that garnered loyalty from families in Brunswick, and of course reelection.

When his deputy explained that Allie Marshall had been to the Montgomery home, the sheriff began to sweat in his air-conditioned office. Learning the sketchy details sent pure adrenaline coursing through his veins.

"I'll take care of it," he barked at his officer, who stepped out of the way. Chief sat up and growled at his harsh tone. Leading the dog by his leash, Gaines stormed from the building.

His tires squealed as he rounded the curves, the speedometer hitting seventy as he raced out of town. By the time he pulled up, a small crowd had gathered in front of the Montgomery home. There was no sign of Allie.

Tall weeds rapped and brushed against Gaines's pant legs as he walked toward the group. The arguing and talking abruptly quit as he stepped into the circle.

"Sheriff." D'Shawn's father greeted him with a handshake. "Sorry to have bothered you with this."

"Where is she?" Gaines asked, breathing hard.

"Gone," he answered, his face darkening. "She left when I told my wife to call you."

Head spinning, fists balled, Sheriff Gaines evaluated the possible charges he could throw at Marshall. Trespassing wouldn't work; his wife had invited her in. Harassment was unlikely to stick because she'd only been there once.

Gaines thought about disorderly conduct. Allie's parole officer would bite on that. It was only a misdemeanor, but it put her on shaky ground. Gladys would have to send her back to Arrendale—or at least a medium-security lockup—while the case was being investigated.

"Gentlemen, could I have a word with the Montgomery family?"

A few of the neighbors frowned, then wandered away across the street. Another raised a hand and motioned for the father to call him before crossing into the next lawn.

"It's okay," the father said to the remaining three men. They nodded and headed down the driveway, heads bent in muted conversation.

The sheriff spread his feet apart, looped his thumbs in his belt, and faced D'Shawn Montgomery's father. "Tell me what happened. Does your boy want to talk? Your wife?"

"No. They're resting. The wife thought she was some kind of reporter. She came in, real polite, talked awhile, and then asked D'Shawn flat out if he'd ever used drugs in high school."

Gaines's heart spasmed. He fought the emotion churning inside his chest. "Drugs?"

"Steroids," he answered. "That Coach Thomas gave him."

Gaines kept his gaze level. His eye wanted to twitch, and he rubbed it hard to keep from letting Montgomery see he was as nervous as a jackrabbit. "And?" he prompted.

"He didn't use anything. D'Shawn didn't use anything," the boy's father repeated, almost as if he was convincing himself.

The sheriff exhaled all of the air from his lungs. "Well, of course not." His chuckle came out flat and cold. "I can call Allison Marshall's parole officer right now."

Montgomery considered this. "Appreciate that. But, you know, we don't need no media circus. D'Shawn has that heart condition. His mother's upset. Her nerves."

At the mention of Montgomery's wife, the sound of a female voice floated out the door. Someone needed help; it wasn't clear whether it was the son or his spouse. There was so much more Sheriff Gaines wanted to ask, but it was clear the family had been through hell.

"Just say the word if you need anything else." Gaines gripped Montgomery's hand. It was a real shame. The way things had turned out for D'Shawn Montgomery. NFL draft picks, nine times out of ten, spent the cash right away. It was a given, like six-year-old kids with a credit card in Toys R Us. There was no on/off button, no stop switch.

D'Shawn had blown that chance all by himself.

And aside from Allie Marshall interfering at what seemed like every turn since she'd been out on parole, there'd been very few problems in Brunswick with former players. The boys after Coach was gone—the ones with big talent—they knew the drill, knew the risks, and wanted the NFL dream like every other kid from Georgia.

The sheriff straightened his tie and got back into the cruiser, taking one last look around the neighborhood. As he cranked the engine and began to drive, Gaines thought back to the last conversation he'd had with Boyd Thomas. The last time he'd seen the man alive.

November 2006

Gaines had been worried about the team's kicker, Kyle Clossner, the brainy senior with a full academic scholarship to Stanford.

It was November, and he'd noted a shift in the boy's demeanor. He'd recently broken up with his girlfriend, cut class the week before, and arrived late at practice. After the coach sent him to run laps as punishment, everything spun out of control.

Clossner's timing. His rhythm. After a third fumbled play, Kyle knocked over a water bucket, ran off the field, and reportedly slammed his fist into a locker. Gaines saw the dent.

After fuming for hours, Gaines confronted Thomas. The sheriff found him at the pharmacy, alone, rearranging stock.

"I thought you said you were done," the sheriff hissed.

Coach paused coolly, holding matching boxes of Motrin. "I never agreed to that."

Crossing his arms tight, the sheriff edged closer so that the coach would have to look at him. Don't give Clossner any more," he'd said.

"No one's forcing those boys." Coach Thomas shrugged. Always so cocky. Certain. And now dismissive. "They have a choice."

"Listen to me," Gaines exploded, clearing the entire shelf of medicine with one sweep of his arm. In an instant, the sheriff grabbed Coach by the collar and slammed him to the wall, pressing his forearm hard into the man's throat.

He'd had enough.

2016

Gaines pushed down the accelerator, urging the squad car faster, as if the speed could help him escape the memories. As the live oak trees whooshed by in the fading sunlight, he attempted to channel the philosophy he'd once tried to live by: *What's done is done.*

Gripping the wheel, the sheriff focused on the positive: Those Mansfield boys did get a stellar season and a whole lot of press for a small school. The community reveled in a much-needed celebration after every win. Brunswick was in the spotlight once again, the team creating the stuff of legends.

The sheriff grimaced. He should be talking about those glory days over coffee at the local diner. Out on the sidelines during practice, lending tips to the coaches.

But when someone was scaring up ghosts from the past, essentially raising the dead, a hell of a lot of good the 2006 season did for Gaines. Or Coach Thomas, six feet under.

FORTY-FOUR

CAROLINE

2016

"How about the library?" Caroline suggested to Russell. "It's quiet there. And I have to drop off some books. They open in about twenty minutes."

Russell cleared his throat. "Are you sure you're okay?"

"I'm okay. I swear. But we need to talk in private," she whispered into the phone.

"I'll be right there," he promised. "See you in about five minutes. Look for me out front, by the steps."

"'K," Caroline said and hung up. She sat for a minute, thinking. Emma was working and she didn't want to disturb her or risk her saying no. She took a Post-it note out of the drawer and wrote, *At the library* and the time, then, *Love, Caro.*

With the note pressed to the middle of the kitchen table, where she was certain Emma would see it, Caroline gathered up her three library books, slipped them into her bag, and eased out the front door. The lock clicked in place behind her.

With barely a sound, she stepped onto the sidewalk and turned toward downtown. The library was a ten- or fifteen-minute walk. She passed the fire department and the post office, as well as a few law offices with shingles hanging on posts. All reminders of her mother.

The jury said she had killed a man. They believed it. They'd sent her away.

Caroline frowned and wandered closer to the steps of the library. The long, low brick structure was one of her favorites, with its tall, mirrored windows and high ceilings. She could get lost there, hide out in the stacks. It made her feel safe and secure.

"Hey," a voice called after a loud car honk startled Caroline.

She whirled at the sound, clutching her books to her chest. "Whoa. Give me a sec." Caroline exhaled, opened the library drop-box, and slid the books inside.

Russell waited as she walked back to him. His hands rested on the wheel, a lock of dark hair falling over one eye. "Jump in. Let's talk in here." He leaned over and pushed open the passenger-side door.

"Um, okay." She walked closer. "What kind of car is this?" Caroline sniffed at the vinyl and leather scents. The vehicle was older, bright white, with a squared-off body style.

"This baby's vintage." Russell winked and stretched out his arm and ran a hand along the dashboard. "Don't even make them anymore."

Caroline didn't know whether to giggle or be impressed. She slid inside and buckled in, closing the door behind her. "What is it?"

"Volare. Chrysler made the last ones in 1980. This was my grandfather's. He had it in Florida until he died a few years ago. It's really my dad's, but he says I'll get it"—Russell signaled and eased out into the road—"if I'm responsible and take care of it."

"Right."

"I've got a limited work permit right now. My dad has me running a few errands for him. It's kind of like probation for a driver's license."

Caroline blinked. "Um, should I be worried about driving with you?"

"No. Remember how I told you we lived outside of Atlanta?" Russell said. "Well, in Buckhead, I got hooked up with a pretty wild bunch of older guys. You know, crazy rich kids who like to drink and party."

She bit her lip and shrugged.

"So, anyway, I got a DUI."

Caroline widened her eyes. "Oh my."

"Yeah." Russell clamped his hand on the wheel. "I've done two driving schools, rehab, almost three hundred hours of community service, and paid huge fines." He glanced over. "So my parents offered me a deal. Move away for my senior year, stay out of trouble, and they'll pay for PT school if I get in."

"Wow." Caroline held his gaze, then turned and pointed at the black device with a spiral cord near the steering wheel. "So, what's that for?"

"It's an ignition interlock thing that I have to breathe into," he said. "It makes sure I'm not drunk. If it measures that I am, the car won't start."

"Couldn't I breathe into it for you?" Caroline asked.

"Would you?" Russell frowned.

"Of course not," she answered, indignant. "I was just asking."

"My parents would ground me for life. Or just send me to some camp for terrible kids out in the middle of nowhere. They've found out every single time I've done something stupid."

Caroline settled back against the seat. "Seriously, Russell? I appreciate you telling me."

"I'm not proud of it." He looked across the seat at Caroline. "I would have told you before, but there was never a good time . . ."

"Or I wouldn't listen," she added and smiled.

"That's true." Russell chuckled.

Caroline pressed her palms against her jeans.

"So, what's going on? What happened?" Russell asked. He focused on the blacktop, then turned off at a small driveway to the left. Shaded with trees, the paved road wound up a hill and ended in front of a bungalow-style home.

"O-kay," Caroline said slowly. Was this his house? Was she meeting his parents? Maybe she should have stayed at the library, but it was too late now.

Russell parked and looked over at her. "Let's sit here first. You can tell me everything. If you want to, then we can go inside."

With a sharp exhale, Caroline began talking. She told him about Emma at the dinner table, how she acted when she brought up June Gaines. She told him about the day at school with the counselor and how she was almost failing science. And she explained about going to talk to Dr. Gaines and the interruption with the sheriff.

"You've had a busy couple of days," Russell mused. "No wonder you're freaked."

Caroline sighed and gave him a lopsided grin.

"Let's talk to my mom. She came home early this afternoon and can help us figure out what to do." He glanced at Caroline.

She frowned and gave a quick shake of her head. It was too much for her to carry around. Caroline felt as if she might burst.

"Come on." Russell motioned. "I promise she won't bite."

Despite her reluctance, Caroline followed him up the stairs. Their home was warm and inviting, a lovely bungalow with a wraparound porch, hanging baskets dripping with flowers, and a wooden swing painted white.

Russell waved for her to hurry.

It was perfect. Too perfect. Caroline's body locked into place.

Her life would never be this perfect. His mother wouldn't understand. "I don't know about this . . ."

"Um, it's okay to be nervous," Russell murmured, coming back across the wooden slats. "It's normal."

But this was not a date. They were investigating. And trying to connect pieces of a puzzle. And sticking their noses where they didn't belong. And they could be making everything more of a mess.

Caroline's throat was suddenly parched. Russell's mother was her mother's boss. She didn't know if Allie and Natalie talked, what they talked about, or if any of it was about Caroline. She bit her lip.

This wasn't just butterflies.

This was roller-coaster-just-before-the-big-drop panic.

FORTY-FIVE

CAROLINE

2016

Before Caroline could say another word, a small-boned woman—a miniature version of Russell with shorter hair and a turned-up nose—opened the front door.

"Hey," she said, smiling. "I'm Natalie. How are you, Caroline?"

"G-good, thank you. Nice to meet you," she said, hanging back behind Russell.

"Don't you two want to come in?" Natalie opened the door wider, making room for them to pass.

Caroline held her breath and tiptoed into the room. She watched as Russell's mother took a seat on the sofa and patted the area beside her. Natalie was tiny and bird-like, graceful in her movements. Russell, with his long limbs, was anything but. He collapsed next to his mother, heaved a sigh, and stretched out. "Have a seat," he told her.

Keeping a safe distance, Caroline took the chair close to the window. Her pulse slowed. Natalie wasn't scary. She didn't look at her like she had two heads or was a bad person; she would live through this.

"So Russell tells me you're helping out at the nursing home." Natalie leaned forward and brushed a piece of lint off her leg. "How do you like it?"

Caroline looked at Russell, who smiled. "It's good. I'm getting used to it."

"It's great experience," Natalie said. "And I guess you know your mom is working in our office?"

"Sure." Caroline squirmed at little in her seat.

"She's talented," Natalie commented. "Really talented."

Caroline cleared her throat as she looked up at Natalie Harper. Clearly, the woman really and truly liked her mother. "S-she was going to be a physician," she said in a soft voice.

"I believe it."

In the awkward beat of silence that followed, Russell put both elbows on his knees. "So, Mom, I was telling you that there's this lady at the nursing home—June Gaines. She used to be a doctor and deliver babies until she got into a really bad accident. Now can't remember a lot of things—like stuff that happened today. And she can't work."

Natalie motioned for Russell to continue.

"So, when Caroline goes in her room, Dr. Gaines always thinks she's someone else."

Russell's mother raised an eyebrow. "Like, an actual person? Or—"

"She calls me Emma," Caroline interjected. "That's my aunt's name. My mom's sister."

Clearing his throat, Russell leaned forward and gestured. "Tell my mom what else she says."

Caroline reddened and ducked her head. "Well, she talks about a baby and someone hurting Emma, some other weird stuff. She's just sure I'm Emma, and she talks to me like she knows me." She hesitated, suddenly feeling this was all stupid. Natalie would think they were both silly kids, on some wild made-up mystery.

"And, Mom, Dr. Gaines doesn't do this with anyone else—get all upset—except for Caroline," added Russell.

"Could it be another Emma?" Natalie asked, looking thoughtful. She didn't laugh or seem to think Caroline was crazy. "Or do you look like your aunt?"

Russell considered this and stared hard at Caroline.

"Um, yeah. We do look alike. A lot more than my mom and I do," Caroline said, still nervous. She played with the hem of her shirt. "And I wouldn't care if Dr. Gaines thought I was Emma, but when she starts freaking out and talking about this baby, it's kind of scary."

"Did you ask your aunt about it?" Natalie shifted to look at Caroline straight on.

"I did," Caroline said, shrugging. "She changes the subject or avoids it, kind of like she wants me to think nothing happened." She lowered her eyes. "It's so creepy. It's like whatever happened is happening over and over when Dr. Gaines sees me. And I think that whatever baby she's talking about . . ." Caroline looked at Russell.

"We don't think the baby made it." He finished the sentence.

Natalie winced. "Why do you say that?"

"She told me—Emma—that I should adopt. That there are other options."

Raising an eyebrow, Natalie clasped her hands tighter. "Oh. I see." Caroline watched Natalie's face change from concern to shock as she absorbed the story. "Well, what about this? If your aunt won't talk, you could ask your mother."

Caroline gulped. "I don't even really know my mom."

Thankfully, Natalie didn't defend Allie. "Why not think about reconnecting now? I know she'd welcome the time with you."

Hesitating, Caroline slid her hands under her legs to keep them from trembling. "Did she say that?"

Natalie cocked her head. "You know, I can't speak for her. I can only tell you what I've seen and heard in my office. Caroline, she cares about you. How could a mother not?"

Caroline's eyes began to itch and sting. She never wanted to cry in front of Russell, but it would be even worse to start sobbing with both of them in the same room.

"I'm so sorry," Natalie added. "And I think you are well within your rights to ask your mom if she knows what happened with Emma."

Caroline pressed a hand to her lips, almost not wanting to say the words. "I-I can't."

"Can't or won't?" Natalie asked in a soft tone. She didn't seem like she was really looking for an answer. She was playing devil's advocate. She looked at Russell and reached over and patted his knee. "Tell her what happened with you."

"She knows about the DUI. And the community service and fines and restrictions."

"Tell her the rest of the story," Natalie prompted him.

The rest? Caroline sat up straighter.

Russell ran a hand through his hair and smoothed it over his forehead. "The bad part, right?" He grimaced and turned to face Caroline. "So I ran with this group of older guys in Buckhead. They all had money; most of them drove Mercedes and BMWs. They were pretty crazy, always drinking, drag racing, stealing stuff, just really nuts."

A wave of surprise swept through Caroline's body.

"This one night, one of them asked me to get some beer," Russell added. "I knew this guy, so I had him buy it. We went to the park, finished off a few cases. We shouldn't have ever gotten back into my friend's Expedition, and for some reason, I was driving." Russell paused and swallowed. "The plan was to pick up some girls."

His mother coughed and frowned.

"Prostitutes." Russell's face turned deep red. "It wasn't my idea, but I didn't back out either. So we picked up three girls, took off for one of the guy's houses. On the way, this huge bus crossed the highway. When I veered out of the way, my car flipped. The Expedition blew a tire, spun out, and rammed straight into another car."

Caroline blinked, wide-eyed.

"One guy died. Another broke his back, and I was pretty bruised up," Russell said. "I was in and out of it for days." Russell paused, staring at his shoes. "What was really terrible—what my mom wanted me to tell you—was when it was all over, the families of the two guys sued me and my parents. They told the police I'd coerced everyone to drink, that it was my idea to pick up the girls, that I'd paid for them too. Everyone had the same story. Except me."

Natalie interrupted. "We had to hire a lawyer and fight it. It took time and a lot of money. But those friends—we can't even call them that now—wanted Russell to take the fall for everything. The death of that boy, all of the injuries."

"What happened?" Caroline was almost afraid to ask.

"The other kids had been in trouble before. Drugs, vandalism, all juvenile offenses. We didn't know that at the time, but with some digging, it came out. That tipped off the judge that this group might not be telling the whole truth." Natalie pursed her lips. "Of course, Russell had just gotten a DUI, so he wasn't any bright, shining example."

"Oh, wow," Caroline breathed.

Natalie nodded. "It took a lot of trust and time, but we got through it." She steadied her gaze on Caroline. "That's why I think you should talk to your mom. This is your life and your family.

Your mother and sister are adults. They can handle some hard questions."

"Okay." Caroline whispered the word. "Even the part about Dr. Gaines?"

"Absolutely," Natalie agreed. "She *thinks* you're Emma. Maybe it's a totally different person and you just look like her, maybe not. But you'll never find out if you don't ask."

Right that moment, Caroline wasn't sure what she wanted. She felt as if she'd stumbled onto a ticking bomb and she was the only person who could try to detonate it. One false move, one wrong clip of the wire, and everything around her would explode.

FORTY-SIX

ALLIE

2016

Allie knew she'd gone too far with the Montgomery family. She might have jeopardized everything. His father had likely called the sheriff or one of his deputies to complain.

She'd have to work fast. What else did D'Shawn know? Had his mother not intervened, Allie thought he might have kept talking. Whether it was football or genetics, something went horribly wrong for a player with so much potential. In her mind, she reexamined his demeanor, the way his muscles didn't respond, the slur of his voice when he answered questions.

Allie took out a thick pad of paper and made a list. Her pen moved over the lines with precision. *Lamar Childree, D'Shawn Montgomery, Sheriff Lee Gaines, and Coach Thomas.* Then there was the mention of the cabin. Did such a place exist?

Allie rubbed her bottom lip, pondering the other options. A sharp rap at the door interrupted her concentration. Allie got to her feet, shaking out the numbness in her legs. She glanced at the clock. It was getting late. A peek outside showed the outline of a man's shoulder. In the disappearing light, the edge of the fabric looked pressed and neat. *Her father?*

Allie held her breath, unlocked the dead bolt, and eased the knob to the right. As she cracked open the door, she saw that it wasn't her father at all. Sheriff Gaines stood waiting on the front porch.

Startled, Allie grabbed the wooden door frame for balance. She half expected the man to grab her and pull her into his waiting patrol car. His German shepherd waited by his side, ears perked at attention, eyes bright in the flicker of the streetlights.

Gaines's brow furrowed with several etched lines. Despite his clean-shaven, shined-boots appearance, there was something about his frame that indicated a deep and thorough exhaustion.

"Miss Marshall." Gaines cleared his throat. "May I have a word?"

Allie forced herself not to tremble. The last one-on-one encounter she'd had with the man had been a decade earlier. That night she'd ended up in jail. She wasn't going to throw the door open, welcome him in, and make a fresh pot of coffee.

"Of course," Allie managed. The air seemed to have been sucked out of the room with a vacuum. She willed the phone to ring or her mother to stop by with an emergency. Anything to get this man off her front doorstep.

Gaines cleared his throat. His eyes, bright and piercing, met hers. "I need to warn you that you're on some shaky ground."

Allie lifted her chin and looked into his eyes. *She would be polite*, she told herself. She would listen.

Gaines stepped closer. "Be careful, Miss Marshall." He gave her a knowing look. "You're poking around where you shouldn't be," he began. "Upsetting innocent folks."

"But, his wife let me in."

"You weren't there as a reporter." Gaines curled his upper lip. "You didn't tell the truth."

"I did, eventually, explain who I was." Allie said the words weakly.

"After you'd tricked them," the sheriff snapped. "They could file a formal complaint." Gaines leaned closer. "They're thinking about it right now."

Guilt washed over her body. Allie tried her best to think of an explanation, an excuse for not telling the truth. She wasn't a liar, or a manipulator, she had gone with honest intentions, but now she had done something that proved otherwise.

"Your probation officer, Miss Williams, would certainly be interested in this little situation." Gaines almost smiled. "I haven't called her yet. But that depends."

"On what?" Allie said, cold creeping down her arms and legs.

"On your cooperation," he replied, glancing behind him at the empty street. Gaines didn't move any closer. He kept a safe distance, waiting for her response.

Allie couldn't help her reaction. Nausea welled in her stomach, churning at the thought of courtrooms, lawyers, and jail. Another sentence. She hadn't done enough to warrant that. She could explain, apologize. This time, she took a step, narrowing the space between them. Allie moved her hand and caught the doorknob, gripping it with all of her might. "Please, if you're not going to charge me—"

Gaines's hand shot forward and caught the edge of the door. "I'm not done."

Allie flinched, blinked up at the man who had ruined her life.

The sheriff lowered his voice. "Back off. Quit digging around in the past."

Anger welled up in Allie. Suddenly, she wanted to slam the door. She wanted to yell and scream and tell him to leave. "And what if the past keeps popping up, Sheriff? Like flyers at my daughter's school?"

"You're just making things worse for yourself." Gaines narrowed his eyes. "If you insist on stirring up trouble, upsetting innocent folks in this town, there's nothing but heartache ahead." He folded his arms. "Is that what you want for your parents? Disgrace? Public humiliation? That's quite a legacy for your own child too."

"Leave her out of this," she said through gritted teeth. "And stay away from her. She's done nothing."

"Watch yourself, Miss Marshall," the sheriff cautioned.

"What I want . . ." Allie took a breath. "Is for my daughter to be safe. I want my family back. And I want my name to be cleared."

Gaines swelled up, indignant. "All of the evidence led to you. You'd been drinking. There was blood on your clothes. Your fingerprints. Skin under your nails. A murder weapon. I did my job."

"The killer's still out there, Sheriff," Allie murmured. "And the truth is going to come out, even if I'm not the one who finds it." She stared into his eyes, waiting for a flicker of fear, a tiny look of worry to cross his face. Anything that would indicate he'd been responsible for leaving Coach Thomas to die.

The sheriff didn't flinch. Allie's throat began to close. "It's true that I didn't care for the coach. And publishing an editorial wasn't the best way to handle what I believed was true—what I still believe. I-I was young and thought I knew everything." She swallowed. "But someone took his life—and left his family without a father. His wife without a husband."

Gaines stared back, stone-faced. "And he was having an affair."

Allie stopped, the air suddenly still around her. "What? Who? Are-are you accusing me?" she sputtered in disbelief. "If you're so sure about that, why didn't this come up during the trial?"

"No. I'm not accusing *you*," Gaines replied evenly.

Covering her eyes with her hands, Allie tried to stop the room from spinning. She needed Gaines to leave. She needed to shut and lock the door behind him. And never speak to this man again.

"What do you remember about that night?"

Everything, Allie wanted to scream. But she waited a beat, telling herself to be calm and answer the question. She didn't need to make things worse. "All I was doing was looking for my sister. She was stopping for something at the grocery store and coming straight to my house. When she didn't show up, I got worried and went looking for her."

"And?"

"She was in the hospital," Allie replied, her tone softer.

"I know," Gaines answered. "My wife was on call. She told me a girl had come in who was in pretty bad shape."

June Gaines had taken care of Emma?

"Well, of course . . . She was attacked," Allie said, hugging her arms to her body. "But you already know all of this. Some drifter who tried to rape her in the park." She hesitated. "And no one ever found him."

"There was no drifter." Gaines tightened his jaw.

Allie stopped. She frowned, trying to make sense of what he was saying.

"Listen to me," the sheriff continued. "According to my wife, your sister had been knocked around pretty badly. She had older bruising—meaning this wasn't the first time. Apparently the nurse who did the rape kit didn't think it was sexual assault."

No drifter? No attempted rape? Allie dropped her arms to her sides, as if they suddenly weighed a hundred pounds each. "I-I don't get it. Why are you telling me this now?"

"Because you're interfering where you don't belong. Again." Gaines frowned. "And because you evidently don't know your sister as well as you think you do. I guarantee there's more to her extra-curricular life than meets the eye."

Allie's lips parted, but she couldn't speak. Her head churned with jumbled thoughts. Her sister, according to the sheriff, was a liar who'd been in a long-term abusive relationship?

No. She wasn't falling for it. Gaines was a master manipulator, trying to throw her off her original plan. She was looking at a cold-blooded killer. A man without conscience. A psychopath deluded enough to convince himself someone else had committed the crime. He actually believed that threatening her parole, along with casting doubt and suspicion on Emma, would take Allie's focus off the sheriff. Allie bit her lip. Gaines was so wrong.

"I'm done here," the sheriff said flatly. He began to walk away, the dog following close to his pant leg. Then Gaines turned and looked over his shoulder. "Stay away from D'Shawn Montgomery and his family. I hear they're saving you a spot at Arrendale. Just in case."

FORTY-SEVEN

ALLIE

2016

Allie sank to her knees and curled up tight, wrapping her arms around her calves. She couldn't make herself small enough. The brave façade she'd put up for the past thirty minutes vanished. Sheriff Lee Gaines had rattled her like a category-five hurricane.

Now there were even more questions, the first of which shook Allie to the core. If her sister wasn't sexually assaulted or raped, the only reason an obstetrician would be taking care of her was because Emma was pregnant. She pressed her knuckles to her bottom lip.

Who was the father, though? And if she was getting hurt, why keep it a secret from her family? What really happened that night?

Allie ran her hands down her face. There *had* been a guy. Someone Emma was seeing.

She gulped. Gaines was certain the coach was having an affair.

Could it have been her sister? Her sister—who had just confessed to her employer that she wanted to *adopt* Allie's own daughter. What was Emma doing? What was she thinking?

Running her hands through her hair, Allie began pacing the

room. It couldn't be. *It couldn't*. She'd confront Emma. Have her swear the affair wasn't true. Make her explain about the conversation with Natalie.

There was no other way around it. Allie snatched up her cell, scrolled down, and touched Emma's number. The line connected and dumped her straight into voice mail. The sound of her sister's greeting was simple, direct, and practiced.

She cleared her throat. "Emma, I need to talk." Allie clenched her teeth, then tried to relax her jaw.

The recording cut off.

"Come on." Allie hit redial and then waited through the menu and options. When the voice mail beeped, she continued. "Listen, call me back when you get this. The weirdest thing happened. Sheriff Gaines came by, asking about you. I just want to know what really happened—that night." She moved her finger to end the call, but then stopped. "I care, Emma. I really do."

Allie hung up and paced the floor. Uncovering a few more details about the past wouldn't necessarily clear her name. It might provide some answers to the Childree family, though, and many like them. She might also right some wrongs about the coach and his seemingly bulletproof reputation.

She needed evidence—something conclusive—to prove her innocence. To pin the murder squarely on Sheriff Gaines. Whatever it was, wherever it was, felt just outside her grasp.

Allie's mind continued to spin with possibilities. What if the coach was also taking steroids? What if that night when Allie had found him, he'd overdosed, fought with Gaines, and had an aneurism? Could a coroner cover that up? Erase the fact from existence?

If Coach Thomas's blood work showed drugs in his system, she might have a fighting chance. If the steroids were plentiful—enough for every member on the team and then some—why wouldn't the coach indulge every now and then?

She stopped mid-step, remembering *why* the steroids were so easily available. The cabin D'Shawn Montgomery had mentioned. Allie ran to her laptop and with shaking fingers, did a search for property records in Glynn County. She looked for a structure—a house, a shack—everything within a reasonable radius of Brunswick.

Coach Thomas's old house was listed among Allie's findings, recorded as sold about a year after his death. There was nothing else under his name any further back.

Allie rapped her knuckles on the desk, thinking. Distance, time, location. The South Carolina state line was only an hour and twenty minutes away; the Florida border was about sixty minutes. Both less than a morning's drive to a cabin and back.

Then it hit her.

The schools where the coach had worked. Allie dashed into the kitchen, opening drawers to find the regional map her mother had left for her. She unfolded it, grabbed at a few pushpins, and tacked the map on the nearest empty wall.

With careful fingers, she plunged a bright red thumbtack into Brunswick, Georgia. Recalling the timeline she'd scribbled out, she placed the next pin in Cottonwood, Alabama, the location of Thomas's first head-coaching job, which lasted a mere seven months. She placed the next in Live Oak, Florida, the head-coaching job that followed. The third pin went in Aiken, South Carolina, just outside Augusta, Thomas's head-coaching position right before Mansfield Academy.

The triangle, based on the pins, formed a possible target. Outside Douglas, Georgia, in Coffee County, seemed the perfect place to hide a bustling steroid operation. The area was wooded, but not overpopulated. Exactly an hour and forty-minute drive from Brunswick.

Allie hurried back to her makeshift office, pulled her chair toward the desk, and typed furiously. She brought up Coffee County property information, plugged in first and last names.

With a deep breath, she hit return.

FORTY-EIGHT

ALLIE

2016

Allie showered and dressed before dawn, had two cups of coffee before seven thirty, and left a message for Natalie explaining that she wouldn't be at work because a family emergency had come up.

It wasn't exactly the truth, Allie thought as she dressed hurriedly. But she couldn't rest—she wouldn't be able to think—unless she was able to get to the bottom of this new turn of events. A quick call to her parents' house confirmed that she could borrow one of their cars.

"I'll leave the key in the mailbox," her mother added. "I have to run, dear. The ladies from church are picking me up for breakfast any minute."

As they hung up, Allie promised to be back as soon as she could.

Before she left Brunswick, Allie made a third phone call, this time to Ben. With her throat strained, she dialed his parents' house—the same landline number they'd had for years. With any luck, no one except her mother and Ben would know she was gone.

When his message clicked on, Allie began to speak. "Ben, it's me. I wanted to tell you . . . If you left me that information about the Childree boy, thank you. I talked to his father, and D'Shawn Montgomery too. I'm heading out of town to check on a lead." She paused. "If something happens to me, I want someone to know."

Under any other circumstances, a long drive would help clear Allie's mind. It used to be, before Arrendale, that with each passing mile, Allie was able to detach from college, medical school, and worries about Caroline.

Green and brown blurred as branches bursting with foliage and dull-leafed kudzu passed overhead, and Allie checked the GPS while she continued north. She swung a right and then a sharp left onto a dirt road, over bumps and uneven terrain.

Her body tensed with anticipation. The back of Allie's neck stiffened; her shoulder muscles contracted. She'd have to peel her fingers from the grooves in the wheel if she held on much tighter.

All at once, the forest and vegetation opened in front of her. In the bright space, midway up the bark of an oak trunk, the corner of a tin roof poked through.

Allie caught her breath and eased the car forward.

She'd almost missed it.

The cabin, tucked back from sight and overgrown with vines and debris, was easy to overlook. Allie parked, thankful it hadn't rained in the last few days; it would be easy to get stuck in the mud after a storm. She checked her cell phone coverage. One bar.

Allie frowned and pushed the car door open, causing a flock of birds to take flight. After a long glance at the ramshackle building in front of her, Allie stepped out of the vehicle, wishing she had a weapon. If there was someone living here, a homeless person or a pack of wild dogs, she wouldn't have any way to defend herself.

Allie eased her way up the half-rotten porch, each step careful and measured. She closed her fist and pressed it to the closest window, making circles on the pane. The grime blackened her hand as if she'd held it over smoky embers. When she'd cleared a place to look through, Allie cupped her hands around her eyes and leaned closer.

No one had been here in ages. Allie noted the shotgun eased against the corner, another hung on the wall. She saw boxes of ammunition, cans of food on the counter, and a bed. There wasn't any sign of even a makeshift laboratory, not even a pot on the stove or bottles of liquid.

She moved in front of the crooked door, pulled her shirt sleeve down over her fingers, and rested her hand on the knob. Allie could leave. Turn around. Go home. After all, no one had thought to search for this place in the last ten years. Even Coach Thomas's wife hadn't bothered, probably because she didn't know or didn't care.

Calling the local authorities would have stirred controversy, too many questions, and involvement by not only local but also state officials. The amount of paperwork and red tape involved in such a job would be mind-boggling and incredibly time consuming. Not to mention the risk of implicating herself, what she needed to avoid in the first place.

Now, Allie was flagrantly disobeying a law officer's command to cease and desist all investigation into the case. What she was about to do would be criminal violation on top of criminal violation. Breaking and entering. Theft, if necessary.

It was too late now. She wasn't going to turn back.

Allie turned the handle and pushed. A gust of hot, musty air hit her face and stung her eyes. She pushed at the wooden door with her shoulder and elbow.

Her eyes took a few seconds to adjust to the darkness. A layer of gray dust covered every surface. Allie checked the living area and the small kitchen. The countertops held cans of beans and vegetables, edges rusted. A sweatshirt with a familiar Mansfield Wolverines emblem hung over the back of one chair. There were posters of the 2006 football schedules tacked to the rough-hewn walls.

Allie stepped into the hallway and checked the two small bedrooms and bathroom. Again, nothing had been touched. A faded quilt was draped over the side of one twin bed. A fleece blanket, moth-eaten, lay across the other.

One door was left. Allie pulled at the knob and turned. It led outside, behind the building. Grass grew in waist-length blades at least a dozen feet back, where the grove of trees stood in uneven rows. She turned to pull the door shut when a flash of sun on glass caught Allie's eye.

She stepped back outside onto a makeshift staircase of cinderblocks. Allie shielded her eyes. Tucked back behind the main cabin, barely visible in the fading light, was another building. Allie rubbed moisture off her upper lip and surveyed the smaller structure.

Her movement set several creatures stirring from the undergrowth. Crickets chirped in the distance, echoing the calls of mockingbirds in midflight.

As she walked closer, fronds of growth brushed at her legs, pulling at the edges of her pants hem and pockets. Intricate cobwebs hung untouched from the edges of the doorway. A spider scurried across the roof's rusted edge, as if anticipating the destruction of its home.

Allie took a hand and swept away the webs and vines. Underneath, she found an unpainted door, double-bolted. Despite its sturdy appearance, the frame gave a little at the slight pressure of one hand.

After a glance behind her, Allie backed up, turned her shoulder, and charged at the opening. With one blow, the door broke into pieces, sending shards of rotted pine flying in every direction. A cloud of dirt swirled from the floor; dust particles hovered in the thick air and fluttered back to the ground. Allie rubbed the dirt from her face and coughed into her hand.

This was the place.

Coach Thomas hadn't gotten rid of a thing. Maybe he didn't care. Or didn't have a chance.

There was a laminar flow hood, vials, and stoppers. Containers of benzyl alcohol, benzyl benzoate, and distilled water. Rows of syringes. Soybean oil.

A rickety stove with four small burners sat next to a sink, the counter next to it stacked with white coffee filters and glass beakers. Cotton balls and rags.

Her eyes, dry and irritated from the dust, rested on a few vials. The labels were faded and discolored, almost unreadable. She could guess what they contained before picking them up. Allie reached for the nearest glass container and held it between her fingers, rolling it to get a better look.

The label said *Equipoise*—EQ, as athletes and bodybuilders often referred to it. Allie rubbed away dirt with her covered thumb, turning the vial over in her hand. The amber-tinged liquid sloshed inside the glass. There was the usual label, seal, and markings from the manufacturer, but nothing to indicate where it came from. A few empty boxes lay on the counter, their labels torn away. Allie drew out her phone and snapped photos of everything. As she lowered the cell and started to slip it back into her pocket, she paused.

There had to be something more. Allie crouched down and opened the cabinet doors. Cardboard, packing material, and tape were crammed inside at odd angles. Piece by piece, she pulled out each scrap. After making a small pile on the floor, she felt the bottom of the black space for anything else. Nothing but dust.

She stood, surveying the room one last time. In the far corner, her eyes landed on a small wooden knob she hadn't noticed earlier. As she walked closer, her throat tightened. Allie closed her eyes and pulled open the narrow drawer.

Inside it lay a few personal items. Gum, a granola bar, deodorant, a comb. A Post-it note with a phone number jotted on it in black ink. Allie stared at the number, debating if she should call. It could be old. It could be nothing. But she couldn't take that chance. Allie swallowed and tucked the paper into her jeans.

There was a pile of light-blue papers, most of them terribly faded. Allie tensed. She recognized the horse's head logo at the top of each page. It was the same company where her father—and many other vet offices, she reminded herself—ordered their equine supplies. She snapped more pictures, feeling sick, disgust rising up in her chest. The coach had destroyed so many lives.

Allie bent over and peered again into the drawer, squinting to make sure she'd seen everything. At the very back, there was something else. With trembling fingers, she reached inside the narrow space and withdrew a faded card. Inside, in her sister's handwriting, were the words *C—I love you.*

FORTY-NINE

EMMA

2016

Emma didn't move from her bedroom when Allie pulled into the driveway. Her own vehicle was in the garage, and she pretended not to hear the doorbell or her sister knocking. Emma exhaled in relief when Allie, after ten minutes, drove away in their mother's car.

After listening to Allie's voice mails from the night before, she'd immediately deleted them, though she couldn't erase what her sister had said in the messages.

Listen, call me back when you get this. The weirdest thing happened. Sheriff Gaines came by, asking about you. I just want to know what really happened—that night. I care, Emma. I really do.

Emma powered off her phone. *Not like this.* The memories rushed back, full force.

November 2006

Emma's wrist was taped with layers of cloth and bandages. A plastic tube snaked from the crook of her arm to an IV pole above her head. Her eyes fluttered open, taking in the sunshine streaming in through the window.

"Oh, you're awake," her mother exclaimed, her fingers trembling, straightening the edges of the crisp sheets. "H-how are you feeling?" She slid a look toward her father, furtive, worried.

She couldn't answer right away. When Emma closed her eyes again, she had the inexplicable sense of floating in a fish bowl, eyeballs larger than life peering through the glass and examining her every move.

Then the memories slammed back. The argument. The angry words. His face. Emma swallowed. Goose bumps raised on her skin. She needed to feign confusion. Amnesia if she had to, until she could figure out if he was all right.

Emma eased her head a few inches to the left, finding the clock on the wall. It was ten o'clock in the morning. The slight motion left her dizzy, as if her body had been dumped into a life-size mixer and spun.

Her father approached the bedside. He laid a hand on Emma's tousled hair, stroking the strands as if she were a child again. His eyes were red around the edges and ringed dark with worry. "Won't you tell us what happened?"

Emma's eyelids closed with the heavy slam of garage door on pavement. Jerky, multicolor images panned through her brain. Muted voices talked in the background, the words lost in an exchange of emotion and tears.

A light touch brought Emma back to the surface of reality. "Your sister—"

It was her mother talking, she thought. She shifted her gaze against the waning sunlight and adjusted her gaze.

"Allie," Emma managed to whisper. They were supposed to watch a movie and have girls' night. And then, when she'd run from the pharmacy, she'd caught a glimpse of her sister. Following her. Spying on her. Anger at Allie had seared Emma from the inside out.

A flash of a memory came vaulting back. Staggering drunkenly toward the hospital ER, just a block away. Inside the medical center walls, on a phone reserved for patients and families, she'd made the call to 9-1-1. Somehow she'd managed to hang up and make it to the emergency room waiting room, where she'd been whisked back to see a doctor after almost collapsing at the check-in desk.

Emma moaned softly. The room went dark again and her parents looked black and shadowy, in silhouettes against the white walls.

"We have to tell her."

Her father's gruff, hushed voice reverberated in the empty space. "Lily, it will upset her. She's fragile . . . She was probably attacked by some maniac who's still on the loose."

Emma moaned again at the noise. Her parents both jumped at the sound. Under the fringe of her eyelashes, she watched as her mother clutched at the edge of her shirt. Her father stood up and began to walk the perimeter of the small room. He never was one to sit still.

"Allie," she repeated, the voice coming from her throat as scratchy as bark.

"Oh, sweetie," her mother breathed out, tears in her eyes. Her hand found her throat, the fingers clutching and grasping at nothing. "I don't know how to tell you this . . ."

Her father swallowed, never taking his eyes off Emma. He put a hand on his wife's shoulder and patted the material of her cotton shirt. The motion was awkward, full of hesitation, as if his touch might break all the bones under her skin.

Their faces looked haunted and gaunt. Though Emma knew it was the harsh florescent light, her father's hair looked more gray, her mother more frail. It was as if her parents had aged a decade overnight.

The words clung to her throat and scraped along her tongue. "Wh-where is she?" Emma croaked.

"There's been an accident." Her mother finally spoke again, just above a whisper. "An incident. We're not sure of all the details." She made a fist and pressed it to her chest as if she were keeping her heart from pumping out from between her ribs. "The sheriff's department's involved."

Allie. The sheriff. What was she talking about?

Emma blinked, trying to focus her vision on her mother's face, attempting to make her brain comprehend what she was being told.

Her mother continued and raised her palms to the ceiling in a helpless gesture. "They think she's done something terrible—"

The hum of the monitors around Emma's head became intolerable. Emma looked at her father, pleading for help, a better explanation.

"I know it's a shock. There must be some mistake," her mother assured Emma, her worried eyes heavy. "We'll find out more soon."

"About what?" Emma looked to her father. He was shaking his head while her mother talked in circles, spinning more confusion than a sudden tornado on a summer day.

"Try not to think about it, honey."

"Lily, stop," her father cut in, attempting damage control. "Emma, your sister can't be here right now." His voice cracked and his face seemed to fall apart in pieces, like rocks breaking off the edges of a cliff and tumbling into the churned ocean water below. First his chin let go, then his bottom lip. His upper lip and the tip of his nose disintegrated next, then his eyes, one by one.

Her parents, both of them, were acting like someone died.

Her father gripped at his wife's shoulder and turned her away from Emma. "The doctor said not to get her excited or upset. Do you think this is helping?" he accused under his breath.

Her mother burst into tears. "How should I know?" She sobbed into her hands, wet, salty emotion dripping between her fingertips. "Are we not supposed to talk about it at all? Not tell our own daughter?" Her voice cracked. "Maybe she knows something we don't. Something that might help Allie."

Eyes stinging with tears, head clouded with snippets of their conversation, Emma clutched at the sheets, pulling them taut. She wanted to yank them over her head, to cover up and hide. She wanted her parents to stop arguing.

"Stop," her father urged. "Please, you're not making things any better."

"What will, Paul? Because right now things are pretty awful." Her mother's temper flashed like a pan of grease on fire, blue and red at the edges, leaping and striking any object within reach.

Emma closed her eyes tight against the sound of her mother's anger.

A distinct, sharp rap at the door and a slight creak of hinges prevented any further argument. Emma averted her eyes and twisted her hands beneath the sheets as a white-clad hospital worker entered the room.

"Good morning," a musical, deep female voice said. Her brisk steps echoed as the rest of the room came to a settled, still quiet.

The nurse's hand grasped Emma's wrist, turning it over, examining for a pulse. IV lines were checked and adjusted. A moment later, a stethoscope found its way to the space on her skin just below her collarbone. Emma could almost make out the *thump-thump-thump* of her own heartbeat. It was fast. So fast it might race out of her chest. The nurse pressed the stethoscope an inch to the left, a centimeter to the right and down.

"How are you?"

"Tired," Emma forced out between her parched lips, making her eyelids heavy. She watched the nurse grow concerned through the fringe of her lashes.

"Dr. Marshall? Mrs. Marshall? Would you excuse us just for a moment?" the nurse inquired. Her request cast a pall over the room, cold and biting.

After a slight pause, her parents walked from the room, their footsteps shuffling and heavy.

"Be right back." The nurse bent over to straighten the sheet across Emma's collarbone. She smoothed it with a light touch and smiled down at her, then turned away to talk to her parents waiting in the hallway.

The door clicked, but didn't close completely.

Thank God someone understood, Emma thought. She couldn't think with her parents fighting. But even from the hallway, her mother's voice floated into the room, rising and falling. "Being held" and "sheriff" were met with firm resistance by the hospital employee.

"I'm sorry," the nurse replied. Then, ". . . time to recover."

Emma heard her mother say Allie's name and then her father interjected, his tone flat and somber. "Coach . . . last . . . couldn't revive . . ."

A shushing noise from the nurse covered the rest of his sentence.

Emma choked on her own breath. *Couldn't revive?* If her sister had something to do with this, then Allie deserved to burn in hell. She would never breathe a word that she'd been there with Coach that night.

She made her lips into the letters of his name. Her tears fell, splashing the sheets, the sound like raindrops landing on a child's watercolor painting, smearing the blues and greens and pinks until nothing but gray smudges remained.

2016

Coach had warned her. At the time she hadn't wanted to believe him, that if word got out it would jeopardize her family's business, ruin her parents' trust. She would be humiliated beyond imagination. Emma pressed her fingers to her brow, thinking back.

"Key people in this community know where I'm getting my supplies," he said quietly.

"And those people know you're involved." Coach pointed his finger at her face to make sure she was listening. *"Sheriff Gaines,"* he added. *"He's just one of them."*

Now it was clear that her sister was investigating the coach's death. First, Caroline's ultimatum, then all of these mysterious trips, and now the voice mail asking Emma to talk after a visit from the county sheriff. Allie had found something.

Gaines had the power to cover it up or make it go away. What was he doing, getting involved now? Boyd Thomas was dead. Everything else should have been buried with him.

Emma walked to her bedroom, bent down, and pulled a tote bag from under her bed. She opened drawers, tossed in clothes for a few days. With a last, worried glance around the room, Emma picked up her keys and a jacket. She could figure out *where* she was going later. She scribbled a note for Caroline, who'd be home in less than an hour, telling her she had to go out of town for a bit. That Caroline should go to Grandma Lily's. *Everything's fine*, she wrote; they'd talk soon.

Almost as an afterthought, Emma paused in the kitchen. What if the sheriff blamed Emma for not controlling her sister, not keeping her from stirring up trouble? What if he stopped by her house, or worse, followed her? Pulse racing, Emma pulled open drawers, rummaged through, searching for something, anything, she could use in self-defense. She laid eyes on an oversize pocketknife, one she could hold in the palm of her hand, hidden. It had a blade sharp enough to slice through corrugated cardboard moving boxes with ease. She'd used it when she'd moved into this very house so many years earlier.

Emma slipped the pocketknife into her jeans. As she hurried to the car, she ran through what she knew: Lee Gaines was an intelligent man. He knew about the steroids, which made him party to whatever laws were broken. And if the sheriff knew Emma loved Coach Thomas, that she had been pregnant with his child, it was likely he didn't care. He would protect his own hide before anyone else's.

Emma cranked the key and started the engine. She pulled out of the driveway and headed east. Right now she needed time to think. She turned a sharp left, exited onto a ramp, and entered the highway. She accelerated, pressing her foot on the gas pedal. The engine raced and the car jerked forward until she eased the pressure.

Tapping the steering wheel with one finger, Emma was certain that all of her sister's digging around had done something to warrant the sheriff's attention, and Emma's name got dragged into it. She sucked in her breath and kept driving. Every so often she glanced into the rearview mirror. Was anyone following her? Had someone seen her leaving the house? With shaking hands, Emma pulled over to the side of the road, cut her lights, and let the car's wheels roll to a stop.

Knowing Allie, she'd want more answers, more information. Her sister might eventually put it all together. And even though it was all Allie's fault for following her and spying on her that night, Allie would still hate Emma forever.

Somehow Emma had to stop this train wreck from happening. *Confront Gaines? Threaten him?*

No, Emma decided. She would do the next best thing.

FIFTY

CAROLINE

2016

Caroline gripped the seat of the SUV with one hand and held her purse on her lap with the other. She was in the backseat, bumping along with Natalie and Russell.

The backs of their heads were identical in shape and color. The son's shaggier and longer. The mother's a bit smaller, the hair shinier. Their postures were similar—a slight cock to the head, left elbows on the armrests. They even sounded the same when they talked and laughed.

Russell turned and grinned, the motion abrupt. "Hey, you okay?"

Caroline jumped. "Sure," she replied, trying to smile while worry pinged in her stomach.

"It's going to be fine," he reassured her and grinned. "You'll see."

Russell was headed in for an afternoon shift at the nursing home. Natalie and Caroline were simply tagging along. It was an excellent opportunity to talk to Dr. Gaines. They could ask a few more questions and make sure they had the story straight before Caroline talked to Allie or Emma.

The nursing home allowed pets to visit, citing the soothing

nature of the animals in nursing homes and long-term care facilities, so Natalie packed up the family dog and one of their three cats. "It's scientifically proven that simply stroking a dog's coat or petting a cat's fur can relaxed and help rid anxiety in Alzheimer's and dementia patients," added Natalie as she grabbed a leash.

It had seemed like a good idea at the time. Now Caroline's pulse began to gallop as they pulled into the parking lot. She tightened her fingers around the seat belt, hesitating before pressing the button to release the metal end. "What if she hates animals?" she whispered at Russell. "What if she's allergic?"

Natalie was already out of the SUV and walking toward the back. She motioned for Russell and Caroline to jump out and help. "It would be in her chart." Russell winked.

Caroline sat inside the SUV, her breath starting to condense on her cheeks in the stuffy space inside the vehicle.

Natalie opened the back hatch. "You coming?" she called out. "You'll roast in there."

Russell lifted the small spaniel out of his cage and clipped on the leash. The dog wagged its tail, tongue lolling to one side of its mouth.

Natalie picked up the smaller cage. A soft mew escaped from inside. "Shh, it's okay. We'll let you get out in just a minute," she whispered. Russell closed the back.

Caroline frowned, not moving. She really might die of heatstroke. Maybe that would be better. It was a bad idea to talk to Dr. Gaines. Caroline scrunched down, the back of her neck wet with perspiration.

The side door flew open. "Come on." Natalie smiled. "We'll go with the flow, okay? And we'll leave if it's a disaster."

Caroline's leg peeled off the seat like pulling Band-Aid strips from taut skin, as if the van wanted to hold her inside. She felt better when Russell slung an arm over her shoulders as they walked inside the air-conditioned building.

Their entrance caused a bit of a stir among the residents. Natalie paused here and there, allowing frail frames to lean forward and squint into the cage. A few of the women clapped their hands at the sight of a furry head and perky ears.

The cat wasn't as thrilled about all of the attention. Russell, sensing her unease, hurried his mother along. "She's getting skittish," he whispered.

Caroline trailed behind, watching the reactions on faces. There were more smiles, more chatter among the ladies and bent-over men leaning on walkers in the corner. The place, in a span of minutes, appeared to come back to life, as if someone had waved a magic wand in the hallway or sprinkled pixie dust.

Russell and Natalie waited by the elevator, both smiling as she joined them. "So far, so good," Natalie whispered as a bell chimed and the double doors heaved apart.

Both animals seemed to freeze until the elevator stopped its mechanical whirring and opened on the second floor. Caroline watched as the dog sniffed at the new air and scents. The cat, now resigned to her fate inside the cage, curled into a defensive ball.

Natalie gave a sidelong glance to the feline. "She'll come around, I think."

A maintenance worker pushed a cart filled with supplies and buckets as they passed. A few of the nurses looked up and smiled.

"Dr. Harper. And hello, you two." One of the nurses' aides nodded at Caroline and Russell. "And you brought friends."

"We did," Natalie said, bending down to check on the cat. She watched as the creature laid back her ears and bared her teeth. "Russell, she's not in the mood for this. Will you and Caroline be all right while I run back to the office with her?"

"Sure, Mom." Russell glanced at Caroline. "We'll be fine."

Caroline felt her body quiver. What would she find out? What would it mean for her relationship with Emma?

Russell went first. He rapped on June Gaines's door, then pushed it open, allowing the spaniel to lead as Caroline followed.

"Hello there. What a lovely surprise!" June exclaimed as they brought the animal into the room. She clasped her hands together and let them drop to her lap, still intertwined.

"Would it be all right if he visited for a few minutes?" Caroline gestured at the dog, who looked at June with bright eyes, lifting one paw, then the other.

"Can he?" June moved her chair forward.

With a deft movement, Russell unclipped the leash. "This is Cocoa." The furry brown ball leaped into June's lap. His pink tongue licked her face. Russell put out his arms as if to grab him and hold him back, but June waved him away.

"Oh, you sweet boy," she cooed and rubbed his head. "This is such a treat. So thoughtful," she mused, scratching the dog behind one soft ear. "It's been so long. We used to have lots of pets, a whole farm, my husband used to say. Now, to whom do I owe a thank-you?" June squinted, her eyes finding the two figures pressed against the wall of the room. "Can you come closer? My eyes aren't what they used to be."

Russell pulled at Caroline's elbow and guided her to the small sofa perpendicular to June's wheelchair. "Ah yes, the man from the exercise department—"

"It's Russell, ma'am." He flushed and adjusted in the seat.

"Oh, and it's the Marshall girl too. How are you, Emma dear?"

"I'm Emma's niece," Caroline explained. "I'll tell her you said hello."

A flicker of confusion registered on her face, but June didn't look away. "How long has it been? How's your sister?" Her eyes softened as she petted the small dog, who was now resting in her lap, paws draped over the side of her legs.

Russell shook his head, indicating she shouldn't argue.

"Fine. She's doing fine," Caroline answered.

"Is she working at the vet office?" June inquired. Her hand paused above the dog's collar, waiting for an answer. "She's going to be perfect for medical school. I just know it."

"Yes, ma'am." Caroline swallowed a lump in her throat.

June resumed stroking her hand over the dog's ears and back. "Now, the person I've been worried about is you, dear. How are you getting along? I know you must be so disappointed."

"I'm fine," Caroline said and glanced at Russell.

"There's no need to try to hide anything. Not from me. I'm your doctor, and you can always discuss things openly in my office." June smiled. "Now, let's talk about your options, shall we?" She settled back in her wheelchair. "When you find someone who really loves and cares for you, you'll be able to figure it out. Both adoption and surrogates are possible."

Caroline stiffened. "Why?"

"The miscarriage caused all kinds of problems," June explained. "You can't have children, Emma. I'm so sorry."

Russell reached for Caroline's hand and squeezed it.

"And I want you to think about pressing charges. Get a restraining order. All those bruises on your right side."

Caroline began shaking.

Russell interrupted. "Right side, meaning what?"

"That he was left-handed, of course. His dominant hand. I noticed it on Emma right away when she came in."

"I see," Russell replied, darting a look at Caroline.

June drew in a breath. "You'll take care of her now? Make sure she stays away from him? I've never quite trusted him. Something about the man."

"Who, ma'am?" Russell pressed.

Cocoa perked up and began to growl in June's lap. She stroked his head and tried to soothe him. "Shh, now. What's all the fuss?" Dr. Gaines bent down to whisper. "It's okay."

A knock sounded at the door. A second later, one of the nurses' aides poked her head in the door. "I hate to break up the party, but Dr. Gaines has an appointment at the beauty parlor downstairs. She'll be back in a while."

Russell clucked his tongue for Cocoa to come. "I have to start my shift soon anyway." He touched Caroline's arm. "I'll walk you downstairs. Mom should be back any minute."

June turned her head. "Thank you so much for stopping by and seeing me. And, Emma dear, come see me in the office on Monday."

FIFTY-ONE

EMMA

November 2006

"Hello?" Emma called out. The pharmacy looked deserted, aisles empty, no one at the cash register. The florescent lights cast a bright glare in her path.

She'd used the nausea as a made-up excuse, something Allie would buy as a reasonable delay. Emma winced at the scent of candles—vanilla, peach, and apple pie—all that seemed so wonderful before pregnancy. Now her lie was coming back to haunt her. Emma stepped away from the aisle, fanning her face with one hand.

"Anyone here?" Emma raised her voice, stepping up on tiptoes to scan the shelves above her head. Her wide skirt swished around her knees. Any sign of life would have been welcome at that point. She started to worry.

The store was clearly open; the sign in front said so in blinking red-and-blue lights. The door was propped open, as was customary on warm fall evenings.

Emma leaned over the pharmacy desk and glanced both ways, almost expecting to find a dead body laid out behind it. Nothing but a scrap of paper lay there. She pressed her elbows and belly to the checkout counter, resting for a moment.

She'd asked, then insisted they meet at the pharmacy. His wife was out of town with the kids. It was neutral ground, untainted, and she didn't want the distractions of the place that held so many memories.

He'd agreed, reluctantly, after she'd wheedled and begged, explaining her father was likely to get after-hours call, as the illegal dog tracks were open Thursday evenings.

"Why doesn't he just shut them down?" Coach Thomas complained into the phone. "Then he wouldn't have to bother with those hounds."

"I-I don't know. Daddy's just that way. The same men who run dogs bring their puppies and kittens in for shots. Daddy sees the horses at their stables." Emma evaluated her answer. "I guess he's not going to bite the hand that feeds him—us."

Coach murmured something under his breath.

"Daddy reads them the riot act if they harm those dogs. He makes sure to tell them he doesn't want to see them back."

"Emma, you just come around 8:50 p.m. I'll be waiting."

The dial tone rang in her ear.

Emma reached over the swinging door separating the front of the store from the back. The latch slid apart easily and fell into place. Without a sound, the divider swung open, allowing Emma to pass through.

She glanced behind her, thought for a moment about locking the glass front doors. No, this wasn't her house or her business. She was here for a reason.

"Hey," Emma whispered and crept toward the back of the building. High shelves were stocked full of Kleenex and tissue paper. Rows of Lysol and cleaning supplies lined the shelves in different-sized bottles and cans.

He was there then, all of a sudden, in the last room she checked. In the single light above a four-legged table, he sat, legs splayed, cell phone in one hand. His gaze was frozen, lost in some world of ice and mist.

Emma took another step.

"Angel, you came." He stood, put his phone on the small table, and rushed over, his hand caressing her neck and the small of her back. He held her out at arm's length and looked her over. "You're looking so fine," he declared and kissed her full on the mouth.

When she came up for air, she started to tell him. About the baby. About her love for him. How she wanted a family and a house and a dog.

"Shh," he cautioned her.

"What is it?" she whispered. Her legs wobbled underneath her. She was hungry again. The thought was constant now, and she couldn't think of much else.

"You've got to be so excited, sugar." He slapped his leg and hooted. "I can see it. A few more games and we'll be at the state play-offs, baby." At the declaration, he spun in place and pretended to spike the ball.

Emma watched as he strutted in front of her, making a muscle sign with his bicep, posing on one knee, then jumping up with both fists extended into a warrior stance. All at once, his actions seemed petty and juvenile, a bit like a clown's at the circus.

"Don't you want to talk about us? The future?"

"There's nothing more important than Wolverine football," he rallied back and struck a haughty stance. "Come on. Show me some excitement. Give me something. Come on."

Emma threw up both hands in surrender. She would let him have his moment of celebration. He was like a kid keyed up after chugging a six-pack of Coke and downing a dozen donuts. It wasn't likely to change as long as they were winning. And there were a few more games to get through till the team made it to the Georgia Dome.

"Did you see them last week? Twenty yard line, ten, then five," Coach described with vigor, his arms mimicking a running stance. "Over the top, in the end zone. He scores! Wolverines score!"

Emma smiled at his antics, trying to pay rapt attention, but she found herself drifting off, away from the room, as she leaned against the wall. She jerked her head up with a start. Coach was still ranting.

"We're ready for tomorrow night." He rubbed his hands together and slapped his thighs. "Oh, do we have some trick plays up our sleeve. And yeah, it's gonna get messy. Those boys over yonder want to play dirty?" He pivoted to make sure Emma was listening. "We're going to bring it on. Make them wish they'd stayed home."

A small, tiny part of her began to fray at the edges, just in places, while she listened to him rant and rave about the next night's game. In that moment, Emma realized she was just part of the crowd, one small bit of his audience. She wondered if it really mattered if she was there or if he just needed someone—a living, breathing female to listen and cheer him on.

Coach was still talking. "Had a little hiccup there, with our friend D'Shawn, but he's back on board. Got him pumped up."

"And after playoffs, will you stop?" Emma finally asked.

"Ma'am?" The coach stopped mid-sentence, mid-pose, mid-breath. His forehead wrinkled, and he waited for her to repeat the statement.

"You will have proven yourself." Emma held up her chin and met his eyes. "Achieved everything you came here to do." Now she wanted proof of their future, evidence that he loved her more than anyone else.

"What did you say?" His tone was accusing and strident. His lips formed a solid, straight line, his nostrils flared. His pat answers, the glib and fresh attitude, vanished. His personality and charm fizzled out like a candlewick doused in water. "Stop? No, I don't think I heard you right."

Emma held her ground, keeping her voice low and casual. She blinked up at him, maintaining an innocent face. "You took this team from a bunch of farm kids and molded them into a group of super soldiers. But if you keep winning, people will start to wonder."

Coach whirled at the jab. "Wonder what?" he barked. "Who do you think you are?" He heaved a breath and regained his composure.

"I'm the person who loves you," she countered.

"Love," the coach scoffed. "This goes way beyond you. It's over your head, girl."

"Girl?" Emma lashed back. "I thought I was going to be your wife. A year, maybe two. Isn't that what you promised me? The house, the yard, a ring . . ."

Coach Thomas stopped, skidding in his tracks. His motion became jerky and robotic.

Emma stared back into his eyes. "Unless that's not what you want. Unless this has all been a big game. And you don't care about me at all."

"You might want to reconsider where you're going with this," he cautioned. "You're treading in some dangerous territory."

It was no answer and she knew it. The gamble was on. No time to stop it, no time to fix it. It was a test of the biggest kind. He needed to decide: trust Emma with everything or not.

"After playoffs, I want to stop," Emma challenged. "Our supplies are way off."

Coach simmered, then began to pace, his face darkening as he let her talk.

"I've had to order more and more." Heart beating double-time, Emma added, "Someone is going to notice."

"Really?" he muttered.

Emma opened her mouth. Before she could utter a sound, Coach yanked her up from the table and slammed her against the wall, sending an old wooden chair clattering to the ground. In one swift motion, he pinned one arm behind her back while he held the other wrist twisted above her head.

"Spoiled little rich girl wants to run the show, does she?" His breath burned hot and acidic on her cheek. "Tell me what to do, how to coach, run my life—is that it? Am I understanding you correctly, Miss Marshall?" Coach relaxed his grip, allowing Emma a second of relief, a reminder that he was in charge.

"Why? Y-you were supposed to love me. We're getting m-married." Emma thrashed in disbelief. "Let me go. You're hurting me."

He tightened his grip on her forearm, fingers digging into the tendons and bone. "Now, where are those lovely manners your mama taught you? I'm not hearing them . . ."

Emma moaned in pain and slunk against the wall. Her arm throbbed. The ache radiated down her arm, through her elbow, and into her shoulder.

"Not so smart, now, are you, princess?" Coach sneered an inch from her lips, unblinking. "Don't you realize what you're doing? Questioning me?" He threw Emma down, casting her off like a used jacket. "You're ruining everything."

He spit on the floor inches from her head. Emma didn't flinch; her body was cement, heavy and thick, attached to the ground.

When she didn't look up or answer, he continued, "I'm the king here. And if I decide I need something or someone, I'm going to take it. Which includes anything I want from your father's office, anything I want from you, anything to win the game and make it to the playoffs. That's what this town wants, and that's what this town is going to get. Year after year after year."

Coach kicked at her shins and aimed for her stomach. Emma shrieked and scrambled to get away from the blow. His boot caught the edge of her abdomen. Searing pain shot through the lower part of her belly, as if the child inside her had cried out in fear.

"If you say a word, I'll hurt you worse than this." He grunted, reached down, and pulled her hair to force her to look at him. His voice was a hoarse whisper. "Do you hear me?"

Emma let out a groan as tears coursed down her cheeks.

"Yes. Yes. Stop, please—" He'd lost his mind. She needed to get away. She needed to save herself. Save the baby. He'd never have to know. She would figure out what to do later.

Coach let go, letting her slump, shaking and quivering, to the floor.

"I'm sorry," she murmured and curled into a ball. The apology wasn't meant for his ears. It was for her father. For her own bruised body. But most of all, for their baby.

He shook his head at Emma in pity, as if someone else had ransacked the office, beat up Emma, and left her for dead. He put his head in his hands and turned away from her, mumbling to himself.

Emma forced herself to ignore the throb of her forearm and the ache below her waist. Using both hands, she pulled herself away from him using the wooden chair that had fallen over, dragging her body. And the coach was still muttering, pacing now, eyes half closed.

On her final hoist, a weakened chair leg came off in her grasp. Breathing hard, Emma scrambled to her feet, tucking it behind her back before Coach could turn around.

"I need to go," she said, just audible above her own heartbeat. She was asking for permission. He wanted to be in charge and needed Emma to be subservient and cowering. She could play the part. "Please."

As she waited for him to reply, she glanced down at her free hand. The forearm above her wrist was swollen twice its normal size. Emma stared at the puffy tissue, the skin covering the veins and tendons beneath. Bruises began to blossom in angry streaks of red and purple. Marks from a man's hand and fingers were clearly evident.

"Please," she repeated. "I won't say anything. I promise—"

"Oh, now you've changed your mind?" Coach sneered.

She kept her gaze on the floor.

"Now you don't want to make me look bad in front of my community, my neighbors, and my players' families? Well, Emma Marshall, I'm glad to hear that, because you are right. You don't want to go there."

Shifting her feet and pressing against the floor, Emma pushed herself up against the closest wall, resting her wounded arm in her lap. She let her gaze fall from his short-cropped hair to his pressed khakis. His neat, orderly appearance, not a fold out of place, every stitch in an even line.

It was so obvious. It had taken this amount of shock to recognize it, though. Allie had seen it, might as well have shouted it from the rooftops. She wasn't afraid like Emma was. Her sister was a warrior, an Amazon. Her sister, who was always right, who always got what she wanted. Who was leaving this awful place and going to make a new life. She was leaving Emma behind. She hadn't even asked if she wanted to tag along. Not even in a joking way.

They were supposed to have tonight, though. Just the two sisters. Popcorn, pillows, and a movie. Allie had cleared her schedule to spend time with her.

Meanwhile, all Coach cared about was himself. How he looked, how he felt, his record of success. Who he stepped on along the way was inconsequential. He hadn't been telling the truth all along. Not to his wife or his kids or to Emma.

"Why?" Emma asked. "Why me?"

Coach smirked. "You're young and naïve, not bad to look at, and your daddy's got all the fixin's we need to get a team to the state playoffs. I just needed a key to get in. Or the code."

Emma winced as she remembered writing it down and handing the information over so freely. Coach reached for a glass of Coke and spun his straw in the ice, taking turns stirring and looking at her.

"Think about it this way. You helped get the team on track to the Georgia Bowl. Couldn't have done it without you." Coach winked.

Emma shifted her weight to one side and pressed her thighs together, still clutching the piece of chair leg. She glanced around at the racks of supplies, the pharmacy boxes, the dispensers and shelves of over-the-counter medication waiting to be stocked.

"Why not use what you already have at the store? Can't you just order what you like? You own a pharmacy." She frowned. "Why not take it? Why ask me?"

She loved him. Didn't he see that? She'd have given him what he wanted, if he really loved her. Why couldn't he see what was right in front of him?

"You're so innocent, so unbelievably naïve," he said and checked his watch. "Ever heard of the DEA? The folks that keep tabs on people like us? Pharmacies? Every pill that comes in and out has to be counted, checked, verified, double-checked. Those idiots are on us every five minutes about this or that. Fill out this form, sign this statement. They can walk in here anytime they please and turn the place upside down. It's the crazy KGB all over again. The government wants to run everything. And you wonder why I'd look elsewhere for my product?" He laughed, shallow and raw.

Emma let out a gasp. Her abdomen cramped like someone had reached in and clutched her insides, then twisted. She forced herself not to cry out again or exclaim at the pain. It seemed to intensify with each pump of blood through her veins.

"Fine. I-I understand now. Really. I won't say anything," she coughed out, her eyes watering. "I need to go, okay?"

"We're clear?"

"Yes," she whispered, maintaining the apologetic look.

"Because, Emma," he continued. "I promise you this. If you breathe a single word, I'll find you." Coach narrowed his eyes. "And when I do, I'll kill you."

Emma gulped, tucking the piece of wood close to her spine.

After a beat, he grabbed his ball cap, turned his head to check the front of the store. "I've got to close up."

Muscles straining, she inched up the wall and straightened her legs. Once on her feet, her vision cleared. She steadied her footing, then took a baby step and caught the edge of the table with her fingertips. Emma let out a small moan, wobbled from side to side, then straightened, keeping both eyes pinned on Coach. He glanced in her direction as he pulled on a jacket.

"I'm fine," she assured him, still hiding the chair leg in the folds of her skirt.

His forehead creased as he reached to straighten his ball cap.

Emma leaned over to grab her purse on her way out the back door. She didn't want to fake too much, just enough for him to come to her rescue.

"Oh." She let out a cry and bent her knees, hunching her shoulders, tucking her chin to her chest.

It was enough.

The coach hesitated, then reached for her again.

This time Emma was ready.

With a battle cry worthy of adrenaline-pumped soldiers, Emma took the chair leg and swung with all of her might.

FIFTY-TWO

ALLIE

2016

Allie tried her sister several times on the way home. Voice mail. She would have to tie Emma down or sedate her to talk about the cabin and the coach. How had she possibly missed all of the signs? She had been so blind—so focused on her moral quest to prove Thomas was guilty of manufacturing steroids and abusing players—that she'd let it cloud everything else in her life.

She bit her lip, regret washing over her body in waves. There was so much she could have done differently.

As she reached her own tree-lined street, she parked her mother's car, grabbed the mail from the box, and headed inside. She locked the door behind her and leaned against it, deciding to check her cell phone for the hundredth time. As she cradled it in the palm of her hand, Allie stared at the screen, debating her next move. She needed to call her father or mother. Path of least resistance first, she decided.

Her mother answered. "Hello?"

"Hey, Mom, it's me," Allie said and offered her the obligatory fine and good when asked. After a lull in the conversation, she dove straight in with questions about her sister. "I'm a little worried," she explained. "Has Emma been acting strangely?"

Her mother made a brief humming noise, thinking. "Sweetie, we've barely seen her. Your father and I thought—we'd hoped—she was spending time with you."

"Well, she has been, off and on," Allie said. "Up until the last few days, she's been here a bit." She pressed her cheek against the cell phone, brushing aside the curtain to glance out the window, hoping to catch a glimpse of her sister's car. "It's not like her to disappear."

"Well, now, I don't think that's the case. Caroline said she left her a note—"

"Caroline's there?" Allie interrupted, scratching at her forehead in frustration.

"She was at the library this morning. After that, she went home, found the note, and called and asked if she could go to a friend's house for a few hours."

"Okay. And, um, you were saying . . . about Emma's note . . ." Allie jiggled her knee impatiently.

"The note from Emma just said that Caroline needed to spend the night with us. That she was fine and would talk to us soon."

"Okay," Allie said, remembering that she still had the mail tucked under her elbow. She withdrew the small pile and placed it on the counter, spreading it out as she half answered her mother. A lump lodged in her chest. There was a letter from Emma. Or handwriting that looked exactly like her sister's. No return address.

"Is everything all right?" her mother asked. Her question was hesitant, as if she really didn't want to know if or why trouble existed between her two daughters. Allie understood. Her mother wasn't a crusader, driven to battle by wrongdoing. Her mother would suffer in silence before bringing an ugly subject to light before God, country, or the population of Brunswick.

"Everything's fine, Mom." Allie squeezed her eyes shut and searched for a good excuse. "I have something of hers and need to return it. That's all." She'd find Emma on her own and deal with the situation before anything else happened. "Can I bring your car back in the morning?"

"Of course, dear," her mother said. "We'll be at the house."

After her mother hung up, Allie flipped over the envelope and pulled at the adhesive flap. She pulled out three sheets of folded white paper.

As she scanned the first page, Allie choked. It was a printout from the state of Georgia, discussing the "Special Needs" adoption category. *Special needs children were those who had been in the care of a public or private agency or individual other than the legal or biological parent for more than twenty-four consecutive months.* Her sister's handwriting was scrawled across the top: *We need to talk about this.*

The other two pages, a policy and a form from the Division of Family and Children Services, dropped out of her hand.

Allie walked the interior of the room in a daze. She kept moving, trying to stimulate some kind of epiphany. Why was her sister acting like this? How could she even suggest this? And where was she?

One fact was certain.

She didn't know her sister at all.

Maybe she never had.

Swallowing her tears, Allie wiped at her face. She needed to go to the office and follow up on the supplies she'd found at the cabin. Allie needed to look back at old itemized billing statements and order forms—papers her father had filed a long time ago. Papers in file boxes that Nick might have taken out to the trash. Allie just hoped she wasn't too late.

After leaving a message for Natalie that she would be stopping by the office, Allie keyed in the code at the back door of the building.

An hour later, after combing through boxes of dusty manila folders and outdated patient files, Allie stumbled on a rusted metal file box in the far corner of the storage room. She'd seen the box before, in her father's office. Under Emma's desk when she'd worked there.

On her hands and knees, Allie dragged the box from its resting place. Heaving it up to the counter, she ran a finger over the locking mechanism. When she pressed the silver button in the middle, the clasp sprung apart and the top opened with a creak. Inside, Allie found paper, all colors and textures, wrinkled, some water damaged on the edges.

She reached in one hand and grasped what she could. A tickle on the top of her ring finger made her jump. Allie pulled out her hand and flicked a spider away. There were likely more where he came from.

Allie fetched a plastic tub from under the sink. With both hands, she picked up the file box, turned it upside down, and shook hard. Dust, grit, and rust flew everywhere, making her sneeze and cough. A few more spiders skittered away. Coins rolled across the surface and bounced to the floor, along with paper clips, used staples, and dried-out rubber bands.

Most of the paper settled into a haphazard pile at least six or seven inches thick. Allie bent over and found the stray pieces, collecting a few with every step. A musty, mildewed smell wafted from the pile.

One by one, she checked each scrap, noting the dates and any markings. Most were order forms, some from as far back as fifteen or sixteen years ago. She recognized the company names and products. There were the usual items any vet office would keep in stock—doxycycline for bacterial infections, valium for sedation, Buprenex for pain. Amoxicillin—another antibiotic—was a frequent order, as was prednisone, an injectable steroid.

Allie placed that pile to the side. She picked up another few pages. Information for owners on rabies shots, a schedule for routine vaccines.

Her fingers trembled as she glanced at the next set of pages. On light blue paper, a horse's head was drawn at the edge of the logo. Equine supplies.

Boldenone Undecylenate. Equipoise, EQ, there were different names for it. Vets used it for weight gain in emaciated horses and to step up testosterone production in stallions. There had been a time when her father had done quite a bit of equine work, and she remembered accompanying him to farms as a girl, watching him give injections, listening to him calm the horses.

The demand for equine services had dropped off some when she came to work for her father as a vet tech in the summer between high school and her freshman year of college. She worked whenever she was home on break, honing her skills, going along on emergency calls.

She paged back—2009, 2008, 2007. She paused and jotted down the amounts in each order. Then 2006. She scanned the pages carefully for this year, then compared it to the prior year's orders. At the bottom of each page, her sister's signature was scrawled.

She'd done the ordering back then, signed for most of the packages, all of the office work Allie and her father couldn't stand. Her mother had done the job forever, but allowed Emma to step in and earn spending money during the summers and then when Emma had quit college. Her mother enjoyed the break, Allie thought, and seemed happy to give the responsibility to someone else.

Emma, of course, would have died before taking a fecal sample, giving injections, or doing a urinalysis. So she stayed behind the counter, ordering and occasionally mixing up drug names like Acepromazine and doxycycline. If she'd make a small mistake, Emma would have tried to cover it up, but Allie was looking for significant changes and increases, especially in the months before her arrest.

Allie thumbed through the 2003, 2004, and 2005 files, taking the pages and organizing them in rows and columns. There was nothing out of the ordinary here. All of the numbers checked out. But after she added 2006, particularly the six months before her arrest, Allie rubbed her eyes to make certain she wasn't seeing things.

She thought hard about any emergencies that would have demanded that much EQ. She rubbed her temples, straining to remember. It had been ten years ago, and nothing came to mind.

Allie pressed both hands on the counter. The orders had increased substantially. There was no mistaking it. And if Gaines had known—known for certain that the coach's plan had gotten out of control, as a public figure and elected official with a reputation to maintain—it was possible the stress would push the sheriff over the edge.

Remembering the Post-it note she'd found in the cabin, Allie pulled out the crinkled piece of paper with the number written in black ink. Rubbing the edge between her fingers, she packed up the papers, slipped them in her bag, and replaced the metal box.

Locking up the building, pulse hammering in her veins, Allie drove to the closest gas station, bought a Coke, and asked the clerk as sweetly as she could if she could use the phone to call her sister.

Busy with inventory, the man shrugged and gestured for Allie to go ahead.

"Thank you *so* much," she replied brightly, offering a too-wide smile. When the worker turned away, Allie sucked in a breath, picked up the receiver, and dialed, praying for a recorded message to click on.

After three agonizing rings, the voice that met her ear was the one she heard in her tormented dreams.

You've reached Sheriff Lee Gaines . . .

FIFTY-THREE

ALLIE

November 2006

After Allie's acceptance to medical school, she felt Emma pulling even further away. Their relationship had always been complicated, but now there was barely a thread of connection between them.

She missed their late-night talks, her sister droning on about modeling and fashion, New York and London runways, the men she was dating. She even missed Emma's ridiculous hissy fits.

Allie had made a mess of so many things—her relationship with Ben, the letter to the editor; she'd infuriated the sheriff. At least blood was thicker than water. They would always be sisters and would always have each other. They were family. And Allie had to try to put things right before she left for med school.

It was early—barely seven o'clock—too early for her sister to be up, but she dialed Emma's number anyway. When her sister answered sleepily, there was the muffled sound of sheets rustling and shifting against the mattress. Allie pictured Emma's hair splayed out in a million different directions, dark chestnut brown against the white cotton pillowcase. She'd rub her eyes, the lids almost closed against the bright morning sun.

"Come on, Em. Caroline's having a sleepover, I'm going to pick up some wine, and I'll have pizza ready. I'll do asiago and mushrooms, if you want." Allie made a drumroll sound. "Plus, the news you've been waiting for. Our double feature will be . . . *Pretty Woman* and *Steel Magnolias*." She crossed her fingers. Chick flicks and homemade pizza were Emma's favorites.

"Um." Emma sounded suspicious. "I love Julia Roberts and all, but is there something you're trying to tell me?"

Allie snorted, then made her voice sound incredulous. "What? There's no deep, dark message." She paused. "I can't ask my sister over for drinks and a movie or two? When's the last time we've done anything together? And I don't mean sitting in the stands for a high school football game either."

Emma didn't answer, so Allie broke the silence. She swallowed and lowered her voice. "Listen, I'm leaving for school. And I may do it earlier than when I'd planned. You know, get out of town, make a fresh start—seeing that I'm so popular. I'm thinking the end of December. Maybe January."

Her sister didn't answer. She was listening, though.

"I haven't told Mom and Dad or Caroline. I have to work out the details first. And I want to spend some time with you before things get crazy. And—"

"Um, okay, okay, enough with the hard sell," her sister said with a yawn. "And what?"

"Well, if you must know, I'm a little worried about you." Allie jumped up to pace the room. "You've been—I don't know—in your own little shell."

"I'm fine," Emma said, sounding amused. "Worrywart."

"Good," Allie said, smiling into the phone. It seemed so long since they had teased each other. This was a good idea. They would have a great time. "So you'll be over at, say, seven?"

Emma began to laugh, then hiccup. "Okay, you're persistent. Do I have any choice?" She hiccupped again.

"Nope."

"Sevenish," Emma said, her voice trailing off. Another hiccup.

Allie hung up the phone, pulled on yoga pants, a soft T-shirt, and her old gray peacoat. After making a shopping list and catching up on the morning news, she shoved both feet in boots, snatched her hat, and called for Caroline.

"Ready, sweetie?" she called out.

Caroline stuck her head out the door of her bedroom. "Can I bring my doll?" Her brown eyes were wide and unblinking.

"One doll," Allie warned, trying to hide a smile. If she didn't limit the toy stash, there'd be twenty-two Barbie dolls in the cart and no room for groceries.

Ten minutes later, they wheeled a cart along the store aisles. "Aunt Emma's coming over to our house?" Caroline asked, stroking her doll's hair.

"She is. We're having a big-girls' night." Allie reached down and smoothed her daughter's hair. "And you're going to Grandma Lily's to sleep over."

"So we're having girls' night too." Caroline grinned and skipped along next to the cart.

"Right." Allie leaned over and kissed the top of her daughter's head. The squeak of nearby buggy wheels made both Allie and Caroline look up.

"Hey, y'all," Morgan squealed over the top of her cart, waving hello. For the first time since the editorial hit the paper, her friend seemed genuinely happy to see her. Morgan air-kissed Allie's cheeks and bent down to hug Caroline. "Who's having a girls' night?"

"Mommy and Aunt Emma. And Grandma Lily and me," Caroline said. She tucked herself close to her mother, clinging to her hand.

Morgan cocked her hip and looked thoughtfully at the contents of her own buggy. She looked up at Allie. "Wish I could come." She smiled. "Daddy's come across some tickets to the Falcons game, so we'll be back in Atlanta this weekend."

"Next time," Allie promised, easing her cart to the side to let other shoppers pass.

Morgan's eyes lit up. "Oh, well, you have got to try this." She swiveled on her heels and eyed the shelves behind her. With one hand on her waist, she ran a finger along the wine labels in front of her. "No, no, no, no."

She plucked a bottle off the shelf, then another. "Yes." Morgan handed them both to Allie.

"The labels are so pretty I can't resist them." Morgan winked at Caroline, then turned to grab a third bottle. "Here's another one you need to get."

"Wait," Allie protested, trying to push the bottle away. "We'll never drink all of this."

Morgan was determined. She placed the bottles in Allie's cart and fluttered her fingers. "Then you'll have extra, now won't you? One has to be prepared!" She glanced at the gold watch on her thin wrist. "Oh. Late, I'm late. Ta-ta, girls!"

Allie leaned against the cart and smiled at her daughter. "Morgan's funny, isn't she?"

Caroline nodded. "She's loud too."

Allie smothered a chuckle. Leave it to kids to call it how they see it. And Caroline was right. Morgan was loud, but she embraced life fully. No one would ever say she was boring. And she was still Allie's friend. Despite the letter. And whatever else. Emma was wrong about that.

With a gentle push of the cart, the buggy wheels began to move along the tile floor. As they moved, Caroline fingered the edge of her shirt, humming softly to herself. She was so adorable; Allie could watch her for hours.

Later that afternoon, elbow-deep in pizza dough, Allie felt a jolt of sadness. She looked around her tiny kitchen, the beat-up cabinets, the rickety table in the center of the room.

It hadn't really hit her, until now, that she was really *leaving*.

Allie covered the bowl with a clean cloth to let the dough rise, then wiped her hands clean, washing them twice to rid her fingers of the sticky mixture. She inhaled the scent of yeast and flour melding together. A pinch of sugar, a dash of salt.

Tonight she needed to spend time with Emma. Just reconnecting. It was way overdue.

As she cleaned up the kitchen, Allie called her sister one last time. Emma picked up on the first ring. "Hey, Mom picked up Caroline. It's just you and me."

"Give me a half hour. I have to make a stop first," Emma said. She sounded distracted, rustling paper and clinking keys.

"What do you need? I might have something here."

There was a pause. "My stomach's just a little unsettled," Emma explained. "Nothing to worry about. See you in a bit."

With a sigh, Allie poured the cabernet, watching as the deep red liquid sloshed up the sides of the glass. Her sister's half hour was more like forty-five minutes or an hour. But that was okay. She could wait.

Her stomach growled with hunger. She nibbled at a bit of Brie on toast, put a few juicy grapes in her mouth. Allie took a sip of the wine, smiling as she remembered Morgan's animated sales pitch about the adorable labels. Allie never should have bought three bottles. But, then again, what harm would it do?

Allie stretched out her legs and took a long drink from her glass. The sweet, dark wine was lovely, she decided. Just right for a night like this. A warm glow spread over her body, the alcohol making its way into her limbs, loosening everything a little bit.

Out of habit, Allie picked up the phone, checked the volume. Was it on silent? Were there messages? Had she missed something? When she flipped over the cell to check, the screen was blank.

She clicked on the television, aimlessly running through the channels. "Nothing, nothing, nothing," she announced to herself after ten minutes of searching. She pushed off her chair, poured a second glass of wine, and considered her options.

Allie would wait another fifteen minutes, then call.

She wandered around the living room, pausing at photos of her and Emma. There was a particular one of the two sisters on Allie's ninth birthday, dressed in princess costumes and tiaras. They were grinning with cake-smeared smiles, clutching each other's shoulder. Beside it, in a wooden frame, was last year's anniversary dinner with Ben. He was so handsome in his navy sport coat and tie. Allie was tanned and laughing, clinging to his arm after he'd told her a joke. She loved that photograph.

Allie adjusted the picture frame and turned to lean on the counter. *Where was her sister?* As she stared out at the dark lawn, Molly, sensing her unease, trotted up close to her leg, sniffing the air.

"What do you think, girl?" Allie murmured, reaching down to rub the dog's head and neck. She stroked her fur, thinking it so odd that Emma still hadn't arrived. Her neck prickled. If something else was wrong and Emma was in trouble, she needed to know about it.

She straightened and took another sip of wine. "I'm such a worrier, aren't I?" she asked out loud.

Molly cocked her head up and raised her ears expectantly. She let out a sharp bark.

Allie grinned, then walked to the front door and opened it. "Don't rub it in, Molly." She watched as her dog bounded outside, then rolled in a pile of dried leaves near the curb. Allie squinted, barely able to see the dog's shape under the thin sliver of moon. Wispy clouds floated across the black sky, the shadows softening the edges of the sidewalk and mailbox.

The night was balmy and warm for November, but Allie shivered in spite of the temperature, clasping her elbows and tucking them close to her body. In the distance, a car's engine revved and whined. Allie listened.

In the far side of the yard, Molly pawed at the ground, nosing at the grass with the dedication of an experienced private eye. A squirrel chattered overhead. Molly growled, then let out a series of ear-piercing barks. A light snapped on in the window across the street.

"Come on, girl!" Allie urged and slapped at the side of her leg. Molly bounded up, eyes shining. She was breathing hard, tongue lolling to one side.

Allie checked the time again. Emma was almost forty minutes late, making Allie officially frustrated and worried. She debated about calling her parents, but they were still at dinner. And there were very few people, if any, Emma would actually confide in.

She picked up the wine glass and poured the remaining liquid into the sink. A few drops hit her black sweater and disappeared. "Great," she murmured, not bothering to blot the stains. She needed to go. Allie grabbed her windbreaker from inside the door. "Come on, Molly. Let's go for a walk."

It took only a few minutes. A lone truck—likely the manager's— sat near the grocery store's entrance, but otherwise, the lot was barren. As an added measure, she walked the length of the property to make sure she hadn't missed Emma's car.

Allie's eyes moved to the still-new sign in the front of a narrow but long one-story building next door. The coach's pharmacy.

She paused. If Emma's stomach was upset, she could have stopped there, thinking it was quicker than the grocery store. She scanned the blacktop. No cars. No sign of Emma.

Molly began whining and pulling on her leash.

"What is it?" Allie allowed her to lead, following the dog's sniffing nose through a row of sparse trees in the far corner of the lot. It was then, looking at the back of the pharmacy, that she noticed a door cracked open. From the opening, a slice of florescent light illuminated a small Dumpster and flattened cardboard boxes propped up beside it.

She turned to leave, but then reconsidered. What if an employee had forgotten to lock up? What if there had been an accident? Just a day ago, her father was talking about a veterinarian's wife who had collapsed at home. No one thought to check on her over the course of nine hours. And by then, it was too late.

Allie's adrenaline kicked in. She tied Molly's leash to a post and gave her a firm command. "Stay, girl."

Gripping her cell phone, she debated about calling the police. If this was nothing, she'd look ridiculous. Allie glanced both ways, picking her way across the gravel, her shoes crunching against the uneven surface. She put a hand on the door and leaned inside. "Hello?"

Allie squinted at the bright lights, shielding her eyes against the glare. She called out again. Silence, then a moan, the sound of something low, came from the back.

Allie didn't think. She bolted into the back of the pharmacy, rushing toward the noise. In the center of the room, a man lay on his side, arms and legs sprawled out like he'd fallen from three stories up.

Letting out a cry, she sank to the floor and felt for a pulse. "Coach?"

At the sound of her voice, his eyes opened, his mouth parted slightly to speak. A thick gurgle rose from his throat. His body tensed, then went slack. The side of his head was cut and bloodied.

With a hand on his back and one on his neck, she tried to ease him into a prone position. Not anticipating his weight and bulk, the coach's body slipped in her hands, causing the tips of her fingers to scrape his skin as she caught him. Gasping for breath, Allie tilted his head back and started compressions, rescue breaths. Again, she felt for a heartbeat. Allie continued pushing on his chest until the muscles in her arms burned. She felt one rib crack, then another.

She didn't stop when noise erupted from all sides. Shouting, feet stomping, doors opening. Hands, several of them, pulled her away, yanked Allie to her feet. Emergency workers flooded the room; sirens wailed. Allie saw Sheriff Gaines, his face grim and cold, jaw set, right before she collapsed.

When Allie opened her eyes, she was propped up in the back of a police cruiser, filthy and dazed. There were streaks of caked blood on one hand, like dried paint. She pressed a hand to her forehead, unable to remember where it had come from.

From the corner of her eye, she caught movement from the pharmacy.

EMTs, each one shuffling his feet like a pallbearer at a funeral. They carried out a black body bag. The contents, lumpy and heavy, were hoisted into the county coroner's vehicle.

Gaines surveyed the scene and turned back to Allie. He reached into the patrol car, grabbed at the crook of her elbow, and shook her hard. "What happened?"

Allie gasped. "I-I don't know. The door was open. I walked in." She inhaled through her nose, fighting the shooting pain. "You're hurting me."

He released her arm, sneering. "You walked in the back, after the place was closed for the night? That's trespassing."

"Something wasn't right," Allie said weakly. "I was only trying to help."

"You must feel pretty at home to just walk in the back door of a business."

Allie recoiled as if she'd been slapped. "Sh-sheriff, I was looking for my sister. She was supposed to be at the grocery store. Her-her stomach was upset. She was late. I was looking for her."

"You weren't looking for her," he erupted. He glowered down at Allie, his nostrils flaring. "You were inside a private building, trespassing."

Anger surged inside Allie. "That's not at all what I was doing," she snapped before she could realize what exactly she was saying.

"Don't you take that tone—" The buzz of a cell interrupted Gaines's retort. He turned away and put a hand down to silence it.

The sheriff locked eyes with Allie, who was fighting to maintain a strong exterior. Below the surface, though, she felt as if her very life force were being suctioned out through an ever-widening hole in her heart.

"Why don't you start by telling me what happened?" Gaines repeated.

Trembling, Allie clasped her hands. "This is all a mistake. Can't you see that?" She searched his stern face with disbelief, then exhaled deeply, blowing all of the air from her lungs.

Gaines drew back and raised an eyebrow. "You just made this easy," he spat out. "Have you been drinking?"

He turned away from Allie and then motioned at a man on his right. "Do a Breathalyzer. Then get her downtown. Reynolds, you transport."

"My dog. She's tied to a post, over there." Allie pointed across the parking lot. She heard Molly barking, mournful, anguished cries.

Gaines gritted his teeth. "Elliott, make sure Dr. Marshall comes and gets the dog," he snarled. All of the officers snapped to attention, many of them older men she recognized from patrols around town and football games. They probably knew her father, maybe even had coffee together on Saturday mornings. Every one of them avoided her gaze.

Reynolds took Allie by the elbow, easing her into the nearest patrol car. He said nothing and kept his grip firm, but not tight. He placed a giant hand on her head, guiding her movement so that she didn't strike it on the door frame. After he recited instructions on the Breathalyzer, Reynolds held the tube for Allie. When she finished blowing, her vision wobbled.

The officer stepped away, and the rear door slammed shut. Allie jumped, then stared, unblinking, at the thick steel rods dividing the front from the backseat.

Reynolds slipped into the front seat and cranked the engine. As the car left the parking lot, she shuddered. Streetlights cast yellowed circles of light on the sidewalks and front lawns. Familiar houses flashed by. Neighbors, people she'd known since childhood, stood half-awake on their front porches, watching the parade of police vehicles and flashing lights.

She was terrified, but forced herself not to cry. They rode in silence to the police station, where she was escorted into a small, windowless room to wait.

FIFTY-FOUR

SHERIFF GAINES

2016

The last time he'd seen June, she'd been fine. Happy, even. More awake and alert than she'd been in years. Gaines choked back a guttural cry, a sound between anger and agony.

On the phone, the administrator told him June's death had been sudden. That she hadn't been in pain. His best guess was a heart attack or stroke. A clot could have dislodged and made its way through her body to her already-fragile brain. By the time anyone realized something was wrong, she was gone.

When he'd hung up from the call, he'd turned on his siren and lights, raced to the nursing home, and pulled into the parking lot. Inside, he'd taken the stairs two at a time, edging past the small crowd of employees around the nurses' station. He'd barely registered all of the people, including the tall, lanky teenager with the dark hair who took off as soon as Gaines arrived.

Chest heaving, the sheriff ran into his wife's room. He skidded to a stop. June looked at peace, he thought, lying in her bed. The aide came in behind him, whispering that the medical examiner was on his way.

"Give us a minute?" Gaines asked. When she stepped out of the room, he knelt in front of his wife and laid his head in her lap, gripping her fragile hand. Tears leaked from his eyes, wracking, silent sobs filled his chest. He smothered the sound in the crook of his elbow.

"I miss you," he murmured, mourning the woman he'd lost ten years before. Then Gaines straightened, sat back on his heels, and sucked in gulps of air. There was more to do before June could truly rest. He owed it to her.

Gaines pulled himself upright, knees creaking in protest. When he opened the door and motioned for the nursing supervisor, she took a careful step toward him and reached to touch his arm, a gesture of empathy. But Gaines didn't have time for that, not now. And because of his job, these people would never question him.

"I have to go. Emergency. One of my men is in trouble. Possible hostage situation. Please take care of what you can," he explained, avoiding eye contact. "I'll be back as soon as I can."

"Of course." The nurse nodded, eyes wide.

He was out of the building and back outside, behind the wheel and driving in less than three minutes. The story was a complete fabrication, but Gaines didn't care. He had to leave, get out of that awful place.

The sheriff pulled into the driveway of his new house and let Chief into the shaded backyard as he gathered supplies for the trip. Gaines made three trips to the garage, loading the trunk with everything he could possibly need.

Finally, the sheriff made sure Chief had enough food and water to last the day. When he knelt down again to stroke the dog's thick coat, his eyes filled with tears. "Good boy, stay."

Chief whined and pawed at the chain link as Gaines drove away. He couldn't watch. He had to focus on the road.

As the miles passed, no matter how much he fought it, his mind drifted back to Allie Marshall. Despite his firm warning, there was nothing she wouldn't do or say to have the investigation into Coach Thomas's death reopened.

So today he would take care of the only other thing he was concerned about Allie Marshall finding. If it was still there. Gaines pressed the accelerator, pushing the engine to respond. The drive didn't take long. There was no music, no radio. An occasional rock or pebble hitting the undercarriage of the cruiser. The splat of an unlucky insect against the windshield. The rub of rubber on the road as he braked around a sharp curve. He flicked on the windshield wipers, sending streams of fluid onto the glass, and watched the parallel black rubber lines cross back and forth across his line of vision, smearing the bug's remains.

As he slowed and turned off the road, the car bumped over the uneven ground. Gaines pulled up to the structure, jumped out of the patrol car, and stared. It was there. Coach Thomas had lied. And the sheriff had convinced himself the one man he couldn't trust had kept his promise.

Near the back of the property, he noticed the adjoining building and did a double take. The door had been broken, split to pieces, as if someone had thrown a sledgehammer right through it. The remaining wooden slab hung precariously on its hinges. The sheriff pulled out his gun as he crept toward the opening and eased inside, bracing himself for someone to jump out of a darkened corner. But there was no one there.

Gaines holstered his weapon and scanned the room, taking in the benzyl alcohol, distilled water, syringes, and glass beakers. Cotton balls and rags sat near a stove with four small burners. He narrowed his eyes. Empty vials of equipoise. Below them, there were footprints in the dust. The sight of them chilled his veins. Allie Marshall had been here. She knew.

Anger welled up inside his chest. Gaines reached for his keys, stalking out to the patrol car, blind to everything but his plan.

Justice, sweet justice, would be watching this place burn to the ground. His own personal Dante's *Inferno*.

FIFTY-FIVE

EMMA

2016

Emma was so very tired. She'd been on the run all day, avoiding her phone, her clients, and her own family. And then there was the stop at the nursing home. As expected, slipping into the private room had been easy. The nurses were busy with charts and medicine checks, the aides swapping stories near the bathroom.

June Gaines had been resting, face up, hands folded across her waist. Her hair was smoothed and coiffed, as if she were to be awakened at any moment for the arrival of a royal guest.

Emma had taken a thick pillow, grasping it firmly in both hands, and held it over the woman's face until she stopped struggling. The minutes dragged by like hours, and Emma's arms ached from fighting. The woman had been stronger than she'd imagined, but gave up the fight after Emma had laid her full weight on the woman, staying there for several more minutes just to make sure.

When she pulled back the pillow, Emma surveyed June's appearance. With a glance around the room, she spied a soft brush on the dresser. Minutes later, Dr. Gaines's hair was brushed and patted into place. Her blouse was smoothed, her hands placed carefully in the same position as they'd been when Emma first walked in the room. She looked close to perfect. And at peace.

Now Emma could take care of Caroline without interference from that awful woman. And Allie—she would take care of sister dear—after she made one last stop.

A short drive later, Emma entered the wrought-iron gate. She made her way up the hill, her shoes pressing into the smooth gravel, making a crunching sound with each step. When she came to the last row from the top, Emma stepped onto the soft grass. With silent feet, she counted the steps, remembering how many it had taken her the last time she'd visited.

It had been years, but not much had changed. The same flowers edged the trees and small flags fluttered in the slight breeze, marking certain resting places. A bench, large enough for two people to sit, had been placed near his marker. She stopped there.

The grave had a magnificent view of Brunswick, with space for his wife and their children. His mother and father were still living, retired in Florida, according to the Internet. Of course, she'd never met them. She couldn't leave the hospital for the funeral.

The community rallied around the coach's wife, taking her enough casseroles and pies for three freezers. Churches collected money for her husband's burial expenses. Someone said a light always burned in the window of their home because Coach Thomas's family had constant visitors. No one wanted to leave them alone.

Two weeks later, the coach's wife sold the house, the pharmacy business, packed up her girls, and moved away. A year later, the high school erected a memorial in his honor. That part proved the most difficult for Emma, a constant reminder of what she didn't have. Of what she could never have. Of what had been taken away.

Perhaps the cruelest blow of all—caring for her sister's child, a bitter replacement for the baby she'd lost. And every time Emma saw her niece, it reminded her of her own losses. She would never be a wife to the man she loved. She would never carry another son or daughter. She could never have the family she wanted.

Waking up in the morning and functioning was effort enough. She lived a respectable life, cared for Caroline, helped her parents: the sister who did everything right. And it still wasn't enough. It would never be.

Allie had everything. She always did. And in the end, she would get Caroline back too.

Emma knew this now. Her niece was like the rest of the human race, like her parents and Natalie Harper and others. They'd forgive and forget, and soon Allie would be back to being the favorite. She'd made inroads already. Caroline was softening; it wouldn't be long before she'd decide that she wanted to be Allie's daughter again. That she wanted her real mother. All children did.

After what seemed like hours, Emma made herself get up and walk to the gravestone. In the grass, she knelt in front of the rectangular gravestone, ran a finger along the edge.

She grasped the small box in her pocket, pulled it out, and removed the top. She reached inside. Time to say good-bye to both of them. She stared at the granite marker, tracing his name with her eyes, her cheeks wet with tears.

Boyd Thomas.

I miss you. I'll always love you. I'm lost without you.

Help me.

What should I do? Where do I belong?

A gust of air blew the tree branches overhead, scattering crisp autumn leaves to the ground like confetti. He answered her through nature, offering a release and a blessing.

Dabbing at her face with the edge of her sleeve, drying her eyes, she almost laughed out loud at his wisdom. *Of course.* One more stop to make, then home.

Gathering all of her strength, Emma held up the cherub figurine, turning it over one last time, memorizing the curves and lines. She turned the little angel to face the gravestone.

"This is your father, sweetie," Emma whispered. "But you two have probably already met." She raised her eyes to the dark sky. "Up there in heaven."

With a gentle sigh, Emma pressed her lips to the delicate porcelain figurine. With a trembling hand, she set it down on the grass, nestling the statuette close to the stone. Her child would be protected here.

As she made her way down the hill and back through the iron gate, the buzz of Emma's cell phone broke the silence. She glanced at the screen, sighing at yet another call from Allie.

She waited for the requisite amount of time to pass, listened for the tone signaling a new voice mail, and listened as she walked.

I've found something really important, Emma. Some real evidence about Coach Thomas and Sheriff Gaines. As soon as you can, I need you to meet me at this address, and I'll show you everything.

After she played the message for a second time, Emma typed the address into her cell and checked the mileage. She sighed heavily. The trip would take ninety minutes, maybe more, all so that Emma could listen to her sister's far-fetched scheme to prove the sheriff's culpability.

Pausing outside her car, Emma debated about the drive and the distance. She was exhausted. She needed to go back to her parents' house, pick up Caroline, and get as far away from Brunswick as she could.

But she couldn't quite shake the urgency in Allie's voice. *Please come.* Her sister had her guard down, anxious to share whatever she'd found. Emma dropped her cell phone into the outside pocket of her bag and fished out her car keys, her fingers tightening around the metal teeth. She squeezed harder, feeling the sharp angles cut into her skin.

It was then Emma's pulse began to race. Fumbling with the remote, Emma unlocked her car and slid inside, cranking the engine as quickly as she could.

FIFTY-SIX

CAROLINE

2016

Caroline was at Emma's, hiding out from the world for a while, despite what she'd told her grandparents about visiting friends. She needed quiet, time to think. She was laying on her bed, staring up at the ceiling, when she heard the tires squeal in the driveway.

Scooping up her cell phone, Caroline jumped up and ran for the front door.

She'd barely reached the handle and swung the door open when Russell stepped inside the house. His eyes darted from corner to corner of the room. "Where is she? Your aunt? Did she come back?"

Caroline paused. "She, um, left me this note and said she was going out of town. I'm supposed to stay with my grandparents." She wrinkled her nose. "It's weird. She's never done that before."

Russell frowned. "I think I saw your aunt leaving Dr. Gaines's room this afternoon. I swear it."

Wrinkling her nose, Caroline hesitated. "That doesn't make any sense. Why would she be there?"

"Listen." Russell touched Caroline's arm. "I don't want to tell you this, but June Gaines . . . She died."

"Wait. What?" Caroline felt her body sway unsteadily.

"I was working, just doing my thing, and I could have sworn I saw you—or your aunt—leaving June Gaines's room." Russell wrinkled his forehead. "I started walking over to see if it was you—like, I thought you'd forgotten something and come back." He stared at the floor. "By the time I got to the stairwell, there was this big commotion behind me. The overhead intercom started blowing up," Russell said. "People were running in and out of Dr. Gaines's room, and then one of the aides told me she died—just like that. They couldn't do anything to help her. Sheriff Gaines came. They called the medical examiner . . ."

Caroline's hand flew to her mouth. "B-but she was fine a few hours ago."

"I know," Russell said, running a hand through his hair. "I just don't think it was an accident." He exhaled and glanced around as if someone might be listening to their conversation. He lowered his voice. "We need to do something. I think we need to tell someone."

Chest tight, head swimming, Caroline hesitated.

Russell bent down to look into Caroline's eyes and reached out for her hand. "But my mom and dad just left—there was some vet emergency on St. Simons and the family couldn't bring their dog in." Russell let Caroline's hand go. "And they can only help so much. Let's at least try to talk to your mom."

Biting her bottom lip, Caroline grabbed her bag and keys, locking Emma's door behind her. She followed Russell silently, slid into the front seat, and held her breath on the way to her mother's rental house.

As they rounded the corner, pulled up to the curb, and parked, Caroline slid down in the seat, causing Russell to flash a worried look in her direction. "Hey, it'll be okay. I promise."

Caroline caught her breath as Russell leaned over and kissed her cheek. The next second he pushed open the car door and jogged to Allie's front porch.

Color rising in her cheeks, Caroline watched him peer into the windows.

For a full two minutes, he didn't move, mesmerized by something inside. Finally, Russell shifted to get a better look. What was he looking at? She strained to see, hoping he might turn around and signal something—some clue about what was inside. When she couldn't stand it any longer, Caroline opened her door, stepped onto the sidewalk, and ran lightly up the porch stairs. "What is it?"

"A map," Russell said, his hands still cupped around his eyes.

Caroline leaned in to get a better look, but the afternoon light made everything shadowy inside the house. "A map?" she echoed.

But Russell didn't answer. He was already down the front steps, sprinting away, before Caroline could ask where he was going. She wanted to call out, yell for him to stop, but that would surely draw attention to anyone driving by who saw the two teenagers. By all rights, anyone with any sense would know they likely had no business being on Allie's porch and peeking in the windows, even if it was her own mother's house. By the time Caroline had thought to glance across the street to make sure the neighbors weren't staring through their windows, Russell opened the front door of Allie's house.

"What the . . ." Caroline's jaw dropped.

"Remember the kids I hung out with?" Russell grinned. "I picked up a few skills along the way."

"I don't think we should—" Caroline's mouth went dry.

Russell took her by the hand and pulled her inside, closing the door behind her. "You can't stay on the porch." He tugged her over to the wall, pointed at the map, and then picked up a notebook with lists made in a woman's cursive handwriting. "Look at all of this," he breathed.

The words swam in front of Caroline's eyes as she tried to focus. She couldn't think. She was inside her mother's house. Russell had just committed breaking and entering.

But Russell was still talking. "This all makes sense," he said. He gestured from the notes to the map on the wall. "The timeline, the locations. All of this stuff about Coach Thomas and Sheriff Gaines. That flyer at the school." He turned to face Caroline. "I think your mom found something." He poked a finger in the center of the triangle. "Something big."

Caroline sucked in a breath and stared at the red pushpin stuck in the middle of Coffee County, Georgia. "But—I don't get it. Why there? And what is it?"

"Come on," Russell said, grasping her hand. "We're going to find out."

FIFTY - SEVEN

ALLIE

2016

Allie was waiting, leaning on her mother's car, when Emma pulled in from the dirt road and parked next to the cabin.

"Finally," she said, relieved as her sister stepped out of the car, blinking into the late-afternoon sunshine. "I've been trying to reach you for days," Allie chided. "I was worried sick."

"I know," Emma murmured, holding the keys in her hand. She fidgeted, refusing to look at anything but the ramshackle cabin. "What is this place?"

"Why don't you tell me?" Allie asked quietly.

"I-I don't know," Emma replied, lifting her chin in defiance.

A sudden gust of wind whistled around them like a warning.

"Fine," Allie said, shaking her head. "It seems Coach Thomas— and probably a few other people—had quite an operation going on here about ten years ago. A little home cooking. Steroids for the football team."

Emma flinched.

"You know, my idea? The one that everyone thought was crazy?" Allie folded her arms tight to her chest.

"Oh great." Emma rolled her eyes. "So, you brought me here to tell me that you were right all along? That's what this is all about? To shove it in my face?"

Allie recoiled as if her sister had taken a swing at her head. "No," she said, shaking her head. "You know what Caroline said to me. You know I had to find who was really responsible for killing the coach. I told you I thought it was Sheriff Gaines." Her voice faltered. "There was a time you cared about my innocence. You said a dozen times that it was all so unfair—the investigation, the trial."

"It's always been about you, hasn't it?" Emma sneered. "You, you, you."

"I—" Allie struggled for an answer. Right before her eyes, her sister had morphed into an enemy, staring at her with something that looked a lot like hatred.

Allie steeled herself. She had come here for answers, no matter how viciously Emma wanted to fight. "This also happens to be about *you*. You and the coach."

"What are you talking about?" Her sister paled.

"All of those secret phone calls, you heading out in the middle of the night," Allie said, choking back nausea at the thought. "It was Coach Thomas, wasn't it?"

This time Emma balked. She pressed her lips together, stuffed her hands in her pockets, and looked away.

"I found something here. It has your handwriting on it."

This got her sister's attention. Emma's head swiveled, her eyes flashing, as if daring Allie to go on.

Allie turned to where her purse sat on the car and withdrew the card. Clutching it tightly, she held it up for Emma to see. "It says 'C—I love you.'" Allie's voice raised an octave. She waited, anticipating, not at all certain her sister would answer. Allie braced for Emma to run away, to jump in the car.

But Emma stood still for what seemed like ages. Finally, she broke the silence. "So what? I did love him."

An electric current ran the length of Allie's body, jolting her with pain. It was true. Somehow Allie found her voice, willing it not to shake. "And what about the rest? What about the steroids?"

Emma shrugged. "Sure, he was giving stuff to the players. D'Shawn Montgomery, some of the others."

Allie blinked as her sister reeled off the information as if they were discussing the merits of using vitamin C to cure the common cold.

"It was supposed to help their performance. He said they needed it, certain players did, and that it would only make things better. It would help them get college prospects and a winning season, guaranteed."

Forcing herself to remain calm, Allie thought carefully about her next questions. "So . . . Dad. Dad was okay with this?"

Her sister wrinkled her nose and offered a righteous look. "Yeah, right." Then Emma pressed a hand to her chest. "Dad didn't know a thing about it. He'd have lost it completely if he found out." She narrowed her eyes.

"What about now?" Allie allowed her voice to trail off. She dangled the question in the night air, hoping for a reaction, needing to hear what her sister would say next.

Emma crossed her arms in disgust. "Seriously, Allie. What? Are you going to tattle on me like I'm in kindergarten?" She scoffed and glared. "You're not going to tell anyone. All it'll do is get *you* in more trouble." She sniffed.

No regret, not a shred of guilt. The sister she had thought she'd known was a complete stranger. A being she didn't recognize. One without a soul.

Emma kept talking. "At first I didn't know anything was missing. I really didn't pay much attention to what I was ordering. I thought Dad was just doing more injectables at the stables. Then one night Coach put vials of some medicine in his pocket. I thought—"

"What? Wait a minute," Allie asked, stunned. "He was taking it—stealing it? You knew? And you let him?" Her mouth gaped open. She forced it closed.

"He said it would help the team." Emma deflected the accusation without a blink, as if Allie's opinion carried the weight of a cotton ball. "You know that *everyone* wanted them to win. Even Mom and Dad. Even you."

Allie dug her fingernails into her palms but kept her face smooth. She assembled the facts in her brain, trying not to explode.

"It was all for good," Emma defended him. "He was doing it to help," her sister wailed, catching a sob in her throat. "You can't see that because you had everything." She wiped at her eyes with the back of her fists. "He was all I had—all I ever had. And then I lost him and . . ."

All of a sudden, Allie couldn't suck in enough air to make her body feel balanced. Everything was floating. "You lost . . . his baby?" Allie asked, not wanting to hear the answer. She was trembling.

Emma raised her eyes and sniffed back tears. "I never had a chance to tell him. He was so upset that night, really angry, not himself at all. It seems so ridiculous now." She choked out a little laugh.

Allie swallowed hard. *She loved him. She believed him. No—it was much more than that. She worshipped him like a deity.*

"We had an argument," Emma continued. "A disagreement. That was all. I didn't feel good, so I left." She drew a long face. "That's when I went to the hospital."

"I don't believe that it was just a disagreement."

As if in slow motion, Emma lifted her head, turning her face to glare at Allie. "What did you say?" her sister demanded.

"You're lying." Allie stepped forward and clenched Emma's

arm tight. Her sister's rape or attack or assault story had been a ruse, a trick to throw everyone off. And it had worked brilliantly. "He put you in the hospital, didn't he? He hit you. He'd been doing it all along. But that night he *really* hurt you. Isn't that right?"

Emma did her best to shake loose of Allie's grip.

"Sheriff Gaines—is that who you were fighting about?" Allie demanded. "Because he was going to stop Coach Thomas's little operation?" She stopped to catch her breath, chest heaving. "Or maybe . . . maybe he was there too."

Like a wild beast caught in a snare, Emma screamed, "Let me go!"

"He was there," Allie said, challenging her sister to tell her otherwise. It all made sense now. It all made perfect sense. "He walked in on the coach smacking you around, didn't he? Got in the middle of it."

Allie held on, the fingers on her right hand going numb. "And then Gaines ended it. Hit him so hard that he died . . ." she sputtered. "And you both left him there." She squeezed harder. "Didn't you?"

Emma cried out, trying to wrench her body away.

Allie let go of her sister's arm.

"He-he wasn't himself that night. I ran. I had to save the baby," Emma began to sob.

An owl hooted in the distance, followed by the flutter of wings. In the fading light, her sister's face crumpled with anguish and grief.

"I know . . . I know he never meant to hurt us," she whispered to herself. "He loved me."

"So did I, Emma," Allie replied, tears welling up in her eyes. "So did I."

FIFTY-EIGHT

ALLIE

2016

In a trance-like state, Emma hugged her arms to her chest. She swayed side to side, repeating the words. "He never meant to hurt us." Sobs wracked Emma's body as she sank to the ground, clawing at the grass and dirt in grief and desperation.

"We could have helped. Don't you think you should have told us?" Allie bent down and touched her sister's shoulder.

Emma sprang to her feet and pushed Allie away. "Don't touch me!" she screamed. "Don't ever touch me."

Stumbling to catch her balance, Allie braced herself against the car. "What's wrong with you?"

"*You could have helped?*" Emma laughed, the sound shrill and tight. "What? You, Mom, Dad—the do-gooders—pitching in to 'help' poor Emma. You can say what you like, but I was never going to measure up to you."

"Emma—"

"Mom and Dad only cared about you," Emma snapped. "You were their favorite. You were going to *medical school.*"

"It's not true," Allie managed to choke out.

"Oh, it is. And I rallied back for a little while once they sent you away, but it was always 'your sister this and your sister that.' It got tiresome."

"What? What did I ever do to you?"

Emma snickered and put her hands on her hips. "Oh, let's see. The pool incident. You let Morgan push me and stood there, staring at me, while I sunk to the bottom. You had to *think* about whether to save me. You should have let me drown." She wiped at her cheeks angrily.

"We were kids, Emma. *Kids.* Sure, we wanted to scare you, get you away from the pool. But after you fell, I was terrified," Allie said. "I couldn't move for a second. But I did jump in and pulled you out. Doesn't that count?"

"You did it for show, to prove, once again, how wonderful you were. Come on, Allie, you were in the stupid newspaper. Everyone was so proud. The angel, swooping in to save her poor little sister."

"That's not fair."

"You're right. It's not."

Allie stared hard into her sister's eyes. "Why, Emma? Why do you hate me?"

"There's a fine line." Emma looked away. "I loved you. I worshipped you. And you were willing to watch me die."

"That's not true," Allie said. The venom in her sister's voice shocked her. "You've got it all wrong." She stopped, blinking back tears. "I'm sorry, Em, if you feel that way. Why didn't you say something?"

"Like it would have made a difference?"

It was then that Allie realized the depth of her sister's hatred. Since they were children, Emma had been adding up her sister's alleged offenses and marking each of them unforgivable, etched in cold, hard stone.

Allie thought fast. She wanted to keep Emma talking. Making

her angry wasn't helping. "Think about it. After that, there was never another mean word or smart remark. Never. I almost lost you. My sister. And it changed me. Don't you see that?"

"No."

"So, all of those days you came to Arrendale. What was that about?" Allie asked.

Her sister turned her head, concentrating on a speck of dust, and shrugged.

"What about Caroline?" Allie demanded. "She never visited after the first few times. Was that you or was that my daughter? Did you tell her not to come?"

Emma shifted her jaw from side to side, considering the question. She wouldn't meet Allie's eyes.

"Let me guess. You told her it was a bad idea. That it might upset her? That she might feel worse after seeing me?" Though she felt like dying inside, Allie fought to keep her voice calm. "You sent me that adoption information. You talked to Natalie about it. My boss. How could you, Emma?"

"She wants me to adopt her. She said it," her sister snapped.

Allie gasped. "She's my child, Emma. I'll need to hear that from her." She was breathing hard, as if she'd just finished sprinting three miles. "What gives you the right to judge me?"

"A jury—" Emma lifted her head.

"You're not on a jury. You're family. You're my sister." Allie lowered her voice.

"Can't choose your family," Emma quipped, her bottom lip thrust out.

Caught up in the argument, Allie didn't hear the rumble of an engine until the Glynn County Sheriff's car was several yards away. She whirled to see Gaines exiting the vehicle, a gun pointed at her chest.

FIFTY-NINE

CAROLINE

2016

"Oh my goodness." Caroline sat straight up in the passenger's seat. At the edge of the woods, Russell pulled to the left side of the road, behind the thickest row of trees just before the clearing.

"Whose cars?" Russell shot her a worried look, turned the key, and pulled it out of the ignition. The last thing they needed to do was draw attention to themselves.

"I think I saw Emma's," Caroline whispered.

"Let's go see." Russell eased open the door and slid outside, beckoning for Caroline to do the same.

They crept to the nearest oak, hiding behind the thick trunk. Three cars were parked around the most run down shack she'd ever seen. Caroline squinted, gripping the bark, her voice quavering. "That's Grandma Lily's car, Emma's car, and—" She turned to Russell, raising an eyebrow.

"Yep, that's the sheriff's car," Russell said, lowering his voice.

"What are they all doing here?" she whispered. "Maybe you should call your mom and dad?"

Russell nodded and dug in his pocket for his cell phone. Glancing at the screen, he frowned. "I've got, like, one bar."

Caroline swallowed hard.

There was a loud wooden creak and the sound of boots on stairs.

Russell yanked Caroline back, pulling her into a crouch. Through the bushes, she could see the sheriff behind her mother and Emma, pointing his gun. She stifled a cry.

"He's going to take them somewhere," Caroline hissed at Russell. "He'll see us. He'll see the car." Her pulse thudded so loudly she could barely hear his response.

"Just wait," he murmured, holding his finger over his lips as he leaned forward to get a better view.

As quietly as she could, Caroline moved in closer to Russell, keeping her eyes glued on the sheriff, her mother, and her aunt.

But instead of forcing the women into the patrol car, Gaines popped the trunk, took out two cans of gasoline, and handed one to Emma and one to Allie. He barked some orders and gestured with the handgun.

With a furtive glance at each other, Emma and Allie began spreading the liquid around the structure, soaking the walls and grass.

"Oh no," Russell said, balling his hands into fists. "What the hell?"

Caroline couldn't move. The scent of rotten eggs filled the air as her mom poured the gasoline on the steps and Emma sloshed it against the shack, Gaines's gaze never leaving them.

When he seemed satisfied that there wasn't another drop left in the cans, grim-faced, Gaines took out a lighter.

"Don't do this," Allie called to him. "You don't have to do this."

"You got out of prison and ruined my life." He raised his voice. "Ten years ago, Coach died. Now my wife is gone." He let out an anguished cry. "I don't have anything to live for."

"But you do," Allie argued with a glance at Emma.

"No," Gaines shot back. "Don't play games with me."

Caroline peered through the leaves and could see her mother's lips pressed tightly together. Why wasn't Emma saying anything? Why wasn't she helping? Her aunt's face had turned ghostly white. Emma's usually bright eyes were clouded over.

"A whole county voted you into office," Allied added. "The *people* elected you."

"You don't care," Gaines snapped back. "You hate me."

"You destroyed my life." She pressed her fingertips to her temples. "I was going to medical school. I was ready to work hard and save lives. I had my daughter to take care of."

Caroline was so consumed with the exchange that Russell had to take her hand and squeeze it to get her attention. He pointed at his phone and mouthed 9-1-1. Russell typed a message, hit Send, then turned the screen so that Caroline could see. The text was to Natalie, with the address, a mention of Gaines, Emma, Allie, and the gun, and *CALL 9-1-1.*

"We've been through all of this before, haven't we, Sheriff?" Allie said.

Caroline stiffened. What was her mother talking about?

"Paying personal visits to people at all hours of the night. Making accusations when, in fact, you're equally culpable for everything that happened," Allie added.

"That's bull," the sheriff blustered. "This"—he waved at the cabin—"all of this was not my idea."

"But you didn't end it, did you?" Allie replied, standing up as straight as she could. "You fanned the fire. You took my editorial—about this place, about Coach Thomas beating those boys—and you acted like I'd accused you of genocide."

The sheriff stared at Allie. "This ends now," he growled.

"It could have ended a long time ago," Allie said. "You could have turned *yourself* in."

"What in the hell for?" Gaines snapped. He took a menacing step toward her, then stopped.

"You were there," Allie retorted. "That night with the coach—"

"No," Gaines interrupted, "I was *never* there with the coach until after we found you. Then I took care of June."

"But you were with him." Allie turned to Emma. "Isn't that right? Isn't that what you said, Emma?"

Caroline squinted. Emma wasn't moving. Her expression was vacant, like she wasn't even hearing the conversation.

Exasperated, Allie turned back to Gaines. "You were there when my sister was there. She said you were arguing—"

Gaines cut her off. "If I had been, I never would have let my . . ." His voice broke. "My *son* die."

As his voice echoed through the trees, Emma let out a sudden gasp. Allie was shaking her head. And Caroline wasn't even sure she'd heard the sheriff right. *The coach was Sheriff Gaines's son? How?*

"But . . . Boyd . . . Thomas." Allie murmured the words and looked up at the sheriff. She covered her mouth, eyes blinking widely.

"Boyd was what his mama wanted to call him," the sheriff replied through gritted teeth. "It's my given name. Boyd Lee Gaines."

There was a cry. Caroline whirled to see her aunt's face crumple.

Allie began to shake visibly. "All of this time." She raised her voice and turned to face her sister. "All of this time, Emma. You knew what happened that night. You were there, you ran away, and you never once tried to help me."

As if brought back to life, Emma began to back away.

"How could you?" Allie demanded.

From the corner of her eye, Caroline caught a flash of silver. Emma was holding a knife, pointing it right at Allie.

Gaines leapt forward and grabbed Emma's hand, forcing the knife from her grasp. Wrapping an arm around Emma's neck, he refocused the barrel on Allie.

"Don't you move," the sheriff said, backing toward the cabin and up the stairs, dragging a kicking and thrashing Emma with him.

In the doorway, Gaines looked like he was gritting his teeth and tightening his grasp on Emma. She scratched at his arms and began to scream.

"Stop it," the sheriff yelled, driving the butt of his gun into Emma's skull.

"No!" Allie cried out as her sister slumped like a rag doll, a trickle of blood running down her face.

Tears streaming down her cheeks, Caroline tried to jump up and run to her aunt, but Russell held her back, wrapping his arms around her and pulling her close. "Shh-shh. You can't," Russell hissed into her ears. "The police are coming. I promise."

Gaines waved his gun at Allie. "Enough of this. Put your back to me. Right now. And get on your knees."

Still shaking, Allie wobbled on her feet. "Don't. Please. Let us go."

"Not a chance," he grunted. "I said, put your back to me. Get down now."

As Allie turned and sank to her knees, Caroline got to her feet.

The movement caught Allie's attention. When she looked up and saw her daughter, Allie's eyes widened. She pressed a finger to her lips, sending Caroline a warning not to move or breathe.

Caroline watched, legs trembling, as the sheriff, with one arm still around Emma's neck, took out his lighter, flicked his thumb to spark a flame, and tossed it onto the porch steps. The dried wood crackled and caught fire immediately.

Satisfied, Gaines watched the fire dance and grow around

the shack. Caroline held her breath, praying for the wail of police sirens. *Nothing.*

As flames licked at the sides of the building, Allie trained her gaze on Caroline, saying a silent *I love you* as Gaines clicked off the gun's safety.

"No!" Caroline screamed.

Emma jerked and stirred at the noise, her eyes flickering open as the sheriff zeroed in on his target.

Caroline began to run, full-speed, for the cabin ahead, not caring if she lived or died. Seeing the teenager caused Gaines to hesitate for a half second—just enough time for Emma to knock his hand away as the bullet discharged from the chamber.

With a sharp crack of thunder, everything in Caroline's world went dark.

EPILOGUE

ALLIE

Almost twelve months after leaving Arrendale, Allie woke without a single nightmare. With a stretch and a yawn, she swung her legs out from under the sheets and stood up. It was early morning, the time of day when the sun first hits the dew-laden grass, making everything look fresh, bright, and new.

It was a time for new beginnings, Allie reminded herself, pulling the curtains open wide and letting the warm rays bathe her face and arms. The house was still. No gurgle of a coffeemaker or hum of the microwave.

Allie smiled and walked toward the kitchen. It was tiny, but airy and white, freshly painted last weekend. She lifted a mug from inside a cabinet and busied herself making breakfast.

She had a full day ahead at the clinic. Natalie was a talented veterinarian and a great boss. They maintained an excellent relationship. Every single day, Allie felt lucky to have been welcomed into her veterinary practice under the strangest of circumstances.

Circumstances that had led her back to Caroline. She was meeting her daughter this morning at Glynn Overlook Park before work. Caroline's change of heart, a decade in the making, had been wonderful and amazing. A miracle that truly began to take shape the night Emma had saved her life.

After being knocked unconscious by the butt of Gaines's gun, her sister had woken to the sound of Caroline's scream. The first thing she saw—the sheriff aiming the barrel in her niece's direction—caused Emma to react in the only way she could, like a parent protecting her child, a mother who would make the ultimate sacrifice for her daughter.

For that, Allie would be eternally grateful.

When the Coffee County police and paramedics arrived at the coach's cabin that summer evening, Emma was taken to the hospital for treatment of a concussion and second-degree burns. Upon her recovery and subsequent arrest, a psychiatric evaluation was performed, deeming Emma fit to be held in police custody. She would eventually stand trial for the death of Coach Boyd Thomas and the murder of Dr. June Gaines.

For months to follow, the town remained in an uproar, the media zeroing in on every new detail revealed about the case.

The law enforcement investigators confirmed that Boyd was indeed the baby Lee Gaines had fathered out of wedlock. The sheriff had met the boy's mother in Atlanta after a high school bowl game victory, expecting never to see her again. The child was barely a toddler when his mother died from cancer. He'd been Boyd Scott then.

After bouncing through foster care, the little towheaded boy had been adopted, and the parents changed his surname to match theirs.

Over the years, Gaines had kept track of the boy, following his high school career, then college, reaching out to him as he began coaching, citing a fondness for a former colleague who'd worked at his first school in Alabama. The men eventually become close friends.

Years later, Sheriff Boyd Lee Gaines made sure that his son returned home.

The night at the cabin, stricken by panic and grief, rather than allowing the authorities to take him alive, the sheriff had allowed the fire he'd set with his own hands to claim his life. Perhaps, Allie thought, it was his way of reuniting with his wife and son.

The scrutiny and stress caused Allie and her parents to transfer Caroline immediately to a new school for a fresh start. Under advisement from her physician, Caroline also met weekly with a child psychologist to try to make sense of all of the trauma from the past year.

After all, Caroline and Allie had loved Emma deeply. Believed in her, trusted her. And Emma had betrayed both mother and daughter in the worst possible way.

Perhaps the cruelest blow came when the investigators handling Emma's case explained to Allie that had her sister only come forward after her trip to the hospital, she could have claimed self-defense, making it unlikely either woman would ever have to serve prison time.

The shock was almost too much to bear. Allie took a brief leave of absence from Natalie's office, spending her days between home, the therapist's office, and the solitude of St. Simons Island before dawn. On her worst days, she ran for miles along the beachfront roads when the pressure of it all seemed too much.

But that December, after settling into her new school, Caroline accepted the idea of meeting Allie for coffee on Wednesdays. Over the next few months, mother and daughter reconnected at a cautious pace, like drops of rain filling a one-hundred-gallon drum.

In May, Caroline surprised everyone by asking Allie if she could come and live with her on a trial basis. When her own parents endorsed the idea wholeheartedly, Allie could barely contain her enthusiasm. The following week, Caroline buzzed with plans for her new bedroom, describing a funky paint scheme and gauze curtains she'd seen in a magazine. They'd been shopping and had picked out bookshelves, a small desk and chair for schoolwork. She was moving in the next day.

The transition to being mother and daughter again hadn't been easy or perfect, but Allie savored the moments, her unbridled joy tempered only occasionally with a touch of regret. Caroline would leave in a few years, off to college and a career path. Allie knew she would let her go, though it would break her apart inside.

After so much wishing that the years would fly by inside Arrendale, it was a conscious effort, a life shift, for Allie to live in the present, the here and now, counting her blessings after many hard lessons.

Looking back, though Emma's betrayal was horrifying and surreal, Allie realized that she, too, had lost her way. She had been so focused on fighting a fight she couldn't win, on proving the impossible to a community who loved its football coach, that she'd lost sight of what was truly important—her family, her child, and her future.

The painful truth, that sharp realization, allowed Allie the first steps toward hope and healing. Toward true forgiveness.

Without it, the past would chain Allie to a dark place, a prison of her own making, with cell walls built of guilt, remorse, and regret. Without forgiveness—for Emma and herself—Allie would never be happy or whole. She could never be the mother she needed to be for Caroline.

Every day, Allie chose forgiveness.

Every day, she chose freedom.

Allie and Caroline made their way near the edge of the saltmarsh, watching for egrets and herons perching near the edges of the tall grass. The air, scented with morning dew and warm earth, tickled Allie's nose. Palm tree fronds rustled in the breeze as the sky glowed first silver, then pink and lavender as the sun rose, waking Brunswick from slumber.

"So I need to tell you something," said Caroline. Her daughter was giving off a serious vibe, which made the back of Allie's neck prickle with worry.

"Sure, anything," Allie replied, flashing a grin. She reminded herself that whatever happened in the future, it would be all right. She could handle it.

"So, Ben came to Grandma Lily's house a couple of months ago." Caroline tilted her head to one side. "He said if there was anything I needed, to just ask. And he wanted to know if you were okay."

"Oh?" Allie smiled, gulping back a twinge of nerves.

"I told him, yes, you were doing great." Caroline smiled up at her.

Allie couldn't reply. To do so would unleash a lifetime of tears. Instead, she smothered a sob and folded her daughter into her arms. At that moment, her life was complete. She had everything she needed. Her life. Hope. A future. And a daughter who believed in her again.

After a beat, Caroline untangled herself and took a step back, causing nearby birds to take flight into the bright blue sky. Through the flutter of wings, Allie thought she heard the scuff of footsteps behind her. Her skin prickled.

"Oh, there's one more thing," Caroline said. She held up both palms and gave Allie a stern look. "Stay there. Don't move."

Allie wrinkled her forehead. "Caroline?" Her daughter inched farther away.

"Shh." Caroline put a finger to her lips. She turned, began walking away, and waved good-bye over her shoulder. "I'll see you at home."

What in the world?

Nothing but the sounds of nature filled her ears. She

concentrated on bees buzzing, the wind rushing through the tall grasses, and leaves rustling overhead.

"Allie."

At the sound of her name being called, Allie jumped and whirled, letting out a gasp.

Ben stood there, watching her, smiling. "So much for the big date," he said.

Allie's eyes filled with tears, flooding her vision. It seemed like they'd had that conversation a million years ago.

"You don't remember? What today is?" With a wink, Ben crossed his arms.

She nodded, wiping her cheeks.

"It was the day after Caroline's first birthday party. She was down for a nap—" Ben moved closer and tilted his head. He gazed down at her.

"And I was crying." Allie shivered, finishing his sentence.

"When I found you, do you remember what I said?" Ben asked, taking a step forward.

They were inches apart. Allie couldn't move. Or breathe.

"Do you remember?" he repeated.

Allie's mind rushed back to the exact moment. *I could tell you the exact day and time. I remember how the air smelled like fresh-cut grass and that the blue afternoon sky was streaked with silver-white clouds.*

Her legs trembled. "Y-you said th-that I didn't have to worry. You would take care of me. And Caroline," Allie managed to reply, her eyes welling up with tears.

Ben reached for her hand. "And that I would spend every day, every waking moment, making you happy. I didn't care about the past. I love you, and that's for always."

With tentative fingers, Allie touched Ben's palm. His fingers closed around hers and squeezed. With a soft touch, Ben wiped at her eyes. "I'm sorry. I know you had this crazy need to prove you could do everything on your own, and you didn't want me to sacrifice my dreams and career, but I never should have let you push me away."

Without pausing to think, Allie nodded. Her heart thudded as Ben cupped her face in his hands.

"Wait," Allie whispered, shaking her head. She pulled back, out of his embrace. "Ben, I can't, not right now. You left. And you didn't come back."

Ben creased his brow. "I was crushed. You broke it off with me and broke my heart, Allie," he said. "And when everything happened, I ran. I was trying to save my feelings. I told myself that what happened with Coach was a sign for me to throw myself into my work and forget you."

Allie shook her head slowly.

"Is there any way . . . Allie? I mean, is there a chance that we could start over?" Ben asked. He didn't move to touch her. He didn't smile or beg or try to plead. It was just Ben, being Ben. The Ben she used to know. The Ben she loved.

"I-I have to focus on Caroline," Allie said, her voice breaking. "It's been ten, now almost eleven, years. I've missed so much." Tears clouded her vision.

When she wiped them away, Ben was nodding.

Allie sucked in a breath. "Can we . . . Let's just see where it goes, okay? One day at a time."

She waited, emotions twisting, as Ben held her gaze. "I understand. You've got it." After a beat, his mouth curved into a grin. "Come on," he said. "Let's go and get Caroline. We need to celebrate."

Allie looked up at him and smiled. This was a first step she could take. "All right. Let's go home."

DISCUSSION QUESTIONS

1. The novel's heroine, Allie Marshall, is a survivor. After being sent to prison, enduring intolerable situations, and fearing for her life, she still dreams of starting her life over and reuniting with her daughter. If you were in Allie's situation, what would keep your hope alive?

2. Emma harbors deep jealousy of her sister, despite Allie's fall from grace. Are any of her feelings justified?

3. Caroline often hides her true personality behind her best friend, Maddie. Why is it so difficult for Caroline to be herself?

4. Despite his ego and tough exterior, Sheriff Lee Gaines makes time to visit his wife in the nursing home every day. Do you believe that he truly loves June or are his actions just a show for the community?

5. Paul and Lily Marshall, Allie's parents, have an extremely difficult time dealing with Allie's incarceration. If Allie were your daughter, how would you handle the public scrutiny and gossip? Would you believe your child's innocence?

6. Ben stands by Allie, vowing to love and protect her no matter what happens in their lives. Did Allie do the right thing by breaking off the engagement? Why or why not?

7. What do you think about Brunswick's focus on high school

football? Have you heard of instances when a player's life might have been put in jeopardy, or safety compromised, in order for a team to win?

8. At the end of the novel, Emma sacrifices her own life in an attempt to save Caroline. Does this, at all, redeem her?

9. How do you imagine Allie's life will turn out after the novel ends?

ACKNOWLEDGMENTS

Deepest gratitude to my talented and amazing editors, Amanda Bostic, Nicci Hubert, Karli Jackson, and Caroline Steudle. Thank you, also, to Katie Bond, Kristen Golden, and Kristen Ingebretson who designed the gorgeous cover.

Lots of love to my mother and father, who encouraged my enthusiasm for reading and books by turning off the TV while I was growing up . . . all summer, every summer. Hugs to my brother Mark, his wife Peg, and their family. I miss you all so much! And to Patrick and John David—you are my world.

To my early readers, Jen McGee, Doug McCourt, and Maxine Kidder—I can't thank you enough for your enthusiasm and encouragement.

To my literary family—Kellie Coates Gilbert, Kristy Cambron, Andrea Peskind Katz, Rachel Hauck, Kimberly S. Belle, Jennie Collins Belk, Sarah Miniaci, Melanie Dickerson, Samantha Stroh Bailey, Jim Kane, Tracie Banister, Samantha March, Jen Tucker, Julie Cantrell, Lisa Steinke, Liz Fenton, Tamara Welch, Suzy Missirlian, Amy Clipston, Lisa Wingate, and Karen Pokras—I am so lucky to have you in my life. Joshilyn Jackson and Anita Hughes, deepest appreciation for sharing your thoughts about my writing.

I am blessed to have the most wonderful friends in the world, among them, Tara Jones, Laura Rash, Jenny Good, Mary Steudle, Simone Armstrong, Chris Hughes, Robert Stewart, April Sanders, Ellen Odom, Cecelia and Chuck Heyer, Simone Armstrong, Jamie Zamudio, Valerie Case, Jana Simpson, Linda and Ted Hicks, Lisa Emanuelli, Heidi Pritchett, Kippie Atkins, Jennifer Gresham, Jessica Sinn, Lora Campbell Roberts, Linda Moore, Tobi Helton, and the entire UA family.

Finally, I am indebted to my wonderful readers. Your reviews, e-mails, and letters mean the world to me! Without you, none of this would be possible.

ABOUT THE AUTHOR

Laura McNeill is a writer, mom, travel enthusiast, and coffee drinker. In her former life, she was a television news anchor for CBS News affiliates in New York and Alabama. Laura holds a master's degree in Journalism from The Ohio State University and is completing a PhD in Instructional Leadership at the University of Alabama. When she's not writing and doing homework, she enjoys running, yoga, and spending time at the beach. She lives in North Alabama with her family.

THE TRUTH COULD COST
HER EVERYTHING.

Available in print, audio, and e-book.

THOMAS NELSON
Since 1798

ENJOY AN EXCERPT FROM LAURA MCNEILL'S

CENTER OF GRAVITY

PROLOGUE

AVA

When your children are stolen, the pain swallows you whole. Logic fades, reason retreats. Desperation permeates the tiniest crevices of your mind. Nothing soothes the ache in your wounded soul.

Right in front of me, my sweet, charmed life fell to pieces. Everything destroyed—a hailstorm's wrath on a field of wildflowers. All I'd known . . . gone. Foolish me, I'd believed in magic, clung tight to false promises. The lies, spoken from tender lips, haunt me now, follow me, and whisper into my ear like a scorned lover.

What's left is emptiness.

Give up, a voice urges. *Let go.*

No! I argue back. My children aren't gone. Not yet. Precious and delicate, tiny fossils, they exist in glass-boxed isolation. Hidden. Protected.

And so tonight, I run. Blood pulses through my legs, my muscles protest; my lungs scream for more oxygen. Thick storm clouds brew in the distance. The rain falls in blinding sheets. The force of it pricks my skin like needles, but the pain only makes me push harder.

I will rescue them.

Lightning flashes across the wet driveway. I skid to a stop and catch my breath, pressing a hand to my heaving chest.

They're here. My children are here.

Thunder booms and crashes, nearer now, and the wind whips my hair. A gust tosses tree branches to the ground. Birds cry and flutter to safety. An escaped sand bucket spins, clattering on the blacktop.

I grasp the railing and pull myself up the steps. At the top, the door is shiny-slick with water and humidity. Mother Nature howls and drowns out my knocking.

"Hello! Can you hear me?" With my palm open wide, I slap at the barrier, willing it to open. I will rescue my children. I will rescue them . . . or I will die trying.

CHAPTER 1

JACK

One Month Earlier
Wednesday, March 24

Every day, somebody somewhere needs a hero.

Think about it. The mom lifting a two-ton truck to save her son after a car crash. The dad—who can't swim—who jumps in the water anyway to pull out his drowning daughter. The guy who kicks down the door of a burning building because his friend's kid is trapped inside.

All of a sudden, getting hurt doesn't matter. There's no thinking twice. Just a gut-pumping, jump-off-the-cliff, no turning back.

For these regular people, thrown into crazy life-or-death situations, there's that one big moment. Then they go back to work, their jobs, or school.

And it's someone else's turn.

I'm only in the third grade, but I've been waiting for my whole life. Waiting for my chance—my moment to be a hero.

An ear-piercing shriek yanks me back to the school playground.

My best friend Mo runs up, breathless. "Emma Dunlop's stuck up in the oak tree." He bends over, chest heaving in the humidity, and puts both hands on his knees. "She's freaking out."

Shielding my eyes, I grit my teeth. The tree's as big as a monster, with twisted brown branches that extend like arms, thick emerald leaves at the fingertips. Spanish moss hangs from the lowest limbs, the ends curling like a snake's tail.

Though I can't see her through the tangle of limbs, I picture Emma hanging on tight to the rough bark. Shaking. Really scared. Trying not to look down at the brick-red clay.

I run a hand through my hair.

She's in trouble. And I know why.

Legend says a man's head—a genie—is hidden in the leaves and branches. Weird, rough pieces of wood make up his face. He has knots for eyes. A bump for his chin. It's for real. I've seen it.

All the kids know the story. If you touch the genie's nose, your wish will come true. Of course my dad doesn't believe in stuff like that and says I shouldn't either. He's a PhD and does an important job at the college. So I guess he knows what he's talking about.

But that's not going to save Emma now. I start to jog, then full-out sprint. At the base of the tree, I push through a crowd of my classmates. Third and fourth graders, gaping, heads tilted, mouths open like baby birds. When I reach the trunk, I squint up and find Emma's brand-new saddle shoes dangling high above me. I see pale, thin legs and the crisp edges of her plaid jumper. And despite everyone talking and whispering, I hear Emma crying. It's a whimpering wail, like a hurt animal.

"Y'all go on back inside now. Go back to class," my teacher says, pushing the group back an inch or two. I end up jostled next to the school librarian, who's holding her hands like she's praying.

Our eyes meet. Mine flicker away.

"Don't even think about it, Jack," she warns.

But I kick off my shoes anyway and grab hold of the trunk. Deep down in my belly, I make myself act like I'm not scared. I don't like heights or even hanging upside down from monkey bars. But Emma needs me. And no one else is doing a thing.

Ms. Martin gasps, but she knows she's too late. I'm out of her reach before she can react. I think hard about one of my favorite superheroes, Daredevil. He's like an Olympic athlete and a master of martial arts. He's blind but uses his other senses to fight crime, beat up bad guys, and save the girl. If he can do it . . .

When I look back down at the ground, my stomach churns like I've eaten too many Snickers bars and guzzled a two-liter of Coke. I push the feeling away. *Climb, Jack*, I say to myself. *Just climb.* When I start to move my legs again, the first few feet are easy. Soon I'm above everyone's heads.

"They're going to get a ladder," the librarian calls out. "Come on down here, Jack Carson, right this instant. Lord have mercy!"

At the sound of her screech, Emma wobbles. Her saddle shoes kick and knock some bark from a branch. *I can't come down now. She's slipping.*

"They've called the fire department," my teacher adds. "Truck's on the way."

I pretend I don't hear her and move closer. My head starts to hurt. My ears are ringing. But I take a deep breath and hold on tight to the tree, concentrating on Emma. She's tiny, a first grader, with brown corkscrew curls and a yellow bow pinned to the side of her head. Her pink cheeks are streaked with dirt.

"Hey, Emma," I say, making my voice calm. "Whatcha doing up here?"

She flushes pink. "I wanted to make a w-wish. For my birthday."

A breeze ruffles the leaves, cooling the sweat on my forehead. My hands, gritty with dirt and bark, inch closer. I can almost reach her. "Well, let's make sure you get to your party."

"But I haven't found the genie." She begins to cry, which makes her body wobble. The branch moves up and down, and she starts sobbing harder.

"Emma," I say. "It's okay. I'll help you."

She snuffles and blinks a few times. "I'm scared."

"I know. Me too," I tell her. "But I won't let you fall. Give me your hand."

Her palm is slippery wet. I grip it and try to smile so that she's not so nervous. "Slide your foot toward me. Then the other one."

I watch Emma drag one foot about an inch. She tries the other one but gets her shoe caught on a bump. I inhale sharply, the scent of dirt and sweat filling my nose.

"Wait. Don't move," I say, squeezing her hand.

Sirens wail. The crowd below grows bigger. I swallow hard. *Daredevil. Be like Daredevil.*

"Hold on," I tell her. "I won't let go."

After what seems like forever, Emma moves her foot closer.

"Can you think of something great, like going on vacation or your birthday?" I ask.

"Or getting a pony." For a moment, she sighs dreamily.

"Right," I say. "Now, let's go."

We begin to climb lower, inch by inch, but my arm muscle cramps. Emma hesitates. I squeeze her hand. I need to get her down. And fast.

"Emma," I whisper. "Look to the right."

The face of the tree genie is right there.

"Oh," Emma breathes.

"Touch his nose, quick."

She reaches out a finger and brushes it, then giggles. Right then, another gust of wind blows through the branches. Her curls tickle my cheek. I almost want to laugh. But I can't. Not yet.

Climbing down is simpler now; the limbs are wider, sturdier. The voices right below us are louder. The last big branch, large enough to hold both of us, is about ten feet up from the ground. We stop here, gasping for breath.

Firefighters are waiting underneath us with a blanket. An ambulance is there with the back door open. Teachers are waving their hands. And saying something.

Jump. They want Emma to jump.

"All right." I use my most grown-up voice. "Emma, I need you to do one more thing."

Her chin moves up and down.

"They want you to let go. So they can catch you."

Emma's arms and legs get stiff. Her eyes widen, and we both swallow a gulp. We're taller than the high dive at Spring Hill Swim Club. I try not to sway when I look at the ground.

"Maybe pretend," I tell her, thinking fast, "that you're a butterfly. Or an eagle."

"How about a unicorn?" She gives me a lopsided grin.

I bite my lip. *Enough with the horses.* I want to get down. This rescue stuff isn't for sissies.

Emma looks at me.

"They're waiting for you, Emma. On the count of three, okay?"

When the firefighter below calls out "one," she jumps, and her uniform billows open like a plaid parachute. She lands square on the blanket and beams in delight. A firefighter reaches in, grabs Emma, and scoops her up.

Emma waves good-bye to me as the firefighter carries her to the ambulance.

"Think you'll get the pony?" I yell after her.

She shakes her curls. "I can't tell you my wish. It won't come true!"

Emma's mother runs up then, crying, hugging, and kissing her.

With Emma okay, the grown-ups turn back to me. Most of

them have their arms crossed and don't look happy. No doubt the principal is ready to dish out a detention or two.

"Dude, your dad's going to freak when he finds out," Mo says and rolls his eyes. "He hates your superhero stuff."

"Don't remind me." Inside, I feel sick. I know that I am supposed to get good grades, play sports, and be polite. My dad isn't a fan of making big scenes.

"It was pretty cool anyway." Mo cocks his head. "Who are you today?"

"Daredevil."

"Nice." He grins and leans against the tree below me, waiting. "You coming down now, superhero?"

I lean back against the trunk, waiting for the firefighters to come back with the blanket. "Yep."

"Go ahead," Mo dares me, raising an eyebrow and grinning.

I hesitate, thinking I'd be crazy to jump. But superheroes take chances, don't they? I'd seen Daredevil jump from this height before. So holding my breath, I let go. Somehow, though, I twist midair and land smack down on my face. Hard.

The belly flop knocks the breath from my lungs. Time stops.

The smell of cut grass makes me want to sneeze. And someone's wearing really, really bad perfume. At least I'm not dead. Everyone is shouting and my ears hurt. There are hands touching my legs and arms. I roll my head an inch to one side. All I can see are shoes. A pair of black heels come closer.

"Jack, sweetheart, can you hear me?"

I push myself up with one arm and swipe at my hair with the back of my hand. "Sure thing," I answer, jaw set at the ridiculous question. Even superheroes stumble sometimes.

"Jack—"

"I'm fine." To prove it, I try to jump up and get to my feet. But like Superman with a mound of Kryptonite in the room, I am so weak that I almost fall over.

The office lady's mouth stretches wide and yawns.

My brain won't work. What is her name? Two of her now? Ink-stained fingers snap in front of my nose. My brain starts to rewind. My knees give out. Everything slides to the right and goes black.

The story continues in Laura McNeill's Center of Gravity . . .